A FEARSOME MOONLIGHT BLACK

A FEARSOME MOONLIGHT BLACK

A BONE DETECTIVE NOVEL

DAVID PUTNAM

First published by Level Best Books 2022

Copyright © 2022 by David Putnam

All rights reserved. No part of this publication may be reproduced, stored or transmitted in any form or by any means, electronic, mechanical, photocopying, recording, scanning, or otherwise without written permission from the publisher. It is illegal to copy this book, post it to a website, or distribute it by any other means without permission.

This novel is entirely a work of fiction. The names, characters and incidents portrayed in it are the work of the author's imagination. Any resemblance to actual persons, living or dead, events or localities is entirely coincidental.

David Putnam asserts the moral right to be identified as the author of this work.

Author Photo Credit: Heather Nada

First edition

ISBN: 978-1-68512-150-1

Cover art by Christian Storm

This book was professionally typeset on Reedsy.
Find out more at reedsy.com

Contents

Praise for A Fearsome Moonlight Black

"A cop's life, whether a rookie or a seasoned detective, is jammed with encounters that are often routine, sometimes disturbing, and all too often life-threateningly dangerous, a grind that takes its toll on personal relationships. *A Fearsome Moonlight Black* pulls back the curtain and takes the reader into that world with in-your-face clarity."—DP Lyle, award-winning author of the Jake Longly and Cain/Harper thriller series

"In this lean, fast-moving cop-novel, you're riding shotgun as Dave Beckett goes from a raw, idealistic young newbie deputy to a cynical, world-weary veteran homicide detective...in a compelling case that spans a decade. You can't fake the realism that underscores every word and scene in this book. Want to know what it's like to be a trainee deputy on patrol in 1979? Then read this book. You will live it...right alongside Dave Beckett, who discovers what it truly means to wear, and embody, the badge. He craves high adventure but discovers the grit, heart-ache and horror of the streets instead. Joseph Wambaugh said you don't work the job, the job works you...and Beckett makes the hard discovery himself, and you're there with him...every grueling step of the way. You may not have graduated from the sheriff's academy, or patrolled a beat in a squad car, but you'll believe you have after riding the mean streets of San Bernardino County with Dave Beckett."—Lee Goldberg, bestselling author of the Eve Ronin series

"Nobody writes cop stories like David Putnam! He lived the job. Read *A Fearsome Moonlight Black* and so will you."—Matt Coyle, author of the bestselling Rick Cahill Crime stories

I

BOOK ONE

"Instead of writing about how cops worked the job, I wrote about how the job worked on the cops."
—Joseph Wambaugh

Chapter One

City of West Valley

Southern California

Early in the winter of 1979, I stumbled upon death four times. The fifth time would shake my world and reverberate throughout my life, a cave echo that never dissipates. A tough year for hard lessons learned. I discovered death never plays favorites. We hope and wish we never have that unwanted visit, and no matter the diversion—the intervention—fate always intercedes, bringing with it grief and heart-wrenching despair.

Cynics call death "Life. It's just what humans do. They die." The hopeful, the skeptics, hide their heads, and whisper, "Not me. Never me. No. No. No." For me as a starry-eyed kid, life didn't have an end. That false and unsavory myth was thrust upon me at an age when I was unprepared to handle it.

At the same time, I learned too late that love and death are inextricably intertwined. Death is forever, and love... Well, love is supposed to be.

The first death came my way one week out of training while driving a single-person patrol car. Twenty-one years old and the department gave me a gun, a fast car, and a large dollop of trust, as yet unearned. If I dwelled upon the responsibility too long the sheer weight from it smothered and made it difficult to breathe. But I was doing it. I was actually driving my own patrol car, a life-long dream. A goal I thought for years was out of reach.

I stopped by my one-bedroom apartment to let Astro out to pee. No pets were allowed, but Astro was a good egg and knew how to keep quiet. I tried to let him out twice each shift. He had the heart of a Rottweiler in the body of a Beagle mix. A cute little guy who preferred love and cuddling over treats.

Astro was bouncing and prancing in the grass section by the hedge when the dispatcher doled out a call as if it were an order for coffee and a donut. "1526 North Calaveras Avenue, unknown problem. Welfare check subject Franklin Shearer, possibly suicidal. He failed to show up for his psych appointment." An odd assignment, the way it came out, and with more experience, I might've questioned it. Would've questioned it. I clapped my hands. "Come Astro, come on boy." I got him back in the apartment and headed for the call.

I parked the new black-and-white 79 Chevy Nova patrol unit one house south of the location on North Calaveras. The front tire screeched against the curb. It was four-fifteen on a warm February afternoon, my first call on swing shift. I walked down the sidewalk, excited and at the same time anxious, keeping an eye on the front of a single-story, two-tone brown house with a composition roof.

The all-grass front yard needed a mow. The shrubs against the front of the house were trimmed and neat. An asphalt driveway led to a front door that stood open; the screen door shut. The sun hung low in the sky, hiding below the peak of the roof and casting long shadows across the yard. In the gathering gloom, a burnt-orange Opel Kadet sat forlornly in the driveway.

I knocked on the aluminum frame screen door. "Hello, Mr. Shearer? Police department. Anyone home?" Not a peep from inside. No lights, the place growing dim with each passing moment. No neighbors came out, curious about the black-and-white parked in their neighborhood.

I tried the door latch. Open. Did I have the right to enter? I thought I did but wasn't sure. Should I call for another unit? No, I didn't want that kind of reputation, "A *Daddy*, holding your hand on every call. Sink or swim,

Beckett, or get the hell out of the pool."

That's what Johnny Maslow said in his last-minute advice outside the briefing room that very day when I stepped into the deep end for the first time, alone. He had been my training officer for the first ninety days; Mike Smith had me for the second ninety. But Johnny had taken me under his wing and became more of a big brother. A brother in blue. Tall and thin, his uniform always impeccable, he exuded confidence that arrived five seconds before he did. A cop's cop. He was tan from being outdoors with his horses, and a hint of a Southern twang that always mixed with his reassuring words.

"Hello? Anyone home?" I took a tentative step inside and stopped a moment for my eyes to adjust. Should I draw my gun? Did the law allow it? This was a safety check. A welfare check. But it was a suicidal person. I could draw pretty fast. I left it in the holster. The way the incident report would read scrolled out from each step, how I would write it "if this happened or that happened."

Sixties-style carpet and furniture filled the living room. On the GE console stereo sat a fishbowl with one goldfish. A typed label on the bowl said "Pescado Oro."

The two bedrooms, clean and neat, smelled of incense and spiced candles, and were without pictures or wall hangings. Each room had boxes stacked against the walls; labels in felt-tipped pen identified household items.

The hall bathroom stood ajar. I stayed to the side of the "the window of death"—that's what they called it in training—and eased the door open with a polished boot. Nothing. Clean, with a whiff of antiseptic.

"Hello? Mr. Shearer? Police department."

Still nothing.

Dispatch came over the handheld radio on my Sam Browne belt. "Paul Four, your status?"

"Code four, still checking."

I moved to the south side of the house through the living room. *Popular Mechanics* magazines fanned in an arc on the coffee table gave the room a dentist office feel. The high-low gold shag carpet was worn and outdated. Three paintings with Asian women playing musical instruments hung on the wall. The entire motif was pure sixties, frozen in time. Mr. Shearer was stuck in the past. I peeked into the empty kitchen on the way to the last room. Nothing there, the counter and sink sans dishes.

A makeshift den—the entrance off the living room—had been converted into a large bedroom that dwarfed a single bed and a short, three-drawer dresser.

I let out a breath I didn't know I'd been holding. The house was empty. Mr. Shearer probably had a second car that he had driven away and, in his addled state, gone off and left his front door open.

I pushed the button on the front doorknob, checked to be sure it locked, and eased it closed until it latched.

With no one home to see, I violated protocol and cut across the front yard as I pulled the HT from my belt. I keyed the mic to speak just as I kicked something in the grass that clinked. I bent down and discovered a set of keys. I looked back at the house I'd just searched and the Opel Kadet that sat in the driveway. The front door had been standing open when I arrived, and the house keys tossed willy-nilly into the grass.

Geeze. I'd missed something.

I didn't want the key to fit the door I'd just locked but it did. I reentered, my mind sifting through all the possibilities. I didn't call out to Mr. Sheerer. Not his time. My stomach clenched, sweat beading on my forehead as I went through the house once more. Instead of just a cursory search, I checked under the beds and in the closets, and even behind the hanging clothes in the two bedrooms.

Nothing. I entered the kitchen that I had only peered into: everything was neat and orderly.

"Huh." Had I let my imagination run slipshod over common sense and this was really as it seemed, an empty house?

I turned to once again leave and noticed some papers lined up on the kitchen table. I switched on the light and leaned over to see. A last will and testament and directions for funeral arrangements. I immediately turned and put my back to the wall, hand on my gun. What the hell was going on?

Use your head, think.

I'd checked and rechecked everything. What was left?

The car's in the driveway, not in the garage.

The garage.

I looked out the kitchen window to the heavy wood two-garage door. The garage was attached to the house with a padlock on the outside. He couldn't be inside. Unless—

What a fool. I'd missed it. I'd almost walked away without checking the garage. Big mistake. But I hadn't seen an interior door to access the garage from the inside. Had I gone right by it without looking for it? I went into the makeshift bedroom, the only room that could have a common wall to the garage. There wasn't any door. I ran my hand over the cheap wood paneling like some kind of fool looking for a secret passage that only happened in the movies.

Nothing.

With the cut-rate room conversion, Mr. Shearer had built a closet attached to the wall. One I'd checked inside on the second tour through the house and had found it without a corpse. I again slid the door open. Shoes lined the floor in two neat rows and clothes hung from a wooden dowel on wire hangers. I moved the clothes aside and stepped back, startled.

A door painted white to match the wall. A door to the garage.

I drew my service revolver. "Mr. Shearer? Sheriff's department. I'm coming in."

Chapter Two

For the next three days I didn't sleep. Not well, at least. I tossed and turned and tangled in sweaty sheets. Nightmare images wouldn't leave me alone. This wasn't how it was supposed to be. Malloy and Reed on *Adam-12* never saw the horror show in Mr. Shearer's garage. I was on the job for the high adventure, not *The Tell-Tale Heart* by Poe. I couldn't talk about it with anyone on the job; they'd think me weak and unable to handle it. I still had six months left on probation. The kind of probation where I could be washed out for just looking at a sergeant the wrong way. I needed to suck it up, get over it.

Those three nights I broke my own rule and let Astro on the bed. I was an immature child who needed his puppy in order to sleep. He didn't overplay his temporary privilege by prancing around on the bedspread happy as a clam, his cute beagle ears flapping as he gloated. He somehow sensed the importance, the need, and as I lay on my back he rested his head on my chest, his big brown eyes staring at me unblinking. "Thanks, pal, you're a good Joe." He didn't answer back. Good thing.

The morning of the third day, after the call on Calaveras, I went for a long run to clear my head. Three miles straight up San Antonio Avenue, where I turned west on I Street. During those three days on patrol, nothing of substance had occurred: burglary reports, stolen bikes, a missing person, a fifteen-year-old runaway girl named Carla Bressler, and a couple of shoplifters. All the mundane minutiae cops deal with while waiting for the real action to kick off. The high adventure I'd always craved.

I made it to Mountain Avenue when I realized I had been subconsciously heading home, the place where I grew up. The last thing I wanted was to talk with Mom. I needed to deal with this on my own. And though I loved her dearly, she could be a little eccentric at times. Dad called it "dingy."

I cut through the large parking lot to the Market Basket where we had always shopped for our groceries, a place that held fond memories, at least until Mom split with Dad. When I was a kid, every month or so Mom took me to the Thrifty's Café next to the grocery for a hot fudge sundae with extra fudge. Sure, I loved the sundae, but I enjoyed the alone time with her more, and that she took the time to be with me.

I entered through the front of the Market Basket to pick up a water, my t-shirt too. My skin rippled with bumps from the cool air. I stood in line to buy the water, worried about odor and what the other patrons in line behind me might think of the humidity emitting from my body.

The clerk, someone I didn't know, kept her eyes on her hands as she rang up the person ahead of me. She wasn't being personable. She wore her brown hair short and pulled back behind her ears. She had delicate features and smooth, perfect skin. I caught myself staring at her because it was safe, she wasn't looking up. Dark half-moons under her eyes and a mouth that didn't smile gave off an aura of unhappiness. She had a ring on her ring finger. Not a wedding ring or one for engagement, but a promise ring with a small red stone. On her right wrist, she wore a tattered handwoven bracelet with little cubed letters that spelled "Cole."

She looked up and caught me staring, her large brown eyes her most striking feature. My breath caught. I knew this girl from high school. Beth. I'd had a huge crush on her. But she'd had a boyfriend all four years. Cole. As if that would've mattered back then. I was never one who could talk to girls. Still wasn't. That was one big reason why I had Astro. I hoped he would do the introductions, break the ice with girls I was too afraid to approach. So far it hadn't worked. Not Astro's fault; he had tried on a number of occasions. I just couldn't handle my end of the deal. But to be fair I'd been too focused on getting through the academy and making it through probation. Right, who was I trying to kid?

She hesitated as she stared. Did she recognize me? My hand all on its own smeared my damp hair off my forehead, as if the small gesture could fix my sweat-soaked appearance. Her expression never changed, and she went back to ringing up food on the conveyor, which hummed, the only sound at the moment. She hadn't recognized me.

When my turn came I handed her the wadded-up five I'd kept in my shorts pocket. I watched her eyes, waiting to make another connection that didn't happen. She handed me my change without a smile. The reason I had not recognized her was that she had always been smiling in high school, as if life had been put there for her alone to enjoy. With Cole, she had grabbed the gold ring and won the game of Life.

Everyone talked about Beth and Cole, the perfect couple, always together. Not just for holding hands. They always had their bodies engaged, side by side, attached at the hip. In my memory, it seemed as if a brighter light always shone down on Beth's face as she looked into Cole's eyes. Friends in my group called it sickening. I secretly envied that kind of love and wondered where it came from. I wanted the same thing. You couldn't buy it in stores and I had no idea where to look. For me, it was more elusive than the Yeti.

Cole had a great job at the General Electric plant in town; he worked nights and weekends on the assembly line cranking out household irons. He drove a cool new Datsun 280Z that gleamed in the sun in the student parking lot. Purchased with his own money. He talked about becoming a manager soon after graduation. He was quiet and unpretentious. He knew he had life by the tail and didn't brag about it. I was jealous of Cole, but also knew he would make her happy based on the way he looked at her, the way he treated her, he'd always be true and not hurt her. This from the lurking romantic inside me. Cole also wore a handmade macramé wristband with Beth's name in little white blocks.

I walked into the warmth of the day and realized Beth had taken my mind away from Mr. Shearer, if only for a moment. The run had cleared my head, and I realized what had bothered me most was whether or not I could stay in the kind of job that put on display a part of life that has always been kept hidden. Nobody outside cop work knows what really goes on. They get up every day, have breakfast, go to work and come home to watch *Gunsmoke* on the TV, with the soap and cereal commercials, thinking that's how life really plays out. When the bad guys on *Gunsmoke* get shot they spin and fall without any blood.

I ran back to my apartment on Flora pushing it hard, a total of seven miles for the day, showered, took Astro out one last time, and then walked the mile to work. I went in the front door of the station and waved to Chuck, the uniformed dayshift desk officer. He buzzed me through. On the left, the patrol captain's door stood open; on the right, the windowed office of the watch commander attached to the dispatch booth. I tried to sneak past both without being seen.

Lieutenant Galbraith rapped on his window and waved me into his office.

Crap. Crap. Crap.

I flushed hot at the thought of standing tall in front of him. Sweat beaded on my forehead from the walk over. Cigarette smoke fogged the watch commander's office, the reek of nicotine enough to gag and burn my freshly exercised lungs.

"Come on in, son, close the door."

Son? Not son. He'd always called me Dave.

Galbraith waved his hand, the cigarette leaving a trail of smoke like a skywriter. His uniform didn't fit him well. He'd lost some weight recently. He wore his thinning black hair combed back and parted on the side, slicked with Brylcreem. "Close the door, grab a seat."

I closed the door like he asked and sat down with great trepidation. What had I done wrong? My mind sped back over the past days I'd been on my own on patrol and could find nothing I'd messed up that warranted a talk with the W/C. At least nothing I could think of.

Galbraith puffed on his cigarette and stared at me. I'd been a cadet at the station for two years before going to the academy and becoming a deputy. I worked with Galbraith most days and thought we had a pretty good relationship. But friends or no friends, if I wasn't cutting it out in the field, they would tell me about it. And if I didn't correct any deficiencies, I'd be washed out.

I waited for him to say something. Sweat ran into my eyes and stung, my body still overheated from the long run and then from the walk over. I hadn't had time to catch up and cool down.

"How you doin'?" Galbraith asked.

"Fine sir."

He stared at me. "You sure?"

"Positive. Why? Is something wrong? Did I screw something up?"

"No. No. I'm just a little concerned. You haven't been smiling like you usually do."

I forced a smile to creep out. "Oh, that. It's nothing. I'm ah, just real focused on getting through probation, that's all."

"You sure that's all it is? Before the other day, you always walked around here like the cat that ate the canary."

Johnny Maslow came from downstairs carrying his war bag with all the things he needed for swing shift patrol, talking to Bukowski. Through the window, Johnny saw me in the hot seat, dropped his bag, opened the door, and came in, a big violation of protocol. "What's going on? What'd you do, Beckett?"

"Johnny, sonofabitch, get your ass out of my office. This is between me and Dave."

"What's wrong? What'd he do?"

"Nothing. It's okay." I said. Johnny was only making things worse.

Galbraith stood and crushed his cigarette in the ashtray. He pointed through the smoke. "Get out, now."

Johnny stared him down, then looked at me. "You sure you're okay?"

"I'm good, really."

He looked back at Galbraith as he spoke to me. "Okay. I'll be right outside this door if you need me."

Johnny would never get promoted; he didn't get along with the bosses. He thought they were only there to "rack a guy up." He left and closed the door and stood watching through the window. Galbraith waited a moment then sat down. He bumped out a Winston and lit it. He no longer displayed the happy demeanor that he had when I first walked in. Johnny had tried to help but did the exact opposite.

Galbraith took a long drag and let it out. "I'm worried about you, Dave. You start smiling again, or I'm going to think there's something wrong. I'll pull you from the field and put you on the desk for a few days until you get your mind right."

That was the last thing I wanted. I'd worked the desk as a cadet. I was a field officer now. No way did I want to go backwards. "I'm good, Lieutenant, I promise." I stood and smiled.

He waved his hand. Smoke trailed behind it. "I'm sorry about what happened. You shouldn't have been sent on that call by yourself, not until you had more time under your belt. That was my fault for not paying attention."

I waved and smiled. "Is that what this is about? That was all about nothing, Lieutenant. Never thought about it again after I drove away. I'm just staying focused on doing a good job, that's all. Just trying to get by."

He finally smiled. "Good. You come and see me if you ever need to talk, you hear me?"

"You got it Lieu, and thanks."

I opened the door and hurried out. Johnny followed me down the stairs right on my tail. "What happened? What'd he say?"

I stopped. He bumped into me. I said, "I appreciate you looking out for me, really I do. But—"

"But what?"

"Never mind. I'm going to be late for briefing. I gotta get changed."

Chapter Three

Mike Smith, my former training officer, Jim Sedge, Ronald Luck, and Joseph Lee were still in the locker room changing into their blue uniforms, getting ready for swing shift and cutting it real close. Joseph Lee worked a traffic car, exclusively. Johnny said a Tom car was a good place for him. Chasing taillights instead of answering calls with unknown dispositions where guns and knives and heated tempers were involved. I had not seen a lot of those encounters in my first six months as a trainee. In fact, the job was nothing like I expected, for the most part slow and unremarkable. I was beginning to believe the description of police work the drill instructor gave in the academy: "It's hours of boredom interspersed with moments of pure terror."

Smith was a short wiry man who carried a six-inch .357 that looked incongruent on his hip. The gun's grip didn't fit his small hand and had a custom extender, so he could choke up on the stock. A cigarette always hung from his lips, one lit right after the other, and his eyes squinted from the smoke when he spoke.

Sedge yelled, "Hey, look who's running late, the Cherry. Image that. That's not like you, Cherry. What happen, your mommy not wake you up from your nap in time? You drink your milk and eat your graham crackers before coming to work with the men?"

I ignored him, unlocked my locker, moving fast, pulling my Kevlar body armor over my head, and strapping the Velcro tight. It had a faint whiff of mildew. At the EOW, end of watch, I needed to take off the cover and wash it with my regular laundry at Smitty's Coin Laundry.

Joseph Lee grabbed his war bag and hurried out; he didn't like any form of conflict. Smith smoked his cigarette and took his time buffing his Wellington boots, one foot on the bench. "How you doin', Dave?"

Why did everyone want to know how I was doing? If they could handle the job so could I.

I didn't slow, tugging on my uniform pants, and lacing up my boots. I knew what he was really asking, how was I doing after the Calaveras call with Mr. Shearer? Smith had been my T/O on phase two of my training—the second three months—he'd been tough but fair and I thought he really cared. I liked and respected him.

"Good. I'm good," I said.

Sedge, who everyone called the "The Walking Waterbed" due to his girth, chuckled. "Heard the FNG got his cherry popped. That true FNG? You toss your cookies at that scene on Calaveras?"

I hated the tag FNG most of all. *Fucking New Guy*. I didn't want to be the new guy.

Smith looked up, squinting in the smoke. The cigarette wagged as he spoke. "Give it a rest, Fatman."

Sedge slammed his locker shut, picked up his warbag, and stopped next to Smith, who continued to polish and buff his Wellingtons to a high sheen, not the least bit concerned that Sedge was blocking the light with his bulk. "For a little shit," Sedge said, "you gotta big mouth." He stood close to Smith, trying to intimidate him with size alone, but missing the backbone to back up his threat. Sedge weighed twice as much as Smith, but Smith carried a beavertail blackjack in the sap pocket behind his leg. An equalizer. I'd seen him lay low a huge biker who'd also taken Smith's size for granted. If there was a line of demarcation for *capable*, Smith was well past it and deep into *devastating*.

Smith slowly took his foot off the bench, let the cigarette sag and hang off his lips, and said, "Keep walkin' Fatman, or I'll knock your dick in the dirt."

Sedge didn't move for a moment, uncertainty plain in his eyes. He didn't want to start something. He must've known about the beavertail sap and that Smith wasn't afraid to pull it, even in the station locker room. What

Sedge feared the most was the empty locker room. No witnesses to keep from telling everyone that Sedge had simply slipped and banged his head on the bench. His acolyte, Ronald Luck, had just hurried out.

I accepted my age and youthful inexperience, but I had expected something entirely different from the cops when I first met them. I'd had an image of professionalism, that they walked and talked like Jack Webb and Pete Mallory, impervious to the everyday world. I was still shocked every time they acted like human beings with regular emotions; envy, hate, love, guilt, and pettiness. They went out in the field every day to mediate other folks' problems when they had to deal with the same things in their own lives.

John Q Public never saw it that way. Cops weren't supposed to be human. But they were. More so, in a way. I found that there were good ones and bad ones just like the people on the street. Some cops wanted to be on the job for the great adventure, some wanted to help people, and some just wanted the paycheck. They wanted to keep their heads down and out of trouble on the long road to retirement, never doing anything more than absolutely necessary.

Sedge hurried out, headed for the briefing room, his bulk filling the corridor of lockers. The swing door swung shut. Smith put his other boot on the bench and buffed it with his shoe brush. I put on my Sam Browne gun belt and worked in the keepers. I wanted to say thanks and couldn't immediately form the words that would only come out sounding weak. "You're going to be late," I said to Smith.

He smoked and buffed and said nothing.

"Thank you," I said, "but I can handle myself."

He looked up, smoke in his eyes, and gave me a huge smile, teeth stained from the nicotine in the constant cigarette smoke.

I grabbed my gear and ran for the door. Everyone in the briefing room stopped laughing and joking to look at me when I entered. What made it worse, I was the only trainee, and trainees sat at the front table, in front of the watch sergeant's podium. I hurried down the row of fifteen veteran cops seated at the tables, four on each side of the aisle. Some of them threw wadded paper balls as I passed. The normal hazing wouldn't end for six more months, when I passed probation. I could then take my place at one of the back tables. When the next trainee came to the department, I promised myself I would never haze him or her.

Sergeant Sid Long, a gruff gray-haired man who never had a good word to say about anyone, said, "It's nice that you could join us, boot." He used his pencil eraser on the watch list. "You know the rule, last one in briefing gets to ride the Beast, unit 109."

The last Oldsmobile in the fleet, a real boat that couldn't get out of its own way and stalled any time you made a hard-left turn. The front seat was broken down from too many butts sitting in it over the years. All the other new Chevy Novas were in the three series: 379, 380, almost to the fours. That's how long the station had held onto the Beast. The administration said it was due to budgetary considerations. All the officers thought they kept the Beast as a rolling penalty box.

Smith came in smoking a fresh cigarette. He dropped his war bag on the table right next to the Walking Waterbed. "Looks like I'm the last one in briefing today, Sid. I'll take the Beast."

I said, "That's okay, I'll—"

Sergeant Long said, "Shut up and sit down, Rookie." Then, "You sure, Smith?"

Smith smiled and shrugged. "The rule's the rule."

Smith had purposely taken his time in the locker room, so I wouldn't be saddled with the Beast. I owed him big. It wasn't just being assigned the Beast. I could handle that, it was the punishment meted out in front of all the veteran officers.

Lieutenant Womack came in and stood at the door at the back of the room. Sergeant Long at the podium said, "Lieutenant, you have something you want to say to this motley crew?"

Womack came into the aisle and stopped about halfway. He kept his uniform immaculate and always had an unlit cigar in his hand or stuck in his mouth. He kept his thinning black hair combed straight back. He'd be bald before too long. He had a round face like a bulldog. As he spoke, he continued to turn and catch everyone's eyes one at a time. He used the hand with the cigar as a pointer for emphasis.

"If for some reason you screw up out there, God forbid, and you go down, just remember that your fellow officers are going to be driving like hell to assist you. They are going to run blindly into a situation that you created." He let that soak in. His words had struck home with me. I could only nod and agree, awed by his words, his commanding presence.

He continued. "If that happens, it's your screwup. You will not roll over and give up. You will fix your screwup if it takes your last breath. You understand?" He waited, then said, "Carry on, Sergeant Long." Lieutenant Womack walked out.

Ronald Luck at the table directedly behind me whispered with a combination of awe and fear, "Jesus H."

Sedge smirked. "He just got back from that officer survival school and has a bad case of 'For reals.'"

From the back table, Johnny Maslow said loud enough for everyone to hear, "Sedge, you're an idiot."

Chapter Four

The watch sergeant assigned me to beat four, a remote beat with a lot of open land, vineyards, and light manufacturing where nothing usually happened. I couldn't help thinking that the watch commander, Lieutenant Galbraith, had something to do with the assignment and put me in the sticks with the crickets until "I got my smile back."

Whoever heard of such a thing? The DIs didn't cover *smiles* in the academy. I wanted beat five, downtown where everything tended to happen. Where *anything* could happen. And even though beats four and five are close in sequence, that's not the way it worked in the beat plan. If something hot went down and beat five needed backup, I was out of position with too many miles in between. The dispatcher would give the assignment to a closer car. As it should be.

Beat four had a small residential pocket on the west side. I hung out there, driving in and out of the same streets looking for something suspicious, a burglar, someone acting furtive, someone who didn't belong. But I wasn't sure how to spot a crook unless he was wearing all black, a mask, and climbing out a window with a pillowcase full of loot. I had so much to learn.

I drove around the small business district at Fourth and Grove hoping for an armed robbery to happen.

A quiet night so far on swing, the three-to-eleven shift. Some domestic disputes, some paper calls; thefts, grand theft autos, a couple of traffic collisions. Based on the radio traffic, Smith and Maslow stayed busy making car stops looking for someone to take to jail. No luck so far for anyone. I didn't have enough experience to spot an offender just driving by, not like those two could. It would come with time. I just didn't want to wait. I wanted to pull the crooks over now and take them to jail. A car stop was like a treasure hunt. You never knew if you were going to find a gun or dope or an obstreperous outlaw wanted in five states. High adventure.

At five o'clock, the sun sat low in the sky casting long shadows in between the oranges and yellows. I found my patrol unit wandering out of beat headed further west into beat one, a beat that all the cops referred to as Sleepy Hollow. Nothing ever happened in beat one. Thank the police gods I wasn't assigned there.

If I got caught out of my area, the field sergeant had the option of issuing a verbal warning or a written, what the officers called an "Ah-shit." For a probationer, an 'out of beat' infraction could carry a much heavier penalty.

The Market Basket was in beat one. Beth worked at the Market Basket. The memory of her, the ones from high school, floated around in my brain: her smile, her large, wonderful brown eyes, the glow that came from having life by the tail. Though, she didn't have that glow when I'd seen her earlier in the day. She seemed broken, her life trod upon. I needed to know what had happened.

If I could just sneak over to beat one, make a drive-by, see if…what? If she was walking to her car to go home? Stupid. Stupid. Stupid. What were the odds of that happening? Slim to none. And if by some crazy chance she did happen to come out headed for her car, no way could I work up the nerve to even say, "Hey."

I went anyway. It was close to code-seven, my lunch break, and if caught, I'd just tell the sarge I wanted to eat at my mom's house and I wanted to get close before I called it on the radio. That weak excuse might fly.

My heart rate increased the farther away I got from beat four. What if a hot call went down in my area? I was out of position. How would I explain that? I couldn't.

At Mountain Avenue, I turned into the parking lot of the shopping center. I made one pass by the front door of Market Basket and should've headed for the exit on I Street. Instead, I made a right to go around the back. I again passed JC Penny, the Kinney Shoes, the News Stand bookstore where I bought all my paperback books while growing up, and finally past the Thrifty's Café and the Market Basket.

The fates shone down on me. She stood outside the double glass doors, one foot flat against the wall, one leg down like a graceful egret as she smoked a cigarette. Her eyes tracked my patrol unit the same as a bird watching a predator approach. The cigarette was long and narrow, a Virginia Slim. I'd worked part-time during high school at a liquor store and could spot cigarette brands from a good distance away.

What now? What should I do? My face flushed hot and my tongue grew thick just thinking about talking to a girl, let alone someone like Beth Abercrombie.

My foot braked, slowing the black-and-white patrol car more and more. Should I just drive by and smile? Maybe say "Hey?" or something like that? The DI, the drill instructor from the academy had said, "Be bold, be curious, stick your nose where it doesn't normally belong, that's how you find criminal behavior. But did that same doctrine apply to women? It had to. Women were wily and cagey and so very unpredictable.

I stopped even with her, not ten feet away, window down, my elbow resting casually on the sill, my insides quivering. She still did not smile and looked a little ragged but at the same time glorious. She took a long drag on her cigarette, her large brown eyes burning holes right through me. Even so, my heart did a little somersault. She let her hand drop with the cigarette and flicked it toward the left front tire of my unit, a sign of disrespect.

She said, "Take a picture, why don't ya? It'll last longer." She turned and headed for the double doors at the back of Market Basket. She still wore the red apron-smock over a white blouse and blue jeans.

She turned into the short alcove that contained the double doors and disappeared from my view. My tongue still wouldn't cooperate, but Beth's rudeness had helped some. I couldn't leave it that way. "Beth?" I blurted. I didn't move the car up to see. With one word, her name, I'd used up my current ability to contact women. I had nothing left in that savings account and wouldn't for days to come until enough interest accrued.

Had she gone back in?

Her head peeked around the corner, her expression quizzical and no longer glum. "Can I help you?" she asked.

The radio dispatcher burped out my call sign asking me to acknowledge. I held up a shaky finger to Beth. "Just one minute, please?" I answered the dispatcher and wrote down a burglary report call back in my beat. While I spoke on the radio Beth came closer, her hand to her red-smocked breast. "You looking for me, Officer? Did I do something wrong? Is my car okay? What's happened?"

The closer she came the warmer my face got. I really needed to head over to that burglary call. I was out of position and it was already going to take longer than it should to get on scene. The watch sergeant and the watch commander would both be paying attention to my ETA.

"Beth Abercrombie?" The only words I could utter as my mind spun out of control, searching hopelessly for what to say next.

"That's me."

"It's me...Dave."

"Dave?"

"Dave Beckett, from Mr. Johnson's World History class, North Hall, third period?" Shut up you fool. What the hell's the matter with you? What, are you in high school? You're a duly sworn peace officer for the state of California. Carrying a gun and driving a black-and-white patrol car and that's the best you can come up with. No wonder women won't talk to you.

I was glad Smith wasn't there to hear such world-class idiocy.

A wonderful smile broke out in Beth's expression. "Dave? Sure. Dave Beckett." She came forward. "How are you doing? I didn't know you were with the police now."

She came right to the window. I took my arm down as if afraid to touch her. I could never touch Beth Abercrombie. She put her arms on the sill, rested her chin on her hands, her smile, her glow, not inches from me. My heart about beat its way out of my chest. How absolutely wonderful. She was smiling. Talking to me. Dave Beckett.

"Look at you, in your nice uniform." She reached in and ran her hand from my shoulder down across my badge.

She'd touched me.

"Yes…I ah…I'm still on probation." Why did I say that? She didn't need to know that.

I wanted in the worst way to sit and talk with her as long as she could on her break, but I felt extreme pressure to be moving toward the burglary report call.

I had had a regular girlfriend in high school, June Davidson, and it was easy to ask her out once we got to know each other. But she'd gone off to college to become a lawyer, and I had not seen or heard from her since. I just wanted to talk with Beth, to be around her, but she was with Cole. I couldn't ask her out even if it was just for coffee and a perfectly innocent conversation.

"I really don't have time to talk right now, Beth, I have to get to a call."

"Oh, sure, sure. I understand." She straightened up, her expression shifting back to glum. She took a half-step away from the car. I wanted her back, close enough to see the specks of gold in her brown eyes. I had never been that close and didn't know about the gold specks. "Okay, see you around then."

She hesitated, waiting for me to drive off. I held my breath, wanting to say something more, still not wanting the encounter to end. Be bold, the DI had said. Take the initiative.

"Are you still with Cole?" My gut clenched at how rude that sounded.

She started to smile at my first words, then heard, "Cole." Her expression drooped. She turned heel and fled into the store.

I punched the steering wheel as I took off for my call, driving too fast through the parking lot.

Chapter Five

I took Fourth Street east instead of the faster route—north to Mountain to the IS10—to get back to my beat and the burglary report call, Beth Abercrombie too heavy on my mind to make the correct decision. Her big brown eyes nudging out all else. Not smart. I needed to be alert, always watching for a car stop. I needed a felony arrest to prove I could do it, that I could handle the streets and that the streets didn't handle me. That's what Johnny said happened to some coppers. The street, an unforgiving mistress, that if you turned away for a second to look somewhere else, she'd reach out and cut your throat. This was all hype and myth. In my time as a cadet and in training I had not seen it.

Smith had a different take on cop philosophy. He said: Unfortunately, cops are like the dog kept chained in the yard and ignored. They take the scraps of food and live in the elements and bark at trespassers, and any bit of attention its owner gives it, it relishes. What makes a cop so noble also makes them do things against self-interest. Smith had a more cerebral outlook on the job and in life and always gave me pause to reexamine my beliefs.

Traffic was light on the surface street. I could roll through the stop signs, cutting my time down a smidgeon.

Up ahead, just before Campus Avenue, an amber light blinked, indicating a traffic stop. A fellow cop had pulled a car over. I had not heard it on the radio. Maybe he hadn't called it out. I wasn't back in beat yet, still several miles too far west. Rule number one on the street, though, is always back your partner. No one ever drives by a traffic stop without checking to see if the person needed help.

Damn. I couldn't put myself out at the stop, not over the air. I would be announcing to everyone my out-of-beat violation. And if I didn't put it over the air, and the sergeant drove by, I'd be in violation of two policies. What a mess I'd created, all to see a girl. How could I be distracted when I'd been so diligent? I turned on my amber hazard light and pulled in behind unit 336. I couldn't remember who had checked out that car this shift.

I got out in a hurry. I'd just check with the officer, make sure he was code-four, then get going. No one the wiser. Maybe it was Johnny or Smith. I moved off the street and into the grass parkway.

It was Sedge.

Of all the people it could've been. One out of fifteen others on patrol.

He stood talking to two male adults that he'd pulled from the car that were sitting on the curb. Wannabe hardasses dressed in denim and black biker boots with chrome chains hanging from their pockets hooked to their billfolds. They both wore their greasy hair long and had similar mustaches, a couple of nefarious bookends on the prowl. Sedge wasn't anything like Johnny and Smith, though he wanted to be. He wanted to make the felony arrests and be a part of the "Big Dog Club." Instead, he always busied himself on the safe side of patrol, writing tickets and running the drivers for outstanding warrants. He never made an arrest on his own. If a warrant popped on the dispatcher's screen, she automatically sent Sedge a backing unit. And he'd await their arrival before trying to take anyone into custody. He didn't handle the streets, the streets handled him.

"You're a bad little rookie," Sedge said when I walked up. "I'm gonna tell your daddy. Sergeant Long isn't going to like that you're out of beat. Tsk, tsk, tsk."

"Yes, sir. Are you code-four? If you are I'll be on my way."

I said it while keeping an eye on the two wannabe thugs. I didn't have a lot of experience with violent confrontations but was always on the alert, always ready. At least I thought I was, even though I didn't know how I'd deal with it when it came. Since I'd been on my own the last two weeks. I had also been on the lookout for that ever-elusive first felony arrest. I needed to prove my worth—that all my training had not gone to waste. Johnny and Smith both found at least one felony every shift, usually two or three. A feat that astounded and at the same time scared the hell out of me. Would I ever make it, be like them? Help to make the streets a safer place?

I moved to the back of the patrol unit where Sedge had emptied the pockets of the two men sitting on the curb: cigarette papers for hand-rolling, two pouches of Bugle Boy tobacco commonly used in the jails, Zippo lighters, a banged-up little black address book, three unused condoms, two buck knives, and an all-steel marijuana pipe, a violation of Health and Safety code 11364, a misdemeanor.

Sedge looked up from his citation book where he wrote out the vehicle code violation, the purpose for his stop. Probably the broken-out brake light lens on the gray primer Dodge Dart. It was a good stop; these two were on the prowl. I'd at least learned that much while riding with Smith.

"Hey, Junior, this is a Big Dog stop. You need to work your way up to one of these." He wagged his hand. "Go on, go write some parker violations, red curbs, fire hydrants, and the like."

"Yes, sir." I picked up the marijuana pipe from the trunk of Sedge's patrol unit. Something didn't look right. It was too heavy for a marijuana pipe. There was a slot on the side with a protruding little handle, both hardly noticeable. I looked at Sedge. He'd gone back to writing the citation, checking the cheat sheet for the correct violation number and description. I shook the pipe. Something rattled. Just a little. I twisted the steel bowl that held the marijuana when in use. The bowl turned. I unscrewed it. The pipe came apart in my hand. Out dropped a .32 caliber pistol cartridge. I looked up shocked. The little handle on the side of the pipe was attached to an interior spring and a firing pin. The pipe was a camouflaged zip gun, a hard felony.

Like a big dope, I stood there for a second not knowing what to do, how to handle it. The District Attorney would throw out the arrest because we couldn't show knowledge that the crook knew it was a zip gun. Or which one of the thugs actually possessed it. Two big hurdles to overcome.

I palmed the .32 cartridge, put it in my pocket, screwed the pipe back together, and set it on the trunk. I stood by and waited. Time was ticking on my burg report call.

Sedge finished writing and went over to the two crooks sitting on the curb. "You can go, Rook. I got this."

The two hadn't seen me messing with the pipe. I'd had my back to them and they were sitting on the curb below sight level. I said nothing and stood by, my hands crossed at my waist, trying to decide how to handle it. I decided on *Be bold, use my initiative.*

Sedge had the driver stand up. Both of them did. I reached back to the trunk and palmed the pipe without anyone paying attention.

Sedge explained the citation and the court date. The driver, the shorter of the two, signed the citation. Sedge tore off the yellow copy and handed it to him. "So, we can go?" The driver asked.

Sedge started to say, yes, but I cut him off and asked Sedge: "You done with them?"

"Yeah, I'm done with them, Rook, why?"

"So, we can go?" the driver asked again. The two started to move toward the Dodge.

I held up my hand. "Just wait a second." I turned to Sedge. "You're done with the contact?"

"Yeah," he raised his voice. "You need to get outta me face, Rookie. I said I was done, okay?"

I stepped in front of the two crooks, stood in a classic interrogator stance, strong foot back, weight balanced over my hips, ready for anything that might happen. My heart beating out of my chest. "Where are you guys headed?" I wasn't sure exactly how to start the conversation.

Sedge huffed, stepped back, and crossed his hands at his waist, his arms resting on his abundant belly. "You're a real ignorant pup, aren't you?"

I opened my hand with the marijuana pipe while watching their eyes. The taller one reacted, a minor twitch at the corner of his eye, at the same time both eyes widened a little.

I pretended to look at the pipe, turning it over and over in my hands, while keeping an eye on him. "I've never seen a pipe quite like this."

Sedge said, "It's a misdemeanor, not worth the time to tag it into evidence. I said I'd let them walk if they cooperated."

I'd turned the pipe end around, holding the bowl like a handle of a gun, and pulled the little steel handle back depressing the interior spring. "What's this for?"

"No, don't." The taller one raised his hands, afraid I was about to accidentally shoot him.

It happened faster than I expected. He shoved me in the chest, spun on his heel, and tried to run. I'd thought I was ready; even so, I almost missed him. I grabbed him around the waist and drove with my legs tackling him to the ground.

Sedge yelled, "Hey! Hey! What the hell's going on? What the—"

On the ground, the thug punched me in the face.

I'd been in scuffles in high school, but nothing as dangerous as this. If he overpowered me and got my gun, he could kill us both. This guy was bigger, thicker, more experienced. I'd grabbed a tiger by the tail. The punch to my eye lit up my world and made me question my chosen vocation. Bright lights exploded in my vision, but I held on tight.

The FBI taught ground fighting in the academy. *In stress situations*, Special Agent Frugalti said, *"If you practice enough you will always revert to training. Practice, practice, practice."*

I was outmatched and knew it. I grappled, fighting hard to get in behind him. Off in another world, in another universe, I sensed Sedge in a fight with the other crook.

When in contact with a superior opponent, you will not lose. You will do what you have to do to overcome the threat. He was the one to choose his path.

I wiggled around and got behind the thug, held on. He clawed at my face. I ducked my head behind his. He tossed me off. We faced each other. He smelled of sour body odor, burnt marijuana, and an acidic chemical. I kicked him between the legs. He bent over. I swept his legs from under him. He rolled around in the dirt. I fell on him, got his hands behind his back, and handcuffed before he came to.

Sedge was bent at the waist, out of breath, his hands on his knees, while his crook ran down the sidewalk. I had a serious urge to go in foot pursuit but needed to stay with the guy I had handcuffed on the ground. I wasn't sure Sedge could handle it.

I wore a huge smile as adrenaline pulsed through my heart and brain fueling pure elation. Now this was the high adventure I'd signed up for.

Sedge came over, his eyes angry. He shoved me. "What the hell just happened? Tell me what the *hell* just happened?"

"Touch me again, Sedge, and—"

"And what? What are you going to do, Rookie?"

I fought the idea of taking it further and telling him what I really thought. I looked around on the ground for the pipe that I'd dropped when I tackled the guy.

"Hey. Hey, did you hear me? Why'd you just attack that guy?" He pointed to the thug lying on the grass just starting to come around.

"Attack that, guy? Are you kidding me? Weren't you standing here when it happened? He shoved me." I found the pipe in the gutter, picked it up. "Here. This."

"A misdemeanor grass pipe. You choked a guy out for a misdemeanor grass pipe. You're in a lot of trouble, bub. I don't know who trained you but—"

I'd unscrewed the pipe, took the .32 out of my pocket, and inserted it. "It's a zip gun."

His mouth gaped open. His shaking hand came up to take it as he realized the thug could have shot him with it. That if things had gone differently he could be lying in the gutter, his blood running out.

I pulled the pipe away before he could take it. He wasn't as angry as I thought. He was scared; the smaller thug almost got the better of him before he broke contact and ran off.

I was still exhilarated and couldn't wait to tell Smith and Johnny Maslow. I couldn't believe how much fun that was, even with my eye swelling, throbbing, pulsing with every quick beat of my heart. The fingernail scratches on the side of my cheek burned. But it could've been a lot worse. I made up my mind that I would get a beavertail blackjack like Smith to carry in my sap pocket.

Sedge closed his mouth, his eyes turned hard. "Give that to me. This is my arrest. I'm the one who stopped them." He held out his open hand.

His uniform shirt was untucked and hanging off his enormous belly. Sweat beaded on his forehead and ran down the side of his large flat face, his white pallor unhealthy.

I looked down at my own blue uniform blouse that was now disheveled and scuffed, a pocket torn.

I didn't immediately hand him the zip gun. He'd told me when I asked, he'd said he was done with the contact. That made it my arrest, my first felony, and a great one. An illegal weapon that would get the thug three to five years in the joint and another one year for the assault on a peace officer. On top of all that I'd taken a dangerous weapon off the street.

I was about to tell Sedge to go take a flying leap at the moon when reality set in. I was out of beat, I had not put out on the radio that I was backing Sedge on his traffic stop. Sure, the arrest would go a long way to moderate those minor violations, but Sedge was a senior officer at the station. And I was barely a rookie.

I handed the zip gun to him. "I needed to show knowledge for the case. That's why I took the .32 out of the pipe, put it back together, and played with it in front of this guy. I kicked the guy's boot on the ground. Be sure to put that in your report, his reaction. It shows he had knowledge, which goes toward possession."

Sedge's expression turned from anger to confusion as he tried to tuck in his shirt. He didn't know how to cover my part of the arrest in a report without making himself look like a total buffoon.

"Look," I said, "I'll write it up in a supplement report to your case. I'll say I stopped by to assist you. You discovered the zip gun and displayed it in front of the crook. It took both of us to subdue him, that's why the other one got away."

His eyes looked confused for a second more. "Yeah, that'll work."

I waited for him to say he'd back me up when asked why I was out of beat. He didn't.

"You got the rest of this?" I asked. "I have to get to my call. I'm already late."

"Yeah, sure. Sure. Go ahead."

I headed to my car, my first felony arrest snatched from my grasp. A great felony arrest.

"Hey?" Sedge said. He had the crook on his feet, putting him in the back of his unit.

I turned.

"Thanks, Beckett."

I raised my hand, tried to smile and couldn't, got in my unit, and took off.

There were drawbacks to the game of high adventure, but I'd been tested and passed. At least this time.

Chapter Six

I made it to the burglary location, and the woman didn't mention my extended response time. Maybe I'd skate on this one. Later, I cruised the surrounding blocks to the station until I thought all the units from swing shift had come in. I slid into the gas pumps and refueled my car. I didn't want to explain my damaged uniform and swollen eye. I took off my shirt and hung it on the briefcase my father gave me for graduation from the academy.

I kept my head down when I entered the station's back door and into the hallway. I only needed to turn in my reports, hang the unit keys on the board, and sneak downstairs to change. In the watch commander's office, Sedge stood with several graveyard deputies, just coming on, and the graveyard sergeant and watch commander.

Sedge held up the unique zip gun/marijuana pipe. Everyone laughed and patted him on the back. I caught his eye as I slinked by. He scowled. It set me back. What did he have to scowl about? Then I realized he would always know that it was really my arrest that he didn't deserve, that he had stolen. He thought that I would eventually tell someone what really had happened, and word would get out. Something I had no intention of doing.

I turned down the stairs, headed for the locker room, still trying to rectify in my brain how in the world Sedge could be angry with me. I decided I couldn't expend any more energy on him. Sedge was always going to be Sedge. I made the first turn in the stairs and ran into Lieutenant Galbraith coming up already dressed in his street clothes, a raggedy tee shirt and threadbare jeans, a Winston smoldering in the hand on the rail. He'd caught me in deep consternation and with it came an expression easily misconstrued for a scowl. I smiled but it was too late, Galbraith had spotted me. What the hell else could go wrong?

The next day I came to work and found myself assigned to beat one. I was swimming upstream but the current shoved back no matter how hard I swam. The next step would be dayshift in beat one, then the front desk. If I continued to follow the downward spiral, I'd blow my probation and be out of a job.

I sat alone at the front table in briefing. No one asked about my black eye and the scratches on the side of my face. Did they think I got into a fight? Like what, in some sleazy bar brawl after work?

Sleepy Hollow. Beat one. Damn. In order to get along with the situation at hand, I needed to put lipstick on a pig, as Dad would say. Paint on that smile, permanently. When briefing broke up, I walked down the aisle between the tables. Sedge threw a wad of paper that bounced off the side of my head. What the hell.

I loaded my unit and took off without talking to anyone.

If there was one silver lining, Market Basket was in beat one. I could work up my nerve, walk in, buy a pack of gum, or a Chick-O-Stick, and apologize to Beth. For what, I wasn't sure. I just knew I had to apologize.

I grew up in beat one and knew most every alley and cul de sac. Some rundown apartments by the freeway might produce a felony arrest. That is if I could pick up the building and shake it hard enough. I'd gotten lucky with the zipgun. I had no idea where to find another felony, especially in beat one. I drove westbound on Fourth Street across Mountain Avenue as childhood memories, one after another, popped up and made me smile.

One day on the way to Market Basket for groceries I sat in the front seat of our Belvedere station wagon with Mom driving. I was ten years old and she'd taken me away from a great book I was reading, *Fear Is the Key*, by Alistair MacLean. She wanted me along just to keep her company while she shopped. That was her excuse. In reality, it was so she could have a child slave to carry the sacks of groceries. She was a wonderful woman who liked to yammer on about this and that, and never liked dead air.

We were eastbound on Fourth, stopped at Mountain Avenue. She told me about how good a nonfiction book was that she was reading, an autobiography of Eddie Rickenbacker. It sounded like something I would like. She stopped mid-sentence as a Toyota Supra sped by in the left-turn pocket. Another car going northbound braked hard. Tires screeched. He laid on the horn. Mom said, "That guy's late for his own accident."

We still had the red signal, but I thought I'd pull a trick on her and said, "Mom? Go."

She said "Oh" and without looking at the signal she let her foot off the brake and proceeded. A few feet into the intersection against the red she caught the error. She braked hard. "David Eugene Beckett!" She leaned over slapping my shoulder. I laughed. It was contagious. She laughed too. "That's a dangerous game, Little Man." A tag she rarely used unless I stepped too close to the line with my pranks.

I drove around my old neighborhood looking for people I knew, a little too proud of the uniform and at having made it through the academy, one of the hardest things I had ever accomplished. Ever would accomplish. We'd started out with a hundred and sixteen recruits and graduated fifty-two.

I pulled over a nice woman with blond hair turning grey driving a blue Volvo, for running a stop sign at D Street and Benson. She immediately apologized for not coming to a complete stop. I couldn't bring myself to cite her and let her off with a warning. She shot me a knowing smile as if she'd gotten away with it before, as if she knew as soon as I stepped out of the patrol I wouldn't be giving her a citation. I needed citations for the end of the month to account for my time; misdemeanor arrests, crime reports, and felonies, it didn't matter which as long as I put forth a diligent effort with designated activities. I needed to write some tickets and make some arrests or at least take a lot more crime report/investigations.

Sedge made few arrests and wrote more tickets than the traffic cars. That's how he accounted for his time. Johnny and Smith never wrote tickets, completed a few crime investigations, and had all felony and misdemeanor arrests. The rest of the cops had mixtures of all four duties. I wanted to be in the same category as Smith and Johnny. I wanted to be a big dog, like Sedge had said. Like Sedge thought he was.

How could Sedge cite so many people when he had to know how much a citation would ruin the driver's day, the driver's month, even his year if his license got suspended for that last ticket?

I got back in the car and cleared the stop with the dispatcher. She gave me a call of a 5150, welfare check at 314 West Armsley Square. My insides cringed. Not another one like Shearer. Welfare and Institutions code 5150 was for a civil commitment of those who were a danger to themselves and others. With just my signatures I could take away someone's freedom, commit them to a 72-hour evaluation by a county psychiatrist. I didn't take that huge responsibility lightly.

Seven minutes later I turned down Armsley Square and right around where 314 West should be. I found some folks on the sidewalk watching something in someone's front yard. One car, a nice kelly-green Jaguar was stopped in the street with the driver out of the vehicle, also looking over the roof at the yard. The old genteel houses on Armsley were large, custom-built jobs, well-groomed with ancient shade trees that gave an illusion of Home Town USA. For the most part, it reeked of big money. At least compared to where I grew up.

I pulled over and stopped in front of the location. Stunned, I stuck my head out the open window for a closer look. A tall thin man pranced around in a perfectly manicured grass front yard. He was naked as a jaybird. He seemed to hear music that wasn't there, music that made him happy enough to frolic. He had dipped his toe into a parallel universe, liked it, and wanted to stay. My job was to try and bring him back to reality.

I advised dispatch that I had a naked man dancing in his front yard and to roll an ambulance for a 5150 committal. Some of the other cops clicked their mics, a form of laughter, viewed as unprofessional and unacceptable by the supervisors. The people on the sidewalk smiled and pointed, amused at the situation, something they could talk about at dinner tonight.

A 5150 contact is one of the most dangerous in the cop's world because the person is so unpredictable. I approached with caution.

I got out and walked to the edge of the emerald-green lawn and stopped. I needed to see if the man would take commands. He stood about six feet tall but was skinny with pale freckled skin in some places and pale white in others where the sun never touched. His hair was neatly coiffed and—

Mr. Simmons. It was Mr. Simmons from high school; he'd taught, of all things, my psych class. The irony of it gave me a twinge of vertigo.

I yelled, "Mr. Simmons?" He stopped his flitting about on tiptoes with a child-like exuberance and turned, losing his happy-go-lucky expression when he saw the uniform. I'd intruded on his world.

"Mr. Simmons, can I talk with you for just a minute?"

Now he looked confused. I took slow steps over to him, talking low. "It's me, Dave Beckett."

"Who?"

"Dave. It's me, Dave. Come over here, let's talk."

He nodded, smiled. "Dave? Do I know you?"

"Sure, you do, you gave me a B in your class, remember?"

He shook his head. "No. No, I don't think I do remember you."

"That's okay, come over here and have a seat in my car, so we can talk."

He looked around as if suddenly aware he stood in his front yard without a scrap of clothing. "The police? What are the police doing here at my house? He looked down at his nakedness, his shoulders slumped. "Ah, hell not again."

"Come on over here, please."

"Can I go inside my house to get a robe or something?"

"No, that's not a good idea. Come over here." Rule number one, always control the situation. Never give your subject the opportunity to arm himself.

A middle-aged woman on the sidewalk said, "Gerome, I'll get it for you."

"Thank you, kind woman. Could you please get my cigarettes as well, thank you? It looks as if I'll be taking another trip downtown. Please, can you lock up for me and feed my cats?"

"Of course."

I gently took the naked Gerome Simmons by the elbow, escorted him to the squad car, opened the backdoor, and had him sit down with his legs sticking out until the ambulance arrived. "I guess you must've been one of my students. How embarrassing. I'm truly sorry you had to experience this."

The woman came out of the house a couple of minutes later with the robe and some Marlboro cigarettes.

"I'm not supposed to let him smoke," I said.

"Really, young man?" Simmons said. "Do I look like a physical threat to you? I know where you are sending me, a place filled with men dressed in white carrying large butterfly nets. I won't be able to smoke for three days, so please allow me this one last request."

"Go ahead."

He stood, shrugged into the robe. I bumped out a cigarette, lit it for him, and held onto the lighter.

He took a huge drag off the cigarette, held it in, and then let it out slowly. "I'm really not a bad person."

"No one said you were."

I remembered a story he told in class, how he won a purple heart in Vietnam. He'd been asleep when his camp came under mortar attack. He jumped from his cot, groggy, grabbed his M16 rifle, and ran from the tent. He held the rifle across his body and slammed into the door frame of the tent door. It knocked him flat and unconscious. In class, he laughed at the silly event, but his eyes told a different story, one of fear and loathing for a war in another country, someone else's war, a story where he had experienced the gruesome and grotesque, the part of life regular humans were not built to endure.

A half-hour later we were talking like old friends about the funny things teenagers did in high school. He talked to me as if I were an adult. He waved goodbye as the attendants lifted him on the gurney into the back of the ambulance. "Drop by and see me some time, Dave." He smiled. "But you're gonna have to wait about three days."

"I'll do that, Mr. Simmons. Good luck."

Chapter Seven

I got back in the patrol car and put the finishing touches on the 5150 form, using gentle, less descriptive language than I normally use, when the dispatcher gave me a code-three run, lights, and siren, to Mountain and Fourth Street, an "unknown injury" traffic accident.

Code-three driving was exciting, I loved it. Traffic accidents not so much. The screaming, the grief, lives forever altered. The siren wailed overhead as I negotiated the turns out of the residential neighborhood and onto Fourth, a wider thoroughfare and a straight shot west to the crash on Mountain.

I was a beat car, not a traffic car. I only caught a crash when the Tom cars were all tied up. Tom-One today was Sedge, of all people. I couldn't help thinking he was off somewhere pretending to be busy, so I'd catch all his crashes. I know it wasn't fair to think that way; Mom always said, "Don't be afraid to feed the dog even if it bites you."

Far up ahead, cars saw my red and blue lights, heard the siren, and pulled over. With the excitement came the small thrill of having just a bit more power than the average person, how I could make folks move out of the way.

Car crash reports were the most difficult for me; they required math above my level of comprehension, with the Delta V, the mass, and velocity mixed in with a bunch of complicated formulas. The investigations were detail-oriented, and if one measurement was off it could defer the cause of the accident to the innocent driver. The Point of Impact, POI, the Points of Rest, POR, the street widths, the lane width, the debris field, all had to be measured and placed in writing in the report as well as in a meticulously drawn scaled diagram. The more serious the crash, the higher the page count, the more detailed the report. Crash reports scared the hell out of me. Maybe this one would be a little fender bender, a "Names exchanged" kind of incident.

From half a mile away, those hopes were dashed. Fire trucks blocked the intersection, and all traffic was at a standstill. Seventy to eighty pedestrians, people from the shopping center, had moved to the sidewalk and corners for a closer look. Ghouls trying to catch a glimpse of human carnage, a way to reassure themselves their day wasn't so bad. I pulled into opposing traffic to get around the stopped cars, drove on the wrong side of the street, and parked blocking northbound traffic, leaving my overhead red and blues rotating.

Half-stunned, I grabbed the department-issue 35mm Instamatic pocket camera and stepped out of the patrol unit. I immediately snapped some photos to memorialize the scene and to give my mind a moment to catch up. The debris field, comprised of bent, mangled parts and cubed glass, started in the middle of the intersection and spread in a widening cone shape northbound for more than a hundred feet. The brute force of this accident, the exchange of energy on impact, had been staggering.

Only two cars were involved. A full-sized baby-blue GMC truck with major front-end damage sat perpendicular to Mountain Avenue on the west side of the intersection blocking eastbound traffic. It hissed and billowed steam. The other car vaguely resembled a root beer brown Ford Maverick and looked as if it might've been dropped from an airplane. There wasn't one smooth part of metal anywhere on the side I could see. All the safety glass windows were shattered or broken out. The deep intrusion into the side of the car all but folded it in half. The crumpled steel no longer held the paint and shined bright in the fading sunlight of the dying day. The GMC truck had T-boned the Maverick at high speed. No way was this a forty-mile-an-hour crash.

Fire personnel stood by the Maverick driver's door not working on the driver. I feared they did it to block the view from the lookie-loos on the sidewalks and street corners. Weak in the knees, I hurried over to them.

The fire captain, with his red helmet and "Hillford" stenciled in black on his turnout coat, handed me a driver's license. "It's an 11-44," he said, the code for a fatal accident. "For your report, we declared him at 1636 hrs."

I took the license from him and could only nod. This was the first fatal I had seen. I had not dealt with one while in training. I didn't want to look at the driver but knew I had to eventually.

I didn't really know where to start. The whole thing overwhelmed my little bit of experience. I looked at the driver's license: Dan Howard, who resided at 1007 North Gardenia Avenue. He was only a few short blocks from home and would never get there now. Would never again pull into his driveway, walk into his house and kiss his wife on the cheek, grab a beer, and watch the nightly news. Today *he* was the nightly news.

His death was now my responsibility. Mine alone.

I had to look at him for the report. I surveyed the scene to get my bearings. Not to see where I stood in the intersection, but to re-establish a grip on my life that seemed, for just a moment, to be spinning out of control. I spotted Beth in her red Market Basket apron standing on the corner. She had her hair pulled back behind her ears, her eyes large and innocent. For some strange reason, seeing her revitalized me. I stared at her a moment longer to get recharged and then walked the few steps to view Mr. Dan Howard. The firemen stepped aside.

Mr. Howard still sat in the front seat but no longer behind the wheel. The entire driver's side of the car had been shoved in, past the halfway point of the car. Howard, a heavyset man, was shoved against the passenger door, his eyes open, his expression plain as if still driving home from work thinking about having dinner with his wife and children and their dog. The point of impact, the instant transfer of so much energy into the side of the Maverick, had simply switched him off. His life's light winked out. He never felt a thing.

After taxes, I took home six hundred dollars a month, hardly enough for a car payment, the rent on my apartment, utilities, and auto insurance. Just enough to eat macaroni and cheese with wienies for dinner. I never minded the lack of pay until three days ago, when I had to handle Mr. Shearer's aftermath, and now this. I wasn't paid enough to handle this much death. Was this job really all about death? Shouldn't it be more about life?

Another fireman handed me a driver's license. "This is the other driver. He's sitting over there on the curb."

"Hold on just a minute." I pulled my radio from my belt, took in a deep breath to steady my nerves and to keep a shaky voice from going over the air. I advised dispatch that this was an 11-44. I asked for a traffic unit. She advised all three Tom cars were tied up and for me to handle, per the watch commander. My worst fear realized.

The fireman said, "That guy said, he was northbound from Holt—"

"Wait." I said, "Holt?" Holt was several miles to the south.

"That's right. He said he just turned northbound on Mountain from Holt when his throttle got stuck."

"He drove this far with his throttle stuck wide open?"

"Yep, ran one of our fire trucks off the road doing it, too, in front of station four."

"Why didn't he turn off his ignition or pull the gear shift into park or neutral?" I knew I didn't have a lot of experience in life, but I could at least see that simple logic.

"I asked him the same thing. He said, and I quote, "It's a new truck, I didn't want to ruin the transmission."

"He made it this far north, doing what, a hundred miles an hour?"

The fireman shrugged. "That's about the size of it. He checks out okay medically, but he still needs to be seen by the ER, just in case." He nodded to the damage of both vehicles. "He could have something going on internally."

Ronald Luck, who worked beat seven, pulled up, parked, got out. "What do you need, boot?"

"Thank you, Ron. Can you snap some photos please?"

I recovered some composure, asked dispatch to notify the coroner, and asked to have them respond ASAP, that the intersection was completely shut down. Fourth and Mountain was a major thoroughfare, and cars were already bumper-to-bumper for miles with the go-home-from-work traffic.

I looked at the other driver's license in my hand: Greg Larson from

Upland. The guy who didn't want to shut his truck off and chose to ride it out. A dumbass decision that cost a man his life. What had he been thinking? Of course, three miles or so from Mountain at a hundred plus miles an hour didn't give him long to think.

"David Eugene?" Someone in the crowd had called my name. "David Eugene?"

My head whipped around.

Mom?

I walked over to her as she stepped off the curb into the street. She wore her usual black pedal pusher slacks and a hand-sewn blouse from a Butterick pattern that made her stand out from all the others around her. More than anything else she liked to create and to be unique. She kept her hair in a beehive with too much Aqua Net hair spray. She always had happy eyes. My friends growing up said she was a babe.

"Mom, get back on the sidewalk." I gently took her by the arm and assisted her.

"My land, I can't believe he—is that man in the other car dead? How come they're not working on him?" I looked around at the people who'd gathered in close to listen to my reply.

I lowered my voice. "What are you doing here? You need to go home."

"Don't you want my statement?"

"Your statement?"

"Yes, I was driving up Mountain at D Street. This guy came barreling up behind me honking his horn. I drove onto the sidewalk or he would've smashed into me. I almost ran over a woman with her stroller getting out of his way. My land, I might've ruined the tire alignment on the station wagon. I really hit that darn curb. Is that man really dead?"

The bastard almost crashed into my mom.

This crash kept getting worse. Two more black-and-whites pulled up. Tom One, Sedge, and Lieutenant Galbraith. What was the lieutenant doing on scene? He never left his office. He wasn't supposed to ever leave the office.

"Mom, please be quiet, just for right now. I'll talk to you later, okay."

"What's the matter, is that your boss? You want me to pretend I'm a regular citizen and tell him what a great job you're doing?" She again stepped off the curb, headed for Lieutenant Galbraith, who was headed our way.

I took her by the arm. "No," I said, a little too harshly. "Please. Please, just stay on the curb and be quiet."

I turned my back to her and walked toward Galbraith, who was wearing his uniform without a Sam Browne belt and had a small Detective Special .38 in a pancake holster on his hip. Was he going to relieve me of this scene because he thought I couldn't handle it? He couldn't do that. Even though a part of me wished he would. What would all the other officers, my peers, think? If he relieved me of the responsibility it would send a message to all the others on patrol that I was still a cadet and not a full-fledged officer, that I couldn't handle my beat. He puffed on a cigarette like a freight train going up a grade. Sedge tailed along in his wake; his big belly's overlap covered his Sam Browne buckle and jiggled with each step.

I needed to handle my assigned call. I veered over to Mr. Greg Larson from Upland, the driver of the GMC who'd caused all the havoc and death. Galbraith and Sedge changed course to intercept.

I told Larson to stand up. He did and immediately started talking fast. "I am so, sooo sorry. I did not mean for this to happen. It was an accident. Really it was. I went through the red light. I couldn't stop. It wasn't my fault. It was the truck. Something's wrong with it. I'm gonna sue the manufacturer, you wait and see if I don't."

The lieutenant and Sedge caught up and stood close by.

I held up my hand to stop Larson from talking. "Are you hurt?"

He ran his hands up and down his torso. "No. I don't think so. I think I'm gonna be real sore tomorrow, though."

So was Dan Howard, the driver of the Maverick.

"What happened?"

"I…I was driving north on Mountain and my truck…my accelerator got stuck. I guess I panicked."

"Why didn't you shut it off or pull the gearshift down into park?"

"It's a brand-new truck. It would've ruined it. If I did that it would've dropped the transmission."

"Turn around and put your hands behind your back."

"What? You're arresting me? It was an accident."

Behind me Sedge said. "Hold on Rookie, you can't—"

Galbraith held up his hand to silence Sedge. Larson wasn't turning around. I took him by the arm, put him in a wristlock, and handcuffed him.

"Dave?" I looked up. Beth had wangled her way to the front of the crowd. My heart skipped a few beats before it caught up.

"You're going to arrest him? My God, it's a horrible thing but it was just an accident."

I didn't have time to explain it to her. I started to escort Larson to my patrol unit. Galbraith said, "Hold on Beckett."

I tried not to cringe. He was going dress me down, tell me I was a fool and too young to be handling this serious of an investigation. Too young to be on the streets unsupervised. I turned to him.

Galbraith said, "What do you need?"

"What?"

"What do you need?"

I recovered. "I need Fourth blocked and the traffic diverted, probably two units. Mountain as well."

"I'm going to jail?" Larson said. I gripped his arm tighter. "Be quiet. I'll talk to you later."

Galbraith said, "Sedge, put this guy in Beckett's unit and then direct traffic." Sedge glared at me. Directing traffic wasn't a fun assignment, it was more a rookie's job. I knew enough not to ask Galbraith why Sedge, as a traffic car, wasn't handling the report.

"What else?" Galbraith asked.

"I need CHP 180s completed on these two cars, I'm holding them as evidence in my manslaughter investigation."

He turned and yelled. "Sedge, bring me your clipboard with two 180s."

Galbraith turned back to me and read my expression. "What? I still know how to fill out a God damn report form." He smiled. "Maybe you better get started on all your measurements. There's going to be a lot of them."

"Yes, sir."

I headed to the root beer brown slab of crushed metal that used to be a Ford Maverick. I took out the yellow lump of lumber crayon I kept in my pocket at all times and marked the POR of the left rear tire.

"Beckett?"

I turned back to the lieutenant.

"That was a nice felony arrest."

I smiled and looked back at the patrol car Sedge was putting Larson in.

"Not him, this crash won't make it past the DA."

He winked.

He meant the zipgun arrest.

I smiled hugely.

Chapter Eight

I didn't sleep well after shift, got up early, and went for a long run to clear my head. The way Beth had looked at me when I arrested Larson for manslaughter for a brief moment made me challenge the way I looked at my chosen career.

A charge that wouldn't stick. I had to arrest him. The DA could take on the onus to let the driver walk on his crime. The right thing to do.

Beth's wonderfully intense brown eyes, her angry words asking me why. The whole scene wouldn't leave me alone and churned round and round in my head.

I automatically turned north, straight up San Antonio Avenue headed for beat one. I would eventually turn left on I Street, west, then traverse the parking lot along the strip center up to Market Basket. It was too early for Beth to be at work. I needed to tell someone, anyone, about Mr. Shearer and Mr. Dan Howard. I needed to explain to Beth why I'd felt the need to make the arrest. And then what? Just how would that conversation go?

Working as a cadet at the station's front desk had been much simpler than working patrol. The station gofer didn't have that much responsibility. Right now, death circled just above my head, a kettle of vultures looking down, ready swoop at any moment. Patrol showed me a part of life I'd never seen, a part of life most everyone had never seen. Cops weren't the keepers of the peace after all, not if the last few weeks were any indication. The patrol officer's only purpose was to keep reality at bay, to keep it from seeping into the perception created by Andy in *Mayberry*, or *Leave it to Beaver*, a kind of life television and magazine ads wanted us to believe in.

The way people really wanted life to be. A parallel world.

I jogged in place at D Street waiting for the cars in the four-way stop to clear. I continued north. The crisp predawn February cooled and dried the sweat. I wasn't out of breath and had plenty in the tank ready to be expended. I increased my pace and pushed it a little.

As a cadet, I got a good grasp from working the front, talking with the folks who came in to report a crime or to ask for copies of crime reports. One of my collateral duties was to fingerprint the teachers for their jobs, the drug registrants, and the sex registrants for their parole requirement. I called them The Good, The Bad, and The Ugly. But life's small sample that walked in the station's front door was just a smidgeon of what really happened out on the street.

And I'd only just started my career. Was it going to get worse? I'd never forget the way Dan Howard looked, shoved into the passenger's side of the crumpled, root beer brown Ford Maverick. I'd never forget his name or his open eyes staring into nothingness as he drove off, into the forever.

I made it to I Street, my tee-shirt now soaked with sweat, my breath coming hard. I ran through the parking lot and looked through the automatic double doors to Market Basket as I went by. The soft welcoming yellow light begged for me to stop and go in even though they were closed for two more hours. I ran to Fourth Street, the north side of the strip mall parking lot, and headed back east without looking at the empty and quiet intersection that hours earlier had been such a gruesome scene. I could easily see how some folks believed ghosts came back to haunt a location.

In that moment I realized all my old, comfortable memories in this town were going to be recorded over with new events, like those flash images of Dan Howard's expression, his death rictus, and Mom almost being a victim. A mild wave of nausea rolled through me. Was this what I really wanted to do with my life?

Then I remembered the fight, the guy with the zip gun, the excitement of catching a felon and taking a dangerous gun off the street, the risk, the very real possibility that I'd lose the fight and he'd get my gun. The great adventure I'd yearned for. That's what the job was really about. The rest of it, all the death, the bad memories recording over the good, were nothing more than unintended consequences I had to deal with. That I *could* deal with. Sure, I could.

But in a few days, the brutal murder of Jessica DeFrank would again shift all my beliefs and forever change my world. A loss of innocence along with an unshakable conviction that true evil did exist.

The long run helped add weight to balance the emotional scales. I made it back to my apartment as dawn peeked out, grays turning to light pinks and yellows. I stood under a hot shower for twenty minutes before dressing, took Astro for a long walk, and then drove to Mom's house at I Street and Benson, right on the border of Montclair, the place I'd grown up. The Pontiac Firebird rode like a dream, an extravagance I'd since realized I couldn't afford, a foolish juvenile gesture I'd mistaken as a milestone in becoming an adult. The car mirrored the color and model James Gardner drove in *The Rockford Files*, my favorite TV program. How juvenile can you get?

The front of our house faced west toward Benson Avenue, one house up from a four-way stop at I Street. In our front yard, Mom had sculpted a six-foot-tall native South Pacific Islander, heavily muscled with broad shoulders and holding a spear. He stood life-size at the corner of the garage, menacing all who approached. On the front of the garage hung three tiki masks she'd created, and like the native they were now fashioned from chicken wire and concrete painted in bright colors. The original hand-carved hardwood tikis had been stolen three times. They looked too authentic and apparently were highly desirable. When she shifted to concrete and chicken wire the sheer weight deterred any further theft.

A vibrant creativity filled my mom to overflowing, an obsession she vented any way she could. She always had different art projects in the hopper, some short-term like paintings and sculptures, others more long-term, the kind she chipped away at whenever the urge struck.

I parked in her driveway, shocked and awed at what I saw. I turned off the quiet engine. I had not been to the house in a week or two. Maybe three. Enough time, apparently, for a seven-foot-tall volcano, brightly painted, to rise from the ground. I walked around the monstrous art shaking my head, marveling at how real it looked. She'd planted banana trees, bougainvillea, and other jungle-type plants I couldn't identify around the base to add to the island mystique. If I squinted I could envision miniature natives, angry and throwing spears at a giant King Kong while the volcano erupted, spewing gray smoke from the cooking cheeseburgers.

Behind the volcano, on the side in between the house, Mom had hollowed the belly where she'd built in a large briquette barbeque grill with a small shelf for food preparation. Amazing. When had she have time to finish something so involved, so large without me knowing about it?

I had come over to see how she was doing with what happened the day before, the crash at Fourth and Mountain. The way Larson ran her off the road, her seeing Dan Howard dead in the crumpled-up Maverick. She hadn't seemed emotional at all. She had shifted her emotional gears smoothly by wanting to give a statement, and by telling my boss what a great job I was doing. She had repressed the incident. The shrink who spoke at our academy warned us about repressing hot emotional incidents and that it could cause problems later in life. I needed to talk Mom into seeing someone about what happened, what she'd experienced.

I knocked at the door before entering. It felt weird to knock at a place where I'd spent eighteen years growing up. I entered. "Hello, Mom?" No answer. The big green Belvedere station wagon wasn't in the driveway. She wasn't home. Down the hall, I stopped at the linen closet for a pillowcase on my way to the kitchen. I was a cop doing a burglary, a little ashamed, but sometimes hunger trumps minor ethical violations. I opened the door to the wall pantry where she kept the canned goods and found a note in Mom's nearly illegible cursive. She'd written:

Mr. David,

Please use this grocery bag. Pillowcases are expensive.

Always yours

Ms. Charlotte.

I looked over my shoulder to see if she'd walked in and caught me red-handed. That's what guilt does for you. I smiled. I thought I'd been fooling her about the canned goods. I didn't think she'd noticed the few cans I'd borrow every now and again. I did intend to pay her back, someday. Wink.

Mom's name was Jo Ann, not Charlotte. She liked to sign her notes to me with names from characters in books we'd both read or that she'd read to me as a child. This one was about a spider with a web, who talked to Wilbur the pig. I smiled at the name. I was an adult now and torn. I wanted to tell her to stop with the childish names. But adults didn't sneak over to a parent's house to raid a pantry. Maybe my growling stomach would let her sign her notes a little while longer.

She had a learning disability and could read just okay. She couldn't spell very well. She did all right with short sentences and kept a small dictionary in her purse for that purpose. I had shopped with her at Market Basket many times when she wrote a check. The spelled-out numbers on the check proved too difficult and she kept a list in sequential order folded in the checkbook. Ashamed at her inability to spell, she held the flap of the checkbook open, covering her crib sheet when she wrote.

I folded the pillowcase and set it on the counter next to the sink where she'd see it as soon as she walked in. I took up her brown paper grocery bag from Market Basket. Some canned goods were set aside from the others. I loaded them up. SpaghettiOs (something I didn't like so much anymore, but she apparently believed I did), and some cans with circle-cut pineapple (those I did still love). Four cans of Le Sueur sweet peas, excellent, but very expensive, and six cans of Campbell's bean-with-bacon soup. The big score, though: ten boxes of mac and cheese. I could survive a long time on mac and cheese.

When I graduated from the Sheriff's academy I had secretly printed business cards with "David Beckett Police Officer." Part of the hazing during training was that I couldn't have business cards until I passed probation (five months, one week, and one day to go). Sedge liked to remind me. "Why spend the money on business cards, Boot? You're just going to wash out and go back to tossing burgers at McDonald's."

I'd never worked at McDonald's and he knew it.

I took one of the cards and wrote an IOU on the back. I signed it Bilbo Baggins. I left it propped against a large orange and green can of yams. She'd see it as soon as she opened the cupboard. She beamed with pride with the largest smile I'd ever seen when I graduated from the academy. She'd like the card.

I drove home feeling better about life in general. Seeing the volcano had done it. Her note. That part of my world would never change, and as long as I had that anchor—Mom at home being Mom—I could handle anything.

I came in through the side door to my apartment and into the kitchen. Astro didn't scamper across the cheap linoleum to come and see me like he always did. Something was up. I set the bag of canned goods on the counter. "Astro? Come here, boy."

I stepped through the kitchen into the small living room. Astro sat on the couch, a forbidden spot, looking guilty. I'd been trying to teach him manners. Weeks ago, while on patrol, I'd noticed the couch discarded for the garbageman in a side alley and came back for it after work with the Belvedere Wagon. It wasn't really all that bad, just a little worn in places. I put a nice Afghan Mom had crocheted on the couch with some throw pillows. Astro looked sheepish. I scanned the room for some other infraction, like peeing on the floor, and noticed light striations in the twenty-year-old high-low carpet.

Mom.

She'd somehow broken into my apartment, vacuumed, and tidied up the place.

"Bad dog, Astro. You're supposed to repel unwanted intruders. What good are you? Huh?" He stuck his nose under a throw pillow and came out with a rawhide chew he'd hidden before I came in. "Oh." I chuckled. "She bribed you. Your affections come awfully cheap, my friend. You should've held out for a beef shank bone."

I couldn't afford to buy him rawhide chews; I could barely afford to feed him. I retraced my steps back to the kitchen to see what else I missed. I opened the refrigerator and found it freshly cleaned and stocked with perishables: vegetables, fruit, milk, cheese, and some Oscar Meyer wienies for the mac and cheese. On the shelf, right up front, sat Mom's famous German chocolate cake. She knew I hated the coconut in the German chocolate and that I really preferred her pineapple upside-down cake. Every time I told her I didn't like German Chocolate she'd wink and say, "Oh, don't be silly, this is a wonderful cake, everyone loves this cake." She could be a tad eccentric.

A note folded in half sat propped against the cake.

Mr. David

Ask that nice girl with the big brown eyes over to your apartment for dinner. She'll love the cake.

Ms. Emilia Bedelia.

The day before, at the crash scene, she must've caught me looking at Beth, heard what Beth had said to me. Seen something in how we looked at each other, imagining something was there when it really wasn't.

Oh sure, after what happened, Beth would come over for dinner at my place? Besides, she had a serious boyfriend, Cole Adler. At least I thought she did. I wasn't entirely sure after the way she'd reacted the day behind the Market Basket when I'd asked about him.

I got ready for work, made a fresh salad, ate it, took Astro out one more time, and walked to work.

Chapter Nine

Halfway through the shift, I caught a domestic out-of-beat. A family disturbance in beat five. I was assigned to back Smith on the call. Domestic disturbances and burglary reports are the most common calls for service, the domestic being the most dangerous of all. Emotions run hot and blur the line between common sense and temporary insanity. A thin line that all too often bulges and snaps. People don't like the authorities coming into their personal space and telling them how to handle their lives.

I pulled up and parked just down from the address, a nice house in a quiet neighborhood at the top of beat five. I'd made it to the call before Smith. I got out and left the amber hazard lights on in case something happened inside and additional backing units needed to get to us fast. I took the baton from the inside door handle and put it in the ring on my belt. It was just after dusk and night had fallen hard. Full dark, no stars.

I needed to be back at the station working on the crash/arrest report from the day before, but dreaded the math needed to complete the investigation and kept putting it off. I stepped onto the sidewalk just as the cherry end of a cigarette glowed hot. Someone stood in the darker shadow created by a big tree trunk on the parkway strip in between the sidewalk and the street.

My hand automatically jumped to the stock of my handgun.

Smith.

I recognized his outline, his scent, the way he stood. He wore Old Spice and smoked unfiltered Camels.

He must've parked around the corner and walked in. He always did things out of the ordinary. Back when I rode in the car with him on training, he'd said, "Always do the unexpected, it'll keep you alive. Never follow a set pattern."

He spoke around the cigarette perched precariously at the corner of his lips. "You're already developing some bad habits, Dave. We talked about this, how it's too easy to become complacent. Don't do it. Don't let your guard down. Develop solid officer survival skills now, before you fall into a groove. You're better than that."

I knew instantly what he was referring to: the amber lights, baton in the door, and parking too close to the house. I did know better, but this was the way Johnny did it and he seemed to do okay on the street. Some said Smith was too paranoid.

"Yeah," I said. "You're right. I'll work on it, I promise." But I'd have to think about it. I needed to develop my own methods working the street. Find my own way.

Smith took another long drag on the Camel. The cherry lit his face in an eerie glow that created dark shadows illuminating his tanned skin. The DI in the academy said cigarettes marked a person with a dim light along with the visual smoke and its scent. I didn't want to point this out to Smith. I liked and respected him too much. To say something would sound juvenile and I was trying like hell to be an adult.

"Come on," he said. "Let's go."

We walked to the front door, neither one of us on the narrow concrete walkway but just off to the side in the grass where someone watching from in the house wouldn't expect us to be. Approaching the house with Smith, I easily slipped back into his paranoia and realized his method suited me. The light above the front door lit us up when we got close and made me hyperaware of the disadvantage. We stood to the side of the door, which is known to all savvy cops as the window of death. I knocked as muffled yelling reached us from inside, a male and female locked in a verbal battle, each disparaging the other with vulgar slurs.

The door abruptly swung open to an angry man dressed in a brown suit, beige shirt unbuttoned at the top, a tan and burgundy tie loose but still in a knot. His eyes carried the glassy blur of alcohol. He reeked of bourbon. He stood six feet tall, a little pudgy, a football player starting to go to fat but still formidable. "Oh," he yelled. "You called the police. Perfect."

Smith waited for me to take the lead, even though it was his call for service. I appreciated the offer to gain additional experience. I raised my hand. "Sir, please step back."

"What? You think you can just come in here without an invite? Not on your life, pal. I know how you assholes operate. You all think you're brothers and lie for each other. No way. Not this time. Assholes, the whole lotta ya."

"Sir," I said, "we have a call to this residence and that gives us the right to enter and check on the safety of the occupants. If you don't step back, we will have to arrest you for resisting and delaying a peace officer in the performance of his duty."

"Son of a bitch." He stomped away, deeper into the living room. We followed him. The living room was a step-down with new plush carpet, burgundy-colored and recently spotted with broken glass and liquids of an unknown origin, glasses, and bottles thrown in anger. The television played a rerun, an old sci-fi movie I'd watched as a kid on Saturday evenings. The entire scene reminded me of the way my mom and dad used to argue.

This was the first week in February and a dried-out Christmas tree lay on its side, the needles brittle and flaking off. The red and blue and green lights on the tree should not have been lit, a fire hazard that could, and eventually would, burn down the house. Presents wrapped with decorative Christmas paper littered the room stomped and mashed, ruined. The expensive furniture sat undisturbed, as if a little tornado had set down here and there limiting the damage.

A woman with bottle-blond hair and dressed in a maroon robe stood by the entrance to the kitchen, one arm under her breasts, holding on tight to her body as if someone, at any moment, might try to steal her away. Her other hand held a tumbler of booze, an amber liquid, no ice, that sloshed when she swung her arm. "Tell him to get out," she said. "I changed the locks and tonight this big bastard just bursts right in." Black mascara lines melted by tears ran down her cheeks. Her eyes, red and puffy, made her a sad clown. Under different circumstances, seen on the street or in her place of business, she'd be a real beauty, maybe even movie-star worthy.

"I'll talk to her," Smith said. "You get his story."

"Excuse me, sir." I pointed to the corner of the living room. "Can I talk with you over here?" Always separate the involved parties when trying to mediate a problem.

He hesitated, looking at his distraught wife, his face flushed red. He pointed a finger at her. "See what you caused. Now the cops are here sticking their big fat noses into our business. Perfect. Just perfect."

"Sir, over here, please." He hesitated for a moment, his eyes locked on his wife. "Fine." He led the way to the corner. Always keep your partner in view. I stood in a strong interrogator's stance, ready, in case he physically went off on me.

"Sir, can you tell me what's going on here tonight?"

"Oh, you know. Don't pretend like you don't know."

"What?" I wanted to look back at Smith to see if he understood what the man meant, but it wouldn't have been smart tactically.

The man raised his hand and pointed at his wife across the room as she talked with Smith. I knocked his hand away, not knowing his initial intent. I took two steps back so I could see the entire room. Smith eyed me.

"Listen," I said to the man. "Keep your voice down and talk to me. Tell me what's going on."

"You're one of them. You're nothing but a shitass kid. I'm getting a drink."

I stepped to the side, blocking his access to the wet bar in the corner. "You going to tell me what's going on, or are we just going to have her side of the story?"

I thought he was going to start yelling again. Instead, his expression dropped and his eyes filled with tears. He stared at his wife. He spoke in a lowered voice with a disheartening tone. "I still love her, goddammit, that's the problem. Can you understand that?" He shifted his gaze to look at me. "I've loved her since the first time I laid eyes on her. You can't possibly know what I'm talking about, loving a woman like I love her."

But I did. I had a crush on Beth the moment I first I saw her sitting on the wall in front of South Hall, Cole Adler next to her, his arm around her shoulders. I knew how it hurt not being able to be with her.

I was new at mediating other people's problems when I still had a difficult time navigating my own. I didn't know what to say, especially about something so personal. I wasn't a trained family counselor. "Why is your Christmas tree still up? Why aren't the gifts opened? What happened here?" Wrong question. I knew it as soon as the words left my mouth.

He turned angry again, his face instantly red. "You know very well what happened here, you little wet-nosed punk. I don't appreciate you pretending like you don't, making me out as some kinda chump."

His voice raised higher with each word. In my short experience, I had never encountered this kind of argument. "I'm sorry, I really don't know what you're talking about."

He puffed up his chest. His face swelled as he yelled, "Don't lie to me. You know. *You know.*" He raised his hand to shove me. I was ready. I grabbed his hand, twisted it into a wristlock, pulled downward, and at the same time kicked his legs from under him. He went to the floor on his belly as I put my knee in his back.

Smith appeared at my side. He put his knee on the man's neck, holding him down while I got the cuffs on him. I stood him up.

He yelled at his wife. "You bitch. See what you caused? See?" His head spun from one side to the other flinging spittle with his words. "You want to know what happened to my marriage? I'll tell ya, I will. I don't care what you do to me."

His wife yelled, "Herb, don't."

"All right, I'll tell ya, sure I will," he said. "I'll tell ya, even though you're pretending like you don't already know. Officer John Maslow is fucking my wife. There, I said it. Now you can take me out back and put a bullet in my head. I know that's how you boys operate. You cover for each other, right? Isn't that right? Come on, let's get it over with. I don't want to live with a wife who wants to fuck officer *John Maslow*. My life's over. Capital O-V-E-R."

His wife rushed across the room and wrapped her arms around her husband's neck, his hands cuffed behind his back. "Baby, I still love you. I told you I'm sorry a hundred times. Please—" She turned to us. "Please, let him go. Don't take him to jail."

I stood still holding Herb's arm, emotionally gut-punched by what he'd said. My friend Johnny had caused all of this chaos. Ruined these people's lives when we were paid to do the opposite. This wasn't the Johnny I knew. My world shifted under my feet yet again.

Chapter Ten

Johnny Maslow's moral turpitude spun round and round in my head and wouldn't leave me alone. I couldn't help wondering if Mom and Dad had separated for the same reasons. In the past I had asked Mom why and each time she changed the subject, pretended like she had not heard the question.

I stayed after shift, four and a half hours to finish the accident investigation. I didn't put in for overtime. How could I? More experienced officers wouldn't have taken as long. I dropped the report in the basket on the counter outside the watch commander's office. Lieutenant Don Hamilton sat at his desk inside the W/C's office carving on a little wooden figurine with an X-Acto knife, the police radio conspicuously silent, the window to the dispatch room slid closed. Hamilton always worked graveyard and always carved during slow nights. He was the nicest guy at the station and had the "graveyard spread," a large stomach with a butt to go with it. Whenever he stood, his too-short legs made him look cartoonish. "Hey, Beckett?"

I stuck my head in the door. "Yes, sir?"

"What are you doing here so late?"

"Paperwork."

"That 11-44?"

"Yes, sir."

"Be sure you put in for overtime. If you have any problem with those skid calculations, bring them to me. I'll give you a hand with them."

"Yes, sir." No way did I have the Vehicle One's speed correct. The big

GMC truck T-boned the Maverick. The Maverick left four perpendicular skids that I had never seen before.

The report would get kicked back at least two times to be fixed—maybe even three or four. It was the longest report I'd written since I'd been on the job. How could I put in for overtime when I screwed up so many times?

"Go home and get some sleep, you've got a shift tomorrow at three."

It was already tomorrow, four in the morning. "Yes, sir. Thank you, sir."

Outside, a damp fog had rolled in. I shivered. hunching my shoulders and wishing I'd driven the Firebird to work. I hurried home, walking the first block, then ran the rest to stay warm.

I pulled my key from my pocket, my hand like ice, unlocked the door, and entered the apartment through the side door that opened to the small kitchen. Astro shot past me, down the steps, across the driveway, and over to the grass area where he lifted his leg.

"Sorry, little guy, that report was a real SOB." He really had to go and stood there longer than normal, every additional second my guilt growing worse. Maybe as a treat I'd fry him up some wienies. If I did I wouldn't have wienies for my mac and cheese. He finished and pranced over, happy to see me, bouncing around on the steps. I picked him up. He licked my face, his unconditional love a real comfort. "Hey, porko, you're getting fat. Maybe I better try taking you on my runs again." I'd tried several times on a long leash. He'd stop and sniff everything, trees, bushes, and fire hydrants.

He licked my face some more. I entered the apartment and found a folded piece of paper on the counter. Mom.

I still held Astro and hugged him. "It's not your fault, boy. Every time Mom sneaks over, she's feeding you like a king. Probably bringing you foot-long meatball sandwiches from Grinder Haven."

I set him down. He jumped up, put his paws on my leg. He wanted me to pick him up again. I unfolded the note.

Mr. David.

I did a bad thing. Please don't be mad. I'll try and catch up with you in the morning. Remember, always keep smiling.

Ms. Pippi Longstockings.

Oh no, now what's she gone and done? I was too tired to think about it. My brain was mush. I knew I'd be dreaming about Points of Rest, and Points of Impact, numbers and formulas that would scroll in an endless parade throughout a restless night's sleep.

I stripped off clothes down to my briefs and crawled under the covers. Astro jumped on the bed. He knew better, but the guilt from leaving him inside longer than normal without a potty break gnawed at my conscience and he won out. He snuggled up and rested his chin on my chest. I liked him there. That was a stupid rule Mom had about dogs in beds. She'd said, "You lay down with dogs you get fleas." As I drifted off to sleep I realized she probably meant something else entirely, something more profound that I couldn't quite grasp in the throes of slumber. I drifted off.

"Police Department. Mr. Shearer, I'm coming in." The gun shook in my hand, as I eased open the camouflaged door behind the clothes in the closet. I tried to grab onto the doorknob, pull it closed. I didn't want to go in. I didn't want to see what was in there, not again. "No. No. No." The door continued to ease open in the slow motion of a cheap horror movie.

"Mr. Shearer?"

Light with sharp rectangular edges from the garage windows illuminated a section of the concrete floor, the dusky yellow-orange sunlight fading fast. The first thing that came into view, a pool of thick red. Pudding-thick, smooth and sickening, it grew larger as the door continued to open, exposing a broader crime scene. Blood. More blood than a human body could hold. More blood than I'd ever seen before.

I swallowed hard. "No. No. No. Please no. Stop. Don't open anymore."

My nose automatically stopped taking in the scent of gun smoke and the cold smell of iron. I took breaths through my mouth.

His open hands came into view; the backs of his wrists rested on his knees. Knees surrounded by that blood pudding puddle. The commercial with Bill Cosby holding up a spoon of pudding saying, "Here's to you, Mom," jumped into the horror film that was playing out, a strange juxtaposition.

Mr. Shearer sat upright on his heels just to the right of the door as it continued to ease open. Then finally came to a stop.

Mr. Shearer didn't have a head.

He had a neck and the bottom part of his jaw, his bottom teeth naked between a purple and bloated tongue.

Bits of skull with black hair littered the floor.

I stepped in, my feet moving all on their own and against my will.

I stopped dead. Bile rose in my throat. At my feet sat a nose, a perfect nose in every minute detail. It looked as if someone had poured concrete around it and this person with the nose was under the concrete slab taking in last gasps of air. My hand, the one with the gun in it, flew to my mouth. I clunked myself across the nose with the barrel. Foolish. But the pain helped to bring me around, not back to reality but to the strange world I'd stepped into.

In front of Mr. Shearer lay a twelve-gauge pump shotgun, one with a long, long barrel speckled with droplets of dried blood. My eyes locked onto a black wingtip, worn but polished to a high sheen. Dad wore wingtips whenever he put on a suit for funerals or weddings. The shoes on Mr. Shearer's feet were the only things in that garage I could relate to.

Mr. Shearer had put his affairs in order by laying out his important papers on the kitchen table, then went into the garage, sat on his heels, stuck the gun barrel in his mouth, and pulled the trigger.

A droplet fell into the blood puddle. The viscous pudding absorbed it without projecting any rings, like a pebble would in a pond. I looked at the ceiling...And wished like hell I hadn't.

I sat bolt upright, breathing hard. Bright sunlight warmed the bed, a reminder of the real world and how I could always just drop off the patrol unit keys, walk out the back door of the station, and leave behind those kinds of incidents, like Mr. Shearer's garage, or people disparaging friends of mine. But those images would forever defile my memory.

Astro stood on the bed, his paws on my leg. He barked once, twice, three times, trying to tell me something. "Lassie, I don't care if Timmy did fall down the well, I'm sleeping for another—"

The doorbell rang again. That's what had awakened me from the Mr. Shearer nightmare.

Had to be Mom coming over to assuage her conscience for the as-yet-undiscovered etiquette violation she'd mentioned in her note. I got up and shrugged into the closest thing at hand, a damp pair of running shorts I'd tossed on the floor the day before.

"Coming."

My stomach growled. Astro bounded ahead of me, made it to the door, and scratched. I ran my hand back and forth through my bedhead hair and up and down my face trying to wake up. I was naked except for the damp running shorts. Mom could sit on the couch and wait until I took a shower and got presentable. I needed to wake up enough to deal with her eccentric behavior— which always required my full attention—or it would sound too much like jibber-jabber.

I opened the door. On the porch stoop stood Beth.

Beth? What the...?

"Oh, I...a—" I said it in concert with her embarrassed explanations that I couldn't hear over my own.

Her face flushed the same as mine. I jumped behind the door. "What are you doing here?" I said it without thinking.

Her mouth hung open mid-word. "Right. I'm so sorry." She turned to leave.

"No, wait. I didn't mean it to sound like an...I mean...I'm not awake yet. Come back. Please. Come back."

She turned and glanced at her watch. "It's ten o'clock in the morn—" She brought her hand down and put her wristwatch behind her back, realizing she was being judgmental. "Oh, I'm sorry, you must've worked late. This is all my fault, I hadn't realized—"

Those liquid brown eyes were bewitching. "It's okay. Really. Just wait thirty seconds, then come in and have a seat. Don't mind Astro." I blocked him from getting out with my foot. "I'll put some clothes on."

"You sure? If you want to sleep some more, I understand."

No way did I want her to go anywhere. She possessed an elegant beauty I could sit and look upon for hours. Then to be able to finally talk to her one-on-one made my week. Hell, it made my entire year. In high school, I had always wanted to talk to her and could never work up the nerve. Now she stood on my stoop wanting to talk to *me*, of all people.

"I was just getting up anyway. Please. Wait thirty seconds then come in and have a seat. It'll only take me a minute to put something on." I didn't wait for her to decline, I eased the door closed till it was ajar and took off for my room, my feet pounding the floor. What was she going to think about my crappy little apartment, the worn-out carpet, the beat-up couch hidden by an afghan, kitchen linoleum worn almost through to the wood underneath?

My heart raced and sweat beaded on my forehead. What was Beth Abercrombie doing at my doorstep? Wasn't she still going out with Cole? They had to be married by now. How had she found where I lived? What did she want with me?

I shucked my shorts and jumped into some denim pants. Maybe she wanted to apologize for what she'd said the day of the crash? I hesitated, pulling on my Rolling Stones tee-shirt, the one with Mick Jagger's large red tongue on the front. No. No. No, not the one with the large tongue. I pulled it off and opted for my old high school basketball tee shirt. No. I wasn't in high school anymore. I pulled out a long sleeve blue chambray shirt from my closet. I started to button it.

Why would she need to apologize? Under similar circumstances, not knowing all the facts, I might've had the same reaction. I hesitated. She wasn't there fishing for a date, was she? No, life didn't work that way. Not where women were concerned. I wasn't ignorant of women; I knew about the silent dance the boy and girl did while courting. I just couldn't hear the music, never could.

From the kitchen, Beth yelled, "If it's okay, I'm going to check your refrigerator for some juice."

I smiled as I buttoned my shirt. Beth Abercrombie was in my house and comfortable enough to check my refrigerator for some—

Oh, geez, Mom's note was still in there with the German chocolate cake. The note that said:

Mr. David

Ask that nice girl with the big brown eyes over for dinner. She'll love the cake.

Ms. Emilia Bedelia.

No. No. I hurried to the kitchen, my shirt half-buttoned, naked chest exposed. Beth stood in front of the refrigerator, the door still open, tipping back a glass of orange juice she'd just poured as she read Mom's note. Astro sat at her feet waiting for some bit of food to be tossed to him. She saw me and quickly put back the note, next to the cake. "Sorry, I didn't mean to be nosey."

Why hadn't I tossed that note in the trash?

"That's okay." My heart was in my throat, about to choke me. I swallowed hard. "You want to sit down?" I held out my hand toward the small table and two chairs. I looked down and realized I was barefoot.

She took her glass of juice and sat at the table. I sat across from her trying to button my shirt with shaky fingers. Astro walked back and forth rubbing his side along her leg. Beth watched me as she drank orange juice with one hand and leaned down to pet Astro with the other. I liked that she was comfortable enough to help herself to some orange juice. Had Mom not made one of her visits, the fridge would've been empty.

"Would you like some breakfast or…or some lunch, maybe?"

She stared at me with those penetrating liquid brown eyes. "No, thank you."

I stopped buttoning. "What?" I asked.

"What?" she asked.

I said, "I…ah, just wanted to know why you're looking at me like that."

She smiled for the first time since I'd seen her all those years ago in high school, a crooked little smile. She used her dimples with her eyes forming a lovely expression that melted something inside me. "I was just curious, that's all," she said.

"Curious?"

She nodded toward the refrigerator. "Do you really know someone named

Emilia Bedelia?"

"What?" I'd been so entranced with her smile that her words entered my brain all jumbled and took a second longer to translate. "Oh, no, my mom thinks she's cute. Not Emilia Bedelia. I mean, that note's from my mom." I heard the words after it was too late. Mom. I'd said it twice.

"That's really cute."

"So, she tracked you down and told you—" The rest of the sentence, the words fled and hid from me.

"Tracked me down? What?"

My face flushed hot. "How did you get here if Mom didn't track you down and—"

She hesitated for a moment, or it might've been a couple of years. "*I* went to *your* house."

"You went to my house?"

"Well, the house you used to live in."

Beth Abercrombie knew where I grew up?

She said, "Everyone knows where you live. You lived in the Jungle Jim house."

The native statue in the front yard, the tikis on the garage, I had heard that's what everyone called it: The Jungle Jim House. She was right, everyone knew where I lived. Mom made sure of that. Having a high-profile house had not always worked in my favor like this time. My mind flitted back to an earlier memory.

Chapter Eleven

1968

When I was nine years old, the black-and-white photo of Butchy Boy Taylor's skinned and bleeding face on the front page of the *Daily Report* made an impression that stayed with me for the rest of my life.

Eight days after Christmas, I rode my brand-new bike to Elderberry Elementary School with my best friend Mike. Everyone we passed looked in awe at that new bike: the butterfly handlebars, long banana seat in leopard print, dual handbrakes, and the real topper—the eye stopper—the three-speed shifter on the right handle. Nobody had one anything like it. And I mean nobody. I don't know how Mom could afford it. She had to love me a helluva lot.

Christmas was her favorite holiday and she saved for it all year long. I couldn't imagine the sacrifices she'd made to give me such a wonderful bike.

I insisted my mom take off the tassels though; they didn't belong on a boy's bike.

This Cadillac of bikes rode all on its own faster than everyone else that day. The wind howled in my ears, my smile so broad my face ached. I flew down the sidewalk, headed for the wide-open school yard. I never rode in the street or the bike would have been taken from me forever.

We circled around and around on last year's side to the school, the L-shaped building that made up the classrooms with the asphalt playground, swing sets, tetherball poles, and the too-tall bounce-ball wall that Karl Purdy somehow scaled the last day of school before we moved on to the upper-grade side—fourth, fifth and sixth graders.

We rode on the familiar junior class side, still scared to death of the upper-grade side, even though we'd already been members for three months. We took turns chasing each other, whipping in and out of the corridors and back onto the playground, a place that held happy memories: school plays and ice cream socials where a slice of any kind of pie or cake with a mound of ice cream cost fifteen cents. Mom always gave me fifty cents for the event, which meant three pieces of baked goods. Heaven on earth.

It could've been the sun in my eyes, or just the thrill of owning such a fine machine. No matter. It happened in any case. I wished as hard as I could to take back that one instant in time where everything in life shifted.

I rode hard along the inside part to the building past the long-ago classroom where I once sat for the first grade in Ms. Butterball's class.

Butchy Boy Taylor came around the top end to that "L" moving fast. One second, he wasn't there, the next he just appeared right in front of me. A fast-moving blur. I didn't have time to hit the handbrake. We collided. Honest to God I couldn't tell you who hit whom first. We slammed into each other at high speed. The perfect intersection to a ninety-degree angle. A second either way and we would have missed. We hit with a slap of metal and a "harrumph" that bellowed from Butchy Boy's mouth, forced from his lungs by the violent impact. I hung on to my crumpled new bike and rode it down to the asphalt. I skidded along, sanding off the skin from both knees and one hand.

I came to rest and lay still for a second, trying to comprehend what just happened. The schoolyard, completely devoid of anyone else, echoed an eerie quiet. The only sound came from my own heavy breathing loud in my ears. That second of silence ended with a horrendous screech from Butchy Boy Taylor.

Upon impact, he had flown over his handlebars. That snapshot image remains today, flash-burned in my memory. The way he flew in mid-air, his arms down at his sides, his body a flesh-and-bone missile shot from a cannon. He landed and skidded on his face.

I lay there looking at him as he struggled to his feet, taking longer than normal. His entire body shook with a fevered palsy. He let loose another gut-wrenching screech. He raised his hands to his head and froze them there without touching. His hands shook. He spun to face me, ten-fifteen feet away, that's when I saw it, the Halloween mask. His crash landing on the asphalt had sanded off every inch of skin and replaced it with the color of the asphalt. His eyes were wide-open, whiter than white against all the black tinged in red. He left his crumpled bike and took off running. Butchy Boy Taylor was fast but I'd never seen him run like that, as if his whole body was on fire.

I tried to stand. I needed to get out of there fast. I was in deep trouble. I'd caused a kid to lose his face.

To lose his face, of all things. He'd left it right there on the playground, the one we'd both played on the year before. Left it for the other kids to find.

Once they caught me, the police would throw me in jail forever. Then throw away the key. Mom had always threatened they'd "throw away the key" if I did something wrong. I wanted to get home before the police chased me down. I needed to tell Mom, tell her I loved her and that I was so very sorry. My hip and knee ached when I stood. Just like Butchy Boy's face, black asphalt had replaced the skin on my knees and one hand. They burned something fierce and wept little red beads that accumulated and ran down my shin. I looked around but didn't see Mike. He'd been right behind me, right? Wasn't he behind me when the crash happened? Where was he now?

Didn't matter. I had to get home, and fast. I picked up my new bike. The butterfly handlebars were bent and cocked to one side. Likewise for the banana seat, skinned like my knees, the all-white plastic underneath reflecting the bright sunlight. Ruined, absolutely ruined. One of the handbrakes dangled, the metal scraped and forever scarred. Tears wet my cheeks and dripped on my arms. I swiped at my nose with my sleeve.

I'd caused a kid to get his face sanded off.

The bike was too mashed up to ride. Fear and instinct told me to leave it like Butchy Boy left his and make a run for it. But nobody else in the neighborhood had a bike like that one. If I left it behind, they'd know I was the one. I watched *Highway Patrol* with Broderick Crawford on television and knew how these things worked. Maybe Butchy Boy hadn't recognized me, not after what happened, how could he? Maybe nobody would find out?

Suddenly the warm breeze alerted me to another problem, an unfamiliar coolness below my waist. I looked down. I'd wet my pants. I kicked my broken bike until my foot hurt. What a little baby. I cried harder. Just like a little baby. I hurried home.

The short ten blocks home went on forever. On the return trip people looked at me from their front yards and their porches; they again looked at my wonderful bike but this time for a different reason. I walked hunched over, not from the injuries but in a feeble attempt to hide my wet pants.

What was jail going to be like? If I even made it to jail. Butchy Boy had a bat-shit crazy older brother, Cary. He was shorter than Butchy Boy, which made him shorter than me by a bit. Even so, he still scared the bejesus out of me with that wild, uncontrolled look in his eyes. They kicked him out of Elderberry for breaking in after-hours and setting a classroom on fire. I didn't know what he did for schooling now, and no one in my group of friends had the nerve to ask.

Cary Taylor had brown hair that hung down in his eyes on one side. He had to keep using scissor-fingers to move it out of the way. He kept his hair longish to cover an embarrassing attribute. All kids have foreheads. Cary though; he had at least a seven-head, long and sloping above deep-set eyes. Those darn crazy eyes.

After school every day, Cary met Butchy Boy at the corner and they walked to the 7-Eleven for a cherry Slurpee that turned their tongues red. I don't know where they got the money to have one every day. I was lucky to get one every two weeks or so, and that was if I collected the deposit on the soda bottles I scavenged. The 7-Eleven was in the opposite direction from my house and that was okay by me, I wanted nothing to do with those two jaybirds. That's what my grandmother Nanny would've called them.

One day awhile back, the two brothers must've run out of money and didn't make the trip to the store. They instead caught up to me and Mike walking home from school. They laughed and cajoled and made fun of my high-watered pants. I had grown too fast over the summer and we couldn't afford new school clothes. Mom offered to sew little skirts at the bottoms to cover my ankles, but I thought that would only make it worse and decided to live with it.

She also made all my tee shirts with the new "Stretch and Sew" method she taught at our house to earn extra money. One newly sewn shirt didn't feel right at school and all day it felt like the material was possessed and kept trying to choke me. When I arrived home that day Mom saw me and started laughing. "Oh, Mr. David (she always called me Mr. David, when all the time I yearned for something more endearing), take that shirt off. I put the collar in backwards." I must've looked the fool all day with high-water pants, glasses, and a tee-shirt with the collar in backward.

I talked Mike into crossing the street to get away from the two Taylors. It was taboo to cross the street and if caught I'd get the strap, but I wanted to get away from Sevenhead Cary Taylor. To my chagrin, Butch-boy and Sevenhead followed.

Mike and I walked faster. It didn't matter the two chuckleheads hurried to keep up.

All of a sudden Sevenhead broke away from us and ran into someone's yard. He ran around willy-nilly in and out of some low shrubs. For a minute, I thought the sun had baked his brain until I realized he was chasing a wounded bird with a broken wing. He caught it and giggled like a crazy person right out of *The Twilight Zone*. Butchy Boy said, "Hey, lemme have it, come on, lemme have it."

"No, I found it, it's mine. Get away."

A car on the street screeched to a stop, a nice midnight-blue convertible with four older boys in it. The guy in the back leaned over the side. "Hey Cary, whatcha got there?"

"It's a bird with a broke wing. What should I do with it?"

The guy slapped the side of the car hard and loud. "Put it under the tire and we'll drive over it."

Sevenhead gave a little hop in his glee and hurried into the street. "Hell yeah, that's a great idea."

I stood there stunned that anyone would come up with such a hideous idea, let alone someone else agreeing to it. "No," I yelled. "You can't do that. Stop it. Don't."

Too late. Sevenhead put the defenseless bird under the back tire and the guy in back directed the driver to back up. The bird crunched, a sound that echoed in my brain for days afterward. I turned and ran the rest of the way home.

That day while walking home with my broken three-speed bike, all I thought about was Sevenhead chasing me down for what I'd done to Butchy Boy and putting *my* head under his friend's car tire. This time I'd not only hear the crunch but would feel the hard rubber crush and explode my head like a grape.

I found my mom in the open garage working on filling toy orders. Her main job was selling Baum Toys on the party plan. She'd take me along on those nightly excursions to the homes of people we'd never met so I could help carry in boxes filled with toys, big boxes painted red with Christmas cards glued to the sides. The customers sipped their drinks and munched on snacks while Mom showed them the toys, giving her always-joyous spiel. Then they filled out the order forms listing which ones they wanted.

A large truck would back into our driveway and drop lots of big boxes filled with toys. I was tasked with unloading the boxes onto shelves in the garage. Using the orders, we filled brown paper bags with each person's request. All the kids in the neighborhood envied me. They didn't know what they were talking about. I was sick to death of those crappy toys.

The day I crashed the bike Mom took one look at me and said, "Oh my land. What happened to you?" I had hoped for a larger reaction, maybe some tears, but she always handled every situation with calm and practicality. At least it seemed that way with her controlled demeanor.

She cleaned up my hand and skinned knees and painted them red with iodine, which burned worse than skidding on the hot asphalt. She kept saying she was sorry about the bike. The unsaid words came out loud and clear: no way did she have the money to get it fixed.

Mom had the prettiest eyes and brown hair with a few freckles sprinkled across her nose. Even at a young age, I knew she was pretty by the way men acted around her. That wasn't just my opinion; she was chosen as the Queen on the television program *Queen for a Day*. She won a brick wall to help keep me corralled, a replacement window for the one I broke, a washer and dryer, and some cash. For years she kept a framed picture on our stereo/television console of the emcee Jack Bailey crowning her. It happened so long ago the photo was black-and-white.

That night I was too tired to eat dinner chicken a la king from a can. Mom asked me what was wrong. I couldn't tell her how my life was over, that I'd be on the run for the ten or fifteen years at least. I couldn't say those horrible words that described what had happened on the playground, on that evil-hot asphalt. She must've thought I was upset over my crumpled bike or the crummy chicken a la king, and let it go.

Had Mom bought our house across the street I would have been in a different school district and attended Vina Danks Elementary School instead of Elderberry. I wouldn't have gone to school with the likes of Butchy Boy and Sevenhead. The whole thing with the bike would never have happened.

With a six-foot concrete native standing at the outside corner of our garage, his long threatening spear in his hand, who wouldn't know where I lived?

It would be a cinch for Sevenhead to find my house, to find me.

The morning after I sanded off Butchy Boy's face I was sick to my stomach at the thought of going to school. I didn't sleep all night, worried there'd come a knock at the door. Mom would get up in her nightgown to answer it. She'd cry when the cops pushed passed her saying, "Where is he? Where's that scoundrel, where's that face eraser?"

Mom always made pancakes and eggs or biscuits and gravy, on the theory a good breakfast was the most important meal of the day. "Mr. David, you're going to school, so you may as well eat." She thought my lack of appetite was a ruse to get out of school. She opened the newspaper. "Oh, my land. Look at this poor child! He looks like the creature from the black lagoon."

I ran to the bathroom. Mom followed me in and stroked my hair as I dry-heaved into the toilet. "You are sick. You're staying home today." I got up and hugged her. I didn't want to cry in front of her; I was too old to cry but couldn't help it. She pulled me away "What's the matter? What happened? What'd you do?" Mom had this weird sixth sense that scared me sometimes.

What had happened with Butchy Boy filled me with a guilt-ridden blackness I couldn't purge, it ate at my insides. I blurted out the whole story, all of it, and finished up saying, "I'm dog meat, Mom. Cary Taylor's going to stick my head under a car tire and drive over it."

She smiled her lovely smile and chuckled. "Pshaw, don't be ridiculous, it was an accident. Nobody's to blame. Those things happen. You're making too much out of this. You'll be fine. Try and pretend like nothing happened, and next time you see this Butchy Boy tell him how sorry you are. That's all. You don't have to worry. It was an accident."

I looked at her like she was from another planet. She really had no idea how the world worked. I was a marked kid. Cary Taylor was going to hunt me down and squish my head. I swallowed hard. "Can you give me a ride back and forth to school? Just for a couple of weeks?" That was my only chance to stay alive. Cary wasn't allowed on the school grounds while it was in session.

"Don't be ridiculous. And you're going to school. I'll get this other boy's phone number and call his mother. You'll see. It'll be all right. I promise."

"Mom, his face is on the front page of the newspaper."

Chapter Twelve

1979

My mind still hadn't gotten past Beth Abercrombie sitting at my kitchen table.

She leaned in, her eyes growing a bit larger. "Did you know you have a volcano in your front yard?"

"I do now. It's new. I just saw it yesterday."

She sat back. "I have to tell you, that's really something. I've never seen anything like it. Except…maybe the Matterhorn at Disn—"

I muttered, "No one has." What does a person say about a volcano in the front yard of his childhood home? What does it say about his family values? I wanted to change the subject but couldn't find any topic as my mind continued to spin out of control.

"You're probably wondering why I knocked on your door."

I nodded, the words still not there. Please, please be here to drop hints for a date. Hints that will give me the nerve to ask.

"I need your help."

I straightened up, pulled my shoulders back. "My help?" She needed my help?

"Yes, I need you to help me find Cole."

"What are you talking about? Find Cole?"

"My fiancé's name is Cole. We dated all through high school. Now he's gone."

"Yes, I know. I mean, I knew you were going out with him and all, but that was three years ago when we graduated. I had no idea that he was gone." I was horribly jealous. And he wasn't even physically around anymore, this according to her. I craved that level of love and devotion she had for him. I would give anything for her to look at me the way she used to look at Cole.

Her expression fell. Sunlight from the kitchen window gave her a soft angelic glow, her face luminous with delicate grace.

"That's right." She said, "He left."

"What happened?"

She looked down at her hands clinging to each other as they rested on the table. "He just disappeared."

"Disappeared?"

She looked up, her eyes fierce. "We were going to be married. The plant, General Electric, laid him off. It's all their fault. Two weeks later he just disappeared." She swallowed down the emotions that rose in her throat, her face flushing red.

"I'm sorry," I said, I didn't know what else to say.

"You're a cop, you can help me find him."

"What…? Oh, yes, of course." Her presence, her words made me forget all about being a cop, my life's dream. A career I'd dedicated myself to for the last five years, a whole quarter of my life on the planet. She knocked on my door and all of that vanished; I was back in high school in front of South Hall watching her cuddle with Cole before class. "I can take a missing person's report, enter it in NCIC, and—"

"That's already been done." She took out a coin purse from her shirt pocket and opened it. Inside she had a credit card, her driver's license, and several other business cards. She removed one and handed it to me.

A police department business card crumpled and a little soiled from being handled too often. The case number was written on the back. Sedge took the report two and a half years ago.

She said, "No one's doing a thing about this. Something's wrong. Something happened to him. I just know it, and no one is doing a thing about it."

"What do you mean? What happened to him?"

"I don't know, that's what I want you to find out."

I hadn't been on the job very long but knew a little about missing persons. If an adult went missing without suspicious circumstances, precious resources were not expended looking for them. Adults had every right to pick up and move without telling a soul, and all too often it happened just that way. I didn't want to tell her that; she wouldn't believe me anyway.

"Is there anything suspicious about his disappearance?"

She snatched the card out of my hand. "Never mind. I thought you'd be different."

"No, wait. I'll look into it."

"You will?"

"Yes, of course, I will. I'll pull the report, read it, and check with the detective who's been assigned to the case."

She put her warm hand on top of mine, her eyes doing a number to my heart and tying up my tongue even more. I'd help her find her lover even if it meant I would never see her again. As long she continued to look at me, and be close enough to touch, I'd do anything she asked. Silly high school crushes had enough power to fly Apollo 13 to the moon.

"Can you tell me what happened?"

"I just told you."

"I know but—"

"No, there was nothing going on between us, we weren't fighting, I swear. That's what that other perverted cop wanted to know."

Sedge.

"What do you mean by that?"

"By what?"

"Perverted?"

"He ah...He...I guess the best way to describe it was that he leered at me." She gave a little shiver. "And he didn't believe a word I said about Cole."

"I'm sorry about that. I'm just coming into this, so please start at the beginning and tell me the whole thing."

"I met Cole when we were sophomores. We were together from that first day, never apart. We love each other. He'd never just up and take off like they say he did. Something's happened."

I waited for her to continue, and when she didn't I nodded. "There are some questions I have to ask."

"Go on and ask them."

"Were you two okay? Did you have an argument about—" I wanted to ask if she suspected another woman but was afraid to incur another glimpse of her anger or make her get up and walk out.

"No. I already told you that. He was depressed, that's all. He'd lost his job when they shut down the plant. We postponed the wedding until he found another job. And sure, it changed our plans, but it wasn't the end of the world. He'd never just take off like that, not without telling me. You have to believe me, something happened to him." Her eyes pleaded.

"I believe you."

"You do?" Her tone softened. "Thank you." She reached out and gently touched my hand. This time a shock wave of heat spread through my body. My heart strummed in my chest, a loud racket that she had to be able to hear. In high school, I'd had foolish daydreams about her being in danger and me coming to her rescue, like some kind of blue knight. Sometimes dreams did come true.

"I'll go in early today and pull that report. Do you have a number where I can call you?" I looked around for a piece of paper. Mom had gone through the entire apartment and put everything away that wasn't nailed down. Beth pulled out a pen from her pocket, her eyes on mine as she took hold of my hand. "Here." She wrote the number on my palm. "Copy that down," she said, "before it rubs off." This was the first time since she walked in that I caught a whiff of the idea that she might be using me. I didn't care in the least.

I didn't have to write the number down; no way would I forget it.

"I'll call you, then."

She stood and took a couple of steps moving through the kitchen toward the front door. I didn't want her to leave, not yet. Not ever. My heart pounded, making my eyes pulse.

"Hey, would you like a piece of cake?"

She turned and smiled. "I would, but I don't like coconut."

"Sure. I know exactly what you mean." She didn't like coconut just like me, imagine that.

"You don't like coconut and you have a whole cake covered in it in your refrigerator?"

"Ah, yeah, right. Kind of crazy, huh?"

She nodded, still smiling. "Call me, Dave. Okay?"

"I will, I promise."

Astro stood at my feet outside on the small square porch while we watched her get into an older yellow VW Bug covered in a film of dust and drive away. She'd decorated the bug's rear with stickers of large petaled flowers.

An emptiness I'd never experienced grew more intense the further away she drove until she disappeared around the corner. I never thought an old crush could rekindle so easily and flame so bright. I got dressed, ate lunch, polished my boots and Sam Browne, then hurried to the station.

In the office, the station secretaries said hello; I knew all of them, friends from when I worked as a cadet. Three constantly kept cigarettes hanging from their lips, the white filters marred with red lipstick. Smoke curled to the ceiling and hung in an even fog bank. The walls and acoustic ceiling were tinged yellow with nicotine.

I pushed the button on the file caddy, a large coffin-shaped machine that rotated shelves with a small motor, until it came around to the H's. I thumbed through the index cards until I came to Cole Adler. I wanted to see if there were any other cases besides the missing person. I found a 242 report, an assault and battery that occurred the night before he was reported missing. The fight occurred at the Bamboo Hut on Holt Boulevard, a bar for the desolate and forgotten. I pulled both reports, copied them, and put the originals back.

The missing person report was pretty straightforward in Sedge's halting handwriting. In my short time with the department, I'd taken many of these reports as a cadet while working the front desk. Sedge didn't do any follow-up on the investigation and merely passed it on to the detectives.

The supplemental report from Detective Fuentes was attached. He had contacted Cole's relatives by phone. They all said something similar to what Beth had said; no one thought he'd take off without saying a thing to anyone, all common remarks for this kind of incident.

At the bottom of the report, it said that the license plate to Cole's car, a newer model Datsun 280Z, had been entered into SVS. If any law enforcement agency in the United States stopped the car, Detective Fuentes would be notified. It was odd that it had not happened in the last three years. No agency had stopped the Datsun. If he had tried to register it anywhere in the US, the VIN, vehicle identification number, would have popped and a DMV investigator would have notified Fuentes. The car had gone unregistered for the last three years. In my mind, this bumped the missing person into the "suspicious circumstances," category.

But in all likelihood, the car probably had been stolen and scrapped for parts. Or Cole sold it to someone who parked it in a barn waiting for the limited edition to grow in value. It could happen that way but not as often as some of the other more heinous reasons.

The 242, the simple assault investigation, was really an incident report cleared as "mutual combat." Cole had imbibed too many Bloody Marys at the Bamboo Hut, then got into a verbal argument that escalated into a shoving match.

Officer Sara Rankin responded and found "One half GOA," gone on arrival. She gave Cole a ride home and left his car in the lot at the Bamboo Hut. Nothing of substance appeared in the report. That's when the car could've been stolen. Undesirables frequented the Bamboo Hut. Cole might've been too depressed to report it stolen and simply caught a bus to parts unknown to start another life. The Mexican border was only two hours south; the car could be in Rosarito Beach that very minute cruising the chicas.

I checked the detective bureau. Fuentes had left for an early lunch. Johnny referred to Fuentes as a "seat-warmer not worth spit." That's why Fuentes had been assigned missing persons, low-profile investigations. I'd check with him later if he ever came back from lunch.

I looked forward to calling Beth with this new information even though the news wasn't good. At the same time, I felt a little guilty for being happy Cole was out of the picture and not likely to return. I was a bad person.

I wouldn't call Beth right away. I needed to think about what to say, and how to say it.

Chapter Thirteen

I changed into my uniform early and checked my mailbox where, just as I predicted, I found the crash report kicked back from the traffic sergeant with enough red ink to make it look like an abstract painting. It'd take two or three hours at least to make the corrections. I settled down in the briefing room to get started.

Too soon, the other swing shift officers began to filter in. Fletcher Fletcher, the man with two last names, nicknamed Twice, had been on days off, and now walked to the front table. He always held a Styrofoam coffee cup or empty soda can in his right hand. He used it as a spit cup for the Skoal he packed in his bottom lip, making a perpetual bulge. Smith had told me that someday Twice is going to need his gun in a hurry and he'll have that cup in his gun hand. The nicotine addiction would kill him. Smith didn't see the irony in what he said, that he was killing himself by chain-smoking the Camels. Twice had come up from an office pogue, a police cadet, just like I did, and Smith had said Twice was the one to fingerprint him for his police application when Smith joined the department. That fact didn't seem to give any extra slack with Smith.

The sergeant hadn't arrived yet. "What are you working on, Rook?" Twice snatched the marked-up report. "Whoeee, would you look at this train wreck?" He held it up for everyone to see. "Lookee here, the traffic sergeant put as much red as you wrote in the entire report, Rook. Hell, the sergeant may as well have written the whole thing for you." He laughed. Sedge threw a wad of paper that hit the side of my face. FNG—fucking new guy.

I no longer had thin skin, and I let their hazing roll off without making my face flush like it used to. I could hold out five more months until my probation ended. Then I wouldn't have to put up with it anymore and I could fire back. I did worry though about what Johnny and Smith thought; they'd been my training officers and my work reflected on them. I said nothing and held out my hand, waiting for Twice to give the report back. He dropped it and grabbed my hand. I tried to yank it back, but he held on tight. "Would you lookee here." He tried to hold up my hand for the rest to see. "He's got a phone number written on his palm. You got a girlfriend, FNG? Is that what this number means? What's her name, Chlamydia Jones?"

The shift sergeant, Long, came in carrying the briefing clipboard. "Fletcher, take your seat."

"No, Sarg, you gotta take a look at this goat fuck of a report." Fletcher chuckled. "I've never seen anything like it."

"Fletcher, take your seat. I'm not going to tell you again." The sergeant moved behind the podium up front and set the clipboard down. Johnny had told me Twice didn't care for supervisors and pushed them whenever he had the chance. He wore the tips of his red shaggy mustache long, almost down to his chin, gunfighter style and a violation of policy. He built cinderblock walls on his days off to make ends meet. He had thick fingers and hands sandpaper-rough. He was a scrapper and would rather fight a suspect than try to use words to defuse a situation. He folded over the first page of my report to a paper-clipped note from the traffic sergeant, his lips moving as he read it. "Oh, my God, listen to this."

"Fletcher, get your ass up here and give briefing."

Fletcher looked down at me as if this penalty was my doing.

"Now, Fletcher."

He dropped the report on the table in front of me. I'd catch hell in the locker room tonight after shift. He had a lot of friends on the shift who'd join in. Fletcher walked slowly to the podium and read the lineup. He said my name with contempt along with my beat assignment, Beat One. I cringed. The watch commander had once again hidden me away in a slow area.

After briefing I quickly prepared my unit and got out on the street. The shift started slow, with paper calls: a stolen bike, an embezzlement investigation committed by an employee from the Kinney Shoe store, and a three-day-old residential burglary where the owner came home from a short vacation in Vegas and found all his electronics stolen—TV, VCR, and an expensive stereo system with Bose speakers, all valued at more than I made in six months.

From listening to the unit radio, Smith had made an arrest for a gun and Johnny grabbed a rolling stolen, a GTA, both great arrests. I was stuck in beat one with a crash report to revise.

When the horizon cut the sun in half and the orange ball cast long shadows tinting everything yellow, the dispatcher started sending units to code seven: dinner. I caught an Unknown Trouble call in beat four. I'd been on the eastside of beat one, so it only took five minutes to drive there. I pulled up and parked three houses down from the address.

In the distance, a woman screamed. My heart rate increased. I pulled up, all the way to the address.

In the low-light dusk, a woman stood in the front yard screaming, a screech that sounded like a cat being run over by a car. I got out and confronted her. She wouldn't stop her hysterical caterwauling. She wore a simple threadbare housedress, mouse-brown hair cut short and in dire need of shampoo. I didn't know what to do. I took her by the shoulders and shook her. "Ma'am? Ma'am, tell me what's going on? What's the matter?"

She came out of her fugue state, her eyes refocusing and seeing me for the first time. "Whaaat? Oh. Oh, the police. No, everything's fine. You don't need to be here. Please go."

"What's the matter? What happened? I'm not leaving until you tell me what happened."

She tried to look around me and down the street. "My son, he took off after my husband, Elmo. That's all. They'll be back soon after they both calm down. Everything's fine here. Really."

"Why's your son chasing your husband?"

"They had a fight."

"Which way did they go?"

She pointed.

"How old are they and what are they wearing?"

"No, it's okay, everything's fine."

"Ma'am?"

"My son's seventeen and my husband, he's...He's forty-seven or forty-eight, I think. I'm not real sure." She gave me a clothing description. I told dispatch to broadcast it to the other units as a BOLO, be on the lookout.

Nosey neighbors had come out to watch. I said to the woman, "Come on, let's go into the house." I gently took her by the arm and escorted her through the open front door. Inside to the left was the entrance to the kitchen. I sat her down on a chair by the table. The kitchen smelled of hot grease and something else I couldn't quite place but knew I'd smelled someplace before. The stove was turned off under two skillets, one containing greens of some sort, solidifying with white lard. The second skillet had fried chicken. Another pan had corn niblets.

"What's your name?"

She wrung her hands, her eyes pleading for me to ease a kind of grief not easily concealed. "Alice Walker."

I took out my notebook. "Tell me what happened."

Her chin quivered. "My son Tim wanted to borrow the car and Elmo said no. Tim is mine from another marriage, Elmo is his stepfather. My son went crazy when he couldn't have the car. They started fighting. More pushing and shoving then, you know, socking." She stood on shaky legs and went to the window by the sink. She pointed. "They ran off that way."

I wrote in my notebook, half paying attention until my mind finally clicked in on the smell that I couldn't identify when I first walked into the kitchen. I looked up, putting my hand on my gun. The scent my subconscious finally kicked out was one I'd detected in Mr. Shearer's garage. Burnt acrid gun smoke. My eyes quickly scanned the room for whatever I'd missed and stopped on little black holes in the refrigerator and the wall that I should've noticed when I first walked in. "Did they have guns?" She didn't answer fast enough. "Did they have guns?"

"My son…He went and got a gun. I didn't know he had a gun in the house. He shot at my husband. Oh my God, you have to stop him."

"Stay right here." I ran for the patrol car, speaking into the radio as calmly as I could, updating the broadcast to an attempted murder and that I'd be doing an area check for the armed suspect and the victim.

I drove around the neighborhood, my head on a swivel. I wanted to find them before anyone else. This was my call to investigate a felony arrest. I also wanted to get to Elmo before he got hurt. Other units cleared their calls and put themselves en route to help. I drove in a widening grid pattern. Five minutes passed. Ten.

Dispatch came on the air and told me to respond back to the location, "unknown problem, woman screaming." I didn't want to go; it was Alice again, and she'd worked herself back into a frenzy. I wanted to find the suspect with the gun. I told dispatch I was busy doing an area check. She came back and said, "Per the watch commander, respond back to the location." Great, now the watch commander would be angry.

I sped back to the address, the engine in the Chevy Nova roaring. I skidded to a stop in front of the location. Alice stood in the front yard, almost in the same place I'd seen her the first time. She was screaming again, only louder this time. The sun was down, the shadows gone as night continued to descend, a process that snuffed out the last bit of visibility. I took Alice by the shoulders and shook her. She continued to scream, hysterical, on the edge of collapse from shock. I shook her harder until her head snapped back and forth. Her screaming finally reduced to a mewing, her eyes still wild. She pointed to the side of the house. I drew my gun and walked to where she pointed. My breathing came faster the closer I got.

Dented metal trashcans obscured my view. Cut shrubs, bundled and stacked on top, made perfect concealment for a lurking suspect. I pointed my gun in that direction and continued to move. In the dimness, I could make out a cedar plank fence behind the trashcans. There was no gate. Whoever was there, I had him trapped. I stopped and was about to call to Tim to come out with his hands where I could see them, when I spotted a pair of shoes on the ground.

My mind all on its own flashed on Mr. Shearer in his garage, the body without a head—a neck with just the bottom jaw and a fat purple tongue. My heart leapt into my throat. Adrenaline dumped into my system and magnified every little detail. I followed the shoes to the ankles, the shins, the waist.

The man lay flat on his back. He had a florid face with heavy jowls. His mouth hung open, displaying yellowish teeth and a purple tongue, swollen large enough to choke a Guernsey. His eyes were wide open, frozen in fright. He was balding with a broad forehead and a weeping bullet hole almost dead center. Alice Walker's husband, Tim's stepfather, lay dead on the side of the house. He had to have been there the first time at the house and I'd missed it. They had run from the house, Tim chasing, cornering him at the cedar plank fence. When he turned, Tim shot him in the head. I took in a deep calming breath and spoke into the radio just as Alice, who'd come up behind me, started screaming all over again. I told dispatch to update the BOLO to a want-for-murder and to notify the watch commander.

I moved Alice to the sidewalk, got the crime scene tape from the trunk, and cordoned off the house just as the sergeant pulled to the curb and got out. I briefed him on what I had.

Two hours later, neighbors in a throng pushed in at the yellow police line tape, trying to get a closer look. They had quit asking questions when I wouldn't answer. Even though the suspect wasn't on scene, it was still considered a "smoking gun murder." The suspect was known and in custody. Smith had grabbed Tim in the park after he'd shot a pregnant woman with the last bullet in his gun. A true psychopath. What a world we lived in, one I had been ignorant of the first twenty years of my life.

The coroner arrived with a gurney and a black rubber body bag. They didn't waste time loading the body and strapping him on. The two attendants rolled the gurney toward the crowd. I lifted the yellow tape as the crowd parted. A small six-year-old kid with blond hair, his hands balled up in his pants pockets, shook his head as the gurney went past him. He said, "You should've given him the keys, Elmo."

Chapter Fourteen

The murder report, for my part, was easy. I just chronicled everything I'd done—two narrative pages. The homicide detectives handled the rest. I cleared the call and headed for the station to take my lunch and call Beth to tell her what I'd found. Maybe if I worked up the nerve, I'd ask her for her address and go tell her in person.

What the little kid said—"You should've given him the keys, Elmo"—banged around in my head, callousness and cynicism juxtaposed with a pure innocence difficult to comprehend and accept as real. Halfway to the station, I got another call from dispatch—"Shots heard." It was out on the eastside of beat six. I headed toward the address.

Shots heard in beat six wasn't an unusual occurrence; most of the area was a checkerboard of defunct vineyards outlined in streets with curbs and gutters for planned industrial complexes not yet built. The address for the call, though, was a residence in an older neighborhood with grass front yards and no driveways out front. The garages were accessed from a back alley. The city trees on the parkway stood tall with interlocking branches that blocked out the ambient light from the stars. There wasn't a breath of breeze and the air had a touch of a chill. When I was a kid I'd trick or treated on similar dark nights with my friend Roger.

This time I heeded Smith's warning, shut down the headlights two blocks away, and slid to the curb four houses from the address. I soundlessly eased the door closed and listened to the quiet night. I moved to the sidewalk and realized all the house lights on the street were dark, causing an eerie blackness to mix with the night's still emptiness. Everyone in the neighborhood had hunkered down holding their collective breath. I got off the sidewalk and moved back into the street, someplace no one expected me to be, and drew my handgun. I didn't use the flashlight; it would give away my location, mark me as a target. After what happened with Elmo, any and all precautions no longer seem so silly. Smith's words about officer survival continued to whisper in my ear. Ahead I counted the houses and their numbers. The address would be at the corner, the one with a naked yellow light over a small porch with two steps, a side entrance to the house. The only house with a light, an island in a sea of black.

I stopped at the edge of the arc cast in yellow, a half step back in shadow. I looked and listened just as a thin man in a raggedy tee-shirt, soiled cargo shorts, and barefoot opened the door and stepped onto the small square porch. In his hands, he held a double-barreled shotgun, the over/under kind.

Mr. Shearer had used a shotgun. I'd seen up close the devastation that weapon could wreak; the neck without a head, exposed teeth and jaw, the purple tongue, and the detached forsaken nose sitting forlornly on the concrete floor. I should've stood frozen like a rabbit right where I stood when confronted by a deadly predator, instead I frantically looked around for cover. None existed. No car, no tree, no trashcans. I was caught in the open.

Now I did freeze and held my breath staring hard at him, hoping he wouldn't look my way, hoping he couldn't pick me out of the shadows. A handgun vs. shotgun was no match; I was outgunned by a factor of ten. My eyes dilated, showing every little detail, his skinned knees, the faded tattoo, an anchor on his forearm, and most of all his blank expression, as if he had not a single thought in his head. An automaton armed with a 12 gauge.

His head slowly swiveled in my direction, and the shotgun came up to his shoulder as he scanned for a target to destroy. His eyes stopped on me. The second they registered recognition I brought up my handgun and simultaneously yelled, "Police officer, drop the gun! Drop the gun!"

I dove for the street, the curb and gutter the only cover, six inches of concrete curb to hide behind. I hit the ground hard as the shotgun bellowed and spit bright orange and yellow. Lead pellets whisked inches overhead, followed close behind by the second bellow, the second barrel. Dirt and a chunk of grass kicked up in the parkway less than a foot away. I got to my knees wondering if I'd been hit and that maybe shock had obscured the pain. I yelled, "Drop the gun or I'll shoot. Drop the gun, now!"

He looked confused, as if he couldn't understand how he'd missed with a shotgun.

I had thought long and hard about having to use deadly force and decided it took three things to shoot in the line of duty: the legal right, the moral right, and the emotional ability to pull the trigger. I stood and started walking toward the man with the shotgun, trying to keep a shaky gun barrel on my target, the skinny man's chest.

He turned frantic. He broke open the shotgun, pulled out the empty shells that cascaded to the grass. He fumbled in the pockets of his cargo shorts for fresh ones and tried to get them into the breech. I ran toward him full tilt. I had to get to him before he reloaded and snapped that breech closed or I would be forced to shoot him. I didn't want to shoot him. As I ran I focused on his hands with the gun. The shotgun shells he tried to load. He dropped one. Left it.

Off to the right, my peripheral vision caught movement. Somehow, I knew it had to be a cop by the way he approached, still too far away to help. The man on the porch looked at me then down at his shotgun and realized he wasn't going get it loaded in time. He turned and entered his house.

"Stop! Stop!" I yelled. If he made it inside, he'd be a barricaded suspect and other responding cops might get hurt trying to get him out.

He started to close the door. I leapt up the two steps to the small square porch and kicked the door. It flew inward and caught the man in the face as he tried to close it. He fell back into the house. I was on him grappling. Johnny Maslow appeared and helped me get him cuffed. Johnny had to have come from around the corner on the other side of the house. We were both breathing hard, not from exertion but from adrenaline.

Johnny slapped my shoulder. "That was fearsome, Dave, absolutely fearsome the way you charged that gun. Never seen anything like it. You coulda shot his ass and been justified but you charged him. You're a better man than me, Gunga Din."

His praise caused my entire body to tingle. Sedge came in, his gun out, his eyes wider than normal, his wide girth filling the room. Behind him came Fletcher Fletcher.

The small living room looked like it belonged to a little old woman. It was furnished with an old couch and armchair, both with yellowing antimacassars, and old area rugs over an older wall-to-wall carpet. The adrenaline started to bleed off, and my awareness returned full force. An LP record played music from the movie *Apocalypse Now*. Next to a wooden rocking chair sat a case containing boxes of shotgun shells with some empty boxes on the floor. He'd been firing for a while. Why did the neighbors wait so long to call the police? Were they afraid of retribution? On the small table next to the rocker sat a bottle of Jack Daniels with a quarter of the brown liquid left.

Fletcher said, "It's my beat, Rook. I'll take the arrest."

"The hell you will," Johnny said. He slapped me on the back, "My good friend Gunga Din is taking it."

Fletcher opened his mouth to argue. Johnny glared at him. Fletcher shut his mouth.

I got the man to his feet. His nose was broken from the edge of the door hitting him. Blood ran down his chin to his shirt. "I need a doctor. I'm going to sue you assholes. You had no right to do this to me. I'm going to sue your assess off. I'll own this shithole town."

Johnny stepped in close, his face inches from the man's. "You're lucky to be alive. You should get down on your knees and thank this kid. He could've shot you full of holes and no one woulda cared. But he didn't and you're still breathin' through your mouth instead of holes in your chest."

The man's expression shifted when he looked at me. Johnny took him by the arm to escort him to my car. The whole incident was surreal. Johnny, as he started to go past, leaned in and half-whispered, "I saw the whole thing, I'm going to write it up and make sure you get an attaboy. You did good, kid." He winked.

I followed them outside to the small porch. For the first time, I noticed what I'd missed on the charge up to the door. On the ground all around the porch lay empty shotgun shells, green plastic hulls that littered the grass like seedlings that if left to pollinate could grow into an evil all its own.

Chapter Fifteen

After shift I quick-walked back to the apartment. The adrenaline wouldn't leave me alone; it pulsed through my body along with the image of rushing a man with a shotgun in his hand playing over and over in my mind's eye. More exciting though, was the way Johnny Maslow patted me on the shoulder. And then said he was going to put me in for an attaboy. I basked in his admiration, something I had yearned for since the first day I met him when I started as a cadet two years earlier.

Incidents like the man with the shotgun also went a long way toward a successful probation, one that edged closer with each passing day. I took B Street west and crossed Euclid without waiting for the signal to turn green, a vehicle code violation. Midnight in the city, few headlights moved on the main artery.

On the next block, the closed businesses sat cloaked in darkness, the doorways caves that contained the unknown. I was so energized I wanted to howl at the moon. Most citizens would've avoided a dark street, but I carried a gun. I was "Fearsome." That's what Johnny had called me. Let the muggers come, bring it on. This was the best job in the world. The moon peeked from behind the clouds. "Awhoooo!"

Once at the apartment I let Astro out to pee and talked to him the whole time, telling him about what happened, about how the world worked, how I had the world by the tail. When he finished his business, he pranced around. My pent-up energy transferred to him in an invisible ray. I guided us inside before Mrs. Kravitz stuck her head out her door and uttered one of her favorite admonishments threatening eviction. The landlord for the triplex, she dealt out her authority the same as a dictator in a minor fiefdom. Her real name wasn't Kravitz; that's just what I called her, after the nosy neighbor on the TV show *Bewitched*.

Inside the apartment, I couldn't sit, so I paced from the kitchen to the living room and back, bouncing a fluorescent green tennis ball on the worn kitchen linoleum and catching it. Astro darted in each time to snatch it and wasn't fast enough. Each miss he gave a happy yip and tried again, delighted to be playing a lively game.

I wanted to drive over to Beth's house, knock on the door. When she answered, take her in my arms and kiss her like she'd never been kissed before. A kiss that would make her forget all about Cole Adler. Why not do it? I was going to do it. Sure, I was.

I headed to get my keys off the counter just as someone knocked at the side kitchen door. Beth? Had to be, my good luck continued to glow bright as the north star. But just as quick the feeling dissipated with reality giving me a little kick in the teeth.

No, it couldn't possibly be Beth. More likely Mrs. Kravitz, dressed in a tattered robe, her hair in pink curlers, her accusatory finger a loaded weapon. I went to the door, took a breath, wiped the huge smile from my face, ready to apologize for bouncing the ball late at night, and swung open the door.

Johnny Maslow's tan face looked at me from ground level. He held a twelve-pack of Miller High Life beer. "Thought you'd be up, kid. Let's celebrate, huh?"

My mouth sagged open. *Johnny Maslow was standing at my door with a twelve-pack of beer.* I didn't think he even knew where I lived. But more than that, his presence meant that I'd made the grade, that I was one of them, a bluebelly, a patrol dog worthy to run with the big dogs.

Johnny climbed the two steps to the small square porch and pushed past me. "Better close that mouth or you're gonna catch flies." He sounded a little down, depressed. He wasn't smiling, and he smiled all the time. I followed him in as his head pivoted this way and that taking in the embarrassingly small living quarters. "Got any chips or pretzels to go with these soda pops?"

"I don't know, let me check."

"You don't know what you have in your own cupboard?"

"No, my mo—" I almost told him how Mom came over with food and also cleaned the place. That would've definitely ruined my high. Johnny would have turned and walked out in disgust at my adult inadequacies. I pulled open the cupboard and discovered Doritos chips, a large bag, my favorite. *Thank you, Mom.*

We went into the cramped living room with the secondhand couch and the ratty carpet and sat down. Johnny cracked open a bottle and handed it to me. I took a drink. I'd only been twenty-one for a few months and wasn't used to drinking; I got drunk easily. The beer tasted great. I looked at the bottle, to double-check if it was really beer. I'd never had a taste for it, but that night beer tasted like ambrosia of the gods. Johnny opened his own beer and gave my shoulder a shove.

"Go on, tell me what it was like. What did it feel like to get shot at with a twelve-gauge at close range? What did it feel like to charge a shotgun? Must've really been somethin', huh? Tell it true."

His words still held an unusual solemn undertone, almost as if he needed a friend.

I couldn't help beaming; this was the best night of my life. I shrugged. "I don't know. It happened so fast."

He sat back and finally smiled, staring at me while his empty hand messed with Astro, who growled and play-bit. His hand would grab Astro's head, shake it a little, and shove him away. Astro loved to play and came back for more. "Why didn't you drop the hammer on that asshole? No one would've said boo over that one. It woulda been clean as a Safeway Chicken."

I took a drink, trying to decide if I could tell him my personal philosophy on shoot-don't-shoot. He'd think me a fool. The light had returned to his eyes, the same excitement I felt for the job.

"It's going to take three things to happen before I can pull the trigger," I said. I waited for him to give the big raspberry. When he didn't, I continued. I held up my hand and ticked off the three things with my fingers. "One, the legal right, which I had in spades. Number two, the moral right, and number three, the emotional ability to pull the trigger." This was something they had not taught in the academy. This was something I'd decided on my own, my personal justification.

With his hand, he continued to dodge and parry with Astro as he took a slug off his bottle. "Kid, you're over-thinking something that's simple. Someone threatens your life or someone else's, you throw down and pull the trigger. You don't take the time to think about it, you just do it. You know that, right? I explained it when we rode together. What else did I tell you?"

"You said if he's good for one, he's good for all six. You give him all six."

"Damn straight. Ouch, this little guy's a real scrapper, but he's got an alligator mouth backed up by a hummingbird ass. All heart and nothing to back it up." He quit playing with Astro and hesitated. "Wait. So, with this numbering system of yours, why didn't you pull the trigger?"

"I didn't have the moral right."

"You didn't have the what?"

"I could see that the gun was a double-barreled shotgun and he'd fired both barrels. His gun was empty."

He chuckled and banged his bottleneck to mine. "That's bold talk for a one-eyed fat man." A quote from *True Grit*. What Robert Duval said to John Wayne. Odd, that he chose to quote the bad guy.

Johnny loved to go to the movies and talked about them all the time, quoted them whenever he deemed fit, sometimes when it didn't apply.

He said, "The code of the old west. I like it. Hey, *Tell Them Valdez Is Coming* is on right now, turn it on."

I turned on the TV. He didn't say anything about the fuzzy screen on the ancient, secondhand set, and settled back on the couch to watch, his eyes alive with excitement. He mouthed the words along with some of the lines. He'd seen the movie many times in the past. I'd read the book by Elmore Leonard but had only seen the movie once. Astro moved to the center of the living room and sat trying hard to obstruct the view. He wasn't tall enough to block out any part of the screen.

We'd missed a good chunk of the movie. At the moment the bad guy had captured Valdez, played by Burt Lancaster. The bad guy, Robert Duval said, "That shot was seven or eight hundred yards." My friend Johnny Maslow said Burt Lancaster's reply in a mocking Lancaster tone: "More like a thousand." Johnny laughed and slapped his leg. "This is a great mov—"

A knock at the front door interrupted him. I jumped up to get it. This time *it had* to be Mrs. Kravitz. I opened the door to find Smith standing on the porch under the porch light. He wore an old leather jacket with worn light-brown creases and had the ever-present cigarette hanging from his lips. He gave me a rare smile. "Hey Dave, you going to ask me in?"

"Sure. Sure. Come on in." I stepped aside. He started to come in and froze when he saw Johnny sitting on the couch. Smith lost his smile. I'd thought they were friends and then realized they probably could've been had they not been competing for top dog at the department and out on the street.

Johnny held up his Miller Highlife, "Hey, Smitty, have a beer with us."

"That's okay, I can't stay long. Dave, can we talk outside a minute?"

"Yeah, sure." I stepped out, eased the door closed so Astro wouldn't bolt outside. I worried what Johnny must think, that maybe we were talking about him.

Smith stood on tiptoes and unscrewed the porchlight, allowing darkness to sweep in and cloak us. A reek of unfiltered Camel cigarettes emanated from his person and hovered around him in a smoky halo. He smiled again. "Heard about how that thing went down tonight. I wanted to come over and...and well...give you this. He handed me a well-used .38 Colt Detective Special revolver, one he had carried for years as a backup in his back pocket.

"I can't accept this. This...this is too nice."

"You don't have a backup, do you?"

"No, not yet—" I almost said, that I couldn't afford one, a weak excuse when it came to officer safety and he knew it. The emotions brought on by Smith giving me his backup flushed my face hot. Tears filled my eyes. I couldn't let him see them. Cops weren't supposed to have emotions, they weren't supposed to cry. I tried to think of something else while swallowing the lump in my throat.

He saw my dilemma and looked away. He said, "Just do me a favor, carry it until you can afford to get the gun you want, okay? Can you do that for me?"

I swallowed again and nodded, afraid my voice might crack.

"Carry it in your back pocket. Some cops carry theirs on their ankle, but the whole idea for a backup is for when you're fighting over your primary weapon. You can't get to your backup if it's on your ankle. And if you have to pick up your foot to get to it you're giving up your balance and the fight will be lost."

I'd heard the speech before and appreciated his concern. "Sure, I understand."

"It's nothing to look at. All the bluing's rubbed off and the checking on the grip is worn down, but she's a shooter. Mechanically sound, I promise you that."

I nodded again. "I don't know what to say. Thanks a lot." I wanted to give him a hug, but cops didn't do that kind of thing either.

He let loose with that rare smile again. "Always remember, they can kill ya, but they can't eat ya." His favorite mantra, he had said over and over when I rode with him as a trainee. He had never been in an officer-involved shooting, maybe due to his diligent officer survival techniques. The city wasn't wild with violence. Of the ninety-five sworn officers, only four had been in a shooting and that was over a span of a decade.

"Thank you. You don't know what this means. Really, thank you." I'll get a holster for it tomorrow."

"Remember, the back pocket is the best place to carry it."

I nodded, still trying hard to suppress my emotions.

"Good. See you tomorrow on swing shift." He turned and faded into the shadowy dimness, night's deepening gradations. I couldn't see where he had parked. Even in his personal life, he stuck to his unpredictability, his special power as a superhero on the street.

I opened the door to find Johnny standing just inside. "What'd he want?"

I held up the .38. "He gave me a backup gun. Isn't that great?"

"Yeah kid, that's great. Hey, I gotta hit the road. I'll see you at shift tomorrow, okay?" He had again lost his smile, that light in his eye. What just happened? The night had been going so well.

"You sure, Johnny? You don't want to stay and finish the movie, have a couple more beers?" I really wanted him to stay.

"Naw, that one beer made me sleepy. Better get movin'. Good job tonight, kid. See you tomorrow, huh?"

"Yeah, sure, Johnny."

I watched him leave. A strange loneliness crowded in, making the air almost too thick to breathe. I put the gun in my waistband, the weight a comfort I'd not known before. Smith had given me his backup gun, an important gift, a huge symbol of friendship and acceptance.

I sat on the couch, opened another beer, and watched *Tell Them Valdez Is Coming*, my eyes on the screen, but my thoughts continued to work over all that happened in one night, the death of Elmo, me charging a crazed man with a shotgun head-on, and most important, two friends coming over to my place for the first time.

What a night. More excitement and experience than I'd had my entire life. I took a long pull on the beer and realized a cop's life runs at a hundred miles an hour and never lets up. What did that do to a normal human psyche? Heck, to the human heart and nervous system? What would Mr. Simmons, my psyche teacher—the naked man that danced in his front yard—say about that life's assessment? I patted Astro, glad he was there for me. I started from the beginning and told him everything that had happened and wished he could drink beer and tell me what he thought. He barked, "Arf. Arf."

Chapter Sixteen

I woke on the couch. From across the room, the hot sun sliced through the window with a light that slashed across my eyes. My head throbbed, my mouth smacked of tacky hops from the beer. I groaned. I'd never drink again. I got up on wobbly legs, the sun too bright to see through the glare. I held my hand up as a shield.

Astro barked. He needed to go out. Empty Miller Highlife bottles littered the floor, little reflective buoys adrift in a sea of gold high-low carpet worn down to the nap. Were all those dead soldiers mine? I groaned, held a hand over my eyes.

Astro barked. "I know pal, I'm on it." I took a step. My foot came down on a bottle that rolled. I slipped, my ankle twisted. I went down in a heap with pain shooting up my leg. The bottles skittered everywhere, clacking into each other, the small living room floor now a giant billiard table without pockets.

I slapped the floor again and again, biting my lip as I tried to eat the pain. Astro barked. I struggled to my feet and hopped through the kitchen. The .38 in my waistband slipped into my crotch and caused a different kind of pain, the dangerous kind that threatened serious personal injury and the real possibility of canceling the family line. I stopped to readjust the gun back to my waistband and opened the screen door.

I'd left the wood door open all night, the apartment unsecured. What the heck was happening to me, I'd always tried hard to be conscientious? Astro bolted out and ran across the asphalt driveway to the grassy area by the hedge that separated our triplex from the neighboring one. He lifted his leg and let go. The sight made me realize I too had a full bladder, and without any warning, my status went from stable to a red alert. "Hurry up, boy, or I'm gonna have to join you and Mrs. Kravitz won't like it."

A car came down the long driveway from the street and honked, the driver stopped to watch Astro do his business. A yellow VW Bug with big flowers on the back.

Oh, my God, Beth.

I looked behind me through the pass-through doorway from the kitchen to the living room at all the empty beer bottles scattered around the floor. Yikes. "Come, boy. Come on, Astro." He finished and ran over to the Bug's driver's door, saw Beth, and jumped up and down giving her his happy bark.

Screw it, let her deal with him. I turned and hurried on a sprained ankle to the living room in a modified hop-run. The pain combined with the hangover headache made it difficult to bear. I grabbed the plastic trash can from the kitchen on the way and on both knees herded the bottles together, trying desperately to get them all corralled and hidden. Now I really had to pee. How could my bladder hold the liquid from all these bottles? I squeezed my legs together and fought the urge to put my hand down to grip my crotch for the added support.

"Hello? Dave?" Beth said through the backdoor screen. She was holding Astro, who licked her cheek.

"Oh, hi. Come on in." I wasn't ready, but what else could I say?

The bottles clinked and rattled in the plastic trash can as I set it down where it belonged. "I'll be right back, please, make yourself at home." I didn't wait for her reply, couldn't or I'd embarrass myself further. In the bathroom, I fumbled with my pants to get them open and again found the .38 in my waistband, about to drop in the toilet. The gun had been clearly visible when Beth came in. I paused. What had Beth thought when she saw it?

Wait, I was a cop, and cops carried guns. But in the apartment where it was supposed to be safe? She must think me some paranoid whackjob. I set the gun on the sink, unzipped, put my hand on the wall for support, stood on one foot, and closed my eyes, stifling a long groan of relief. What a sight I made: a sappy-grinned kook with a gun in the bathroom, standing on one foot taking a leak. I finished up, came out of the bathroom, and on the way tossed the gun on the unslept-in bed.

Beth stood at the kitchen sink filling the coffee pot with water from the tap. She didn't turn to look at me. "Looked like you just woke up, so I thought I'd make you some breakfast, if that's okay?"

"Yeah...ah...sure."

"Have a seat. We can talk while I cook some eggs." She wore a nice floral dress and sandals. She had wonderful feet, perfect and delicate with a ring around the big toe of her right foot.

I limped to the table and sat down. She had set out two aspirin and a glass of water on the small table. *She knew*. Was last evening's debauchery that obvious in my appearance? I gobbled the aspirin and drank the glass of water down, thankful for her thoughtfulness.

She looked around and found a frying pan in the cupboard, put it on the stove, adjusted the blue gas flame, and dropped in a butter tab to sizzle and melt. She pointed to the trash can. "Looks like you had quite the party last night. I hope there were more people here besides you and Astro?"

She didn't know me well enough to be judgmental, or maybe that was my headache doing the thinking. I didn't usually have a callous edge in the morning.

"I found those bottles in the trash when I got up this morning. I think Astro is a closet drinker. I'm going to get him into a program."

She chuckled. "I guess we can be glad it's beer and not the hard stuff."

"A couple of friends came over. Friends from work, I mean."

She nodded as if she didn't care who I fraternized with. But I wanted her to care.

She wanted to ask what I'd found out about Cole, the whole purpose for the morning visit. I wasn't so sure I'd tell her, not right away.

What was I thinking? Of course, I would. I'd tell her anything she wanted to know whenever she asked.

"Oh, you had some friends over? That's good news." She smiled. She had a wonderful smile.

"That a regular thing? With your friends?"

"No, something happened at work and we wanted to talk about it."

"Oh."

She didn't follow up and ask what happened. Didn't matter now, I was too embarrassed to tell her what I'd done, what happened with the man with the shotgun, how he'd fired at me, given me both barrels. Or tell her what happened with Elmo. About friends coming over for the first time, about the .38 Colt given as a gift, and the importance it held in my world.

Suddenly, the memory of the way Elmo's dead eyes stared into the fading dusk flashed back. Elmo had been on the side of the house the first time I confronted the woman in the front yard. A dead man, a murder victim, not fifty feet away and I had not known it. I swallowed down the bile that rose in my throat. I didn't think I'd ever want to talk about that again. I wanted to shove that into the darkest closet in my mind, slam the door, lock it, and throw away the key.

I got up, hobbled to the stove, and leaned on the short counter as I looked at her. My heart throbbed, then a half-second later my foot throbbed. With a guitar, we could play a rumba. She looked up from tending the eggs, smiled. My heart did that flutter thing again. She had the most beautiful eyes I'd ever seen. She stared at me for a long moment, a stare I didn't want to end. My eyes all on their own moved down to look at her lips, soft and inviting.

I shook myself, "I...I pulled that report on Cole."

She hesitated and went back to tending the eggs with the spatula. She'd seen me sneak that peek at her lips. My face flushed hot with embarrassment.

"That right?" she said. The toaster popped up. She dropped the toast in the pan to stay warm while the eggs finished cooking. The eggs crackled and popped in the melted butter. She tried to pretend that what I had to say about Cole wasn't a big deal.

"Yeah," I said.

I hobbled to the table and sat down. She came over with the pan and spatula and shoveled onto the plate two perfectly fried eggs and two golden pieces of glistening toast damp from the butter in the pan. She went to the stove and set the pan down, then came back and sat in the chair; the entire time my eyes never left her. She put her hands together in her lap and watched me. "Your eggs are getting cold."

I was suddenly starved and started eating. She looked on. She was trying for reserved restraint and failing miserably. She wanted to know what I knew.

She said, "I heard something yesterday."

"That right?" I tried to talk without showing yellow yolk.

"You remember Mr. Simmons from psych class in North Hall?"

"Sure, I do."

She leaned in to pass on a tidbit of small-town gossip. "The other day he flipped his lid and danced naked in his front yard. Naked. Can you imagine?"

I took a bite of toast. "You're kidding me?"

"Nope, heard it straight from Donna Humphry, she lives right down the street from him. The poor man. But the irony, right?"

"Yes, that really is something."

She stood and took my plate over to the sink. I was only half-finished. She rinsed the plate and remained with her back to me, not speaking. She waited, pretending to look out the kitchen window at something important. I got up and limped over to her. I wanted to take her in my arms and hug her; instead I stood close and leaned in just a little but not close enough to touch. An inappropriate distance for our current relationship, but I didn't care.

She smelled wonderful, fresh like a spring day, and *Irish Spring* soap clean. My voice came out in a whisper. "Beth, nothing's changed. There's nothing new in the report or the investigation into Cole's disappearance." Just saying his name brought out a jealousy I had no right to own. "He just took off. I…I don't think he's coming back."

She finally turned to the side to look into my eyes, emotional pain plain in her expression. I didn't want to see her hurting. Her chin quivered, her eyes welled. She had depended on me to tell her something else, something she wanted to hear, some good news. She nodded ever so slightly, moved in between me and the sink, put her arms around my waist, and slowly rested her head on my chest. I held my arms out, startled, not expecting it, and finally eased them around her. I pulled her in tight and hugged her, the hug every bit as good as I imagined it would be. Better. My own emotions swelled. I wanted to find Cole and kick his ass for continuously hurting her for so many years. The selfish bastard, running off like that.

We stood together a long time.

I never wanted it to end.

My shirt turned damp with her tears.

She whispered into my chest, "I'm a romantic fool, aren't I? For not moving on? I know I should forget him but it's just so damn hard."

"No, you're not a fool." The words caught in my throat. I wanted her to be a romantic fool, but for me, not for Cole. She looked up at me, her body warm against mine, her eyes wet. The DI's words from the academy echoed in my brain, *Don't be a fool, shitbird, take the initiative.* I slowly moved my lips toward hers, giving her plenty of time to step back and slap me for even thinking about something so insane at such an inappropriate moment. I was scared to death. Her eyes stayed on mine. I brushed my lips against hers, the whispered touch from a butterfly's wing. Tingling shot up my spine to the top of my head. I closed my eyes and kissed her. Her body melted into mine. The most tender kiss I had ever experienced, and I never wanted it to end.

She finally broke away not looking at me, her face wet with fresh tears. Seeing her in pain caused a little ache deep inside. She swiped at her nose with the back of her hand. I moved quick, tore off a paper towel from the roll on the counter. She tried to take it from me. I took her hand in mine and with the other gently dabbed her tears, my eyes on hers. I hoped I hadn't gone too far. "I'm sorry," I said. "I shouldn't have done that."

She pulled her hand away and put it flat against my chest. She had to feel my heart going a thousand beats a second. "Don't be silly. I liked it." Her voice a little husky. "I liked it a lot."

"You did?"

"Of course, I did. You're not very confident for being a cop." She gave me a half-hearted smile. "I better go."

"Can…can I call you?" I tried for confident.

Her smile tarnished a bit. She didn't answer. My heart sank.

I said, "But maybe not right away, okay?"

She nodded. "Yes, that sounds about right."

The brush-off, easy to identify.

I hobbled with her to the door. God, I didn't want her to leave. If I let her get away, I'd never see her again. That damn Cole still had her in his iron grasp and he wasn't anywhere within a hundred miles. Maybe she would never get over him.

I hobbled down the steps right behind her, my mind spinning out of control looking for a solution, anything that would keep her close. "Did you know that Cole got in a fight at the Bamboo Hut the night before he disappeared?"

She whipped around, eyes flashing with promise and hope. I was a selfish cad for tossing it out there like that, for no other reason than to tempt her. "What? The Bamboo Hut?" she said. "No. No one ever told me anything of the sort. What does it mean?"

It meant, based on her reaction, the kiss we shared had little or no significance. A dark cloud moved in, snuffing out the last bit of elation, snuffing out the remaining warmth of that wonderful kiss. I struggled to hold onto the memory.

But still, I wanted to hold her close. Kiss her again no matter what the cost. "I don't know," I said. "The cop that responded to the call left Cole's car in the lot and gave him a ride home. That was two and a half years ago."

Beth took a quick step over and grabbed my hand, clutched it too tight. I was a fool for wanting her. She'd never give up on Cole. She came from rare stock, soft and warm and beautiful, a penguin who mated for life.

But I didn't mind being her fool.

"What do you think it means?" she asked. "It has to mean something, right?"

"It probably...it probably doesn't mean anything at all." I needed to back up the denial with additional data and couldn't. I should never have let the genie out of the bottle. I'd never get him back in. Cole's drinking in a bar and getting into a fight backed up the premise he was depressed and angry and looking to change his life.

"It has to mean something. Are you going to do anything about it? Is there anything you can do about it? Talk to somebody?"

I was a total heel. "I can look into it, if you want me to." I'd have said anything to keep her close, keep her on the line even if I was the one left dangling.

"Yes, please. Thank you, Dave, really." She leaned in and gave me a chaste kiss on the cheek. A *chaste kiss* after what we'd just shared in the kitchen.

I *was* an absolute fool.

Chapter Seventeen

After a short nap and lunch, I took Astro out one last time, then wrapped my ankle in an ACE bandage as tight as I could without cutting off circulation. I forced my swollen foot into my boot and laced it loosely. The nap and three tall glasses of cool water alleviated the hard edges of the hangover. I drove to work instead of walking, not wanting to aggravate the injury any more than I had already. Getting in and out of the cop car all night would be bad enough. I wouldn't be able to chase anyone if they ran. Unless the crook was in a wheelchair. Twisting my ankle, on a beer bottle of all things. My hangover throbbed behind my eyes and my mouth was dry. I needed more aspirin and another tall glass of water.

I'd had a wonderful night with Johnny and Smith coming over. Then the morning started out sensational with that kiss but went downhill fast with Beth's rejection. In my mailbox at the station, the crash report had been kicked back yet again. This time it didn't have quite so much red ink.

Sedge came by in civilian clothes, a huge bright floral Hawaiian shirt that could have worked as a sail on a boat to Tahiti. The brightness put the hurt on my bloodshot eyes. I turned away. He peeked around my shoulder at the rejected report.

"Huh," he said. "I've been thinkin' about that zipgun caper and decided even a blind pig can get lucky and find an acorn." He grunted, laughed, and moved to the stairs headed to the locker room to suit up for the shift. Maybe he was right. What did I know about the street? What did I know about women? I swallowed down the hangover bile that rose in my throat. I didn't deserve the .38 in my back pocket, the great honor Smith had bestowed upon me.

To revise the crash report—doing all that math for the skids and Points of Rest—made my head hurt even more. I wanted to shove the report back in my mailbox, deal with it tomorrow on my day off. I'd never drink again.

Only I couldn't put off the report; I had to act responsibly.

Detective Fuentes came out of the detective bureau and crossed the hall to the officer's counter where I stood, anger plain in his expression.

"I hear you're nosin' round one of my cases? You need to concern yourself with gettin' off probation, Boot, before you go messin' with things you know nothin' about. You understand, *Boot*?" Beth had called him asking about the case.

"Yes, sir."

He stood glaring at me a moment more, then turned and headed back into the bureau. Perfect, what else could go wrong today? He didn't want me to solve one of his cases and make him look bad. Like that would happen. Cole had just moved on. He was living in Portland, or Denver, Tucson maybe. Someplace where he could start fresh where no one knew him. Lots of people did it.

The backdoor, around the corner, opened. Twice's loud voice echoed down the hall before he appeared with Ronald Luck in tow, another officer coming in to work swing shift.

"Hey, lookee here, it's Beckett the boot."

Twice set down his hard-plastic box with all his gear next to the armory doors. The box had a hook that hung from the back of the patrol unit passenger seat and acted as a desk of sorts. About half the officers at the department used them.

"Whatta ya got there, Boot?" He jerked the rejected report from my hand, the pages already rumpled and slightly smudged from being handled too often.

He slapped me on the back. "Not again. You gotta be kiddin' me. You got it kicked back two times in as many days? You ain't worth a damn, are ya, kid?"

The day shift lieutenant, Womack, came out of the watch commander's office, "Dave, this was left for you at the front desk."

"Thanks, Lieutenant." I took it from him. Twice grabbed at it, a pink envelope that smelled of lilac with my first name written in cursive writing. I yanked it out of his reach. The lieutenant wanted no part of the everyday banter and grab-ass. He retired into his office. Twice tried to get the envelope from me. I turned my back and covered it like a quarterback protecting the ball while getting sacked.

"That from your girlfriend, Boot? You gettin' a little a stink finger, are ya? She got a nice set of sweater puppies?"

The letter had to be from Beth. I wanted to read it right then but had to contend with Twice and his vulgar mouth. Twice had his arms around me, his strong hands trying hard. His warm breath on my neck smelled of mint from the lump of *Skoal* in his lip. His bushy red mustache brushed against my shoulder.

"Let it go, Fletcher, or I swear I'll…"

He took a step back, stunned, and looked at Luck. "Looks like our little rookie is finally growing a set of balls." He jerked the .38 from my back pocket. "What's this? You think you're a big dog now and need a backup? Puh-leeze."

I squared off with him, fists clenched. He realized he crossed a line. He opened the cylinder and let the rounds fall to the floor. He jerked the cylinder closed, turned the gun around, and handed it back butt first. I took it. We glared at each other.

Ronald Luck, an acolyte of Twice, said, "You know what Fletch, I'd like to see him fuck. Wouldn't that be something to see? All gangly arms and legs, like some kinda porch ape tryin' to pick up a greased football. Huh, Fletch?" Luck swung his arms wildly and kicked out his legs.

Twice smiled and turned to Luck. "You're not kiddin'. I'd pay good money to watch this geek get after it." He punched Luck in the arm. "Come on." They entered the stairwell and headed to the locker room. I couldn't wait to get off probation. I'd tell him what I really thought. I got down on one knee, a little kid picking up his marbles. I gathered in the bullets Twice ejected from the .38.

I looked around for someplace safe to open Beth's letter and couldn't think of one, not one totally safe from prying eyes. I'd have to wait until I went into the field. Maybe I didn't really want to see what it said, afraid she'd spelled out what she'd meant at our last meeting. I headed for the stairs and passed Twice's patrol box sitting on the floor by the armory. I looked up to see the watch commander sitting at his desk busy approving reports. I hesitated, angry about the letter. I knew what Beth had written; a Dear John. Sure, had to be. Now I really didn't want to open it. She'd had time to think over what happened in the kitchen. How stupid, to kiss her like that. I'd blown it. Now she would tell me with nice flowery words. I wanted to punch the wall. I headed down the stairs to the locker room.

Briefing went off without a hitch; at least the hazing remained at a moderate level, a few paper balls to the side of the head and a couple of crude comments about a phantom girlfriend. I had to be making her up; no girl in her right mind would go out with me.

The sergeant talked about a rash of burglaries on the southeast side of the city in beat two and three with no leads. Auto theft was up; he read off three cars to BOLO, be on the lookout for. And a missing juvenile that might be a runaway. Each officer got a handout with a color picture of Jessica DeFrank; a beautiful girl with baby-fine blond hair and blue eyes. She was fourteen years old. The most common age for a runaway. The photo caught a delicate vulnerability in her sweet face. I stared at her eyes a moment too long. Her friends last saw her walking home from school with her older boyfriend, Amos Butler.

The sergeant called out the beat assignments and I drew beat one again. Smith had been called in early to work overtime on dayshift to cover a hole in the schedule for someone who'd called in sick; he wasn't in briefing. I had hoped to thank him again for the .38. Later, I'd track him down for coffee.

All twelve patrol officers from briefing tramped up the stairs in a long string, talking and joking, camaraderie that in five months and seven days I'd be a part of. I stopped at the officer's counter to replenish my posse box with blank report forms and cassette tapes to dictate the narratives.

Around the corner and down the hall by the back door, the officers' noise level rose. Something was happening. I stepped to the corner to have a look. The swing shift patrol officers, which included Twice, Sedge, and Luck, all stepped aside with their backs to the wall to let pass three prisoners. Newly arrested suspects that Smith had brought in. Two were my height, six-one but broader through the shoulders with thick arms, jutting jaws, long greasy hair, and outlaw biker tattoos prominent on their arms: skulls, crosses, and women with large bosoms.

The third one could've played linebacker for the NFL. No shirt, his tan skin covered in a light film of dust. He had a broad chest and a narrow waist, the kind of guy Johnny Maslow called an alligator wrestler. Even handcuffed the guy was intimidating. The thought of going up against him alone sent a shiver up my back. To shoot him would only make him mad. A .38 bullet in his case would be grossly inadequate. Smith, at five-nine, looked like a Lilliputian next to Gulliver. He ushered all three into the holding cell. How the heck did Smith take this guy down? Plus the other two—all at the same time?

Swing shift patrol officers congratulated Smith and patted his back and shoulder as he passed. I pushed my way into the holding cell area as Smith took the cuffs off the man-monster and told him to get in the cell. The man looked down and scowled at Smith before turning and going in. Smith kicked him in the ass with a dusty boot. A violation of department policy. It wasn't like Smith, he never deviated from the book and always followed regulations to the letter. This guy had to have angered him. He started to uncuff the other two while keeping his eyes on the monster in the open cage. The other officers moved on to load their patrol units, to get out on the street, and handle the backed-up calls for service. The three suspects reeked of body odor, cheap wine, and burnt marijuana.

"What'd you get?" I asked.

Smith shoved the last one in with the other two and swung the heavy barred gate closed with a loud clang. "It's not a big deal. I was patrolling beat six, in the vineyards, and came across a car way out, off G Street. You know that stretch of dirt road along that hedgerow of eucalyptus, in the middle of nowhere?"

"Yeah, I know it." I patrolled there every time I was assigned beat six, hoping to find a duck—an abandoned stolen car that had been dumped.

"I came upon these three degenerates in the process of kidnap and rape."

"Are you kidding me? Was it Jessica DeFrank?" I held up the flyer.

He looked at it. "Nope, but these animals grabbed this other poor girl off the street and took her to the vineyards. Thirteen years old. Had her down in the dirt about to do the hucklebuck when I rolled in."

The man-monster inside the cell said, "It wasn't kidnap, she wanted—"

Smith spun and glared at him. The man shut his mouth.

I said, "How did you…ah…I mean—" I didn't know how to ask without sounding like a rookie or worse, a total twit.

He gently took me by the arm and escorted me from the cell area into the hall. "I threw down on 'em, that's all."

"All three of them. By yourself?" I blurted. "They could've rushed you and—"

"Having a gun and drawing down on someone is only the half of it, kid. You have to make them believe you'll drop the hammer on 'em. We've talked about this."

"I know we have, but how do you do it? Make them believe it?"

"By believing it yourself. If *you* don't believe it, neither will they. They'll take your gun away from you and stick it up your ass."

He winked and shot me one of his rare smiles. "Don't sweat it, kid, when the time comes, you'll figure it out. Trust me."

But if I didn't figure it out, what would be the consequences? Smith had never been in an officer-involved shooting. I wasn't sure how he made them believe he could and would pull the trigger. Johnny had never been in one either. It was a very limited club.

I didn't have his confidence that when the time came I would act appropriately. The night before, when I confronted the man armed with a double-barreled shotgun—that he'd fired at me—I had pointed my gun at him, which did nothing to deter him. He tried his best to shoot me dead.

Maybe he had seen that I didn't have it in me to pull the trigger, like Smith had said.

I wanted to ask Smith how he handcuffed them by himself. And many other questions. But he was all done talking. He let his smile slip away, his expression going neutral, where it remained most of the time. He walked down the hall to brief the watch commander.

Chapter Eighteen

The pink envelope from Beth didn't fit in my uniform shirt pocket. I stuck it between my body armor and shirt and zipped my shirt back up. Pink and smelling of lilac. The envelope stayed there close to my body, giving off a kind of glow. Maybe I was wrong and she'd had time to think about that kiss. Maybe she wanted to give up on Cole and test the waters of a new relationship and that's what her lovely words would say. The thought of that option came with a warm glow.

I loaded my patrol unit and headed to my beat. I'd not driven five blocks when the dispatcher gave me a call, in beat four, Sedge's beat: "Suspicious circumstances, unknown problem." I didn't mind covering for a lazy officer who didn't care who handled his calls. This sort of call was what I loved about the job: the mystery of the unknown.

The address bordered on beat six, a Holiday Inn right off the IS10 freeway.

Halfway to the location, the dispatcher updated the call to a 927d, a dead body. During training, I'd handled a dead body at the Capri motel on Holt Boulevard. Like most people, I'd stayed in motels in the past and had never stopped to think that the room I'd stayed in could've been a room where someone had died.

Smith said it happens all the time. "People are born to die, and they have to do it somewhere."

No backup unit was assigned. This wasn't an in-progress call, not one assessed as dangerous. Since I had already dealt with dead bodies in my limited experience, I could handle this one. People died, paperwork had to be filled out, a number issued, "a soul ushered out to make room for another." That's the way Mom looked at death. "There are a limited number of souls available. The more births there are, the more people have to die."

Mom, you gotta love her.

Folks out front came and went from the parking lot and lobby as if nothing important had happened. Life went on. The sun had crossed its zenith, the sky a cloudless bright blue. I parked in the red zone in front and entered a lobby filled with yellows and browns, wall coverings, and furniture worn and tattered with age. The desk clerk, a plain-looking woman with mouse-brown hair, gave me a vacant stare.

She said, "Room 212, the manager's up there."

She pointed as if I knew the way. Even though new and inexperienced, I caught onto the heated emotion she'd tried to mask. She wasn't used to people dying in the hotel rooms.

I nodded. "Which way?" I wanted a more definitive direction. She again pointed. I probably should've gotten her name and asked her what she knew about what had happened. I followed her finger, went out the door and up the stairs. Ten rooms down on the second floor, the harried manager, in a brown suit, and a woman housekeeper in a brown and gold uniform stood outside room 212.

The manager brought his hand up and pulled it toward him. "Over here, come quick. It's a murder!"

I hurried. My leather creaked with each step. My heart thumped hard. "A murder?" I said in a harsh whisper as if this revelation needed to remain a secret. This was supposed to be a dead body call. I approached the room's open door and peered into the dimness as the manager, a middle-aged portly man, mostly bald with sweat beading on his forehead, stood by, wringing his hands.

"You sure?" I asked.

The manager shrugged, too stressed to confirm his unlikely and heinous assumption. The victim had just died of natural causes, and these two were mistaken, merely caught up in death's mystique. Sure, that had to be it. They weren't experts on the causes of death, and murders didn't happen all that often in a small city, right?

The housekeeper stood in the hall with her back to the wall and seemed indifferent as she puffed a cigarette a little too rapidly.

"What happened?" I asked, just in case it actually was a murder. I wasn't sure what I was supposed to do next.

The manager continued to wring his hands. "Can we keep this out of the papers? I'm going to need a report number for corporate. How does this work? What happens next? How long is the room going to be tied up? Are you going to shut down this entire hallway? This has never happened to me before."

Happened to *him*? Someone was dead and all he could think about was how it impacted him and his job?

I pulled my D-cell flashlight from the sap pocket at the back of my leg. The dull yellowish beam tried hard to cut through the dimness in the dark room. I didn't want to reach in and turn on the light; it might disturb fingerprints. Rumpled sheets and bedcovers partially concealed a woman lying on her stomach, her long smooth thigh stuck in the air in an abnormal position. She wasn't moving. Crap.

"Who found her?" I asked, while my mind spun around and around thinking of what I should do next. Words screamed in my head from the academy instructor: *Don't contaminate the crime scene.*

The manager said, "Olivia here found her when she opened the door to make up the room."

"Has anyone else been inside?" One question I knew would later be asked of me.

The manager—whose nameplate identified him as Herb—looked sheepish. "I went in...just to...just to be sure. You understand?"

"Next time call it in and stay out."

"Sure. Sure. What are you going to do?"

"You sure she's dead?" I asked.

"Ah...What? Ah, no. Olivia, did you check to..."

I'd mistaken Olivia's indifference for shock. She didn't answer her boss and continued to stare straight ahead. She wouldn't be any use as a witness until later after she returned to this world.

"Stay here." My training kicked in and answered my own questions as to what to do next. I followed my flashlight beam into the room. I couldn't smell anything from outside the door, but automatically shut off any sense of smell and breathed through my mouth as I entered. Not a smart thing to do; a good investigator used all his or her senses.

I had the deadly "tunnel vision" the academy staff had warned us about. Knew it and couldn't do anything about it. I was too entranced with what lay on the bed. I stared straight ahead without looking to either side for any kind of threat. I focused on that long smooth thigh, hoping this was all a mistake. That the woman was semi-comatose with alcohol, and any moment she would roll over, be indignant about me violating her privacy, and utter a string of invectives. Come on, roll over. Please roll over, pull the sheet up to your chest, your hair a rumpled mess, and yell at me. Please. Please yell at me.

I came to within three feet of the bed. My head swam with vertigo. Now I knew why the manager and the housekeeper declared this poor woman dead. She was hogtied. She lay on her stomach, her feet tied together and then tied to her wrists, which were also tied. She was naked, the cleave of her small bottom peeking from under the sheet.

At twenty-one years of age, I had little to no experience with naked women. Embarrassment flushed my skin hot. I wanted to cover her and couldn't, not without violating the strict rules of evidence.

I couldn't see her face.

The suspect had put a pillow over her head. He didn't want to see her eyes when he fired the bullet through the foam. Black/gray gunpowder and stippling marks surrounded the little dark hole in the white cotton pillowcase. A small, insignificant dot, but still big enough to end a woman's life.

First, before you do anything, confirm the victim is dead. The voice of the instructor from the academy rang in my head. I reached out with a shaky hand and lifted the pillow...and wished I hadn't. She had delicate features, a pretty woman. Her face was to the side, her mouth agape, the tip of her pink tongue protruding past blue lips. Her open pale-blue eye had an opaque film and stared off, into the netherworld. The bullet had entered her skull just above her ear. Blood caked the shiny brown hair. I put the pillow back, pulled my handheld radio from my belt, and called it in.

Jubal Butler, the same homicide detective who'd responded to the Elmo killing, arrived within twenty minutes. All three of us, myself, the manager, and the housekeeper stood in the hall waiting for him to amble his way from the stairs.

"Another one, kid? You're bad news, you know that? A real jinx." He spoke with a gravelly voice from decades of smoking and didn't smile even though he had to be kidding about being bad news. It wasn't my fault, I only answered the calls given. If anyone or anything could be faulted it would be the wheel of fate. And why did he have to talk that way in front of the witnesses? He was way out of line and unprofessional.

Butler didn't have much hair on his bald pate, tanned, with age and sunspots. His mustache had streaks of gray. His suit had put in too many years of service and slipped past its retirement date without telling Butler. He didn't wear a tie and the collar to his sports shirt, open at the neck, was a bit frayed. He hooked his thumb over his shoulder. "You get their information?" Meaning Herb the manager and Olivia the housekeeper. He spoke as if they weren't there.

"Yes, sir," I said.

He turned to them. "Thank you, folks. Could you please wait downstairs until I come down and talk with you?"

Herb nodded. "Sure. Come along, Olivia." He took her gently by the arm and escorted her away.

Butler lit a cigarette. "Come on, kid, let's see what we got." Sweat beaded on his forehead and I caught a whiff of sour whiskey when he passed. Alcohol apparently went hand in hand with law enforcement. We were a pair to draw to, handling such a serious crime scene with my inexperience and his impaired ability.

Sweat ran into my eyes and stung.

I really didn't want to enter the room again but again told myself this was only a small part of the job I'd signed up for. Butler led the way with a trail of white smoke coming over his shoulder. In the academy, they told us never to smoke in a crime scene, chew gum, or eat, especially in a murder scene. It wasn't my place to bring it up to a veteran detective.

He stood at the bedside taking in the scene, then pulled the sheet back and removed the pillow. The whole scene should've been photographed before he moved anything. The woman was now totally naked and vulnerable, trussed up with the cord cut from the curtains. I was embarrassed for her. What a horrible way to die. Alone with no hope of assistance coming from anyone. Tied up, unable to move, a pillow placed over her head, and shot. As the pillow descended to block out the last light she'd ever see, what had she been thinking as she waited for a bullet she knew had to be coming.

Butler stood there looking at her. "I guess there's no chance of clearing this one as a suicide, huh, kid?" He turned and smiled, showing teeth yellowed from too many cigarettes. I walked out.

Little did I know that the murder of this poor woman would be a harbinger of what was to come.

Chapter Nineteen

As soon as I cleared the call, the dispatcher told me to "Ten-nineteen the W/C"—return to the station and check with the watch commander. While on probation a call like that came as an ominous request. I could only hope it was something simple like the watch commander had caught onto my limp—my sore ankle that I'd tried too hard to mask.

Maybe he wanted to know if I was okay to work patrol injured. Or, worst-case scenario, the request was about a work performance contract, what they put you on just before termination. The way the crash report kept getting rejected was enough to get anyone on probation washed out. I didn't like walking the tightrope.

I parked out back and walked into the station. I knocked on the door frame to the WC's office. "You wanted to see me, sir?" Lieutenant Womack was known as a fair and impartial manager. He kept his red hair combed to the side, and his glasses made him look more like a professor than a cop.

"Yeah, Dave, come on in and close the door."

Close the door? Not good.

I stood in front of his desk. He leaned back in his chair and smoked his pipe while looking up at me. "Sit. Sit."

I sat. The hot seat.

"Take it easy, I'm just checking up on you." Just like Lieutenant Galbraith had. They had to be talking to each other about me.

I let out a longer-than-normal breath.

"You doin' okay?"

"Yes, of course. Why? Am I doing something wrong?"

"No, you're doing great. I just wanted to check on your state of mind."

This was the second time staff had done this. Did he do this kind of oversight for the seasoned officers? Or was he just worried about me because of my age? Didn't he think I couldn't handle the job? This wasn't good. I'd have to watch my step even more in the next five months.

He banged his pipe in the ashtray on his desk and dug around in the bowl with a pipe tool to clear it out. "You caught two murder investigations back to back. That doesn't happen. The city averages eighteen to twenty-five murders a year and you caught two of them in a row. For that to happen—those are some long odds. In fact, it doesn't ever happen. Not has as far back as I can remember."

Maybe he wasn't singling me out after all and this was one of those unique situations, one that I happened to be wrapped up in.

He did stop short, though, of saying that I wasn't seasoned enough to handle so much death. Maybe he was right. Maybe the age requirement for the job should be moved up to twenty-five instead of twenty-one. If he added in the suicide of Mr. Shearer and the fatal traffic accident with Dan Howard, I'd had more than my fill of Doctor Death. And my career had only just started.

"Thanks for your concern, Lieutenant, I do appreciate it, but I'm handling everything just fine."

He smoked and stared for a moment as if waiting for me to crack, start babbling, and foaming at the mouth. He said, "Butler called me, briefed me on that 187 you just caught at the Holiday Inn. Pretty gruesome."

I could only nod and swallow hard; the image of that poor, hogtied woman flashed back on me, vivid in every detail. How she was alone in that drab hotel room filled with shadows, grays, and blacks, the colors of depression and despair.

He again waited. He finally leaned forward and flipped over a sheet of paper on the desk, moved it toward me an inch or two. I sucked in a breath. *A work performance contract.*

He smiled. I relaxed.

"Johnny Maslow has been singing your praises. You did a damn fine job last night with that shots-fired call. Maslow wrote this. I think maybe he flowered it up a little too much, but I'm happy to approve it." He slid it the rest of the way.

The adrenaline that had been masking the hangover symptoms bled off, allowing the nausea back in and the constant ping of the headache to return. I relaxed and tried to focus on the attaboy in front of me. In it, Johnny described what happened in the shotgun attack, my actions at the scene. He used wonderful long phrases with frequent and carefully chosen adjectives that made me smile and brought a warm glow in my chest. Johnny was a good friend.

The lieutenant continued to watch me and puff on a freshly lit pipe. "Thought you might like that. The last couple of weeks for you have been unusual and it won't always be like this. Trust me, it'll all even out soon and you'll get into an easier rhythm."

I didn't know what to say. "Thank you, sir, for your concern."

"And don't let that attaboy go to your head. One awshit wipes out ten attaboys. It's not fair, but that's the way it works."

"Yes, sir. Thank you, sir."

"You need to sign at the bottom and make yourself a copy, if you want one. The original goes in your personnel file. Good job, Dave." He extended his hand. I shook it. All of a sudden this was again the best job in the world.

"Oh, one more thing. He picked up a piece of paper from his Inbox and handed it to me.

It was a teletype 'stop and hold' warrant for Leon Zachary Pierce. I shrugged. "What's this?"

"Seven weeks ago, you arrested Melvin Hobbs for drunk driving. He didn't have ID when you booked him. The Jail fingerprinted him. It takes that long for the fingerprints to catch up to the arrest. This one happened to come back with his real name and a warrant for murder.

I sat back down, stunned. I'd had a murderer handcuffed in my car and let him get away with a drunk driving citation. He was out among the lambs because of me.

"This kind of thing happens all the time," the lieutenant said. "I just wanted to let you know so you can be alert and be careful out there."

"Yes, sir. Thank you, sir."

Twenty minutes later I was back on the street driving the black-and-white, basking in the warm glow of Johnny's complimentary words. It didn't last long. The tied-up murdered woman jumped into my thoughts. I never had such conflicted emotions, the kind that flip-flopped this way and that, trying to tear me apart from the inside.

I didn't even know the woman's name or where she was from.

I had to find out her name. I had to make her real and not a prop in a scene that would turn into a caricature.

I needed to find out what had happened to her. Who did it and why, or I didn't think I'd be able to sleep ever again. I'd ask Butler if I could help on the investigation, even if it only meant running and getting his coffee, picking up his dry cleaning. Anything.

No one should have their life snuffed out in such a violent manner. Whoever did it needed to pay for that poor woman's death. I turned back toward the Holiday Inn headed east, out of beat. I'd risk the policy violation. I'd go back to the scene and talk to Butler.

I came to a red stoplight at Fourth and Grove just as the dispatcher gave beat four, Sedge, a, "211 in progress at the liquor store at Fourth and Grove." An armed robbery and I was right there, on scene. I was also a long way from my beat, but didn't hesitate. I picked up the mic and told dispatch I was 10-97, on scene. She cleared the air for emergency traffic with a code 777.

I turned on the overhead red lights and busted through the intersection as I tried to see across the tops of all the parked cars at the northeast corner, in the parking lot of the strip center, and all the way to the liquor store. How lucky could I get, I was right on top of the call. My heart raced. My pupils dilated, making everything more distinct. I pulled into the parking lot and zoomed too fast, row after row, through the parked cars. If someone stepped from between them I wouldn't be able to stop in time. Over by the liquor store, a man in a green smock ran out waving wildly. He had black slicked-back hair and a narrow black mustache. He saw my black-and-white racing toward him. He pointed south and jumped up and down. I pulled over with the window down. "What did they look like?"

"Did you see them?" He had an accent of unknown origin.

"No. What did they look like?"

"You didn't see them? How could you not see them? Jesus H. They just ran out."

"What did they look like?"

"How could you have missed them?"

I put the car in park and opened the door. He pushed it closed. "Two white guys wearing Pendletons."

"What color?"

"Brown and…and, er, gray. Yeah, yeah, they were brown and gray."

I took off. He had to jump back or get his feet run over. I made a left on Fourth, leaning into the windshield trying to see. I'd entered the strip center parking lot from the west, which meant the two suspects had to have gone east. Three long blocks of commercial buildings strung out along the northside went all the way to the IS10 freeway underpass where the commercial buildings continued on the other side.

On the south side of Fourth, though, there were lower-income residential homes, perpendicular streets that bumped into Fourth named after California counties, like Amador and Calaveras. I picked up the mic and broadcast what I had learned and told them the area I was checking. I couldn't see the suspects anywhere. I drove down the street past the underpass, turned around, and came back. Two other units checked the area: Johnny and Sedge.

Anxiety gave me the jitters. Dejected and a little depressed, I headed back to the store to talk to the victim and to get a better description and DOT, direction of travel. The man at the liquor store couldn't add anything more other than both suspects were armed with handguns. He was angry that I had not seen the suspects exit the store, almost as if he thought I'd lied about it or that I said I didn't see them because I'd been too scared to confront them. He was entitled to his opinion.

Now I wanted to find these guys more than ever. I got back in my patrol unit and went from business to business, making sure the suspects had not ducked inside one of them. A longshot for sure, but I had nothing left. In all likelihood, they had a car laid off somewhere close and had gotten away clean. The closer I got to the freeway, the more it became apparent I was wasting my time, getting in and out of my patrol car like some kind of fool. My ankle didn't like it either. The other units cleared the call and returned to their beats.

The adrenaline had bled off forty minutes into the business checks and made my folly all the more obvious. I decided the restaurant at the end of the third block would be the last. I pulled up and double-parked in front of the double glass doors. Folks inside eating Monte Cristo sandwiches, stacks of pancakes, Club sandwiches, burgers with fries, and chocolate shakes stopped mid-bite looking out the windows at the kid-cop.

Inside, a hostess in a gold uniform with white lapels and a nameplate that read "Penny" offered a menu. She asked if I wanted to sit at the counter.

"No, thank you. I'm looking for two guys wearing brown and gray Pendletons. White guys. They would've come in almost an hour ago."

Penny looked tired and pointed with the menu to the alcove left of the front doors. I took several steps over and looked into the alcove and found thirty-five or forty people drinking coffee, talking, eating, taking a meal break, most all them working men who didn't care about the cop and continued to eat and gab. At least eighty percent wore Pendletons.

Terrific.

I stepped back to the hostess. "Which ones are acting funny?"

She'd lost interest in my plight, snapped her chewing gum, shrugged, and pointed to two men who had not looked at me. "Looks like those two only ordered coffee and they've been here for a while."

"Okay, thanks."

I walked over to the two men, my hand on the stock of my gun. "How you guys doin'? I want to talk to both of you. Please stand up and walk in front of me outside." They looked like all the rest of the men in the alcove. Average height and weight with brown hair. They could blend in anywhere.

"What's going on? We didn't do nothin'. Why you pickin' on us?"

My resolve wavered. This was stupid. I'd catch an awshit out of this for sure. They looked at each other as if trying to decide to do what the kid wanted, the one standing in front of them playing cop. My mind spun. What would I do if they told me to go pound sand? What would Smith do in a situation like this?

Finally, they slid from behind the table and walked ahead of me to the front door. An unseen energy hummed in each of them. Were they ready to bolt at any second? Or was that my overactive imagination? Outside, I ordered them to put their hands on the car and step back. They complied. I put my left leg between the legs of the first one, put my left hand on the back of his shirt coat, grabbed a handful of it for at least some control, and reached around searching his waistband first. My hand came across a gun.

I froze for a second, one that lasted for several hours. I made my choice. I yanked his gun out, shoved him over the hood of the car, stuck his own gun in his back, and yelled, "Don't move or I will shoot you."

I took a half-step back, pulled my radio from my belt while covering them, and asked for backup. Sirens started from a couple of miles away. The suspect I took the gun from said to his partner, "I told you this was a dumb idea."

Johnny got there first, coming too fast, and laid down a long skid that roiled with white smoke before he turned into the parking lot. The front of his patrol unit banged up and down in the driveway. He jumped out with his shotgun, racked it, and pointed it at the two propped on the hood of my car. "Don't you move!"

Twice pulled up next, got out, and drew his service revolver. More sirens still headed our way. Sedge pulled in.

I handcuffed the first one and laid him down on the ground. I found the second gun and handcuffed the second suspect before I allowed myself to breathe.

Johnny came around the car, the shotgun butt resting on his hip. He patted my shoulder. "Good job, kid. Damn good job."

I tried to pretend like it was nothing and to keep my body from shaking.

I said, "We need to bring the victim by for an infield show-up."

Johnny said, "Twice, you can handle that."

"He's the rookie, let him do it."

Johnny glared at him. Twice, bold and brash, did not want to mess with Johnny Maslow, not when Maslow used that well-known scowl. He got in his patrol car and left to get the victim. Johnny patted me on the shoulder while looking at Sedge, who was standing close by. "Looks like this blind pig keeps finding those acorns."

Sedge got in his patrol car, slammed the door, and took off.

Chapter Twenty

I booked the two robbers at the West End Sheriff's station and drove back to the police department. The case was a slam dunk; the liquor store owner identified both suspects. They had the store money in their pockets, plus half-pints of Old Granddad and packs of Salem cigarettes that also came from the store during the robbery.

Butler was already back at his desk in the detective bureau, writing the murder report. He looked up when I walked in. "Hey, kid, have your side to this report done before you go home tonight."

"I will, no problem." I stood at his desk, not knowing how to broach the questions that were burning a hole in my brain. He stopped writing, snuffed out his cigarette butt, bumped out another, a long brown Mores, and lit it with an ancient Zippo that had the Marine Corp emblem. He leaned back in his chair. "Can I help you kid? I'm kinda busy here."

I really didn't want to know, but at the same time, I had to know. "What's her name?"

He stared at me with brown eyes that had seen too many murders. Uncaring, vacant eyes.

He nodded. "I understand where you're comin' from, kid. I do. But you really don't wanna get into it if you don't have to, not right now. There's plenty of time left in your career to get jaded and cynical. Go and enjoy the streets before that happens. Because it's gonna happen. Nothing's gonna stop it. One day soon it's gonna jump right up and slap you in the face, and you're gonna look around and say, 'What the hell am I doin' here?'"

I swallowed hard. "I need to know. Please?"

He looked at me and puffed on his long brown cigarette. Finally, he leaned forward, took the face page report he'd been working on, and handed it to me. I could hardly read his jagged script and had to decipher it. The typist would clean it all up when she retyped the whole thing.

The woman's name was Elise Stoner. Thirty-two years old. She lived in Phoenix and had flown to West Valley on business. She was five foot five and weighed a hundred and eight pounds. The synopsis at the bottom of the page said that she'd had a drink at the hotel bar and had left by herself between eleven-thirty and midnight. She wasn't seen again until Olivia Contreras from housekeeping found her in the morning, trussed up. Preliminary examination by the deputy coroner revealed that Elise Stoner had been sexually assaulted.

I handed the face page report back to him. "Any ideas on who did it?"

He smirked. "So far it looks like this one's gonna be a whodunit. The hotel is too transitory. It's too close to the airport and the truck stop and it's right next to the freeway."

The 76 Truck Stop in beat six was huge, almost a city in itself, and nationally renowned. But a better descriptor than renowned would be notorious. Every kind of criminal passed through that truck stop, a festering sore on the butt of the city.

"So, you're saying this was random?"

"Too soon to tell right now but that would be my guess. One of those real headscratchers."

"Is there anything I can do? Can I help with the case?"

"Kid, you don't even know how to investigate a stolen bike yet. Give it a few years, okay?" He waved his hand, "Now let me get back to it."

"Yes, sir. But if there is anything I can do, let me know."

I had no idea where to start to investigate a murder, especially one where there were so many suspects. Butler was right, it was a real head-scratcher. I needed to do something though to take my mind off Elise Stoner.

I could look for Jessica DeFrank. I wouldn't be stepping on anyone's toes if I tried to find out what happened to her. Even if she did just run away.

The rest of the shift went by in a fog. I handled the insignificant calls for service: a barking dog, a disturbance between two neighbors over a fence and a property line, and of course a stolen bike. The entire time I couldn't get Elise Stoner out of my mind. The way she lay there bound up, naked and innocent, the look in her open eye, the tip of her pink tongue protruding between her bluish lips. Thirty-two years old. What a horrible waste of life.

In between calls, I tried to track down Jessica DeFrank. I went to her house and re-interviewed her parents, who had nothing new to report. Jessica's mother was worried, said that Jessica had never done anything like this before. Her mother managed to pass on to me a little bit of her urgency and paranoia, her fear for her only child. The inside walls of the house held a family history in framed pictures, an evolution of Jessica growing up. Elise Stoner's mom and dad probably had the same thing in their home.

I handled an in-custody, a citizen's arrest, a fifty-five-year-old named Al Winthrop who'd shoplifted lacy bras and panties at the JC Penny's. Afterward, I drove to two different homes that belonged to Jessica DeFrank's friends and talked to Sara and then Berry. They both backed up the mother: this wasn't something Jessica would do. I drove to Chaffey High School and got out and walked around the campus hoping I'd find her tucked away in one of the common nooks kids used for making out. No luck. The search only reminded me how recently I'd gone to school and graduated three years before. I hadn't contacted Jessica's boyfriend yet and would have to do that when I came back from days off. The shift was over, and it was time to go home. Jessica would probably return by then.

In the locker room, after shift, Smith and Johnny for some reason weren't there, both probably held over on late arrests. The officers not in Twice's clique congratulated me on nabbing the two liquor store robbers. I would've enjoyed the attention, but I only wanted to get out of the station. While I changed from my uniform into civilian clothes, Ramsey, a short, blond-haired officer relatively new to the street, told a story about Sergeant Sid Long that I eavesdropped on. Any other time, when I wasn't so focused, I would've thought it funny.

I still had not opened the pink envelope. I took it down from my locker shelf and stared at it. When I looked up I caught Twice looking at me.

"That from little Suzie Rotten Crotch? Haven't opened it yet, huh? You scared, rookie?" He smirked.

I stared at him, tried to make it a glare like Smith had done to the three in the vineyard, but had nothing to back it up, no experience, no reputation. What had I done to Twice to make him act that way toward me?

Twice laughed, slammed his locker, and bumped my shoulder on purpose as he went by.

I stopped at a liquor store on the way home. I probably wouldn't have, had I walked to work. I pulled out a six-pack of Miller Highlife, "the Champagne of bottled beer," from the store's refrigerator and set it on the counter. My wallet told me this sort of extravagance wasn't in my budget. This would be the last night. I wouldn't drink again. I just wanted a little fortification when I opened the letter from Beth. The clerk, a balding forty-something man with a comb-over asked for my ID. I showed it to him and wondered how much longer I'd have to put up with the humiliation. I was a street cop, for crying out loud, entrusted with a gun.

I couldn't help myself. I drove by Beth's apartment all the way to beat one. No way would she be out and about this late. I just needed to…I didn't know what I needed. I was nothing but a fool and headed home to my dog.

Chapter Twenty-One

At my triplex, I drove down the driveway and parked by the backdoor to the apartment. Barking grew louder when I shut the Firebird down. I looked to the right. The inside back door to the apartment stood open and Astro, on the other side of the screen, barked and jumped, excited to see me. The apartment was dark. I hadn't left the door open. I locked it when I left. Didn't I? I had been severely hung over and the memory was a little cloudy when I tried to call it up.

I quietly set the six-pack on the steps and left Beth's envelope on top and sideways between the bottlenecks. I drew Smith's .38 from my back pocket and opened the screen door. Who could be inside? Mom? But why sit in the dark? Why not turn on the lights? Mom wouldn't be at my place at a quarter after midnight. I could identify all the cars on the street and in the parking area for the triplex, nothing suspicious. Maybe there had been three robbers with brown and gray Pendletons at the restaurant and I'd missed the third one. Now he wanted revenge. He was inside, "lying in wait," a term in the penal code that when attached to a murder got the suspect the death penalty. The death penalty for him wouldn't do me a heck of a lot of good if I were dead.

The old kitchen floor creaked underfoot as I took easy steps toward the passthrough doorway that bordered the living room. Astro's claws skittered too loud on the linoleum as he followed along jumping on my leg demanding attention, apparently unaware of the threat. I peeked around the corner. A dark shadow sat on my ratty couch. My heart took off at a gallop. I brought the .38 halfway up, afraid to point it at him, afraid it might be an ignorant friend who didn't know the danger of prowling a cop's apartment.

"Who is it?"

Nothing.

No answer from the man made the question *friend or foe* lean more toward foe.

Suddenly, the cherry-red glow of a cigarette illuminated the man's face, leaving gray and black shadows, a portrait in a black-and-white film. In the stillness, his cigarette made a barely audible crackle as it burned

I let out a breath. "For God sakes, Johnny, I could've shot you." I turned on a light.

He held up his arm to block his eyes. "Wish you wouldn't do that."

"How'd you get in?" But I knew. When I rode with him on training, he'd shown me his lock pick set and told me never to do the kind of things he did.

He'd picked a lock to a room at The Landmark hotel, a place inhabited by dopers, prostitutes, and derelicts who'd lost their way in life. Back in its heyday, The Landmark catered to movie stars who stopped over on their way from Hollywood to the speakeasies and casinos in Big Bear. An out-of-the-way place the law had not yet touched. At the time, Johnny had been looking for a fugitive with a felony warrant. In that case, it wasn't necessarily wrong to enter with a lock pick but came awfully close.

"Turn off the light, would ya, kid?"

I left it on, a little angry that even though we were friends, he'd violated my privacy in such a rude and blatant manner. I nudged Astro with my foot. "Hey, some guard dog you are." He barked and bounced around, then bit my shoe thinking we were playing. I set the gun on top of the TV. Johnny held up a half-empty bottle of Jack Daniels. "Here, have yourself a pull."

"No, that's okay, on the way home I stopped and picked up a six-pack." I went back through the kitchen and opened the screen door. The six-pack on the steps was gone and I'd only been in the house a few minutes. I walked around the parking lot and out to the street. Not a soul to be seen. What the heck? There was hardly any crime in my neighborhood. Damn sneak thieves, I hated them. It had to be a neighbor, and that made it worse. If the neighbor did it as a joke, it wasn't funny. I'd been craving a beer since I pulled the six-pack from the liquor store reefer.

I had a little Hibachi barbeque that I sometimes set up on my steps. One evening I was cooking a couple of burgers for me and Astro, and I went in the apartment to get some seasoning. came back out and the burgers were gone. Had to be the same crook. A real jokester. Then I realized the envelope from Beth was gone as well. What a kick in the teeth.

Back inside I sat on the couch fuming about my bad luck before I realized something was bothering Johnny. He wouldn't break into my apartment, sit alone in the dark, and drink Jack Daniels unless something serious had happened.

"What's goin' on?" I asked.

He nudged me with the bottle. I knew better than to drink the hard stuff. I took it from him and set it on the coffee table. "Tell me, what's going on?"

Astro lay at my feet, tired of waiting for attention.

"Nothin', kid. Don't Bogart that bottle, hand it back." He shoved my shoulder.

"You've had enough." How had he gotten from the station over here and this drunk in such a short period of time?

"That right? You my mother now?"

Nothing on the street bothered Johnny, not since I'd known him. He was a rock. This had to be a woman problem, or something on that order of magnitude. I remembered the domestic call I'd handled with Smith, and the man who claimed Johnny had been having sex with his wife, how Johnny had ruined their marriage. Maybe tomcatting around had caught up to him and bit him in the butt. He'd finally fallen in love and she'd shunned him.

I needed to cheer him up.

He leaned over, his movements clumsy, and grabbed the bottle of Jack off the coffee table. "Sorry, Mother, tonight, Johnny's going to be a bad little boy." He tilted it back and took in two long glugs. He wiped his mouth with the back of his hand, the air now heavily scented with whiskey. "Ah, that's better. Really takes the edge off what ails ya, huh? You sure you don't want a pull? Heard you drew another bad one today. Go on, take a pull. You'll see what I'm talkin' about."

Elise Stoner. There she was again, brought to the forefront of my thoughts. Thanks a lot.

I didn't want to talk about it. About her.

"Hey," I said. "You hear what happened to Sergeant Long tonight on the 459 call?" Johnny let out a small sample of his regular smile.

"No, but I'm sure, you're going to tell me." His eyelids drooped a little, another symptom to his drunken state.

"The call was a burglary in progress. This woman came home and found her house burglarized and thought they were still inside. Twice, Sedge, and Luck responded along with Sergeant Long. I guess this woman—the reporting party—was a real looker and Long sat on the couch right next to her patting her hand telling her it would be all right while the other three searched the house."

"Other three." Johnny said, "Never thought of it that way before just now, but you're right. They're Larry, Curly, and Moe." He chuckled. "Go on."

"They cleared the house and left. Five minutes later dispatch sent them right back to the location. I guess the crook had been hiding the entire time behind the couch the sergeant had been sitting on with the RP. And when the cops left he'd jumped up and took off."

Johnny laughed and laughed. He laughed too hard. It was funny but not that funny.

He gradually calmed down, and again wiped his mouth with the back of his hand as his eyes bored into me. The intensity of it made me shiver. I took the bottle and tilted it back. Fire burned my mouth, my throat, and all the way to my stomach. I coughed until my eyes watered. Johnny laughed and shoved me a couple of times.

I recovered and wiped my mouth with the back of my hand like he had. "What's going on, Johnny?"

He stopped laughing.

"Nothin', kid. It's just been, you know, Bad Day at Black Rock."

Another reference to a movie.

"And...and sometimes, no matter how hard we try, ghosts always come back to haunt us. Nothin' new, I'll get over it."

His words scared the heck out of me. I knew exactly what he was talking about. Two weeks ago, I wouldn't have. Two short weeks ago my life had been my own. Now I wasn't so sure. It now belonged more to Dan Howard, Elmo, Shearer, and Elise Stoner.

Chapter Twenty-Two

The next morning, I found Johnny sleeping on the couch, the dead Jack Daniels bottle on the floor just below his hand. Without his eyes open and missing his smile, he looked ten years older, a full-grown adult that had no business being friends with the likes of me. I let Astro out and found the six-pack right where I left it the night before on the steps, minus the beer, the bottles empty. Beth's envelope gone. I didn't give two hoots about the beer, but that envelope really frosted me. I should've opened it and read it when I had the chance.

I had two days off. I could put another six-pack out there and watch and wait for the sneak thief, catch him in the act, and pounce. Make him give back the note from Beth. My first surveillance. The thought of catching him brought out a smile and a small thrill.

Astro finished up and came in. I scrambled the last of the eggs and put some coffee on. Johnny shuffled into the kitchen and sat at the table. The same place I sat the morning before with Beth. I divided the eggs evenly and poured us cups of coffee. He wrapped his hands around the cup, sipped with his eyes closed, and let out a little groan. *"Gracias, mi hombre."*

"You want some sugar, I'm out of milk."

He opened his eyes. "No, thanks, this is great. Sorry about that little 'poor me' fest last night. That just doesn't happen. I don't know what got into me."

I didn't know what to say and shrugged. All of this was out of the realm of my limited experience.

He opened his eyes and watched me as he sipped, not touching his eggs.

His probing eyes made me uncomfortable even though I considered us friends.

"You want to talk about it?" I asked. My question sounded alien even to me.

"You have a degree in head-shrinking I don't know about?" He said it with a straight face. I didn't know how to take it. He put his plate on the floor without having touched the eggs. Astro tore into them, gobbling down every last scrap before I had a chance to nix it.

"Thanks, that's probably going to give him the runs."

Johnny let a whisker of his usual smile creep out. *"De nada."* I smiled back, and his smile died without a whimper.

Johnny asked, "What are you doing today?"

"I have to go back in and finish that 11-44 I got kicked back for the second time."

"I'm workin' today, I'll come in and give you a hand with it."

The other officers would see Johnny helping me. I'd had my fill of ridicule and harassment, had enough to last two lifetimes. "Thanks, really, but I think I need to get this on my own."

"I understand." He stood to leave. I wanted to talk to him. I needed to talk to him.

I blurted it out too fast. "Hey, ah, you ever have—" I couldn't finish. All of a sudden, I'd turned into one big horse's ass looking for solace in the wrong place.

He sat back down, picked up the pot of coffee, refilled his cup, sipped it, and looked at me. "Go ahead, hombre, finish what you were gonna say."

"We can talk, right?"

"You know we can."

I nodded, thought about the words first, something he'd taught me. "You ever have one of those calls that keep coming back night after night and won't leave you alone?"

"We all do, Dave, that's part of the job. It gets better. It's tough at first. But we all have a really bad one tucked away, shoved back in that closet in our brain, the one that we keep locked tight at all times."

"You have one?"

He nodded.

I waited. I was afraid to bare my soul.

He said, "Okay, we going to do this, now?"

I didn't answer.

He looked out the kitchen window to the small parking lot of the triplex, his eyes no longer taking in the scenery, no longer taking in any information at all. "You tell anyone, and I'll deny it and then kick your ass."

I still didn't answer him.

"This one, it was a call, shots fired, man down on Budd street, the two-hundred block east. I was already on Euclid, northbound. I was right there, right on top of it. I rolled up and…and this was when I was brand new, still wet behind the ears. It was an apartment with the garage doors facing the driveway.

"In this driveway, a Hispanic man was on his knees, tears streaming down his face. In his lap, he held his fifteen-year-old son. He'd been shot in the back several times by gangbangers. They'd used a .380, the shell casings were right there on the sidewalk. He was dying in his father's arms. The kid had been lung-shot. Large red pieces of tissue and blood came out of his mouth as he convulsed, creating a small red pyramid on the hot asphalt. There was nothing anyone could do for him. The despair was…well it hung in the air thick as fog and to tell you the truth, I didn't know how to handle it. That bugged me for a long time. I've tamped it down over the years. Now it's more like a brain itch. Time does that for ya if you let it."

Johnny quit talking. I waited, my mind visualizing the scene he'd just described, and tried to put myself in his shoes. Had I not lived through the two prior weeks I wouldn't have been able to relate. Now I related too well and didn't like the things the scene conjured.

"Your turn," Johnny said.

I swallowed a lump that rose in my throat, at the same time trying to smother rising emotions before they spawned unwanted tears. "You really want to hear it?" A stall. I didn't want to bare those raw feelings. My voice cracked. "I've had four in the last two weeks. Four." Mr. Shearer, Mr.

Howard, Elise Stoner, and Elmo, who'd died over his damn car keys.

Johnny sat back in the chair, his mind busy behind his eyes, trying to figure out which four I was talking about. Cops out in the field chasing calls and looking for arrests listen to the radio as background noise in case someone yells for help. Otherwise, they are self-contained in their own little world, only obliquely aware of what goes on outside their realm of interest.

"That's right," Johnny said. "I didn't even think about it. All four of those were tough ones. You're going to get days or weeks like that now and again. One at a time though, not all bunched in a cluster like that. You just drew the short end of the stick this time, getting four in such short order."

A huge pressure lifted just telling Johnny my problem and him simply acknowledging it.

"Don't focus on those bad scenes. Think about the good times. Look at the way you faced down that guy with the shotgun and how you took down those two bandits, that was great police work. That had to feel great, didn't it? This other," he waved his hand in the air, "it's the castor oil we all have to take in order to play the greatest game in the world."

He leaned closer. "Hunting men. Hemingway said that once you've hunted man, and liked it, there is nothing else you can ever do. Don't worry, kid, I can see it in you. You'll get through this little blip and soon you'll be out there, takin' down the heavies and lovin' every minute of it. Hell, you've already made some great arrests. It's funny how some cops come into more shit than others. It's just the way the job works. There's a name for it, Shit Magnet. That's what you are, hombre. We don't have any at the station right now. They usually move to larger departments, so they can blend in easier."

"I'll never leave this department. It's my home." I didn't want a moniker like Shit Magnet and would be more careful in the future to avoid getting involved in sensational events.

"Don't talk too soon. You're still brand new and don't know the lay of the land."

I waved that thought off. "I want to find out what happened to Elise

Stoner."

"Who?"

"The 187 at the Holiday Inn."

He lost the light in his eyes as he turned serious. "You best keep your nose out of that kind of thing until you got some time under your belt and know what you're doing. Ol' Butler will slap you down he catches you sniffin' around his case."

"Yeah, I already got that feeling."

"Let it go for now and when you make it to homicide—if that's what you want to do—and the case is still open, you can pick it up and run with it."

"You think the case will still be open by the time I make detective?"

Johnny smirked as he stood. "Kid, with the kinda luck you've been having lately, you'll make detective before I do. Shit Magnets are like that." He patted my shoulder as he went by. "Thanks for the use of your couch, hombre, and the breakfast. See you at the station."

"Yeah, see ya there." He didn't answer the part of the question about why the case would still be open.

My ankle still hurt but was much better; overnight the swelling had gone down. I had to take a run to get things straight in my head. I wrapped the ankle and headed south on San Antonio Avenue instead of north where I'd be tempted to go by the Market Basket to see if Beth was working. I didn't know what her note had said. In all likelihood, she'd written that she wanted some space. Me showing up where she worked would make me out as a stalker.

I couldn't get her out of my head, her eyes, the way she smiled. It had been stupid to steal that kiss. What was I thinking? I ran a five-mile circuit, cut over on a side street to Euclid north, then east on D Street back to San Antonio. Astro bounced around, happy to see me as if I'd been gone a month of Sundays. He made me smile.

At the station, I tried to slide by without the lieutenant seeing me. I grabbed the rejected traffic accident report from my mailbox and headed for the stairs. I passed the bulletin board, which jumped out and caught my eye with two large red arrows pointing at something tacked to the cork.

The envelope Beth had left at the station for me, the same one taken off my back stoop. I took it down and checked inside. Empty. In primitive scroll the culprit responsible had written in black loopy felt-tipped letters:

"Oh, Davey, I LUV you TOO Maach."

I looked around to see if anyone was watching as I seethed. If I let on that I was mad, the others would see the weakness and pile on. It was one of the rules of the jungle. I'd seen it too many times while working with them when I was a cadet. The best thing to do—which was also the hardest thing to do—was to keep quiet and pretend it never happened. Had I not come in on my day off the envelope, with the ugly propaganda, would've been on the board for two days.

I headed down the stairs to the briefing room, the only place in the station to spread out the complicated crash report and work on it. I couldn't focus on the report no matter how I tried. I knew who had taken the Miller Highlife and the note from Beth, and he was going to get away with it.

Two hours later I looked up from a math problem with a skid that dealt with mass and velocity and an ugly delta-V, and found the briefing room filled with swing officers. I'd been concentrating too hard on the algebra problem. I had planned on getting out before briefing started to avoid the usual grief. I didn't need hazing on my day off. Johnny and Smith both sat quietly at different tables behind me. Johnny didn't even nod. He played the rookie-training officer game. If he acknowledged me it would just make things worse. He'd lay low for five more months, then we could be friends at the station.

Twice, Luck and Sedge came into briefing all at once, a couple minutes late, Sergeant Sid Long right behind them. Sedge immediately wadded up a piece of paper and hit me in the head with it.

Sergeant Long said, "Beckett, what are you doing here? You're not on the roster."

Before I could answer, Twice yelled from the back of the room, "He's working on a career case, Sarge."

"A career case?" Long asked.

"Yeah," Twice said, "It's a case he's going take his entire career writin'." Half the room broke out in laughter.

Long smirked at the joke. "Beckett see me after briefing."

"Yes, sir." I turned to the side. With my peripheral vision I watched for incoming paper balls while waiting for briefing to get over so I could finish the report. I wouldn't get anything done with everyone looking at me sitting up front.

Twice picked up his round cardboard container of Skoal, slapped it against his palm, pulled off the top, and took out a dip. He stuck the lump in the front of his lip just as Sergeant Long started calling out the beat assignments.

Twice spit the mouthful of Skoal all over Luck, who sat in the row in front of him.

"Fletcher," Long yelled. "What the hell's the matter with you?"

"Yeah," Luck said, as he jumped up and squeegeed off his uniform. "What the hell?"

Twice sniffed his Skoal container. "Some asshole loaded my chew with pencil shavings."

Smith laughed. "You sure it's pencil shavings? How would you know what those smell like? You don't write any reports. You kiss them all off."

"You do this, Smith? If you did I'm gonna—"

"Settle it after briefing," Long said. "The both of you sit down. Now."

Chapter Twenty-Three

Briefing ended, and everyone filed out. Sergeant Long didn't stop on his way out to remind me about seeing him after briefing. On my day off when I wasn't getting paid, I didn't feel the need to take his verbal abuse. I finished the last algebra problem in the report, confident I had it all right this time, and shuffled all the pages together.

I turned to leave and found Smith standing by the door to the briefing room. He closed it and walked to the front table. Smith was shorter than most cops at the station and he carried a six-inch .357 that looked incongruent on his hip. His brown hair was cut in seventies style and hung down across his forehead. He had boyish looks, but two decades of smoking had ruined his skin and teeth and aged him beyond his years. He pulled up a chair at the next table and sat in it backward, his arms resting on the top.

"Hey," I said. "What's shakin'?"

He let a smile slowly develop and shook his head. "Kid, it's not good to poke the bear, especially when you have five months left on your probation."

"What are you talking about?"

He didn't answer right away. Then: "I think you know what I'm talking about."

He waited for me to cop to something he thought I'd done, an interrogation technique he'd taught me and now was trying to use on me. "Never mind about that. Now here's how this other thing is going to go: you're not going to ask me where I got this, and the subject is closed as of right now. You understand?" I didn't but nodded.

He waited some more and finally unzipped his uniform shirt, reached in, and pulled out a pink folded piece of paper. "I rescued this for you." He handed it to me, then got up and walked toward the door. The note from Beth. I should've told him thank you, made him understand how much getting the note back meant to me. Instead, like some kind of kid on a kindergarten playground, I blurted, "Did you read it?"

Smith froze and slowly turned around, his smile huge. "What do you think?"

"Ah, heck."

"Exactly. You better not mess around. Call that girl, she expects you to take her to dinner tonight."

My entire body tingled over his words. I looked down at the folded note in my hand. It wasn't a Dear John letter after all.

Smith hadn't moved. "Dave, you remember your rules of evidence?"

"You know I do."

"Then quit acting the fool and go wash your hands. Do it right now. If I can figure it out so can he. And remember, if you wrestle a pig you're the one that gets dirty and the pig's the one that has the fun." This was an adage he repeated a number of times when I was in the car training with him. He turned and left through the briefing room door.

I slowly brought my hands to my nose. He was absolutely right, I should've thought of it on my own. My hands smelled of mint, tobacco, graphite, and wood. I scooped up the crash report and hurried to the bathroom to wash my hands.

Out in the Firebird, I unfolded the note:

Dave:

I'm so sorry. I don't act normal around people anymore, haven't for the last two years. I know I have to close that chapter of my life and find it the most difficult thing I've ever had to do. I love Cole too much to say goodbye, to give up on him. But I must. And I will. The way he just up and left without a word, it makes me think that I did something wrong, that all of these feelings of emptiness were my doing. And now, I can't help believing that love is a sin that carries with it nothing but pain.

I should have told you this in person. Please don't think me cowardly. I do need to move on and you're the only person who knows about all of me. If you are willing to take the risk, see where things go, maybe we can go out some time. Maybe tomorrow night before I lose my nerve? Dinner? Coffee? Whatever you think is best. I hope I haven't screwed things up so much that you won't give me another try. If you want, come by my place about six.

Beth

I couldn't believe it. In the enclosed Firebird I put my head back and howled and pounded on the steering wheel.

I stopped at Greenwoods, the uniform store everyone used, and bought an ankle holster. I wanted to take Smith's advice about where to carry the backup gun, but carrying it in my back pocket the last few days hurt my butt. I still had time to kill and drove to the station. In the basement, the department maintained a shooting range where officers were required to qualify once a month.

Department policy dictated that before I could carry a backup or off-duty weapon I had to qualify with it. Officer Luck worked patrol two days a week; the rest of the time he was the department range master. He also had a federal firearms license, an FFL, and sold guns at a discount to coppers. A real gun freak. His garage was purportedly lined with gun safes, one reason why his wife had recently left him. He had one or multiples to every make and model, including assault rifles.

I walked into the range unscheduled. Luck had his feet on the desk reading a *Soldier of Fortune* magazine, or so it seemed. The magazine he was really reading had slipped past the bottom edge of the *Soldier of Fortune.* Part of a naked woman peeked out, a woman with a large bosom. Luck had put on a little fat since he'd last purchased his uniforms. He didn't have on a Sam Browne and carried a gun in a pancake holster on his hip. He had a flat face and wore wire-framed glasses that made him look sharp, intelligent. He kept his hair cut short on the sides with a part on the right side.

I cleared my throat. He jumped, pulled his foot off the desk, and fumbled the two magazines. The nudie fell to the desk. He grabbed it but not before I peeped the title, "Women of the Amazon." I held up the .38. "I need to qualify with this."

"What? Oh, sure, sure. Fill this card out."

I took the card from him.

"I need to inspect your weapon."

I handed it to him.

I filled out the card while he looked the gun over.

While I was a cadet working the front desk and playing department gofer, Luck took twenty days off for a screw-up on patrol. He was allergic to work, according to Johnny Maslow, and kissed off whatever calls he could get away with. One Sunday morning, call intake received nineteen calls of smashed car windows all on one street. Some teenagers had hung out their car window with a ball bat and shattered all the parked car windows. Luck handled it and later bragged one too many times that he had talked all the victims into believing it wasn't a crime, that "atmospheric conditions, the rapid shift from sweltering summer day to freezing night, had caused the windows to shatter." Word somehow got back to the watch commander. Range master was a good place to hide him.

He handed the gun back to me. "That's a real shooter. I recognize it. It used to belong to Smith."

"That's right, he gave it to me as a gift."

"It's good to have him as a rabbi, he's going places on this department. Here's fifty rounds, go ahead and shoot at fifty feet."

I took the box of shells, my mind mulling over what he'd just said. I never thought Smith would do anything but patrol. He was too good at it. A natural. Why would he want to work his way up the ladder, work a desk?

I fired the .38 and instantly fell in love with the gun. I'd have to buy something for Smith to thank him, even if it was only dinner at the cat taco stand.

Chapter Twenty-Four

I pulled the Firebird over at five-thirty, two blocks down the street from Beth's address, not wanting to be too early. In the time since I opened the note, I stayed busy getting a haircut and trying to decide on the best flowers to bring. This after a long internal debate whether flowers were even appropriate. I had no one to call and ask, no one to lean on with questions about girls. My father wouldn't know, and didn't matter—I had no idea how to contact him.

I tapped the steering wheel to "Smoke on the Water" by Deep Purple that played in my head on a continuous loop. I stared down the street at her apartment door, time passing far too slow.

I was scared to death Cole would suddenly appear before I had a chance to knock. He'd be wearing an African Safari hat, a khaki shirt with big pockets, and soiled cargo pants from riding too many elephants. He would not have showered or shaved, having somehow sensed the love of his life about to go on a date.

Twenty long minutes later I tamped down a bundle of jittery nerves and pulled forward and parked in front of her apartment. I grabbed the daisies wrapped in green florist paper and walked slowly to the door. I knocked. The door opened immediately. Her sun-kissed hair was pulled back on one side with an abalone-shell barrette. She wore a light touch of lipstick.

She was absolutely beautiful. I could stand there and stare at her forever and started to until she said, "Are those for me?"

"Oh, right. Here."

She took them and put her nose close. "They smell wonderful. Let me get them into some water. Come in. I'll only be a minute." Her small studio apartment had cinderblock walls and throw carpets on the bare concrete floor. Two plants in custom-made pots hung from the ceiling in macramé slings, the plant vines almost touching the floor. The walls were hand-painted murals that depicted a 180-degree seascape and looked professionally done. On the coffee table sat a sculpture, glued together smooth rocks and seashells that made a small cottage on a bluff. Beth was an artist. My mom was an artist. Was that why I was so attracted to her? Had I instinctively sensed it?

She put the flowers in a vase filled it with water and set it on the kitchen table. She wore a new kaftan that accented her hair, and sandals.

"The painting on the walls, it's really beautiful."

"Thank you." Her face turned a light shade of crimson. "You really think so or are you just saying that?"

"No, I'm absolutely serious."

She came over to me, and on tiptoes, gave me a kiss on the cheek. "Well, if you're *absolutely serious*, then maybe I can believe you. You ready to go?"

She befuddled me and stole the words right from my brain. I nodded, took her hand, and walked her to the Firebird. I closed her door and hurried around and got in. I started up the car, still flustered with what I was supposed to do and say, the confusion like a hundred bees buzzing in my head. "Is Italian okay?"

"Sure."

"Good." On the drive to the restaurant, I checked my side mirrors and rearview too many times, needing something to do. I didn't want to stare at her too much. Were my armpits sweating, staining my dress shirt? Did I have on too much cologne?

I headed south to Holt Boulevard to "Vince's Restaurant" where Mom had worked when she met my father. Inside, they kept Vince's dark. The smell of red sauce and garlic and parmesan filled the air, a comfortable, familiar aroma. I put our name in with the hostess. We sat on the red vinyl bench waiting for a table. I suddenly realized I had not thought through the location of our date. On a number of occasions, I'd seen Twice, Luck, and

Sedge come to Vince's for their code-seven break. I should've driven to an entirely different city. Oh please, please don't let those idiots come tonight. The next problem popped up: money. I didn't know if I had enough to cover the tab. I could always put it on the credit card. I never used the credit card; I kept it strictly for emergencies. This qualified as a full-blown emergency. I could pay it off later.

I stood and paced. Beth stood, took my hand. "Is everything okay?"

"Yes, sure, why?"

She laughed. "You look like you're about to jump out of your skin."

"I just want everything to work out, that's all."

"Dave, you've already kissed me."

"What? Oh, you mean before."

"That's right. Why do you think I'm here? Right now?"

"That kiss?"

"That's right, so relax, okay?" We sat down. She patted my leg. "You're starting to give me the jitters."

I took a deep breath. She was right, I was being foolish. Her eyes scanned a wall-sized framed portrait of Vince's Restaurant depicting a scene when it first opened. She moved over to have a look, holding my hand, dragging me along. "This is amazing work," she said. She checked the right corner and read 'Jo Ann Beckett.' "Oh my God. Dave, is this your mom who painted this?"

"Yes." I really had not thought the location through. How was I supposed to know Beth was an artist as well? I waved my hand. "All the pictures on the walls are original Becketts. Mom used to wait tables here. This is where she met my dad. Then she painted this picture of the restaurant and the owners liked it so much they commissioned her to paint the rest of them."

"And you brought me here?"

Oh, dear Lord, I *really* had not thought this through. It seemed the most natural place to take her. The restaurant was where I was most familiar and comfortable. The confusion returned "This is not…I mean—"

She gave me a large dose of wonderful innocent eyes, put her hand on my chest. "Take it easy, cowboy."

The hostess called my name and escorted us to a table. On the way Beth held my hand; hers was warm and soft. I couldn't believe I was on a date with Beth Abercrombie. A dream come true. We sat at a small table in the corner with a candle illuminating our faces.

"I want you to promise me something," she said.

"What?'

"After dinner you take me around the restaurant and show me all of your mom's pictures."

I suddenly grew a spine—as Twice had put it—and said, "If I didn't know any better I'd think you only like me for my mom's paintings."

She smiled coyly. "You're not only cute, you're sharp as well. Ah, you're blushing."

She gave me the shivers. "I promise, I'll show you the pictures and if you want, I'll take you to my mom's and introduce you. Wait, you've already met her."

We said it at the same time. "The volcano."

We laughed.

"I'd love to meet your mom again and talk to her but only if you're absolutely serious about doing it."

"I guess I'm going to get that one for a while."

"I think it's a little early in the relationship to be meeting your mom, but maybe another time." She picked up a piece of cheese bread and took a dainty bite.

She was going to keep me on my toes the entire night. I liked that about her.

She suddenly turned serious.

"What's the matter?" I asked.

"Have you ever shot anyone?"

"No, and I don't think I ever will."

"Really? Why?"

"The vast majority of police officers go through their entire careers without shooting their guns. Real life is nothing like what's on television." I had learned that lesson the hard way in the last two weeks.

"Oh. But it's still dangerous, right?"

"It might be if we weren't so highly trained. Statistically, it's far more dangerous to be a clerk in small, all-night markets or gas stations."

"You're kidding, right?"

"No, I'm not. That's true."

"What percentage?"

"What percentage for what?"

"How many cops shoot their guns on the job?"

"Of the whole US? Maybe, one or two percent."

"I guess you're right, television isn't a good representation of what really happens. And that's good it's not." She squeezed my hand.

At the end of the night, I walked her to her door and kissed her goodnight, a kiss every bit as good as the first one. I walked two feet off the ground back to the Firebird, got in, and started it up. That's when I realized she had not mentioned Cole one time all night. Maybe she *was* serious about moving on. I waited until I was a block away before sticking my head out the window, into the wind, and howling at the moon.

Chapter Twenty-Five

Two weeks went by in a flash. I loved patrol. Life got back to normal just like the lieutenant said it would. I made four more felony arrests, one from a call and three from car stops: one gun, one for Mexican brown heroin, and one for possession of stolen property—power tools taken in a burglary. What Johnny said was true, I loved hunting the bad guys. If at the end of the shift I didn't have a felony arrest, I stayed out a little longer. One of those times the watch commander got me on the secondary frequency and told me to bring the car in so the next shift could go out. I took the subtle hint and after that I came in on time; the anxiety of not having a felony arrest at the end of the night worked on me like an itch I couldn't scratch.

On my days off I took Beth to dinner and the movies. In no time I was close to maxing out the four-hundred-dollar limit on my one and only credit card. I'd trimmed my budget down until moths flew out of my wallet whenever I opened it. I'd have to make another run to Mom's pantry. I'd been putting it off. Responsible adults didn't conduct pantry raids on their parental unit's home.

I also made regular stops at the police station on my morning runs to pilfer the stale donuts in the breakroom. I stocked up on boxes of mac and cheese, the off-brand, twenty-five cents per. I tried to fool Astro with some second-rate dog food, but he'd have none of it. He went on a hunger strike, the little butthead. He was actually eating better than I was. He didn't feel bad for me. I could read the look on his cute little mug, saying I was the one with the girlfriend so suck it up, buttercup. Even so, life was grand, better than it had ever been.

Except some late nights after swing shift. If I wasn't tired enough and couldn't fall right to sleep, I stayed up and watched reruns of *Cheers*, and *MASH*, not looking forward to confronting the people who populated my dreams—night terrors: Dan Howard, Elmo, Franklyn Shearer, and Elise Stoner. I'd tried to lock them in that closet in my mind like Johnny said, but for me, it didn't work that way. Not yet.

I had let the investigation into Cole Adler drop and I didn't follow up on the Bamboo Hut lead. I felt a little guilty, but Beth never mentioned it again. I didn't let the search for Jessica DeFrank die off, though. I continued to look for her in between hunting bandits and felons. To no avail. She had simply disappeared, and the case cleared as "a runaway, no suspicious circumstances."

Two weeks after I'd begun dating Beth, Mom invited us for dinner on my next day off. A big test. Mom was a little eccentric and hard to take sometimes. If Beth could get along with Mom, well...

Now I didn't mind beat one as much. I could see Beth when she took her breaks.

One night I slid the patrol car to the back door of the Market Basket. Beth came out and over to the open window as she always did. She leaned in and gave me a kiss. The sun had set on the other side of the store, creating long shadows in back intermingled with fading yellows and oranges.

I said, "I can't stay, I have to take Code-Seven, or I won't be able to eat. It's starting to get busy with calls for service."

"I can get you something from inside. What do you want? A sandwich from the deli?"

I couldn't let her pay for my meal. My stomach growled too loud at the prospect. "That's okay, I have to let Astro out anyway. You still up for dinner at Mom's tomorrow?"

"You bet, cowboy. Looking forward to it."

"Okay, don't say I didn't warn you. I have to get going."

As I started to leave, she said, "Ah...Dave, you wanna stop by my place after work tonight?"

We had never met after work.

Of course, I wanted to. Stunned, I didn't answer as fast as I should have. I said, a little too eager, "It would be late, after eleven-thirty, at least, and—?"

She looked at me funny like I'd missed a lobbed ball over home plate.

"Oh," I said. "Oh…sure. I'll come by."

"Good." She tapped my arm twice—her touch electric—turned, and fled into the store. I watched her go, watched until the glass doors closed behind her. I drove north through the parking lot in a daze. Had she meant what I thought she meant, or had I read into the offer?

I made it back to the apartment in record time and let Astro out. Through the kitchen window, I watched him do his business by the hedge while I prepared dinner, mac and cheese sans wienies. The entire time my mind went over Beth's every word, her every mannerism during our short conversation. Was she really saying what I thought she was saying?

The dispatcher on the radio broke into my thoughts. "West Valley units be advised, 211 in progress at the Market Basket, 1110 North Mountain. Units responding?"

The Market Basket? I opened the screen door. "Astro, get in here, now." He ran in. I pulled the boiling water off the stove, turned off the burner, and ran for my patrol unit parked out back. Mentally I went over where all the other patrol units were on calls and realized I was the closest. I got onto San Antonio Avenue and gunned the car, blowing through all the stop signs northbound. Dusk settled in. The last shadows from sunset disappeared, leaving behind that eerie light that ushered in the night.

Beth worked at Market Basket. A fact my mind tried not to dwell on or risk severe emotional overload.

I picked up the mic and asked dispatch if she had an update on the 211 and told her that I was breaking from code-seven to respond. She said, "Two white males, both wearing denim jackets, both armed with handguns, fled out the east door of the location. They pistol-whipped a clerk and are now being chased by the box boys eastbound from the location."

Pistol-whipped a clerk?

I picked up the mic and asked, "Confirming the suspects are armed with handguns?"

"That's affirmative."

"Are the box boys armed?"

The dispatcher paused, as the question I asked finally sank in. "Negative, the box boys are not armed."

I tapped the siren when cars tried to go through the stop sign as I approached the intersections.

A clerk had been pistol-whipped. It couldn't have been Beth. How many checkout clerks were there? Six. Seven. A one-out-of-seven chance. What was I thinking? They were all people, all of them would be a victim of a violent crime. I had to put that from my mind and pay attention to the call. The DI's words came back to me: "Be professional—stay alive."

Other units were responding, along with Sergeant Long.

Five streets ran perpendicular to the back of the Market Basket. I had a one-out-of-five chance of picking the right one. I made my choice and did a long sweeping turn to westbound Rosewood, the tires screaming to stay on the street. A car was stopped six long blocks down, barely visible, in the middle of Rosewood. I pushed the accelerator. The 1979 Chevy Nova leapt forward. Houses on both sides zipped by until they turned into a blur. I kept my focus on the car stopped in the middle of the street.

A man got out on the driver's side. He spotted me barreling toward him. He waved wildly and pointed south toward a house. I skidded to a stop and told dispatch that I needed a code-three backup, that I was in foot pursuit of an armed suspect, even though I'd yet to see one. I bailed from the car before she acknowledged my request. I ran toward the house where the man from the other car had pointed.

Behind me, he yelled, "He tried to take my car. He stopped me in the middle of the street. Be careful, he has a gun."

An elderly man came out his front door as I ran toward him, my service pistol in my hand, held down by my leg. He pointed through his house and whispered loudly, "He's in my backyard."

"Can I go through your house?"

"Of course." He turned too slowly, or my adrenaline had sped up things too much. I couldn't wait for him, deviated from my direct course, and vaulted his chain-link gate into his back yard. The man's dog charged me for violating the territory he'd been sworn to protect. I didn't have time to mess with the dog and charged him right back yelling. He backed down. The owner called the dog from the back door. I ran to the fence, stopped, and listened, only hearing my own rapid breath.

Then came the sound of someone jumping a fence. I jumped over it and ran to the next fence to the east, did a quick peek, moved down, and peeked again. I went over. The same sound again. He was yard-jumping. I still had not seen him. I vaulted the fence and moved to the next one as darkness fought dusk. We kept at it, four yards, five. The sixth one I didn't hear him go over. I did a quick peek, moved, did another, and didn't see him. He could be lying in wait. I went over. I still had not seen him, and then I realized there were no sirens coming to assist.

I jumped over.

In the dim backyard, night closing in, I held my Smith and Wesson Model 15 Combat Masterpiece in front as I scanned the entire backyard, peering into the thicker shrubs where he could be lurking and at any second fire from ambush. This person without a face, without a body.

Muffled words came to me. I looked to the patio on the residence. Inside the sliding glass doors, a white male adult wearing a denim jacket held a crying black child, no more than four or five years old. The man held him around the neck with a gun to his head.

Chapter Twenty-Six

This was the guy who robbed the Market Basket where my mother shopped, where I had shopped all my life. This was the guy who pistol-whipped a clerk at the Market Basket, a clerk that could well be Beth. This was the guy who held a small child around the neck with a gun to his head.

"Quit chasing me or I'll shoot the kid!" His words louder now. More pronounced.

"You shoot the kid, and I'll shoot you." I didn't know what else to say, this was all new to me. It would be new to anyone at the police department. It just didn't happen this way.

I had confidence in my ability to take the shot. Even so, in a blink, a thousand thoughts spun through my brain. In marksmanship, I rated number two in the academy behind an ex-marine from Palm Springs PD. But was the sliding glass door I'd have to shoot through the new safety glass that would shatter and not deflect the round. Or was it the old type, solid, the kind that sheered? If so it would be anyone's guess where the bullet would end up.

"Quit chasing me!"

I only had one option that I could see. I lined up my sights on his head. He now looked down the barrel of my gun. He shoved the kid down and ran for the front door. I ran to the side of the house and vaulted the cedar plank gate. As I went over, in the front yard, four or five people yelled, "There he is, get him. Get him."

I popped into the front yard.

Five houses to the right—or west—in the middle of the street, four box boys wearing red smocks from Market Basket ran east toward me. "All right. The police." They yelled. "He's right there. Get him. Get him."

I took off running to the left, going through the front yards, the suspect only three front yards ahead, the gun visible in his hand. I had the legal right and the moral right, to shoot him. I just didn't have the emotional ability to pull the trigger. What scared me most in that split second was that I didn't know if I would ever have the emotional ability. Then what? Chase him forever?

"Quit chasing me or I'll kill you!"

He started to go between the houses again, to yard jump, to go over a fence and wait for me, shoot me from close range as soon as I came after him. I yelled, "Stop or I'll shoot!"

He ran down the driveway toward another cedar plank gate. I stopped and took a shooter's stand. "Stop or I'll shoot!" He mounted the gate, starting to go over. "Last chance." I didn't want to shoot. I pulled the hammer back to single-action as another stall. He reached the top of the gate. One second more he'd be gone. Out of view. I tapped the trigger. The gun bucked in my hand. Oddly, it sounded more like a cap gun. The man in the denim jacket spun in midair and landed with his butt atop the gate. He teetered at his waist, facing me.

White gun smoke hung in the still air.

To the left, the box boys yelled, "Shit." Life had gotten too real. They turned and in a full sprint headed back the way they had come.

Leaving me alone.

On the cedar plank gate Denim Jacket yelled, "Oh, my God, you shot me. You shot me."

I took two steps closer and stopped when I saw he was still holding the gun. He was trying to lure me closer. No way could I have hit him. Not a moving target, not in the low light, not at that distance. "Drop the gun, now."

"Help me. You shot me."

"No way did I hit you, not from here. Drop the gun or I *will* shoot you."

I pulled the hammer back again for another single-action shot. His eyes grew large; he knew I wasn't kidding. He looked at the gun in his hand as if he finally realized the reason for my insistence. He pulled his arm back to toss the gun. When he did he lost his balance and flipped over the fence out of view. He flopped hard on the other side. I ran to the gate and did a quick peek over.

Denim Jacket was on his belly, one arm under his body, the other akimbo. He'd had the money from the Market Basket in a brown paper bag stuffed inside his jacket. When he hit, the paper money fanned out around him on the concrete. Blood, in a widening puddle, came from underneath him and mixed with the money, red blending with dirty green. The bullet had found its mark. I'd hit him hard.

I yelled, "Show me your hand."

"Help me." This time his words faded off. He was going into shock. He wasn't going to comply. Was he playing a game? I climbed the cedar plank gate. From on top, I yelled again, "Show me your hand."

He didn't reply. I came down on him with both knees. He grunted. I holstered my gun, pulled his arms behind his back, and handcuffed him. "No, don't handcuff me. Help me, I've been shot. You shot me."

I stood looking around. I had no idea where we were. I hurried behind the house to the sliding glass door where the drapes stood open. Inside, a scared woman in a nightgown ran by the living room to the hall and out of sight. I yelled, "Call the police." A second later a door inside slammed. I pulled my HT, my handheld walkie-talkie. Took a breath and tried to keep the panic out of my voice. "West Valley Paul One, I've been involved in a shooting. I need code three backup."

"All units stand by, West Valley Paul One has been involved in a shooting. Paul One what is your ten-twenty?"

I keyed the mic. "I don't know. I'm on a street behind Market Basket. I started on Rosewood, but I chased him through a lot of backyards."

Johnny came on the radio. "Hold, on Dave, I'll be there in two minutes. Two minutes. You hold on." Sirens lit up all over the city.

I started to hyperventilate and looked around for someplace to sit. The homeowners had a wooden picnic table and benches in their backyard. I stumbled over and sat. Time slowed even more.

Pretty soon Johnny's voice from the street floated into the backyard, barely audible over the rush of blood that pounded in my ears. "Dave? Where are you?"

"Over here. I'm over here."

"Keep yelling."

I did.

Thirty seconds later, Johnny's face popped over the cedar plank gate. I had never been so happy to see anyone. He disappeared. His voice came over the radio. "I got him, 822 West J Street. Eight-two-two West J Street."

Johnny didn't jump the fence; he was too pumped. He kicked it down. He hurried in a quick walk over to me, grabbed my hand, and shook it. "Good job, Dave. Damn good job." He turned, went back to Denim Jacket, got down on one knee, grabbed a handful of his hair, and lifted his head. "Good-bye, asshole."

It wasn't the right thing to do, in fact it was morally reprehensible, but at the same time, it was the best thing he could've done for me. He had validated my decision to shoot.

Chapter Twenty-Seven

One second dusk tinted the world; the next, night slammed down, black and thick. Johnny sat on the picnic table bench with me spewing inane words, not knowing exactly what to say, as sirens skidded to a stopped in front of the house.

"Beth," I said. "Who at the store was pistol-whipped?"

He knew instantly what I wanted. He shut up, stood, pulled his HT, and stepped away from the table to talk into it.

Paramedics arrived. They worked in a feverish attempt to save the bandit's life. They set their gear down next to him and went to work cutting off his clothes, starting an IV, and talking to the hospital. I watched, entranced. I'd caused him to be lying there semi-naked on the concrete, blood leaking from his body, pooling. The paramedics kneeling in it.

He no longer spoke or moved. I was scared to death that I'd killed him. No matter the justification, I didn't want him to die. Please don't die.

Sergeant Long appeared at my side holding out his hand. "Beckett, I need your gun."

Johnny came back. "Come on, Sid, let him keep his gun."

"You know the policy and procedure. I have to take custody of his gun."

I stood on shaky legs. "It's okay, I understand." I pulled my gun and handed it to him, stock first.

Long said to Johnny, "You stay with him. Take him to WVCH and get a blood draw."

Johnny didn't argue. He gently took me by the elbow. "Come on, kid, let's get this done."

Long followed and stopped by the paramedics, who were busy working a trauma suit onto the suspect's legs. They'd pump it full of air to apply pressure to keep his blood up in his core. Long said to Johnny, "Then take Dave to the station and wait with him, okay Johnny?"

"Sure, Sarge."

We walked together past the gate Johnny had kicked in, then down the long concrete driveway. Almost to the sidewalk, I stopped, took the yellow lumber crayon from my pocket—the same one that I used to spot the tires on the Dan Howard traffic fatality—and marked the spot on the driveway where I stood when I pulled the trigger. My mind worked on its own trying to picture how I was going to write the report. We got into the closest cop car and drove to the hospital for the blood draw.

Johnny didn't know what to say. He rambled on about women and horses and a simple burglary report he'd just taken. I couldn't blame him, though the lack of substantial communication between us sickened me even more. He pulled into the back of WVCH and parked in the same place we'd parked when I was on training and pre-booking a felon or getting a blood draw on a drunk driver.

This time it was for me.

Inside, they ushered me into a cubicle and pulled the curtain. I sat on the gurney and waited my turn. Within minutes Johnny, on the other side of the curtains, was talking to the nurse. He found out the suspect I'd shot was critical and had been transported to a level-one trauma center at Loma Linda hospital.

Beth suddenly appeared between the curtains. She froze and stared at me. Her eyes filled with tears. She slowly came toward the gurney. I slid off and took her in my arms and hugged her. The world righted itself. I whispered, "You're okay. I was so worried."

She nodded, her words choked up. "It was Sharon. They took her to X-ray. I rode in the ambulance with her. She's going to need stitches on her face. It was just horrible. Horrible. We were scared to death. Are you okay? Are you hurt?"

"I'm fine. They just want to take some blood for a BAC."

"BAC?"

"Blood alcohol, to see if I've been drinking."

She pulled back to look at me. "They think you've been drinking?"

"No, it's routine with any officer-involved shooting. It's for later so the defense can't claim recklessness or diminished capacity on my part. And for the civil trial after that."

"Civil trial?"

"If there is one."

She put her head back against my chest. I wished I wasn't wearing body armor underneath my shirt; it threw up a wall between us. I wished I'd not told her I never intended to ever shoot my gun in the line of duty. We stayed that way a long time.

An hour later, with a cotton ball taped to my inner elbow, I sat in the chair in the detective bureau at Fuente's desk. Fuentes was the investigator who handled grand theft autos. Johnny sat on the crimes against persons desk with his feet resting on the chair seat. The adrenaline had long since bled off, and my body continued to shake. I didn't want anyone to see such blatant vulnerability.

Lieutenant Womack stuck his head in the Bureau office, the long cord from the watch commander's office stretching across the hall, the phone receiver to his ear. "Johnny, the investigators want Dave back at the scene to show them where he was standing when he fired."

I stood and took out the piece of yellow lumber crayon and showed it to him. "I marked the concrete driveway where I was standing."

Womack's mouth dropped open a little as his mind processed this new information. He said into the phone, "Look for the yellow crayon mark in the driveway." A minute passed. Two. Womack said, "You sure, Dave? That's close to sixty-five feet from the gate."

Johnny smiled, shifted to his Burt Lancaster imitation in the movie *Tell Them Valdez Is Coming*, and said, "More like a thousand."

I looked at Johnny, flopped back in the chair, and started laughing. More of the nervous hysterical type, but laughter just the same. Johnny had been trying to cheer me up and had succeeded. He was a good friend. He laughed right along with me. Womack looked at us both like we'd lost our minds.

I was interviewed by two homicide detectives from San Bernardino County Sheriff's Department in the captain's office. They first put me at ease with a lot of small talk, then asked me to tell them what happened, starting with when I got up that morning, everything I'd done, step by step, not leaving anything out. Even how much butter I put on my toast. This was to get me relaxed and talking in a smooth, even flow before we hit the speed bumps. They called chasing down an armed robber/kidnapper that I had been forced to shoot a "speed bump." I did as they asked. In the end, they assured me this was a clean shoot—"Squeaky clean."

Johnny stood waiting outside the captain's door when I came out. He reached to my arm and tore off the cotton ball taped at the inner elbow from the BAC. I'd forgotten it was there. How stupid to leave it there so long. "Come on, kid, let's get you home." I followed him down the hall.

"Hey?" Lieutenant Womack said. I turned. He came from around the corner of the glassed-in watch commander's office. He drew his own service revolver from his holster and handed it to me stock first. "I'll get yours back to you as soon as ballistics is done with it."

I didn't know what to say. "Thanks, Lieutenant." I put the gun in my holster and snapped the safety strap over the hammer. Somehow, I felt whole again.

Johnny pulled behind my apartment and made no move to get out.

"Aren't you coming in?" The words slipped out before I'd thought about them, a cardinal rule violated, one Smith instilled in me during training. Rule number two on the street: "Never let your mouth overload your ass." Number one was to keep your head down and know where you are at all times. I'd violated the "know where you are at all times" rule on Rosewood in that backyard where the shooting occurred.

The soft glow from the Unitrol and Motorola lights lit Johnny's face. The shadows in his age-wrinkles made him older, somehow sadder, as if he'd lost his best friend in the world. But he hadn't; I was sitting right there. I really needed him to come in and have a beer. I didn't need him to talk as much as to just be there. Get drunk again and sleep on the couch. It wasn't too much to ask.

He eased out that knowing smile. "You gotta ride this bronc on your own, kid. Go on now, get out. I'll see you tomorrow."

How could he do that? Just the night before...what had he called his minor breakdown, his confession of sorts..."Oh, poor me?"

I opened my mouth to say something rude when he pointed. I followed his finger to the kitchen window to my apartment where a warm yellow light spilled out. Beth's concerned expression peered into the night.

I looked at Johnny. "Oh."

He chuckled. "You bet, 'oh.' Go get 'em, tiger. Talk to you in the morning."

I opened the door. Before I closed it, he said, "Hey, kid?"

"Yeah?"

He smiled. "Keep your head down."

Chapter Twenty-Eight

Beth opened the back door to the kitchen as I came up the steps, Astro jumping at the screen to greet me. My eyes never left hers. I still wore my uniform with my Sam Browne gun belt hanging off my shoulder, the lieutenant's gun in the holster; the violence the gun represented incongruent in the presence of such a beautiful girl. I stepped inside, set the belt on the table, and took her in my arms. I held onto her with my face buried in the crook of her neck, smelling her flowery scent. She felt so natural. So perfect. Without asking, she'd come to my apartment to wait for me.

She finally moved from the doorway, shut and locked the door. She took my hand and guided us to the bedroom. Astro had gotten tired of waiting and played with an old knotted sock on the living room floor, snarling and rolling on his back, the sock an evil badger attacking the homestead. The dog had a real imagination. Then he saw us and tried to follow along.

Soft music was playing in the bedroom where she'd lit two candles that were not mine, the shadowy light filled with unspoken promise. She stood in front of me and slowly unbuttoned my blue uniform shirt.

She startled, took a step back, her hand to her mouth. "Oh, my God. You wear that monstrosity every day?"

She had to have known it was there. She must've imagined it as looking like something else, thin and lightweight. Or she'd just pretended it wasn't there.

"Yes, it's body armor, threat level three, with a trauma plate." I had not needed to say the additional description, but her reaction brought on an unjustified need to explain.

She slowly nodded, her eyes back on mine as she came in close again. Her hands caressed both sides of my face. She went up on tiptoes and gently kissed me. She moved her hands to the uniform and slipped the shirt off my shoulders. I realized I was the boy and should've been undressing her. I knew that much at least. That's the way it was done in the movies.

My fingers tried to unbutton her blouse and lost their nimbleness. She pulled loose the Velcro straps that held the body armor in place. I lifted it over my head and let the Kevlar drop to the floor. The tee shirt underneath was damp from sweat. My skin prickled with goose flesh. She pulled the t-shirt over my head and ran her hands up and down my chest. She backed us up to the bed. We fell backward, her on top. Her hands went behind her back and released her bra, let it drop off. She started to lean down to kiss me. I put my hand gently on her chest. The candlelight flickered in her eyes.

"What?" she whispered.

"You're God awful beautiful." I pulled her down and kissed her. The kiss heated up. I rolled over on top of her. She let out a cute little yelp.

Astro whined at the bedroom door, wanting in.

She pushed off a little and shucked off her pants, then helped me with mine; her skin—all of it—hot to the touch. Her hand, hungry, felt down between us and grabbed hold of me. I tried to slow her down, to savor the wonderful moment. She'd have none of it and positioned herself, wiggling until I entered her. My back arched. We moved together as one. The elation was pure and all-encompassing. I had never been so happy. So...so alive.

Suddenly, I hesitated. The night's events shoved their way back into my life. The smell of gun smoke and blood. Standing on that driveway, gun in hand, trying to make the most difficult decision I had ever had to make, I realized I felt alive then, too.

Beth's fingers gripped tighter in the back of my hair. "What?" she whispered. "What's the matter?"

I looked down at her. "Nothing. I...I think I'm in love with you."

Her chin quivered, and tears filled her eyes. She nodded and pulled me back into another kiss, one I would never forget.

The next morning, I wanted to stay in bed and watch her sleep but couldn't. An anxiety like I had never felt before continued to plague my nerves, until I rolled to my feet, got dressed, and went for a long run. I came back near exhausted, soaked to the skin with sweat but at least a little more relaxed. Beth met me at the back door, put her arms around me, and kissed me. She didn't flinch at the wet tee shirt and whispered. "Why don't you get a shower? Your breakfast is in the oven keeping warm."

"Sorry I was gone so long."

She smiled. "Go on, get your shower."

My stomach growled. I opened the oven door with Astro at my side, also curious. He was a little foodie. I always worried his stomach could override his survival instincts and one day he'd jump in the oven after the prize.

Pancakes, eggs, and bacon. She'd gone to the store while I'd been running. Was it the Market Basket? I looked at the clock: one in the afternoon. It had been a longer run than I thought.

"Shower first." She closed the oven. "Go on."

I walked through the small kitchen, into the hall, and into the bedroom, thinking how strange it was to have a girl in my place telling me to take a shower. A girl who'd I'd spent the night with. The first time I'd spent the night with any girl. Until that night I'd always dropped the girl off at her house, wondering what the alternative would be like. Now I knew and couldn't wait to continue.

I grabbed some clothes, went into the bathroom, started the shower, stripped down, and got in, the water a wonderful sensation on my skin. I'd just put in the shampoo when the shower curtain opened. I bent at the waist, my hands going to cover my private area. Beth stood naked and unabashed, smiling. She stepped in and pulled the curtain. "Silly boy."

Thirty minutes later, with shaky legs and wrinkled skin, we dried each other off. I got dressed. She sat at the table, wearing my tattered robe, and used a towel to dry her hair. The plate of eggs and pancakes had dried out; it didn't matter, I drowned it all in syrup and ate, never taking my eyes off her. She shot me a coy smile. "Hey, quit that."

"Quit what?"

"Looking at me like that."

"Looking at you like what?"

"Like I'm some kind of apple fritter fresh out of the fryer."

She even knew my favorite donut. Without warning her smile shifted just a little. Or maybe I imagined it. I thought I caught something fleeting behind her eyes. A hidden emotion. She got up, went to the stove, came back with the coffee pot. She refilled my cup and sat down. She reached out and took my hand. "I thought you got like a week off after…after—"

"I do."

"While you were on your run your captain called. Said that the new thinking on things like this is to get right back on the horse. That's the way he put it too. Get right back on the horse, of all things."

"What?"

"He wants you to come in for shift today."

"Oh." My stomach suddenly soured at the thought. I had not been mentally preparing for this. Maybe the captain was right. Maybe it would be better to get right back out there so I didn't have much time to ponder it, to let it erode away my confidence.

She squeezed my hand, "He also said that if you need the week to take it."

I sat back and looked out the window, trying to decipher my emotions. Which would be better, work? Or time off?

Chapter Twenty-Nine

I parked the Firebird behind the station and sat behind the wheel watching other officers coming in to work swing shift. They wove their way through the cars, carrying war bags and plastic-wrapped uniforms from the dry cleaners. What were they going to think of me? Would they act any differently? I almost wanted it to be like it had been the day before with the rookie harassment, paper balls to the side of the head; at least that way I knew where I stood. I understood those rules. The way things were supposed to be.

I wouldn't act any different around them and see what happened. I went in the station through the back door and forced myself to make eye contact with whomever I met. I was *a shooter of man* and didn't know how I was supposed to feel, how I was supposed to act.

Officer Luck said a quick "Hello," as did a few others. A couple of them gave me a pat on the back as I went by. They didn't know how to act around me, either. I made my way straight to the watch commander's office and went in without knocking. Lieutenant Womack sat back in his chair and smiled. "Good to see you, Dave. How you holdin' up?"

"How is he doing?"

Womack's smile tarnished a little, but he managed to hold on to it. "He's in intensive care at Loma Linda, too critical to be moved to the county jail ward."

I nodded, the lump in my throat starting to diminish. He was still alive. "What's his name?"

"Come in, close the door."

I did as he asked.

He opened a file on his desk. "His name's Gary Hussey. He and his partner robbed the Farmer's Market on Holt yesterday in Montclair, and a pharmacy here in the city where they shot the pharmacist. The pharmacist is in critical condition in Loma Linda as well."

I shot a guy named Gary Hussey.

The lieutenant was trying to make me feel better about what I'd done.

"These are a couple of bad dudes, Dave. They had it coming. We're working on who the second guy is. We have an idea, and we have a team out looking for him right now."

"Thanks, Lieutenant." My voice cracked.

He nodded, not knowing what else to say. He again looked down at a report on his desk. "You hit him just below the tailbone, the bullet went through his prostate, upper and lower intestine, and lodged in his chest."

This part wasn't helping and was a lot more than I wanted to know. I couldn't imagine what kind of pain that must've caused Gary, what it was still causing him. "Thanks, Lieutenant. Can you keep me posted on the guy's status?"

"Sure, if that's what you want."

I nodded, opened the door, and headed down the stairs to the locker room to get ready for the shift. I was running a little late after sitting in the parking lot and then stopping to talk to the W/C. The locker room was almost empty. A couple of stragglers grabbed their gear and hurried out. They'd stopped talking when I came in.

On a bulletin board in the hall outside the briefing room, the lieutenant had posted a sign-up sheet for overtime. Gary Hussey had to have a round-the-clock cop on his door at Loma Linda. Easy kickback-read-a-magazine overtime. I needed the money as bad as anyone else, took out a pen, and added my name to a couple of slots on my days off.

When I entered the briefing room, everyone turned and clapped. The lump rose in my throat again but for a different reason this time.

Sergeant Long came in walking fast and stood at the podium. His always-gruff demeanor faltered. A rarely seen smile tried hard to squeak out.

"Beckett, you can't sign up for the Loma Linda overtime."

Confused, I looked around at the other officers. Johnny smiled. Smith kept his expression neutral as always. Long said, "It's a conflict of interest. You can't benefit from shooting someone in the ass."

Everyone in the room laughed and slapped the tables.

I drew beat six a little glad that it wasn't beat one. I wasn't ready to drive around Fourth and Mountain, the Market Basket, or the entire area surrounding it. Maybe the W/C did it on purpose.

Beat six was the largest beat, geographically in the city, but the least populated. Basically, there was the truck stop and miles of abandoned vineyards.

For the first hour, I drove around in long, empty streets with the vineyards on both sides, the whole area on track to eventually handle light manufacturing. I put the HT on the dash tuned to CLEMARs—California Law Enforcement Mutual Aid Radio frequency—listening to the team chasing down leads on Gary Hussey's partner who'd evaded arrest the night before. I wanted to be in on that hunt and felt that I had an absolute right, after what I'd been through, a feeling that had no true basis or merit.

I took a stolen semi-truck report at the truck stop, then wandered in closer to beat four to maybe poach a felony arrest in the low-income apartments right off Vineyard Avenue where a couple of dope dealers had set up shop.

Beth said she'd make dinner if I could get away about six. The thought of her back at the apartment gave me a warm glow.

I'd burnt too many calories on the long run and stopped at a market at Fourth and Vineyard. I bought a bag of salted peanuts and a bottle of coke. I drank off a good slug of the coke and poured the salted peanuts into the bottle, a trick Smith taught me. This way I could eat and drink with one hand, keeping my gun hand free. I started to get into the patrol car in front of the small market when two guys pulled up in a baby-blue Baja Bug. They got out and headed into the store. The one with longer hair stopped and said, "Hey, man?"

I paused and stood. "Yeah?"

He pointed east. "There's a car parked in the vineyard. Looks funny. Know what I mean? Like it's stolen or something."

"What kind of car?"

He shrugged. "Orange...burnt-orange, Pontiac maybe. Or GM, you know." He shrugged again. "Just thought, you might want to know."

"Where?"

He waved his arm. "Way out there, man"—he swung his arm north and south—"on a dirt road off the asphalt that runs this way. There's a long row of tall trees and a bunch of junk people dumped out there and shot up, a couch, some barrels, things like that."

I knew the place. It was where Smith had caught the kidnap/rapists. "Thank you, I'll check it out."

The dirt road was at the outer edge of the city, past the truck stop. The city was fifty square miles and it would take fifteen minutes to get there. I headed east, the sun in the rearview mirror setting on the horizon threatening to end the day in a blaze of orange. I took my time.

Twenty minutes later I slowed and eased off the asphalt onto the dirt road. The row of eucalyptus trees started half a mile farther up. No burnt-orange Pontiac in sight, unless it was hidden in the trees. I drove slowly, giving the car's suspension enough time to absorb the chuckholes without banging it up too badly. "Take care of your equipment and your equipment will take care of you." Another Smith axiom.

I'd been up the same road a thousand times, and knew when to move to what side to avoid upcoming ruts and holes. This trip would be a waste of time. There wasn't any car. If there had been it was gone now. The shot-up refrigerator and the two shot-up fifty-five-gallon barrels sat in the same place on the left. The hedgerow was a popular place for illegal shooters.

I made a five-point turn around in the narrow dirt track just as the spectrum of light from the sunset caught just right. I flashed on the memory from the night before. The one where I raced up San Antonio Avenue running the stop signs trying to get to the call. The smell of blood and gun smoke. The look in Gary Hussey's eyes as he accused me of shooting him.

My stomach soured. I threw the car in park and jumped out, trying to keep from losing the peanuts and coke I'd eaten, glad I was out where no one could see me. Sweat beaded on my forehead. I closed my eyes and took in deep cleansing breaths until the moment passed. I started to get back in when the fading sunlight glinted off something on the other side of the hedgerow of eucalyptus trees. I walked away from the patrol car, moving right and left trying to see through the trees, trying to see what was there. A car maybe? Burnt-orange?

I picked my way through the row to the other side and found nothing but miles of emptiness. Sand and abandoned vineyards.

And a slit trench someone had just dug, the dirt freshly piled up on one side. Orange and yellow sunlight knifed through the hedge of huge eucalyptus trees, creating shadows, an illusion of sharp shadowy teeth eating the trench. A white and pink object stuck up from the hole, clean and new and incongruent. I couldn't take my eyes off it, my feet moving on their own to get a closer look. I didn't want to go any closer and yet my feet kept moving. My hand dropped to the stock of my handgun, the lieutenant's handgun, the one he'd lent me until mine came back from ballistics.

With each step, more of the slit trench came into view. When the eyes don't want to see what they're seeing, mixed messages are sent to the brain and come out jumbled. *Clear plastic. Skin. Blue denim. White and pink sneakers. Long brown hair.*

For one interminable moment, I stood at the end of the slit trench, no air getting to my lungs. The world had come to a complete stop and I wanted to step off.

My mind caught up as my eyes digested the scene. My hand yanked the gun from my holster. I spun around.

In a fraction of a second, my mind registered the flat side of a shovel that twanged off my face, blinking out all light. I fell backward slowly. Falling. Falling. Without ever landing.

I woke to clumps of dirt—shovel loads sliding across my body, the weight already too much to bear, making it difficult to breathe. Smothering. The darkness in the world spun round and round. A concussion.

I opened my eyes. My swollen and bloated nose touched clear plastic. On the other side of which was a girl. I'd recognize her anywhere, from her photo: Jessica DeFrank. The missing girl. No longer missing. A milky film covered her once-beautiful eyes. I threw up Coke and peanuts. Choked and gagged on it.

Another clump of dirt landed with a smothering weight. I turned my head. The man stood at the end of the trench shoveling in the fresh dirt. The last rays of sunlight backlit him, obscuring his features and making him nothing more than a thin shadow with a shovel that looked more like a scythe.

"Stop it," I croaked.

Another clump of dirt.

My arm was pinned to my side by the weight of the dirt.

A clump landed on my face, blocking out the last bit of light. I shook and sputtered and gasped for breath. Dirt fell off. Light returned. I wanted to just close my eyes and go to sleep. Let someone else deal with this problem.

The next clump covered poor Jessica's face. The dirt rattled the plastic.

Lieutenant Womack's speech whispered in my ear, the one he gave as he stood in briefing, cigar in hand: *If for some reason you screw up out there, God forbid, and you go down, just remember, your fellow officers are going to be driving like hell to assist you. They are going to run blindly into a situation you created. It's your screwup. You will not roll over and give up. You will fix your screwup if it takes your last breath. You understand?*

I took in a long breath and let out a yell. At the same time, I shoved my arm deeper. Down along my leg, the only place I could get my arm to go.

Another clump landed on my face.

"Aaah! Stop it! Stop it!" I choked and gasped. My hand found the .38 Smith had given me, the one in the ankle holster. I yanked it loose and used every ounce of strength I had left forcing my arm up through the loose, heavy dirt.

My hand broke through, the gun pointed at the shadow not six feet away. He froze mid-toss.

"Say good-bye, asshole." I fired again and again. The shadow stuttered-stepped backward as each round thumped into him. The gun clicked empty.

I'd fired all six. *If he's good for one, he's good for all six.* The shadow had moved back six or seven feet but still stood on his feet. He wasn't human. He was the devil. Pure evil that couldn't be killed. My arm went limp. Darkness closed in again.

I woke a second time to blackness and found it difficult to breathe. It wasn't a nightmare; that would've been too easy. I was still in the slit trench with Jessica. Tears burned my eyes.

"Bastard. You bastard."

Some strength had returned after my little dirt nap. I wiggled my shoulder until enough dirt fell away that I could get a full breath. More strength returned. I wiggled and clawed and pulled my way out of the trench. I couldn't stand, not without losing my balance and falling on my ass. That was the concussion. The full moon with an odd brightness blanketed the miles and miles of empty vineyard. Blood, an eerie moonlight black, dripped from my head and face and mouth, the sandy ground taking it all in, hungry for it.

I crawled on my hands and knees to get away from the trench. The shadow wasn't where he should've been, dead or dying where I'd shot him. He'd disappeared. How could that be?

I reached for my HT. I'd left it on the dash of the patrol car where I'd been listening to CLAMRs, the hunt for Gary Hussey's partner.

I crawled. Rested and crawled some more. Crawled miles and miles, it seemed, when it was only seventy feet to the patrol unit on the other side of the hedgerow.

From ground level, I reached into the car, pulled the mic, and asked for help. I couldn't keep the sobs from slurring my pleas. This time I knew my location.

II

BOOK TWO

If you can meet with Triumph and Disaster. And treat those two impostors just the same.
—Rudyard Kipling

Chapter One

Eight Years Later. 1988

Homicide Bureau

"I said I'd pick her up at five-thirty sharp. What do you want from me?"

My fingers gently rubbed the scar tissue along the left side of my face, above and across my eye. The doctor had said he could make it like new with plastic surgery, but I declined. I wanted it left alone, a reminder of what had happened, an ugly chapter in a life that had never gone as planned. A bit of scar crossed through the brow and down to the corner of my eye. It gave me a haggard, dangerous appearance that at times had helped in my job.

I had Lucy for the weekend. Beth just wanted to give me grief; she liked to get me jacked up. We'd been separated for six months and according to her, "pending divorce." I hoped, for Lucy's sake, that we could work it out; she was only five and needed both of her parents. In a heated rage, I'd been the one to walk out and now regretted it. I still loved Beth. I'd tried everything to get back into the house, but Beth would have none of it. She now lived to press my buttons.

"You're not here tonight," Beth said on the other end of the line, "I'm taking you back to family court to get full custody, pending the divorce."

I gripped the phone receiver and closed my eyes. "I told you, my team's not up, and we have nothing going on right now. I'll be there." She knew as well as I did that homicides waited for no one. Two could come in at any time, and the rotation would reach down to my team.

"Don't disappoint her again, Dave." She hung up.

I looked up to see if anyone had noticed the loud conversation. The large room was divided into four quadrants with half cubicle walls and desks, four teams of four detectives with a sergeant for each. Homicide teams that rotated the on-call. To the left was the glassed-in office of Lieutenant Sims, who ran all four teams. He was a good friend, but I'd recently stretched that friendship to a breaking point. Family conflict did not help matters.

Jaime Lopez, across the room on Team Two, held up his receiver. "You off the phone now, Dogman? I got a call for you by name."

"Who is it?"

"I'm not your secretary, pendejo. Line three."

They all knew I didn't like the tag Dogman, but there was nothing I could do about it. I picked the phone up and punched line three. "Beckett."

"I was told you're the guy I need to talk to."

I eased back into my chair and put my boot on the desk. "That right? Who's this?"

"Out of that whole big county of yours, I'm told you're the man to call when someone needs something done. Dirty Dave Beckett."

Another tag unjustly awarded and impossible to shake. "This some kind of joke? I'm hanging up." The other detectives in the division liked to pull gags.

"Wait. This is no joke. I need a big favor."

"I'm not in the habit of doing favors for phantom callers. Who is this?"

"I'm a detective with Riverside County."

"Name?"

"I think it'd be better if you didn't know."

I dropped my boot to the floor and sat forward. "You've got my attention."

"I've got a warrant for manslaughter that I need served in your county."

"I work homicide, not fugitive."

"This is a favor, and like I said, I was told you're the one to handle this. The guy's name is Oscar Sanchez. Hispanic male, 4/26/61." He paused, waiting for me to check his story. I put the phone to my shoulder and tapped the information into the computer. Sanchez popped with a manslaughter warrant just like he said. "Okay, I'm with you. Now tell me why this is a special handle?"

Another long pause of dead air.

"You want my help or not?"

The unknown detective said, "Okay, look...ah. Okay. Sanchez is a major asshole. We had him set up in a ten-kilo meth buy-bust. We slid in one of our regular informants to do the deal, a real good dude on our regular payroll as a contract player. The deal went down bad. Sanchez tumbled to the surveillance. There was a pursuit and a crash. This happened down in Elsinore. Our informant was killed in the crash. The DA would only file manslaughter instead of murder. We know where Sanchez is but—"

Another pause.

"But the way you got to it isn't kosher."

"That's right, a black-bag wiretap. You didn't hear that from me."

"So, you can't serve the warrant because you're too close to it and it would be too easy for someone to figure it out and track it back."

"Right. You in?"

"I'm always up for a little game of fox and hounds. Give me the address."

"Excellent."

I wrote it down and at the same time hit print to get a copy of the warrant.

"Beckett?"

"Yeah."

"This informant that died, he was a good dude."

"You said that already."

"If Sanchez so much as reaches for a comb—"

"I'll do what I can."

"Thanks."

I hung up, grabbed my war bag, and headed to the big board. I signed out without putting the address, just "The High Desert." Lieutenant Sims saw me leaving, got up from his desk, and came to his door. I hurried. I didn't want to lie to him and was gone before he could yell at me.

Chapter Two

I headed upstairs to the Violent Crimes office. I'd need someone to cover the back door of the house. Jimmy Mora understood the way I worked. We became friends the usual way in the cop world. One day during in-service training—the quarterly qualification and legal update—the instructor called Jimmy's name. He was absent. At the time, I only knew him from tilting a beer with him once at the Crazy Chicken Bar. At break, I signed him in, and during a video sneaked out.

I drove to his house and found his front door ajar. I called out. No one answered. I got worried, pulled my gun, and eased open the door. The interior looked like a pool party bomb went off, beach towels, sunscreen scattered about. The furniture was pushed to one side, and empty beer bottles littered the floor with empty chip bags, chips, guacamole, and sour cream smeared into the carpet. And the true cause of the party bomb going off: two empty bottles of Jose Cuervo Gold.

On the couch lay a drunk naked woman on her stomach, her long black hair a nest covering her face. Jimmy Mora was a lucky man. I covered her with a beach towel and continued through the house. The back door stood open. I took a peek in the back yard and froze.

Jimmy Mora lay naked on the dirt, his arms around a tree trunk, his hands handcuffed. I ran to the side of the house out the gate and to the trunk of my car. I came back with my Polaroid and took several snaps from different angles. I put the camera back, uncuffed him, got him up and walking around.

We made it back to in-service training before the video ended. I sent him one of the snaps in an interoffice mail envelope with his name, labeled "Personal," and a note that said "You owe The Dogman lunch for one month."

On the second floor, directly above homicide, the Violent Crimes office mirrored the floor plan below. I moved through the cubicles to Jimmy Mora, who sat at his desk with his feet up talking on the phone. When he saw me, he said into the phone, "Hold on." I handed him the printout. His eyes scanned it. He said into the phone, "Babe, let me call you back." He hung up and shrugged, "Manslaughter, fifty-thousand-dollar bail, big deal. They're a dime a dozen. We handle murder warrants, bank robbers, and carjackers."

"This is a special handle." Cop-talk for something that could go *cowboys and Indians*, and you didn't make it to the Violent Crimes Team unless you were a cowboy.

"Why didn't you say so?" He jumped up and yelled to his crew, "Let's roll, compadres" Two other members on his team popped up over their cubicles.

"I was kinda thinkin' it'd be you and me."

"This is my team. They've made their bones. You don't need to worry." He grabbed his war bag. "Where we goin'?"

"Phelan."

The other two team members came around to Jimmy's cubicle, carrying their war bags. They were new. I only knew them from passing in the hall. If Jimmy said they were okay, I was good with it. Jimmy's team was the only one subsidized by the FBI. They were cross sworn as US Marshals. They had one FBI agent on the team, Samuel T. Brown. I'd met him. He was a suit-and-tie-wearing stuffed shirt who spoke to crooks as if they were regular people, which never got him anywhere on the street. I tried to stay away from him. I was happy he wasn't around to butt his nose into our raid.

The four of us headed out, weaving through the cubicle farm headed to the stairs. We almost made it out the door and to the stairs when Samuel T. came up the steps, wearing denim pants and a long-sleeve white dress shirt, starched and ironed with sharp edges. "Where are you going?" he said to Mora, as he scowled at me. Apparently, he didn't like his team having anything to do with The Dogman.

"No big deal," Mora said. "We're just going to help homicide serving an arrest warrant."

"Good, I got some time, I'll tag along."

"Ah, man," I said.

Mora turned, shrugged, and gave me the look that said, "Nothing we can do about it."

Outside, I headed to my car.

We stayed on the tactical frequency all the way through Cajon Pass. We sped by the offramp for Institution Road, and GHRC—Glen Helen Rehabilitation Center—and for the umpteenth time in the last two weeks I thought about stopping in for a visit. Like all the other times when the urge struck, I quashed it. I didn't need additional headaches and that would be a huge one.

After forty-five minutes of driving, the conga line of three unmarked cars turned down an abusive dirt road. Ten more minutes, the house came into view. A big house for the area that sat on a steep knoll by itself with a narrow dirt ridge that led to it, the only access. A perfect bandit hideout. I should've called for a helicopter. But who knew? I led the way in and stopped at the opening to the front yard. I got out as the others gathered around, guns in their hands.

"I'll take the front door." They were professionals, nothing else needed to be said. They knew what to do. We deployed on the house. Samuel T. stayed with me, the worst possible scenario.

The house was newer, but the desert wind and the constant shift from freezing to sweltering heat had already taken its toll on the wood and stucco. There was nothing green planted anywhere around the house, nothing but dirt and sand. I handed the warrant to Samuel T. as I knocked.

Samuel T. said, "This is an arrest warrant, not a search warrant. We can't force entry."

I knew having him along was going to be a problem. I said nothing.

Samuel T. asked, "How did we get here? Why do you think this guy is inside?"

I looked at him as I knocked again, louder this time. "An anonymous phone tip."

"That was a long drive for nothing, let's go."

I knocked again louder yet, my fist shaking the door and the house. To my right, by the corner of the house, Mora waved at me. I hurried over. He said, "Someone came out the back." I moved that way at a fast clip with Mora and Samuel T. following.

Around back, one of Mora's new guys had talked with a white male who'd come from inside and was walking back to the house when I came up. "Hey, hold on." He stopped.

The man wore work boots, shabby denim, and a long-sleeve plaid shirt, tattered and ready for the rag bin. His hair was long and greasy, his face pocked with acne scars. The back yard was cluttered with concrete blocks, and a huge concrete formed fountain lying on its side never hooked up.

He turned back. "I already told this cop, the guy you're looking for isn't here. I don't know him. Never heard of him. So, you can just leave. Now."

I walked up to him, Mora and Samuel T. right behind me. I said, "It's not that I don't believe you, but we need to take a look inside."

"Not gonna happen. Leave. Now."

Samuel T. said, "Come on, let's go."

Mora and his two guys waited to see what I'd do. "You have any ID?"

"I'm at my own house, in my own yard. I don't need ID. Now get out of here."

"He's right," Samuel T. said.

I suppressed the urge to spin around and slap him; assault on a federal agent wouldn't go down well with Lieutenant Sims.

I held up the arrest warrant. "I have this, and I have reason to believe he is in here. That gives me the right to ask you for your ID." The man came over and took the warrant. I let him.

He handed it right back. "This guy is six foot two, I'm five-ten. He has brown hair and green eyes, I have black hair and brown eyes. Now get off my property before I call your boss and tell him you're violating my civil rights.

Samuel T. said to Mora, "Come on, get your guys, we're out of here."

Mora, to his credit, held his ground. He was going to wait and see what I would do and back me up if I needed it.

I said, "We're not leaving until we check inside for this guy."

The man turned heel and headed for his back door. I made a tough decision. Well, not so tough. "Hold it," I said, in a commanding tone.

One of Mora's men stepped in front of the man, stopping him. Everyone looked at me.

I said, "Wait. Listen. Did you hear that?"

Samuel T. said, "Don't do this."

I said. "Someone's in the house destroying evidence and attempting to evade arrest. Breach the door."

The man yelled. "No! No!"

To his credit, Mora didn't crack a smile and remained professional. "Take the door." His two guys moved up, kicked it in, and entered, guns drawn and at the ready. Mora followed them in. I stayed with the homeowner, unsure if Samuel T. would detain him if he tried to run.

Samuel T. said, "You're going to hear about this, Detective Beckett. This time you're finished."

"I figured as much."

Mora came out of the house a few minutes later chuckling and shaking his head. "You're guy's not in there." He grabbed the homeowner in a wristlock and handcuffed him. "But this guy's got a three-room meth lab with eight 22000 mil beakers, all of them bubbling. Biggest lab I have ever seen. Might be the record for the county. Great bust, Dogman."

I'd been had; the detective who'd called knew there was a lab and had played me.

I turned to smile at Samuel T., but he'd already stomped off, headed for his car and, I was sure, to the closest phone.

Chapter Three

We had to wait for narcotics, a forensics crew, and a hazmat team to drive to the location and secure the residence. The two new guys drove the homeowner/suspect to Victorville Station to book him. Thirty minutes after Samuel T. left, my pager buzzed with "1021 62L 911," code for "Call the boss right away—he's mad as hell." The house didn't have a phone hooked up. The lieutenant would have to wait. It was probably better to wait and give him a chance to cool down.

Mora brought his car to the front yard by the front door, got out, and opened his hood, the engine still running. From his trunk, he took out a small ice chest. "You hungry, Dogman? I got enough for two. *Burritos con carne y papas.*"

His wife's burritos were famous, only a fool would turn one down. "Sure, thanks."

He took out two foil-wrapped burritos and laid them on the engine manifold to heat, a poor man's microwave. He pulled out two ice-cold beers and handed me one. I handed it back and shrugged.

"Oh," he said. "That's right. Sorry, man." He fished out a coke and handed it over as my pager continued to buzz.

Mora took a tug off his beer and pointed the bottle at the pager on my belt. "Sounds like you might be in a little trouble, *mijo.*"

"Yeah, this time I'm afraid I might be in a lot of trouble."

He pointed his beer at the house and shrugged. "Not for this. I heard the guy in the house destroying evidence just like you did. Screw Samuel T. Brown."

"It would've been a lot better if the house hadn't been empty and someone else had been in there who could've made a noise."

"Lot of wind out here howling. It was an easy mistake. The court allows for mistakes like that. My guys will go along with it."

"I'm not so worried about the FBI. Sims will smooth that over. It's that lab in there. There just had to be a lab. That's the way my luck's been running."

Mora leaned under his car hood and turned the burritos. "I don't understand. Talk to me."

"Narcotics is going to have my ass over this one. They're already mad at me. In fact, I'm on double-secret probation after the last caper. Sims isn't going to have a choice, he has to drop the hammer on me."

Mora smiled. "I'm all ears."

"It's a long sad story."

"What, you got someplace you gotta be?"

"Okay." I moved to my car, sat on the hood, and took a drink of coca-cola. "I was working this case, you probably heard about it. A body dump in Summit Valley. Two dudes, taped hand and foot, shot back of the head and shoved in a truck bed with a camper shell. Then the truck was lit on fire. Not much to go on. Most of the evidence was burned. It was linked to meth in the high desert. I thought I'd shake the bushes a little and serve some search warrants, throw out a wide net and see who floated to the surface, find someone who wanted to talk. It was one affidavit with seven search warrants."

"That's a pretty wide net. I think I remember hearing something about this."

I nodded. "Anyway, we hit this one place in Apple Valley, a high-dollar house being used as a slam pad. Sixteen people were in there. One was this guy, the only one wearing a suit and tie, said he was into real estate, said he had a reputation to protect. He wanted to trade his way out of the arrest. He gave me his name, but I couldn't find him in the system. I told him I'd take his information and if it panned out I'd let him walk.

"After I identified him, that is. I only had him on a misdemeanor, but he didn't know that. Turned out later, after I took his fingerprints and ran him, he came back with an out-of-state attempted murder warrant. Anyway, he said he knew of a house that had pounds of meth, guns, and lots of cash. Said one of the guns was a machine gun. You know as well as I do these guys always say there's pounds when it's ounces or even grams.

I put him in the car and drove him by a place he pointed out in Apple Valley. Real nice pad up in The Knolls. There were seven cars in the driveway, all expensive, newer or classics. All of them high-dollar. I grabbed a few plates, went back to Apple Valley station, stashed the dude in a cell, and ran the plates."

Mora, leaned under his hood and picked up a burrito, tossed it back and forth in his hands, and tossed it to me. It was too hot to eat. I set it on my hood to cool. Mora toughed it out with his, peeled back the foil, and took a bite. My mouth watered watching him.

He said, "Go on."

One of the cars came back to William Jones. Bill Jones. I ran Bill Jones and came up with a warrant for a million dollars out of San Diego for ADW, assault with a deadly weapon."

Mora chuckled. "You didn't have a date of birth, so how do you know you got the right Bill Jones?"

"You want to hear this?"

"How many Bill Joneses were there?"

I smiled. "Twenty-seven with warrants."

"Oh man, I can tell right now this is going to be a good one."

"I know. And how was I to know the caper here at this place with the lab was going to turn out the same way. It's going to look like I did it on purpose when it was just an unlucky coincidence.

Mora laughed, took a drink of his beer. "Tell the rest of it, *mijo*."

"So, I'm going to cold-knock the door at the house in The Knolls with all the cars, try to get in for a look-see using the warrant as a ruse. Which is absolutely legal. I tried to get one of the dicks at Apple Valley to go along as backup and—"

"And they wanted no part of it."

"That's right. So, I call narcotics, tell the on-call team sergeant, Stevens. I tell him what I have, the dope and guns, and what I intended to do. I wanted to play by the rules and give them the opportunity to come out and play. Once he heard the Bill Jones thing he laughed at me and said good luck."

I picked up the burrito from the hood, unwrapped it, and took a bite. It was delicious, with beans, rice, potato, tender beef, chilies, and a heavenly mild red sauce.

Mora said, "So you knocked on the door."

"Yeah, I went and knocked on the door. This guy answers. I give him the spiel about Bill Jones. He says Bill Jones doesn't live there. I point to the car and ask, whose car is that? He says, Bill's. I say Bill who? He says Bill Jones. I show him the arrest warrant and tell him I just want to cruise the inside of his house to see if Bill is inside.

"He finally lets me in. Nice place. Everything inside is brand spanking new, everything. Some of the stuff still had the plastic on it. Like he won the showcase on a game show: furniture, appliances, the whole shiteree. I walk through the house, it's as clean as a Safeway chicken. As soon as I walk into the master bedroom I smell dirty socks. I turn around, thank him, and leave."

Mora took a bite of his burrito and muttered, "Meth."

Meth has two smells, depending on the process used to make it: dirty socks or apple blossoms.

I nodded, took another bite of my burrito. "I go back to the station and call Sergeant Stevens back. He laughs at me, tells me good luck getting a search warrant on dirty socks. I call a judge who knows me, knows the way I work, knows that I have testified in his court as a narcotics expert in the past. And I ask him flat out, would he give me a search warrant based solely on my nose. He says sure, why not. Then I can tell people I signed a warrant for dirty socks. I write the affidavit and warrant and call him back and get a telephonic warrant."

Mora said, "Now the Apple Valley dicks want to go because you have a warrant."

"That's right."

"Did you call Stevens back and tell him?"

"No, and that's where I made my mistake. Because of the weapons, we hit the place hard and fast. I took the ram. We all exited our cars and ran to the house. The guy I spoke to earlier had come to his door to see what was going on. He opened the door just as I ran up. He slammed it. I threw the ram. And just let it go. It took down his door. I was on him. Caught him in the hall in front of his master bedroom. He was going for a gun. He resisted arrest and I had to hit him with my gun."

"Of course, you did. What'd you get in the house?"

I smiled, took a bite of burrito, chewed, swallowed. "Six pounds of meth, fifty thousand in cash, a cheap Tec-9, and a bunch of assault rifles. I seized all the cars in front of the house and backed a truck up and took all the furniture. All of it under the rules of asset forfeiture. I found a couple of receipts for storage places and wrote an addendum Then I called back the judge, who was tickled pink at the seizure. He signed the addendum and we scored, chemicals to manufacture meth and a t-bucket funny car worth a 100 grand."

"All of that sounds great to me, *mijo.*"

"Except that homicide had better stats that month for narcotics and asset forfeiture than the entire narcotics division. It caused a huge stink. And Stevens took it in the shorts for waving it off. And now, you think this house has the largest meth lab seizure in the history of the county? No, I'm in the grease, big time."

I lost my appetite just thinking about what Lieutenant Sims was going to say. I wrapped up the half burrito to eat later. I pulled out the pager and checked the pages: seven from Sims, all 911s. I held it up to Mora. "I better get down there and face the music. You mind covering this?"

"Sure, Dogman, no problem."

I moved around, opened the door, and started to get in.

"Hey *mijo*, keep your head down."

"You too."

Chapter Four

I dumped my undercover car in the vast parking lot behind headquarters and walked in the back door to the Homicide Bureau. Kenny Willis saw me first, stood up, and clapped. All the homicide dicks in the office stood to look and then started clapping. I couldn't help but smile. I raised my hand and waved like a princess riding in the backseat of a fancy red 57 Chevy Nomad convertible on a hot fourth of July parade, a princess about to be unceremoniously deflowered.

I walked into Sims' office, closed the door, and sat in the hot seat in front of his desk. He was so mad he didn't look up from writing in his Red Book day planner; in all likelihood, the entry listed the name Dogman with lots of expletives. I felt bad that I had put him in such a precarious situation. I sat and took in the uncomfortable silence, understanding it was part of the penalty, the guillotine poised over my head. Had I stopped to talk to him on the way out of the office he would've talked me out of the foolhardy stunt. But, *what was life without a little adventure?* A Johnny Maslow axiom. I missed Johnny and our days together riding in a patrol car.

Sims finished writing, closed his planner, and sat back giving me the mad-dog stare that I deserved. The applause when I entered the office from the guys in the bullpen had not helped matters.

I'd left the city of West Valley right after the shovel to the face incident and laterally transferred to San Bernardino County Sheriff's Department, a much larger place. Trying to disappear. With my street experience, I made detective right away and eventually landed in homicide. Now I wished I'd stayed in that small-town environment. I might still have my marriage, and not, yet again, be in the grease.

Sims was ten years older, with a svelte runner's build he got from running at lunch and in half marathons, a leader on a Baker to Vegas team. He wore an impeccable dress shirt and silk tie that I could never afford. He shaved his tanned head and had intense green eyes that now lasered right through me.

I knew enough to wait for him to open the conversation. I had to look away. My eyes wandered to the coat rack behind him where he hung his dress Ike jacket and a *just-in-case* long-sleeve dress uniform still in dry cleaner plastic, already set up to be worn with his badge and nameplate pinned to the shirt.

A while back I had noticed that uniform on the coat rack where he always kept it and saw an opportunity. I sneaked in one day when he was out and replaced the nameplate from *R. Sims* with one I had the uniform shop make ahead of time: *Lou Kemia*. It was one of those jokes that ran like a silent torpedo, one that you never knew when it was going to explode. I forgot all about it.

Unfortunately, the way my luck went, Sims wore the uniform to an awards banquet and sat at the same table as the sheriff. Now whenever a member of the executive staff—the deputy chiefs, assistance sheriffs, under sheriff or the sheriff—pass him in the hall, they call him Lou. He cringes each time and mutters my name in vain.

I smiled at the memory.

Sims said, "You think this is funny, Beckett?"

"No, sir."

"The commander of narcotics is up for Deputy Chief. He is mad as a hatter over this. Especially after you'd been warned to keep your nose out of their business."

"Yes, sir."

"Cut out that 'sir,' crap. It's not going to help you here."

"Okay, Bob."

He gritted his teeth and leaned forward over his desk. "Son of bitch, Beckett, I can't cover you this time. You really screwed the pooch and now you sit there and make jokes?"

I said nothing.

He sat back and took in a couple of deep breaths. The redness left his face. "Look, the FBI's involved too, so now it has to be investigated by IAB. You're suspended pending board of review."

The words came as a sock to the stomach. I knew it was going to be bad, but not suspended. "Lieutenant…I…I—"

He lowered his tone to consoling. "There's nothing I can do for you."

My hand, all on its own, moved to the chain around my neck, my fingers finding the small medallions: one was Astro's dog license tag, the other, my two-year AA chip. "Work is the only thing that keeps me straight."

"I know," he said, "and I'm sorry."

"This thing is all blown out of proportion. Talk to Mora, he'll tell you."

"IAB will be doing the interviews. I'm ordering you not to talk to anyone about this investigation until it's adjudicated. Turn your active cases over to the senior man on your team. Your team sergeant is on vacation. You are to stay at your home from eight in the morning until five at night and subject to verification."

I stood, turned to leave, my legs tingling. I turned back. "How long?"

"You know how these things work, a month, maybe two."

Dizziness made the world around me warble like a heatwave. Two months alone in my small apartment. No way. No chance. Can't happen. I wouldn't make it through to the other side, not this time.

He must've seen my face lose all its color. He lowered his tone. "Dave, I guess I could give you desk duty."

I turned back, anxious to grab at any life preserver tossed my way. "That'd be great." He had that offer in his back pocket all the time and only wanted me to see the downside first—how bad it could get.

He pointed at me. "I'm putting my ass on the line for you. Do not screw up again."

"No, I won't. I promise."

He walked to his file cabinet and took down a huge map of the county, glued to a board.

"No," I whispered. "Not the Bone Detective."

"I'm sorry, but it's the only way I can make this work. I have to tell the chiefs that you're in the penalty box. Answering the division phones at your desk isn't going to be enough."

He handed me the map, which had eight hundred and fifty-four little red flags, each indicating where human bones had been discovered in the county—open cases. Unidentified victims. San Bernardino County is the largest county, geographically, in the contiguous United States. Twenty thousand square miles, with a long freeway through the center of the desert running all the way to the Nevada border and Las Vegas.

It was said that if every murder victim buried in the Mojave Desert were to stand up, it would be a forest too dense to see through. Eight hundred and fifty-four was the count so far, with more turning up all the time. The Bone Detective was a thankless, dead-end job no one wanted. Boring. Capital B, capital Oring. But the worst thing about being awarded this assignment was that, historically, it ended careers. It was jinxed. Some thought it had to do with the ghosts of the victims. Pure folly.

I took the board with the bone map glued to it and exited his office. Now all the detectives stood and this time clapped at the new downturn in my career. Trying to make light of it. I pasted on a fake smile and waved like a deflowered princess and walked back to my desk. I propped the map on the shelves above my desk, just as Sergeant Wilks from team three came over and handed me a pink While-you-were-out slip.

"Leg bone found by a resident. His dog brought it to the back door. It's gonna require a door-to-door neighborhood check for other pet dog activity in the area." He chuckled, and said, "Good luck, Dogman. Arf."

"Thanks, Sarge, I hope I can return the favor sometime." I got the nickname Dogman by wearing Astro's dog tags around my neck. All those other dumbasses didn't understand the love of a good dog. This new assignment was too apropos.

The pink slip said the leg bone was found in Phelan, at the top of Cajon Pass. I had just come from that direction, Phelan, where the meth lab was found. The day was spiraling out of control. If I didn't pull out of the tailspin, I'd auger in for sure, burst into a ball of flames, and scatter shrapnel across the countryside. It wasn't fair, but sometimes when life fed you lemons, you had to go looking for someone worse off. I grabbed my war bag and marked on the big board "Out, at "Phelan, bone hunting. Arf."

A place I had no intention of going.

Chapter Five

I pulled into the GHRC parking lot, shut off the Mustang 5.0—a county ride—and sat looking at the concertina barbed wire and ten-foot-tall chain link fence that surrounded the facility. Over to the right at the guard shack, a deputy checked in a food-delivery truck in the sally port, looking underneath it with a handheld mirror on a long pole.

I grabbed my custom leather notebook with the steno pad inside, a common tool of a homicide dick, and got out. I had to make this visit look official. I went to the trunk and secured my gun and asp rather than using the gun lockers in the guard shack. I'd learned *that* important lesson while riding with Smith as a trainee. We'd just booked a crook for possession of tar heroin when a 211 silent robbery alarm was given to us. I ran to the patrol unit and jumped in. Smith had stayed with the car to write reports. We took off. He knew my error and wanted to ram home the lesson in the worst possible way.

We arrived on scene at the bank, pulled up, and jumped out. My hand went to my holster and found it empty. In my haste, I'd gone off and left my service revolver in the gun locker at the jail. I would never forget that feeling of being unarmed and vulnerable. Smith was good that way about knowing how to train the ignorant. I'd learned a helluva lot from him. At the time, I pulled the unit shotgun, my face flushed hot with embarrassment. The call was a false alarm. But what if it hadn't been?

I walked to the GHRC guard shack. I'd been there before for other interviews of suspects and witnesses already in custody, serving time. My gold star clipped to my belt and the worn leather notebook in my hand was all the new jail deputy securing the gate needed. His hair was shaved close on the sides and he had a babyface. He could pass for sixteen. How did he keep from getting eaten by the inmates? Maybe that was why he was on the gate.

He handed me the visitor's badge and the clipboard to fill in. Under "reason for visit," I lied and wrote homicide investigation. He took the board back and buzzed me through. I took the concrete walk to the main office which, had it not been surrounded by fencing and guards, could've been any regular business enterprise out in the real world, like a ball-bearing or cardboard-box manufacturer.

Instead of ringing the bell at the front desk, I pushed through the swing gate like I knew what I was about. I found this method worked best when trying to bamboozle the unsuspecting. I needed to get through this part quickly before a more senior deputy in the facility started paying attention. I moved right to the watch deputy desk. I didn't recognize him. I picked up the visiting board from the in-box tray and filled it in.

He said, "How you doin', Detective?"

"I'd appreciate it if you put a rush on this visit. I've got three other interviews and they're all in Big Bear. That's a long drive."

"Sure thing." He lost his smile when he read the board I'd handed back. "I'm sorry, sir, this inmate is red-flagged, marked as an escape risk with visits approved only by the captain."

I took out my Sheriff's homicide business card and handed it to him. "That doesn't apply to me. I'm not a friend, or attorney, or relative. I'm one of us."

"I know but—"

"I'm a deputy just like you. Are you saying that deputies can't talk to him either?"

"That's right. This inmate has caused us nothing but grief, and the captain has ordered no one to talk to him. He's a dangerous murderer, and I'm sorry but the captain's off the facility."

"Right, and I'm a murder detective and if the captain were here he'd let me conduct my interview." I could see in his eyes the logic starting to sway him.

"All right," I said. "Gimme your phone, I'll call my captain and he'll give you the go-ahead. But I'll tell you right now he's a busy man and won't like the disruption, especially for something so chickenshit."

"Okay," he said. "You can go on back."

"Great. Instead of waiting on a rover, why don't you escort me to the blocks, so I can get this over with and get out of your hair."

He grabbed his keys and led me into the bowels of GHRC. With each hard door and gate we passed through, the jail turned dimmer and gloomier. The walls were cinderblock and covered in multiple coats of institutional beige paint. The floor gleamed from being mopped and waxed every day, something to keep the inmates busy. But still, a familiar odor, one only found in custodial facilities, hung thick in the air. More an essence, a combination of sour body odor with a tinge of vomit and a large dollop of despair. The kind of odor a gallon of pine cleaner couldn't mask.

The watch deputy said over his shoulder, "You'll have to do the interview from outside his cell, he's a red suit. He's also a suicide risk with a twenty-four-hour watch and a fifteen-minute observation paper log."

"That's cool, standing outside the cell will work just fine."

Down at the very end of the hall, in front of the last cell, a deputy on overtime sat in a chair. What a horrible assignment, sitting eight hours watching a human in a cage and under direct orders not to talk to him. The entire row had been left empty because of one inmate. We came up on the overtime deputy, who stood. I tried to see into the cell. It was too shadowy to see anything other than indistinct lines and shadows. For some reason, the interior light was off. Probably by order of the captain, to mess with the inmate.

I hooked my thumb over my shoulder, "It's okay, take a break. Go get some coffee."

The overtime deputy looked at the watch deputy, who nodded and said to him, "Come back in thirty minutes."

He had not bothered to ask me if thirty minutes would be satisfactory. He wanted to reassert at least a smidgeon of his authority. That was okay by me. I wouldn't be that long. I only had one question. A big one.

I sat in the chair vacated by the overtime deputy and let my eyes adjust to the dimness in the cell. The two deputies made it to the end of the row and disappeared out a hard door that clanked shut. Silence prevailed along with the pervasive stink.

Hands appeared first on the bars, knuckles, and long fingers. Then the familiar face moved from the gloom and into the dim light between the bars. He said, "Hey, kid, long time, no see."

"Hey, Johnny."

Chapter Six

I flashed back to all the great memories riding as a trainee in Johnny Maslow's patrol car, a nostalgic wave that made me lightheaded. A wondrous time of awe punctuated by heart-pounding thrills and fun like I had never experienced. While at the same time learning to be a good street cop. How had it all ended this way? I knew, and just didn't want to accept it. Johnny had a love for women that superseded all else. His desire and lust short-circuited his common sense. That's what had happened to Johnny. He loved women too much.

To see him in a cage caused my stomach to churn.

He had long hair, pulled back in a ponytail, the way state prisons allowed. His always-tan skin was sallow, his teeth yellowed from smoking too much. He never smoked before. He looked nothing like the Johnny I used to know. Except in the eyes. His eyes still had that lust for life. I didn't know how he maintained it with what he had ahead of him, life without the possibility of parole. He'd been convicted by a jury of his peers for the rape and murder of Elise Stoner, the woman at the Holiday Inn.

I took out two packs of menthol cigarettes and set them on the crosspiece between the bars.

"Thanks, kid, I'll be careful with them."

They were contraband. Hand-rolled Bugle Boy was the only accepted tobacco in GHRC. From my other pocket, I took out two cans of Skoal and set them on the bars. His eyes lit up. "My friend, you are a gentleman and a scholar but a poor judge of whiskey." It was a saying he had regularly tossed out while on patrol. Another wave of nostalgia, like a gut punch.

He took one of the cans and knocked it against his hand, opened it, and fed into his lip a large pinch that bulged. He smiled again. "You know this stuff will kill ya." He chuckled and coughed. He moved deeper into his cell and came back with a white Styrofoam cup to spit in. He sat on the edge of his bunk and crossed his legs at the knee, like a woman would wearing a tight skirt. He banged one of the packs of cigarettes against his hand, tore off the cellophane and foil, bumped one out, and lit it, doubling down on the nicotine. He was as nervous as I was. He put his head back and blew out a cloud of white smoke. "You know you could get days off for smuggling contraband into the jail?"

I smiled.

He said, "How did you know I'd taken up smoking?"

I shrugged. But he knew. There wasn't anything else to do in prison but smoke.

I finally spoke. "Heard you've been giving the guys here a hard way to go."

He shrugged. "Eh."

I said, "What are you doing at Glen Helen?"

"Road trip."

This was a term used by hardcore cons. If you knew the right people or you could have money put on another con's books, you could get that con to have his attorney issue a subpoena as a character witness in that con's trial. It was a break from the world where nothing ever changed. A road trip was a con's vacation.

But it was a lie. He'd come hoping to see me. I wasn't a rookie anymore, and I had an idea what he wanted. I received an interoffice mail envelope two weeks ago from GHRC, one that contained a kite from Johnny. A kite was a note passed in a prison or jail. Johnny had sweet-talked a deputy into dropping the kite in the county mail. The note merely said, "Come see me. We'll talk old times."

Going to see Johnny meant nothing but trouble. But now, what did I have to lose? I was the Bone Detective. I'd been righteously boned.

He smoked and spit into his cup. I waited.

He finally took the unfiltered menthol from his lips and picked a bit of tobacco off his tongue, his eyes mere slits from the smoke. "You know, kid, people take their lives for granted."

He waited for a comment from me that wasn't forthcoming. I wasn't a *kid* anymore, I was twenty-eight years old and a homicide detective—sorta. I didn't know if Bone Detective counted anymore.

He continued. "I never stopped to think about that old saying, 'spending a day,' you know what I mean? Doing this or that. Like, 'I spent the day going to the zoo,' that kind of thing. But now I can see its full meaning. When we're born we're given a certain number of days to spend; it's our only true currency. Most everyone I know, well, knew, out in the real world—even me—took it for granted and foolishly *spent* my days—wasted them. That was back then. We only have so many beats of our hearts. I've wasted seven years of heartbeats in hellholes like this. Think about that. Seven years in a concrete pen."

I couldn't help but feel sorry for him while he made his case, trying to lure me in and doing a crappy job at it.

At the other end of the row, the hard door popped open. I'd been found out. They were coming to toss me the hell out. Johnny pinched off the tip of his cigarette and fanned his hand to disperse the smoke.

At the end of the hall, the watch deputy and watch sergeant came onto the row headed my way. Johnny stood, stuck his face between the bars as far as it would go, pulling the skin tight in an attempt to get closer. "Listen. You and I both know—we've both heard it a million times on the street. Dave, I didn't do this thing they say I did. I swear I didn't."

There it was. He floated it out between us like a big bloated Goodyear blimp.

Johnny had been arrested for the murder of Elise Stoner while I was recovering in the hospital from the injuries inflicted by a shovel-wielding murderer that I'd let get away. One they never caught. By the time I was released from the hospital, the news hit me hard. My good friend and training officer arrested for a murder investigation I'd seen first-hand. The horrible wasted life of a beautiful woman.

I couldn't rectify the two in my head. After I heard he was arrested I never went to see him again. I couldn't even go watch his trial. Maybe that was why I'd come to visit him now: guilt. He'd already been in prison seven years. I couldn't imagine what that was like for him. An ex-cop mingling with those he'd put away, worried at any moment he'd be confronted and killed. And worse, a man like Johnny, who lived to love women.

Johnny talked in a fast whisper. "You go through life thinking all you have to worry about is cancer, or the pox, or some misanthrope sticking a shiv between your ribs on a domestic call. When all along I should've been looking for a broken justice system doing me in. Dave, please?" He stuck his hand out.

I stepped back, not wanting to touch him. As if the act would transfer some of that poison that made him kill Elise Stoner, a weird poison like something out of a Stephan King novel.

The watch sergeant and the watch deputy walked up. The sergeant said, "Beckett, what the hell you are doing in my jail?"

Johnny and I both started to talk at the same time. I held up my hand silencing him. I said, "As of this afternoon, I am officially the department Bone Detective and—"

Johnny cut me off. "And he thought he'd come and milk me for all the bodies I buried out in the desert. Right kid?"

The sergeant's expression shifted. "Oh. I didn't know." He looked at the watch deputy. "Why didn't you tell me that part?"

"Sorry, I didn't know."

I said, "My fault, I'm tired and I forgot to mention it."

The sergeant said, "No problem. Next time just clear it with me, first. I need to know you're on the facility talking to this asshole. He's a special handle."

"I understand, it won't happen again. I was just leaving."

Johnny said. "Come back tomorrow and I'll you give another one, a place to dig in Hesperia. X marks the spot for buried treasure." He winked, and at the same time gave the watch sergeant the finger.

I held up my leather notebook and pointed it at him. "Don't hold your breath, pal." I said it more for the watch sergeant's benefit, me and Johnny playing our parts.

I walked away. He yelled from behind me, "Check it out, kid. Do it for me."

I did owe him for that night on Rosewood when I shot the Market Basket robber, the way he grabbed the handcuffed Gary Hussey by the hair, lifted his head, and said, "Goodbye Asshole." Then he'd stayed with me, sat with me on that picnic bench in that Rosewood back yard, kept me from emotionally floating away. He was right I owed him plenty.

Chapter Seven

I pulled in front of our house in San Antonio Heights, a rambling ranch-style made of red brick. It had been painted white too many times, making the brick almost indistinguishable. Two acres for horses around back, with a white rail fence in horrible disrepair. Bare dirt surrounded most of the property. I never had the time to put in the landscaping we'd talked about when we bought the house.

It was a bank repo, or we could never have afforded it on my salary. I'd found out about the place while on the job. My team had been called out "after the fact." One of the worst kinds of investigations, playing catch up. A patrol deputy took a dead body report. A sixty-four-year-old man named Robert Munden who sat down on his couch and died while watching reruns of Dukes of Hazard. The morgue was backed up and the pathologist didn't get to the autopsy for two weeks. That's when he found a small bullet hole in the back of Mr. Munden's head.

The suspect had stood outside the house with a .22 rifle and plugged Mr. Munden with one round, killing him instantly. I found a small hole in the window screen. The suspect had put the rifle right up to the screen when he fired. I ended up arresting the neighbor, who pleaded guilty to murder-two. Munden had left his trashcans at the curb several days after pick-up; he did it every week. He also "played his goddam television too loud."

I liked the neighborhood and the house, and as soon as it went into foreclosure I contacted the bank. I left the hole in the screen and never told Beth the history. She was the sort that would contract a bad case of the heebeegeebees if she knew someone had been murdered in her living room. I'd come to accept murder as a way of life. Nothing any different than switching off a light.

I sat in the Mustang and watched from across the street. Beth and Lucy moved about in the house doing everyday domestic things. I ached inside, missing those simple *things*. Why had I walked out? I had to get control of my anger. At least now as the Bone Detective, I would have more time to spend with Lucy. *Spend time*. That's what Johnny had just talked about. I didn't take my time with Lucy for granted. I just didn't have enough of it. I still loved Beth with all my heart.

The problem with Beth and me started six months back when I tried to buy her a diamond tennis bracelet for our anniversary. I couldn't really afford it, but they were small diamonds and she deserved a nice gift for putting up with me. I stood in front of the display counter at the jewelry store and I took out a little-used credit card from my wallet, one we kept just for emergencies. The clerk came back and told me the credit card was maxed out and the credit card company said to hold the card. Mad as hell, I headed home, driving as if the car were a bullet fired from a magnum handgun. The biggest mistake of them all. I should've waited, cooled down. I went home and confronted her while fuming.

Lots of tears and screaming from both of us. Lucy was the big loser. I fell asleep on the couch and found all my clothes and stuff strewn in the front yard with a big note written in purple Crayola on the living room glass table: "Get Out!" I didn't argue, just complied.

Now I sat in the Mustang in front of the house wishing again for the millionth time to have that day back, to sit down with her calmly and discuss the credit card like a normal couple. For the last six months, I had avoided thinking about the credit deficit, at least not in any depth. I sat forward in the car seat as I realized I'd somehow missed a big piece of the puzzle. Before the split-up, I had not noticed anything new around the house: no new clothes or furniture, nothing like that. Where had twenty thousand dollars gone? During our domestic argument six months ago, I had not given her the opportunity to explain. Or maybe she didn't want to. But in any case, I had never found out the reason for the deficit.

I didn't like what I was thinking. I started up, turned around, and drove to the Rancho sheriff's station. I called the credit card company and found all the charges for the last four years, 20k worth, came back to only one company called Alliance Investigations located on Foothill Blvd. in Rancho Cucamonga. Instead of calling them, I drove there to confront the people in person. Taking money from an unwitting housewife needed a personal touch. She'd had to have hired them to follow me.

She didn't trust me. I had not given her any reason not to. Though there were several times I couldn't blame her for thinking otherwise, long stretches of time where I stayed out on an investigation running down the clues, letting them take me where they may. The longest had been forty straight hours. Homicide dick was not conducive to a healthy family life.

Most murders occurred after the bars closed, two or three o'clock in the morning, that's when the pagers sounded dragging us both from a sound sleep. I'd be gone for at least twenty-four hours, usually more. I kept clothes at work, and an extra suit to change into when the one I wore turned sour. Why *wouldn't* she think I had strayed? I had not told her how much I loved her, not enough times. Not in a way to make her take it as a truth. We had slipped into an easy way of life, going through the motions, frivolously spending our time.

Alliance Investigations sat in a small strip mall between a donut shop and a pawn shop. I walked in the door and froze. The place only had two desks, both occupied. Ronald Luck sat in one and Sedge sat in the other. What the hell? In small towns, the same people continually run into each other. In the real world, there are six degrees of separation between contacts. In a small town, it's two to three. The two sitting there like a couple of goofs proved it.

Both wore cheap suits that might've been purchased from Goodwill. Sedge's obesity bulged out the sides of the armrest. He had a half-eaten Abba-Zaba candy bar in his hand. He wouldn't be able to stand quickly without bringing the chair with him. At least Luck had shaved and combed his hair.

Apparently, Luck and Sedge had quit West Valley Police Department to start their own PI agency. I'd lost touch with my old department and had no idea. I stood for a moment, staring. I had been funding their little endeavor through my unsuspecting wife, their victim.

They both smirked and looked at each other when I walked in. I wanted to pound them both and took several steps before good sense reined me in. Something wasn't right. These two, buffoons to the tenth power, couldn't have been following me around or even checked on my history without me tumbling to it. And I wouldn't get the information I needed by pounding on either one of them.

I couldn't stomach Sedge at all, so I took a seat in front of Luck's desk.

His smile gradually disappeared as I stared him down.

One night while riding with Smith on training we stopped in at The Iron Skillet for code seven. The restaurant allowed you to smoke anywhere inside and not just in designated areas. We sat down and spotted Luck off duty wearing his civvies, sitting with a woman in the corner booth. He got up when we entered and came over and shook our hands like we were old buddies. He lowered his voice and said, "Help me out here, if it comes up, I'm an emergency room doc at West Valley Community Hospital, okay?"

Smith said, "Get away from me, Luck."

"Oh, it's gonna be like that?"

Smith gave him the evil eye. Luck turned around and went back to his lady friend, his wife at home waiting for him. And *he* was investigating me?

Sitting in the chair in front of his desk, I knew Luck would be the weak link. I continued to stare. He squirmed a little.

I said, "You going to tell me what you two are doing for my wife?"

Sedge said, "That's privileged client information. Why don't you go ask her?"

"I'm not talking to you, Sedge." I said it without looking away from Luck. I said to Luck, "You're going to tell me what I want to know."

Luck moved around in his chair, not knowing what to do and looking scared.

Sedge said, "You get out of here right now, Shovel Face, or I'll call your boss and tell him you're causing a 415 at our business." He put his hand on a black wood baton propped next to his desk, one he'd carried on the job. He wouldn't have the nerve to call me that name without a weapon. He thought the baton would keep me off him. He was wrong.

Luck had a cut-down military artillery shell as an ashtray on his desk. I picked it up and threw it at a framed picture on the wall, one of those popular motivational shots of real men climbing Mount Everest. The glass frame shattered. "Go ahead and call it in, let's see who my boss believes."

Luck jumped in his chair when the picture shattered.

I stood, knocking the chair back. "Tell me. You have twenty thousand dollars of mine, and I have a right to know."

"Tell him, Sedge," Luck said, his voice shaky.

Sedge shook his head and smirked. "It's not our fault your wife has hot panties for a guy named Cole Adler."

The name staggered me.

She wasn't having me followed. She was still looking for her ex-fiancé, Cole. We had a daughter together and she still couldn't let the guy go. Spent twenty thousand dollars trying to find him.

Chapter Eight

My wife was emotionally broken. How could I stay angry with her? Cole Adler would never come back and tell her what had happened between them or why he left without a word, traveling to parts unknown. I stopped at the flower shop and picked up a bouquet of her favorite, lilies. I pulled in front of our house and sat in the car, afraid to go in. I was a cop who chased murderers and I was afraid to talk with my wife, afraid to be permanently shunned. Well, I *was* a cop who *used* to chase murderers, now I chased scattered bones. I got out and trudged to the front door. I had a key but knocked anyway. The door swung open too fast. Beth wore a nice dress and she'd recently had her hair done. Her brown eyes blazed with anger. "You're late."

I held up my hand. "Hold on, just give me a minute, okay, please? I want to talk."

"My attorney said that if you're late I don't have to let you take Luce."

A rage deep in my gut started to smolder. "Look, can you just hear me out, please?" I brought the flowers from behind my back. Her expression wavered, softened just a smidgeon. I had a chance. Maybe.

"Can I come in? Please?"

"Please Mommy, please let him come in." Lucy came from behind and tugged on Beth's dress."

I went down on one knee. "Hi, there Pumpkin." Lucy also wore a dress, one with different colors of blues and white lace. She had a blue ribbon in her blond hair holding back natural curls. I was a little biased, but she was the most beautiful kid in the entire world. She took two quick steps and jumped. I caught her in one arm and stood. I closed my eyes and hugged her as I held out the flowers. I wanted back in the house more than anything I had ever desired.

Beth accepted the flowers and looked at them while she thought about it. "Okay, but only for a minute. And this means nothing." She shook the flowers.

"Sure." I said, "I understand.

Over by the sliding glass door, a flap popped open. A doggie door. We didn't have a doggie door. We didn't have a dog. I wouldn't allow it. When Astro died, the loss hurt too bad. I didn't want to go through it again. This new dog bee-lined right at us, barking. Lucy squirmed in my arms until I put her down.

"Willy Wonka. Daddy look, we got a dog. I named him Willy Wonka." She headed him off before he got to me and went for an ankle. I had read to her, *Charlie and the Chocolate Factory*.

The dog looked just like Astro. Lucy had begged and begged for a dog. Beth must've just gotten Willy Wonka to stick it to me a little harder. And she got a dog that looked just like Astro.

I gritted my teeth.

Beth hid a smile behind the flowers as she pretended to sniff them. My emotions were always easy to read, easy to manipulate, something Beth said she loved about me. I was like a puppet to her puppet master. Not fair.

Lucy took up a sock with a knot at the end and played tug of war with Willy Wonka. The sight brought back old Astro memories and made me realize I'd been wrong about not getting Luce a dog. I sat at the kitchen table and tried to calm down. Beth was winning in her game to drive the stake into my heart.

"Okay," Beth said. "You have three minutes. Talk."

In the living room area, Luce said, "Mommy, be nice."

Beth looked from Luce back to me. "Okay, then three and a half minutes."

"I'm sorry," I said.

"You've said that before. What's changed?"

"I was a fool."

"I'm listening."

I took a couple of cleansing breaths and unclenched my teeth. "This whole thing...is my fault."

A bit of a smile peeked out, a portion of the old Beth that I loved. "That's all well and good, but there's the other thing that's still standing between us."

"What are you talking about?"

"Your mistress."

"My what?"

"You love your job more than your family. She's a woman I can't compete with."

My face flushed hot as I fought the rising anger. I looked away from her and counted to ten. My job was *my mistress*, oh my god.

Beth said, "Your time's almost up."

I couldn't help it, I spoke through clenched teeth. "It'll be different this time."

"I don't believe you."

"Beth, I've been bounced off the teams."

Her mouth dropped open as her eyes gradually softened. Her hand inched across the table and touched mine, soft and warm. "I'm sorry, I know how much that job means to you."

"Will you give me another chance?"

She got up and walked into the kitchen, opened a cupboard, brought down a vase, filled it with water, and put in the lilies. "Call me for a date."

I smiled hugely. I'd finally broken through. "I'm taking Luce for some ice cream, you want to come with us?"

"No, I mean a regular date."

"Got it."

"Call me."

"Got it." She wanted romance. I could give her romance, that would be easy. I loved her. Even more now that she'd finally lowered her shields.

"Daddy, I don't want ice cream. Can we just stay here and play with Willy Wonka, you and me?"

The kid was smart; she saw the ice queen starting to melt and wanted to help. “Sure, Pumpkin, if it’s all right with your mom?”

“Mommy, please, please?”

We both looked at Beth. She nodded.

Chapter Nine

The next day I didn't go into the office at headquarters. I needed to stay invisible as long as I could while choppy waters calmed. I pulled into the Glen Helen Rehabilitation Center at nine a.m. Before I got out I called the homicide division secretary. Gail put me on the big board with my location.

In GHRC, the same watch deputy sat at his desk. "Good to see you again, Detective."

I signed in. "Could you tell your sergeant I'm on the facility and that I'm talking with Johnny Maslow?"

"Can do. Come on, I'll take you back."

I stopped at an empty desk and grabbed an aluminum-framed straight chair. The watch deputy didn't say anything about it. On our way back into the bowels of the jail, he said, "You really think he'll give you anything?"

"It's like playing the lotto, you can't win if you don't buy a ticket."

"Yeah, I guess that makes sense."

"I'll give it a few go-rounds and if nothing comes of it, so be it. Better than tramping through the desert looking for bones."

He let me through the last hard door and closed it behind me. I relieved the overtime deputy sitting in front of Johnny's cell. I set the chair down and sat in the existing one. I opened a travel-sized chess set I'd brought and put it on the empty chair.

"Good to see you, kid."

"I thought we'd play a little chess, get to know each other again; it's been seven years."

He smiled big, his bottom lip loaded with Skoal. I took two more cans from my pocket and handed them to him.

"Thanks," he said, his smile huge, his eyes glowing brightly. "You remember that time someone loaded ol' Twice's Skoal can with pencil shavings? That was really something, wasn't it?"

I said, "Yeah, it was good for some shits and giggles." Did he know who had spiked the can? Smith had been the one to warn me to be careful with Twice, that he wasn't anyone to mess with.

Johnny stuck his hand out through the bars to shake. I hesitated and shouldn't have. He was in for murder, the kind of person I chased. I'd interviewed many killers, but this one was different. At one time we had been good friends, and now I found it difficult to rectify this new relationship. I couldn't help thinking that when death brushes by you it leaves something behind, something contagious. I shook his hand and smiled.

"Thanks for comin', kid."

I put the little plastic men on the chessboard. Johnny lit a cigarette, the smoke easier to take than the jail's perpetual reek. He was freshly shaved, and he'd trimmed his nails. He looked a little more like the Johnny I used to know, and it brought back a memory of something he'd said when I was his trainee; at the time I took it as him being a little too jaded and cynical toward the job.

Over a cup of joe and apple fritter at The Hole in One, he'd said, "You and I both know what life really comes down to, don't ya kid? It's blood and bone. When life's delicate balance is ruptured, the trapped soul is released to go do what it was meant to do in the first place. We're all trapped here in this...this in-between place."

Murder didn't mean much to Johnny because life didn't mean much to him. The statement presented a huge mark against him in whether he'd actually killed Elise Stoner. Back when he'd said it I'd let his words slide on by, dismissing them as a cynical bias toward unsuspecting victims, as if they deserved what they got.

He said, "I don't know that much about chess." I recognized the comment, one of his tactical ploys. *Whenever possible throw your opponent off balance.* He couldn't help doing it, tactics a part of his internal makeup that had kept him alive on the street. He'd forgotten he told me he'd been a chess club captain in high school. It reminded me that he'd used tactics and manipulation to get me in the chair in front of his claustrophobic jail cell. So far, he was winning, and I hadn't made one chess move yet.

I barely knew a knight from a rook, I just wanted a distraction while I spoke with him about Elise Stoner—something they taught in Homicide 101. He had court appeals pending, and technically I couldn't speak with him without his attorney present. Johnny knew his rights, but he was the one who'd invited me. He was the one who had something to say. I took a black piece and a red piece, put them behind my back, then brought them out in closed fists for him to pick. He chose black.

What I really wanted to ask would snip the last tenuous threads of trust that connected us to the wonderful friendship, the unique bond we'd created in the patrol car. I wanted him to stand close to the bars and remove his shirt. I wanted to see if he was the one. If he had killed Elise Stoner, why not Jessica DeFrank too, then hit me in the face with a shovel and toss my limp body in a slit trench? Then bury me alive. This wasn't a large jump in logic, and I couldn't let emotions cloud my judgment. I needed to know.

I wanted to see if the six rounds I fired from the .38 Colt had left any marks, divot scars. But that didn't make sense either. If I had hit him six times, he wouldn't have been able to cover those severe injuries, not without hospitalization. Or leaving an obvious blood trail.

We both moved pawns to open the game. Moved several more times while we thought out our next move, none of them concerning the board game.

He said, "Heard you got married?"

"Ah...if you don't mind, let's not talk about my family."

"I understand." He smiled hugely. "It's funny, I trained you when you were greener than snot, and now look at us. You're a big-time sheriff's homicide detective. Good for you, kid."

"You going to tell me about Elise?"

His breath caught. He pulled back into his cell a little, half his face in shadow. "It's going to be like that?"

"It's got to be, and you know why. My boss knows I'm out at GHRC, but not who I'm talking to. If he finds out, I won't be talking to you anymore."

He nodded. "You're going to be in the grease if he finds out. So, we need to get on with it. I get it."

"That's right."

He put the cigarette to his lips and pulled in a deep lungful; the red cherry tip glowed, the barely heard crackle from the burn loud in the dead quiet. His eyes locked onto mine.

"What do you know?" he asked, smoke coming out of his mouth, mingling with the words.

"Why don't you pretend I don't know a thing and start at the beginning?"

He stared at me for a moment, choosing his words carefully. "I'll tell ya true, I don't know what happened. Not for sure. One day I'm working patrol lovin' life when I get a ten-nineteen to see watch commander. I walk in and there's Jubal Butler, homicide for West Valley. Twice is in there too as backup, smug as all get-out. I guess they thought I might freak or something. I didn't know from Adam's ox what was going on, but if they thought that nefarious Twice was going to throw a bag over me, they had another thing comin'."

I moved my knight. "Then what?"

Johnny calmed, his tone lowered. "Twice cuffed me after Lieutenant Womack put his hand on my shoulder and told me to take it easy. I gotta lot of respect for Womack. Butler took me into the interview room." He shook his head. "And I tell ya, kid, I had no idea what it felt like sitting on the other side of that desk until Butler read me my rights while my hands were cuffed behind my back. I couldn't breathe. There wasn't enough air left in the world."

I knew that feeling. I experienced it with a face full of shovel and lying in a slit trench next to Jessica DeFrank, dirt being tossed in on my head.

Johnny pointed his cigarette at me. "What an eye-opener, huh? Butler was the department homicide dick and I knew I was in it up to my nose. I'd done some sketchy things in my time, crossed over into that gray area to put a crook in jail, but nothin' close to killin' anyone. I swear. You know me, Dave. You know how I work. I'm a straight shooter, always have been."

I nodded for him to move a chess piece. He moved his rook and put my knight in jeopardy.

I stared at him.

He said, "I wanted in the worst way to know what it was all about. Like I said, Butler, he read me my rights and I invoked. I wanted to play him a little while, find out what was going on, but knew it wasn't the right move, that I'd know soon enough. I didn't know until I drew a public defender at the arraignment two days later. Murder. Elise Stoner. I couldn't believe it. It was a sock to the gut, I'm tellin' ya."

"Why did you have a public defender? Why not go with a high-dollar sharkskin suit?"

He broke eye contact and looked down, ashamed. "Me and Mia, we split the sheets. She did me rotten when she left."

Mia was his wife.

I remembered that domestic when I backed Smith on the call at Christmas time, where the husband accused Johnny of stepping out with his wife. Johnny liked to run in the fast lane and it finally caught up with him. He'd crashed and burned, big time.

He said, "I made the mistake of letting Mia handle the bills. She didn't pay the mortgage for six months, let all the bills go, real strategic like, as far as timing. She walked out with six months of my salary and left me with the clothes on my back. I lost the boat, the horses, the horse trailer, the whole shiteree."

A public defender had to have put on a no-nothing defense, the reason Johnny was convicted. But why? I didn't have all the facts, not yet.

He hesitated and looked at me. "I'm sorry, man, I was all caught up in my problem and haven't asked you if they ever solved who hit you in the face with that shovel."

I sat back and let out a long breath. I didn't want to discuss ancient history, at least not something so emotionally painful. I couldn't muster the nerve to ask him to take off his shirt. "No." My voice cracked. "They never caught who killed Jessica DeFrank." I took his knight, sacrificing my rook to expose his king.

I'd worked hard to get into homicide, forsaking everything else, including family. I wanted to learn the craft, become a crackerjack investigator, and then go back in time for Jessica, look for a little bit of justice. I blamed myself for her death even though I couldn't have prevented it. I guess it had something to do with being in the slit trench with her, eye to eye, her silent entreaty to make right what had happened to her.

I finally made it to homicide and continually told myself that I needed more experience, putting off, again and again, reopening her case. Now I had my chance, as if karma had stepped in to kick me in the head. If I had to go back to West Valley PD to reopen the investigation into Elise Stoner, I might as well stick my nose into the Jessica DeFrank affair. What else could my boss do to me? The West Valley PD wasn't going to appreciate a sheriff's dick sticking his fat nose in their business, especially into a closed case. Especially a bottom-feeding Bone Detective.

He nodded and moved his bishop to block.

"You still haven't told me what happened, what evidence they have on you. Elise Stoner was just passing through town. To make a solid case they had to place you at the scene, with motive and opportunity. What did they have?"

He looked up at me, his eyes filled with grief and sorrow and at the same time a seething rage. He shoved his hand outside the bars, knocking over all the chess pieces. I stood and stepped back. He slowly rose, his hands on the bars, knuckles turning white. He stuck his face between the bars, his eyes intense. "I knew Elise. I had sex with her the weekend before at that same Holiday Inn."

Chapter Ten

The next morning, I made the trek up Cajon Pass to the high desert and then headed west to Phelan. I had to pick up the human leg bone, one task I never thought I'd be asked to handle. To say it out loud sounded like something from a sitcom. My thoughts should've been on the leg bone case, how to track the rest of the bones, identify the victim, determine homicide or undetermined.

Or, I should've been thinking about what Johnny Maslow had said, the bombshell revelation about having sex with the murder victim, Elise Stoner, the week before her death in that same hotel. Instead, my mind continued to see little Luce on the floor playing with Willy Wonka, an Astro lookalike. The image brought warmth and joy to a world that of late had soured with too much murder and mayhem. A world with a faulty bureaucracy that couldn't get out of the way of itself and allow real police work that champions justice for those not with us.

Phelan sat in the foothills on the lee side of the San Gabriel mountains, the backside of Mount Baldy. Yucca, Joshua trees, and cedars populated the gently rolling hills. Houses on five-, ten-, and twenty-acre lots broke up the landscape, accessed only by long, rutted dirt roads. The sky glowed bright and blue as the Caribbean Sea, the sun a burnished yellow orb overhead. The Mustang threw up a dusty rooster tail that could be seen for miles.

I found the address and pulled up the long gravel driveway. The house was a doublewide mobile and had a large redwood deck off the front. The redwood cost more than the mobile home. The deck would have a wonderful view of Baldy Mesa and the El Mirage dry lakebed far down in the valley, a view of all the beautiful dust devils and color-laden sunsets. A big Hollywood movie production company had just shot a Mel Gibson movie called *Lethal Weapon* down on the flats. The scene, a hostage trade for Danny Glover's daughter, one that involved a helicopter, limo, station wagon, and various other cars, was a huge undertaking.

The Victorville deputies told me all about it. At night the movie people kept the special weapons used in the scene locked in a jail cell at Victorville station. I wondered if the Phelan residents watched the scene play out from their foothill perch—the fake pursuit of the stretch limo, the helicopter pilot bouncing the skid off the roof of the car. Something that would never happen in real life. This imitation of life, only a few miles from a murdered victim's leg bone and as yet undiscovered grave.

Before I could open the car door, two large Rottweilers charged, angry at the intrusion into their domain. Their fat paws mauled the paint on the door and threatened to crash through the safety glass. They smeared the window with slobber that dried quickly in the heat, baking abstract art into glass.

An older woman with a small hand spade, wearing a worn gardening apron, came from around back and yelled at the dogs. The dogs left the car and ran to her side. She kept her distance, ready to flee if the need arose, a tactic used by those living far from civilization. She'd also have a shotgun close at hand.

She held her arm up to shield the bright sun from her eyes and yelled, "Can I help you?"

I unclipped my badge from my belt, rolled down the window, and held it up, the sun reflecting off the gold star.

She nodded in an exaggerated manner while waving. "Let me put up Brutus and Cleo. I'll be right back."

She disappeared around the mobile home. Less than a minute later she reappeared, pulling off her cotton gardening gloves. She had a faded blue bandanna tied around her head to keep back her gray hair and sweat out of her eyes. She looked to be eighty-five but was probably sixty-five or so. The hot, arid desert tended to shrivel and age the human body and count the years the same as a dog's.

I got out and offered her my hand as she approached. "Dave Beckett, deputy sheriff. I'm here about your leg bone."

She smiled with her gray eyes. She took my hand in a firm grip, one with callouses and strength for such a delicate bone structure. "Silly, it's not my leg bone, both of mine are accounted for." She swiveled her hips like a starlet on the red carpet. "I'm Ms. Collingsworth, would you like some iced sun tea?"

"Yes, that would be great."

She stepped back to let me lead, another tactic used by the desert wary. She might not have been aware she was doing it. I changed my opinion of her and decided she probably had a small handgun somewhere on her person and knew how to use it.

I sat on redwood patio furniture in a place where she could keep an eye on me from the inside. She tinkered in the kitchen and came out with a tray loaded with two large glasses of tea and a bowl of white sugar. "It's already sweetened, so give it a go before you add more."

"Thank you." I tasted it. "Perfect." I guzzled half; the liquid cooled all the way down. "So," I said, "your dog brought you a human bone?"

"That's right, night before last when *Jeopardy* was on, Brutus tried to come in the house through his dog door. He made a helluva racket. He couldn't get through because of the long bone in his mouth. He's brought me gifts before, rabbits and rats, one time even a fresh-kill coyote. That dog's a real keeper." She smiled, not taking her eyes from mine, and took a sip of tea.

"You live here by yourself?"

Wrong question. She lost her smile. "Why?"

"For my report. I have to be thorough or my boss will take a big bite outta my butt."

She nodded as if she understood, but didn't answer the question. She toasted with her glass. "That's alliteration."

"What?"

"I was a school teacher for thirty-five years, taught high school English. 'Big bite outta your butt.'"

"That's why you live in the boondocks, you've had your fill of the obstinate and obstreperous of our species, ones full of blossoming testosterone and acne?"

She smiled. "You've had some education."

"Hardly. I love crosswords and Scrabble. Do you know if any of your neighbors have had a similar treat brought to them by their dogs?"

"As a matter of fact, I knew someone would eventually come here to pick up my bone and ask that same question. So, I saved you some time and called around."

"Thank you."

"Old Man Oliver has a foot. He says it still has some skin on it. An entire foot with skin, and I only got a bare leg bone." She took a piece of paper from her pocket and slid it over to me. "Here's his address. He's waiting on you."

Do you know where Brutus and Cleo could've found your leg bone?"

She'd gotten up and for the first time turned her back to me as she stepped over to the slider, the outline of a small gun plainly visible in her back pocket. She must've been a real pistol of a high school teacher, her students made better for it. She disappeared through the slider and came right back with a brown paper bag, the top of a femur bone sticking out. She handed it to me. I realized at that moment how far I'd fallen. It was my own fault. I suddenly couldn't get enough air and I was sitting outside.

I stood. "Thank you for your good citizenship, I mean for calling this in. If Brutus finds any more, please call me personally. Here's my card."

"You haven't finished your tea"

"As the department's bone detective, I have a few other stops."

"I understand, thank you for coming by." This time she shot me a look difficult to decipher. I shook her offered hand. "Thank you for the tea." I turned and took the wooden steps that led to the ground and the driveway.

"Dave?"

I shielded my eyes with my arm and looked up at her standing on the redwood deck.

A corona of sunlight surrounded her head. She said with a straight face,

"I just realized, that title actually makes you a Bone Dick."

My mouth sagged open. "Why, Ms. Collingsworth, that isn't a euphemism."

She smiled and waved with her fingers. "Come back anytime, Mr. Bone Dick, and we'll play some...Scrabble."

Chapter Eleven

As I drove through the Cajon Pass, the ugly desiccated foot and leg bone in the trunk wouldn't allow me to think about Luce or Beth. Johnny's entreaty to help now looped round and round in my head; the look in his eyes, the tone of his voice as he swore he had not killed Elise Stoner, ate away at my certainty that he'd done it.

At the bottom of the pass, instead of heading east to headquarters I took the San Bernardino Freeway west. Twenty-five minutes later I pulled into the front of West Valley Police Department's visitor's parking. I patted the trunk with the foot and leg as I went by. "I'll be right back Mr. Doe, don't go anywhere." Someone needed to speak for him (or her) and I'd be his advocate.

Inside the lobby and to the left, the department kept a wall-size showcase with photos that depicted officers who had earned medals for valor while working the streets. I focused on the counter as I approached. I didn't want to see the photo of me holding the gold-stamped certificate draped with the medal for shooting Gary Hussey. It reminded me too much of my failure, taking the shovel to the face and not catching the killer who'd put the plastic-wrapped Jessica DeFrank in the slit trench. Tossed dirt on her and me. I could still taste the dirt in my mouth and throat. He was still out there on the street.

Old Joe Keneally worked the front desk, dressed in an immaculate class A uniform with razor-sharp creases. His hair cut regulation, as well as his mustache, now showing more gray than brown. He was on the desk when I was a cadet and we'd become good friends in those two years working together in the front office.

He'd worked as a postal carrier before taking the cop job. Ten years back he had a stroke while on patrol. He blacked out and crashed his car into a telephone pole. Human Resources tried to retire him, but Old Joe had too much pride. The chief went to bat for him, and the city relented with the stipulation he never again work the field.

His face lit up with a huge smile when he saw me. "Hey, Dave." He got up from his desk, came around, and offered his hand. I shook it. "How you doing?" he asked.

"Great. You look the same."

"That's right, nothing ever changes at Old Joe's front desk."

He always considered the lobby his domain, his microcosm of the street where he kept the peace and did his part. Human Resources thought the job sheltered him from the hazards of regular police work. But not Old Joe. He asked everyone who entered his domain for their ID. He ran them for warrants before helping with their issue.

Some months he rivaled the number of arrests made by Smith and Johnny. More than a few times he got into a real donnybrook in the lobby arresting an obstinate criminal. Now he had enough time on the books to retire but said he intended to ride his desk into the sunset. Some cops preferred to ride loyalty and dedication right to the grave rather than give up and sit in a lazy boy nursing a brown bottle, awaiting their personal visit from the Grim Reaper.

The phone on his desk behind him rang. He never let it go more than twice before answering. "Who you here to see?"

"I need to get a homicide report." Even cops from other agencies needed to sign in and wear a visitor badge behind the locked doors of the station entry.

Old Joe held up his finger and with his other hand grabbed the phone from his desk. "West Valley Police Department, Officer Keneally, how may I help you?" I'd heard those same words a million times while I was a cadet working alongside him. A nostalgic wave washed over me. Back then was a simpler time, full of hopes and dreams. Why had I ever left the police to go to the Sheriff's Department?

Old Joe listened to the complaint. I pointed to the side lobby door. He nodded and pressed the solenoid release. The door buzzed. I yanked it open and waved.

In the hall, I passed the open door to the captain's office, the place where homicide interviewed me after I shot Gary Hussy. The captain wasn't in.

Homicide reports and the murder books weren't kept with the regular reports. They were in a locked room just outside CAPs, Crimes Against Persons. I'd have to ask the CAPs lieutenant for access. I didn't know what to use as an excuse. If I ruffled any feathers, the CAPs lieutenant would call my lieutenant and ask what the hell was an SBSD detective doing sticking his big nose where it didn't belong. My specialty of late.

But I knew the CAPs lieutenant from before, and Langford wouldn't give me any trouble. I walked into CAPs and looked over at Jubal Butler's desk. My breath caught. Fletcher Fletcher, a.k.a. Twice, was sitting where Jack Butler should've been. Apparently, Twice had made detective and they put him on the homicide desk. Sometimes life wasn't fair. Butler must've retired. Technically, I would have to work the case with Twice.

"Hey, Dave, how are you doing?"

I turned around. Smith was wearing a suit that looked strange on him after only seeing him all those years in uniform. I shook his hand. "Hey," I said, "how's it going? Good to see you."

"Heard you're working homicide for the sheriff."

"That's right."

"Come on in, take a load off."

I followed him into the lieutenant's office. He went behind the desk, took his suit coat off, put it on a hanger, and hung it on the hat tree behind him. I smiled. My luck had just shifted for the better.

"Have a seat." He wore his six-inch .357 in a shoulder holster under his left arm. It was too big for him; the barrel end hung past his belt.

I sat. "Congratulations on making lieutenant, you definitely deserve it." Lieutenant was his third promotion since I left—detective, sergeant, lieutenant. He was moving up fast. He'd be chief before too long.

"Thanks. Is this visit business or pleasure?"

"Both. Haven't been here in a long while."

"Yeah, since you left seven years ago. You forgot where you grew up."

"Busy. Life always gets in the way."

"I know what you mean. How can I help you?'

"I'm the new bone detective for the SO and I'm making the rounds checking missing person cases and homicides trying to match them to our John Does or similar MOs."

"Excellent, it'll be great working with you."

"Do you mind if I take a look at your homicide files?"

"You looking for any case in particular?"

I couldn't tell him that I wanted Johnny Maslow's file without causing a huge dust-up, so I lied. "No." A knot grew in my stomach over it. I liked Smith. Respected him.

"No problem, you know where we keep the files, help yourself. I just ask one thing."

My breath caught. "Yeah?"

He smiled. "If you get any good leads, you let me know about it."

"Absolutely."

I stood and shook his hand again. What I wouldn't give to again work a patrol car with him. I hurried down the hall and into the alcove to the file room door. File cabinets lined the alcove filled with the less-important reports. At the first cabinet, I pulled open the top drawer all the way and found the key to the homicide report room where it had always been kept. Lazy man's security.

I opened the door and entered the file room. Homicide has no statute of limitations so every homicide in West Valley is kept forever. Or until the suspect dies in prison or is executed. And even those reports are never purged because no one keeps up with the dispositions.

Unsolved missing persons were also kept in the same room. Sometimes missing persons turn into homicides. I found and pulled the file on Jessica DeFrank. I wasn't there for that one but wanted to take a look anyway. Next, I pulled the Elise Stoner file and found it strangely lacking in thickness. I started to leave and decided to pull Cole Adler's missing person report to show Beth, more as a peace offering.

I again started to leave when I remembered something from my first homicide class about suicide investigations made to look like murders. The instructor had a slide presentation about how difficult it was to commit suicide with a shotgun that had a 36" barrel and how the victim would have to manipulate the trigger with his naked toe.

Since I took that class, one thought continued to resurface and nag like an itch I couldn't reach. Had I missed something on my first suicide investigation? Was it really a suicide? I couldn't remember if Franklin Shearer had his shoes on or how long the barrel was to his shotgun. I grabbed his file as well and then jammed out of there.

Chapter Twelve

I picked up Beth for our dinner date. She wore a new yellow and white dress that I had never seen, her hair freshly clipped and coifed, her eyes alive with anticipation. Beauty radiated off her in an aura. She smiled at my reaction. She liked to drive the relationship, and my reaction put her firmly in the driver's seat. I didn't mind. The sight of her when she opened the front door to our house made my heart skip and added joy that had not been there seconds before. Getting all fixed up for our date meant she really wanted to put our relationship back on track. The thought of having missed so many of her wonderful smiles was tragic.

I opened the car door to the county Mustang and held it for her. Juggling two households, I couldn't afford a second car, not with the registration, insurance, and car payment. Inside, the car smelled of cheap pine tree from the air freshener I bought at the car wash. The sour scent of street urchins I'd had in the car for work fought with the pine tree, both trying to escape. The car ran like a top but had too many miles, with faded paint and upholstery.

I drove toward our favorite restaurant, The China Gate in Upland, where we'd had many good meals. She loved the sizzling rice soup and egg foo young. I wanted her to remember the nice times when everything was new to the both of us. With the window down the warm wind blowing on my face I was happier than I had been in a long time. What the hell was the matter with me? Why hadn't I given in sooner? Bullheaded stubbornness almost ruined the best thing I ever had in my life.

She talked about how well Luce was doing in preschool and how she thought we should enroll her next year in private school to the tune of twelve thousand dollars. A thousand dollars a month. The number caused the car to involuntarily jerk to the right and my head to whip around to look at her.

"What?" she said. "You don't want the best for her?"

"You know better, but babe, I'm not made of gold."

Her face closed off and returned to the Beth of the last six months, angry and bitter.

"I'm sorry," I said, "I didn't mean to sound so harsh. Let's see how things go, okay? Can we do that?"

She stared at me, letting the moment pass, letting both of us come down several notches. I wanted to say, "Can't we just have a nice evening together without fighting?" but knew that would light the fuse and she'd blow a gasket. I needed to tiptoe around certain topics until I could get us both on firmer ground.

After another mile, she said, "You can still get a lot of overtime working patrol and you can study for the sergeant's test and put in for a promotion this year."

Her expression lit up again. She'd always talked about being a regular family with regular work hours. Not an absentee husband who chased wet-brained murderers who liked to shoot each other at three in the morning. She really didn't understand me at all. I didn't like the smoking-gun murders or the heat-of-passion killings. I loved to work the guy who thought he was smarter than the system, someone who meticulously planned out his heinous enterprise believing there was no way he'd get caught. A crook like that was an adversary worth chasing.

I spoke before I had the chance to think it through. "I'm not going to be working patrol."

This time *her* head whipped around, her eyes suspicious. "What?"

"Wait. Just let me explain. I…I can still take the sergeant's exam. And I will."

"Tell me," she demanded. She could read me like no one else.

"I…"

"You lied. You're still on the teams."

I pulled into the parking lot of The China Gate, spotted an open space, and parked. I shut the car down and turned to her. "Now wait, just let me talk before you jump off a cliff."

"Don't you dare talk to me like that. Are you or aren't you still on the teams?"

"I'm the Bone Dick."

Shock filled her expression. "You're the what?"

"I'm not chasing homicides anymore, I have been dropped from the teams. I still work under the umbrella of homicide but...wait...wait. It's an eight-to-five and I pick my own hours. I'm working the bones. Cold cases."

Her face flushed. "You lied to me."

"I didn't, I swear this is going to be like a regular job. The same as if I was an accountant or any other eight-to-fiver."

She crossed her arms and stared out the windshield doing a slow burn. She hated anything that even resembled the homicide bureau. In her mind, I had purposely misled her.

"Take me home."

"Wait? Can't we just talk about this?"

"Now, Dave."

I tried to keep from blowing up. She was being unreasonable.

I said, "I was saving this as a surprise for after dinner—"

She leaned over, her eyes intense. "Some cheap little bauble is not going to get you out of this...this deceitful attempt at...take me home right now, or I'll get out and walk."

I wanted to kiss her, but it would just get me a slap across the face. I reached behind the seat and pulled out an old file folder.

She turned and opened the door. I put my hand softly on her shoulder. "Wait. I think this will prove my sincerity."

With her leg out the door, she looked back at my eyes and not the folder in my hand, searching for the truth in my words. She pulled her leg back in, the door still open a crack. The invisible buzz of her anger calmed. She finally broke eye contact and looked at the file. "What is it?" Her tone down-shifted from high speed to a bit softer.

"Here." I proffered it again.

She closed the door and took it, her eyes searching the faded file in my hand until they settled on the name affixed to the tab: *Cole Adler*. "Oh, my God. Dave?" Tears filled her eyes. In that moment, I knew everything was going to be okay. I was happy. She was happy, but I was green with jealousy. I wanted to throttle Cole Adler until he turned blue.

She took hold of the file but did not try to take it from my hands, too afraid of what she'd find.

I said, "It's not cleared," and realized she might not understand the police jargon; cleared meant the case was still open. Cole was still out there somewhere, living his life and a major thorn in my ass.

It didn't matter. She shook her head that she understood, causing a single tear to roll down her beautiful cheek. Her chin quivered. She pushed over and hugged me, her head next to my shoulder buried in my neck. A lump rose in my throat and tears burned my eyes. The file had shown her that I knew about the 20k in credit card debt, that I knew all about her silent crusade to find her ex-lover in her fruitless search for closure. It told her that even with all of that I still loved her. Part of the obstacle between us had been that ugly secret, the guilt fueling her angst and anger more at herself that she'd turned outward. Turned toward me. She moved her mouth up to my ear and kissed it. "You know," she said, "I have always loved you? This...this—"

I pulled her back, so I could look in her eyes. "I know," I said, "and I understand." I kissed her, a kiss filled with enough passion to light the car on fire with spontaneous combustion.

Chapter Thirteen

I rose from deep slumber after a vivid dream, one where I was in a cop car racing to a call of 'man with a gun.' I wanted to get there first, siren blaring, adrenaline pulsing in my eyes. I couldn't find the location. I didn't recognize any of the streets that flashed by. Anxiety straggling, choking.

I sat up on the couch in *my* house and looked around confused. Through the windows, I could see that it was still dark. How had I gotten there?

I rested my hand on the back of the newer couch, one different than the one on which they had found Robert Munden sitting shot in the back of the head, but still a couch, set in the exact spot where he'd been murdered. I looked closer at the window, at the screen and the small .22 bullet hole, unnoticeable unless you knew where to look. It seemed I couldn't get away from murder; it always lurked close by, a beast waiting to feed on an unsuspecting victim.

The phone rang again. Beth came out of the bedroom clutching her robe closed with both hands, a move that saddened me, a move that said we were no longer intimate, that I had a longer way to go to repair our relationship. The end of the date, hours before, I'd thought I'd at least softened her up a little.

We'd come home from The China Gate and found the sitter reading *Charlie and the Chocolate Factory* to Luce and her new dog, Willy Wonka. I paid the sitter and sat with Luce in her bed and read to her until she fell asleep, her soft golden curls warm against my chest. I dearly missed putting her to bed and would do anything to be back in the house, if for no other reason than to be with my daughter and to watch her grow into a young woman.

I'd come down the hall after putting Luce to sleep and found Beth at the kitchen table going over the Cole Adler missing person's report. I sat on the couch and watched her go over the report three times cover to cover, her finger following along, each word mumbled silently on her lips. She didn't realize what her obsession did to me. I must've fallen asleep, deeply concerned that I couldn't compete with another man who was somewhere out there in the world. Someone who could, at any minute of any day, walk back into our lives and reclaim his prize: my Beth.

And with Beth would come my daughter. I knew what I had to do. I couldn't have that emotional blade poised over my head. I had to find Cole and put that whole chaotic relationship to rest. Live with the consequences no matter what they may be. In all likelihood, Cole had his own family by now and what I feared would be moot.

"Are you going to get the phone?" she said, anger in her tone.

"What time is it?" I looked at my watch: three o'clock in the morning. That's why she didn't answer it. The ringing phone this early could only mean one thing, a homicide, and she knew it. She knew that I had lied to her about leaving the teams, or at least she thought I had.

"It's not for me," I said. "No one knows I'm here."

She stomped over to the blue Princess phone mounted on the wall and grabbed it. "Hello?" Her face flushed hot. She shoved the phone away as if it might burn her hand. "It's for you. It's work."

I still wore all my clothes and shuffle-stepped over to her trying to shake off sleep that clouded my world like an intravenous drug and at the same time figure out what was going on. It couldn't be work. I checked my pager clipped to my belt. No one had paged. "Beth, I don't know what's going on, but it can't be work."

She handed me the phone. "I want you out of here."

I nodded, not wanting to inflame the situation, not at three o'clock in the morning. I loved her more than humanly possible. She stayed close trying to listen to confirm her assumption, so she could take her anger to

DEFCON 4—the nuclear option.

I said into the phone, "Who is this?"

Heavy breathing, then a little smirk. "Trouble in paradise, Romeo? I wake you, Shovel Face?"

"I'm hanging up." It was only a ploy, I had to know who was creating the rift in my already tenuous relationship with Beth.

The caller said, "I know what you're up to. I'm going to drop a dime to your boss."

He'd said enough for me to recognize the voice. Fletcher Fletcher. "Twice, what the hell are you doing calling me at three o'clock in the morning?" But I knew. It was the time of night where a man is at his lowest ebb, his most vulnerable hour. A time when law enforcement chose to serve high-risk search warrants, the best opportunity to catch their prey, literally with their pants down.

I said, "I don't know what you think you know, but I'm just doing my job." No way could he know what I was doing in the homicide file room.

"You pulled the Johnny Maslow file."

Maybe he did know.

It wasn't a big leap. Johnny and I had been good friends. Neither of us got along with Twice. I didn't want to acknowledge anything to him; he might have the conversation taped. I knew I would if I were trying to trap someone. "I don't know what you're talking about. I'm the Bone Detective just doing my job. I got permission from your lieutenant. You'd better check with Smith before you step on your dick any harder than you already have. How did you get this number?"

I had already worked at the Sheriff's Department when we bought the house and the phone number wasn't on file with West Valley…oh, Sedge and Luck, they had gotten it from Beth when she'd hired them to find Cole Adler. They were all colluding. Twice had waited until three in the morning to make the call and wreak more havoc.

I said, "Do what you think you need to do. But don't ever call here again." I hung up.

Beth's expression softened. "That wasn't work?"

I shook my head.

"I'm sorry, I shouldn't have jumped to conclusions. You're in trouble for getting Cole's file?"

"No, you had every right to be angry. I know what I was like before. I'm not like that anymore. I promise. And I'm going to make you believe me. I'll show you I'm not like that, just give me a chance."

She let go of her robe that parted revealing shadows lost to me for too many months and enflamed my desire. She stepped in closer, went on tiptoes, and kissed me. The kiss intensified. Our breathing turned rapid. I picked her up and carried her to the bedroom, easing the door closed behind us.

Chapter Fourteen

The next day, I relieved the overtime deputy sitting in front of Johnny's cell, turned the chair around, and sat in it reversed with my arms resting on the back while a slow burn of anger seethed in my chest looking for any outlet.

"Good morning, kid."

"Not such a good morning from where I'm sitting. I read the case file before taking the ride over here."

"Oh, I see."

"Do you? I don't know why I even came."

Johnny Maslow had blue-gray eyes with streaks of black, and a killer smile. Probably also a killer's smile. He didn't smile now but he let me have a large dose of those eyes that pleaded for relief. He hated being locked up like an animal. I hated seeing him that way. For the most part, anyway.

The lack of lighting—dimness shadowed the rest of his features the way a director would in a horror movie. Flop sweat mixed with the sweet tang of Skoal wafted from the cell. This was his last meeting with me and he knew it. Johnny Maslow wasn't a stupid man, anything but.

"Then run it down for me, Dave. I haven't heard it for a while. What's your take on what *I* did?"

"Don't lay it off on me like that. It's not just my take, the prosecutor and the jury saw it the same way."

He moved up close, his knuckles on the bars blanching as he gripped them to control his own escalating anger. His tone came out low, his words a knife honed sharp that cut through to my deepest emotions.

"I understood when the department threw me to the wolves," he said. "I understood what the District Attorney did at the trial even though we'd been friends; she was just doing her job. And the jury, well, they were led down the primrose path with a carrot and fancy words blown up their dresses and up their asses.

"But you, Dave." He clicked his tongue twice. "I thought you'd at least hear me out, hear what I had to say before you passed judgment. That you of all people might believe in the railroad job someone hung on me. We rode in a cop car together, you and me, watched each other's backs, trusted each other with our lives. And this is what I get from you? I trained you. I taught you how to be a cop, you little wet-nosed punk." The last sentences, he raised his voice. Little bits of spittle flew from his mouth, his eyes wild.

I boiled over, my face flushed hot with guilt and anger. And a little shame. Why had I even come? I stood. The chair slid forward and banged the bars. I pointed a loaded finger at him. "Your business card was in her wallet. In Elise Stoner's wallet."

"I told you, I'd slept with her the week before she was killed. We met in the bar. I troll that bar for the ladies after work. You know me, that's a weakness of mine. I admit that much, but I'm not a killer. I'm not. I gave her my card for her to call me when she next came to town."

"'J. Maslow' was written in her day planner for the date and time she was killed. Bound up, raped. and brutally murdered. A pillow put over her head and shot point-blank with a .38. The same caliber most commonly carried by cops. You carried a .38 on patrol."

"I didn't do it."

"Her mother called the night she was murdered and heard you arguing with Elise. She testified that she heard Elise call you by name, 'Johnny.' Elise yelled for you to get out."

"Dave, please."

I pulled the chair away from the bars and set it against the wall. "Tell me something I don't know. Tell me something that's not in the report or the court records or I'm gone. And I mean for good."

He slowly moved his head back and forth in the negative.

"Have a good life." I turned and started to walk away. His arm came out of the bars as I passed, an arm desperate to escape, an arm that wanted me to take it along with me into the light of day and freedom.

"I loved her. Wait, Dave? I loved her. I'd never kill her. I fell for her. Hard. I fell hard. She loved me. I thought she loved me."

I raised my hand still walking down the long hall toward the hard door and waved over my head.

"She was using me."

I kept walking.

"All right, I was there that night, at the hotel. You wanted to know something. Okay, that's it. I was there, I admit it to you. I've never admitted it to anyone else."

I kept walking down that long empty row of cells trying to get to the hard door and away from him and the emotional pain.

"I found out she was using me, Dave. That's why I left." His voice rose so I'd hear him. "She wanted me to investigate a suicide…a dude…some… ah…dude named Sheehan or Shearer or something like that."

I froze, the breath knocked out of me. I slowly turned. Johnny had his face pushed as far into the bars as he could, his arm stretched out, his fingers splayed.

"Yes, that's right, she wanted me to look into a no-nothing, go-nowhere suicide because I was a cop at West Valley. That's why she was there. She said she was sure it was a murder. That this dude—Sheehan, or Shearer—was murdered. But she wouldn't tell me why she thought that." He spit the words out fast and frantic, words that came as a gut punch. I started walking back to him while I fought to get air back into my lungs.

He talked faster yet. "Yes. Yes. That's right, she told me I wouldn't believe her if she told me why she thought this Sheehan or Shearer had been murdered. I loved her, Dave. I'm not shittin' ya here, I did. Then I find out…well, once she asked me to help her I… She only wanted to be with me because I could help her with some bullshit suicide. It ripped my guts out. I'm tellin' ya, it hurt like hell." He stopped, took in a deep breath. "You know how it is, everyone thinks their loved one couldn't possibly kill themselves. It's the same old story."

I stopped in front of his cell and stared at him. Johnny knew the game, he knew better than anyone how to manipulate people, make them do what he wanted them to do. Was he using me now?

"Tell me one thing," I said. "Tell me the truth about this one question. If you consider us friends, you'll do this one thing and tell me true."

He took a half step back and composed himself, swallowed hard to get ready. He no longer reeked of desperation, now he concealed it like a chameleon. "Okay. Shoot."

"Did you know I was the one who investigated the Franklin Shearer suicide?"

His mouth sagged open. He didn't have to answer; his eyes told the story. He had not known of my involvement. He put his hands back on the bars. "I swear to God, I did not know that. You have to believe me, Dave. I didn't know. I never looked into it. I was wrecked over her using me. I was in a fog over it. Stumbling around in the dark. I loved the hell outta her. You know. You saw me that night."

"I what?" My mind spun out of control, searching back for memories of seven years ago.

"I came over to your place that night to talk to you about her. We drank some beers, remember? You were the only one I could spill it to."

"We never talked about you being in love with Elise Stoner."

"I know, once I got there it hurt too much to talk about it. I was…I was kind of ashamed about the whole mess. We watched TV and drank beer. I fell asleep on your couch. Remember?"

"Yes," I said it without much effort behind it as I tried to pull up that dusty memory. "You're sure it was the Shearer suicide she wanted you to look into?"

"Yes, I remember now because it was like wind shear."

What he said could only mean one thing. The Shearer suicide was somehow related to Elise Stoner's murder. How could it not be? Otherwise, it was too large of a coincidence and those didn't happen in homicides.

I came out of my trance. "Take your shirt off and show me your chest."

"What? Have you lost your marbles?"

"Take it off."

He paused for an interminable moment, his eyes burning into mine. He nodded and pulled his shirt over his head.

Chapter Fifteen

I steered the Ford Mustang once again through the Cajon Pass, a steep grade that led to the high desert, the window open, warm wind blowing on my face. At the summit's 4000-foot elevation I passed the turn-off for Hwy 138 that led to Phelan and kept going into the Victor Valley. All things seemed to be leading to the high desert, a vast landscape, the largest part of San Bernardino County's twenty thousand square miles.

My pager buzzed. I picked it up and pushed the button. It was one of the new pagers that received text messages. What would technology come up with next? The electronic leash was bad enough; now it talked to you with text. Nag, nag, nag.

Lieutenant Sims from homicide, my boss, soon to be ex-boss had typed: *You come to HQ right now or I'm putting out an APB on your ass!!!*

Twice had been true to his word. He'd called Sims about me working the Elise Stoner case without authorization. I didn't have much time. No time at all, actually. I turned the pager off. Smith would've said I was hiding from responsibility. Johnny would've said, "Good for you, damn bureaucrats don't know their head from their ass when it comes to real police work."

I took the off-ramp to Helendale; Bell Mountain stood in the distance to the east. The urban sprawl of Victorville dropped away as I continued west, the sun high in the washed-out blue sky. The desert sun bore down on everyone and everything, turning the world into a desiccated piece of shoe leather.

How could a homicide dick live in the middle of nowhere? When I worked West Valley as a cadet and then a cop I didn't have a lot of interactions with

Jubal Butler. No one did. He came off gruff and angry all the time. Johnny had said it was because he was a juicer. Butler drank on the job and didn't want anyone close enough to smell it. Too many cops used alcohol to numb the emotional pain from all the blood and bone that came with the job. I should know.

I had to pull over several times to check the Thomas Guide, a book of maps, to see if I was on the right road. The asphalt had turned from cracked and unmaintained to washboard dirt that vibrated into my wrists and up my arms if I drove too fast, and threatened to jerk the wheel from my hands. The Mustang undercarriage took a real beating at thirty-five miles per hour, so I slowed to twenty-five. Slow going when I needed to hurry.

No signpost pointed out road names, so I had to count them. I made a right in the middle of the desert, drove a few miles, stopped, went back and retraced my steps, tried another one. In the distance, a doublewide mobile home appeared through the dust-laden windshield. This had to be Jubal's place. Old Joe had given me the address without asking any questions when I called the West Valley desk. I couldn't ask Lieutenant Smith for the address without getting an earful about trust and friendship, and of course, experiencing the guilt that came along with violating that trust. What Old Joe did say though was "Good luck. You're not going to like what you find out there."

A rougher road that served as a long driveway slowed the Mustang down to five mph. Tall cottonwood trees surrounded a manmade lake the size of half a football field. The lake had a dock and a forlorn rowboat that drifted, tethered on a long rope. The trees' bright green leaves shimmered in the breeze and the water reflected the bright sun like a mirror, a small oasis in the middle of the desert. Between the lake and mobile home stood a huge metal garage with two fifteen-foot-tall doors. One door stood open, exposing to the sunlight the back of a long motorhome. Soon the unrelenting sun would rot all the petroleum products—the plastic, vinyl, rubber tires, ruin them.

I pulled up and parked in front of the mobile home, which had a newer wood handicap ramp leading to a wide porch. In a couple of years, the same would happen to the ramp if it wasn't painted soon; the brutal sun would warp and erode it to splinters.

The sliding glass door opened. The curtains fluttered. A shotgun barrel stuck out, pointed right at me. "Get your ass back in the car and get the hell outta here."

"Jubal, it's me, Dave Beckett."

"I don't give a shit who you are, get off my land or I'll cut you in half."

"I need your help with a homicide."

No reply. The shotgun shook with a palsy. I hoped he didn't have his finger on the trigger. I couldn't see any of him, just the double-barrel looking huge and ominous like that night on Calaveras Street.

"I don't care, get the hell off my property. I'll count to ten, then I'm pullin' the trigger. Don't think I won't. Don't make that mistake. It'll be your last. One. Two. Three. Four."

I couldn't walk away; not without talking to him.

"Five. Six. Seven. I'm not kidding. I'm within my rights to blast you out of your shoes."

I took a chance and cringed, waiting for the buckshot to penetrate my body and toss me into the desert like a rag doll. "You made a big mistake in one of your homicide investigations."

The curtain slid aside and out popped Jubal's face, much lower to the floor than it should've been. "The hell you say?" He no longer had hair, not even the stubble; his bald pate glistened with sweat and glare from the bright sunlight.

I held up the Elise Stoner file. "It's right here."

"Show me some tin."

I unclipped my sheriff's star and held it up for him to see; the bright sun intensified the gold and reflected against the side of the white metal of the mobile home.

"If you're gonna be an asshole about it, come ahead."

Out of habit I pulled the Sheriff's hand-held radio from the charger in the car and walked up the handicapped ramp, sweat stinging my eyes, the wood creaking under my feet. My pager buzzed again, Lieutenant Sims with another threat. Nag. Nag.

I hesitated at the sliding glass door. Without a breeze in the lee of the mobile home, the curtains hung straight down. Jubal didn't really have the right to shoot a trespasser, but once I stepped across his threshold he did. I took a deep breath and pushed in. The dim light wouldn't let me see until my eyes adjusted. The place smelled of cat urine, garbage, and metabolized alcohol.

As soon as my eyes adjusted I realized what Old Joe had meant. Jubal sat in a wheelchair minus two legs, his clothes soiled. In his lap sat a 4-inch blue steel .38 revolver engraved with the West Valley City emblem, his name, and the words "For thirty-five years of service," all inlaid in gold. On the couch next to his chair sat the empty mahogany box with a molded red felt lining. Next to it, a partially opened box of shells missing six bullets.

The living room area and the kitchen looked as if a trash-laden tornado had blown through leaving mostly liquor bottles, empty mac and cheese cartons, and empty cans of tomato soup. The counter and sink were piled with dishes writhed with cockroaches and dive-bombing flies.

"Don't bother to sit. You're not gonna be here long."

On the low living room table next to his chair sat an old black-and-white framed photo of a regal woman with a dazzling smile. He kept her picture close at hand.

I brushed all the trash off an easy chair and sat down.

"What'd I tell ya about sitting? Get the hell out, I changed my mind." He waved the .38 at me like a white-gloved traffic cop.

I didn't move and stared at him.

After a time, he calmed down. "Ah, what the hell difference does it make?" He set the .38 back in his lap, picked up a tall green glass, and took a long gulp. On the low table next to the framed photo was a tall can of grapefruit juice and a plastic half-gallon jug of cheap vodka. He drank greyhounds. I found it difficult to believe this was the same man I knew back at the cop shop.

"Well, aren't you going to comment on the place, how nice it is?" His sarcasm didn't carry a smile.

I said nothing.

He took another long slug and smacked his lips from the tart drink. He held up his glass and waved it like a magic wand. "You wonderin' about these?" He waggled his stumps. "Diabetes. That's right. Some joke on me, huh? Big frigging joke."

I wanted to wait for him to continue; I would've if he'd been a crook during an interview. "I'm sorry."

He nodded like he'd heard it too many times before. "You wanna know what happened?" His adrenaline had worn off from the interloper intruding into his world and now his words came out a little slurred.

I nodded.

"Like some kinda fool I thought the job was my life and spent it foolishly chasing assholes who killed other people, a noble cause, and all that crap. When I should've been paying attention to life speeding on past. I was too dumb to reach out and take hold as it went by." He stuck out his hand and made a fist. "Now look what's it gotten me. No legs, shittin' myself in this chair, and a rig in the garage I can't even drive." His gaze dropped to the picture of the regal woman. Tears filled his eyes. "And worse, much worse I—"

A lump rose in my throat, I was about to join him in tears. I couldn't take it anymore and said, "Elise Stoner."

He looked up, his glistening eyes boring into me. He took a drink and waited a moment. "I knew that's what this was about, that asshole Johnny Maslow and his damn women."

"What do you mean by you knew what it was about?"

He took another drink and smacked his lips while he thought about it. "That was three or four years ago and—"

"Seven."

He paused again as he tried to calculate the time that had slipped undetected through his fingers. "If you say so." He held up his glass like a toast. "I admit, I wasn't at the top of my game back then but—"

"But?"

"That killing was too pat for my liking. Too easy."

My breath caught as I waited for more.

"I worked murders a long time, you know that, and I never seen one that just fell into place like that one did. I just thought the turn of the wheel, the click of fate, and it was my turn to draw a slam dunk case. The kind you just needed to walk through to the DA."

"That why the file was so thin?" Johnny might be an asshole, but he also might be right. "I think Johnny deserved more than that."

"Don't lecture me, Sonny Jim. No sir, not until you walked a mile in my shoes." He wagged his stumps without a smile.

I waited him out.

The flush gradually left his face. He shrugged. "You know how it is, once you got the guy by the balls, why look further? If it walks like a duck, talks like a duck, it's a damn duck, am I right?"

I nodded. "Tell me something that's not in the report."

He reached for a pack of unfiltered Camels on the table, bumped one out, and lit it with a Zippo that had the Marine Corp emblem, then snapped it closed with a flick of his wrist. He puffed and stared at me. "Nothin'. I always put everything in the report and never leave anything out. I never worked that way and don't appreciate the accusation."

"Okay, then if you had the time, or if you could do it over again, what would you do different?"

He squinted from the smoke, the Camel barely hanging on to his lips as he reached for the file. "You're asking me the same question, just round about."

I handed it to him. He opened it on his lap. He scanned and turned pages. He shook his head.

"What?"

"This case was just too solid."

"Gimme something."

He shrugged. "There isn't anything. To tie it up with a nice yellow bow, I guess I would've called the Stoner family and asked for a writing exemplar of Elise's writing to compare to the writing in her datebook. The entry about meeting Johnny Maslow that night she was killed. But that didn't really matter 'cause I had the mother's statement, she heard Elise use Johnny's name."

I knew all of that, I'd read the report.

I sat forward. "Why even ask for the exemplar? That means you think this might be a railroad job?"

He looked up and smiled for the first time since I came through the door; it changed his personality. "That's why you're here isn't it, Sonny Jim? Questioning my work."

"I'm not questioning your work. You did a great job on this case but—"

"Something stinks. That's it, isn't it? How many murders have *you* worked?"

I didn't want to tell him I'd worked homicide for the last four years. I nodded, opened the second file I brought in, and handed him the photos I had developed the night before.

Seven years ago, West Valley PD issued every patrol cop a Kodak Instamatic camera to photograph crime scenes. The pictures were not developed unless the case went to court or further investigation was needed. It was too costly to develop every photo from every investigation. In the case of suicide, there was no reason to get them developed. "What do you think of these?" While I had an expert in front of me, I might as well get a second opinion.

He took the photos, looked at them for a couple of seconds, and handed them back. "That right there is a staged murder."

Chapter Sixteen

T*hat right there is a staged murder.* Words I had not wanted to hear. I too had known the truth as soon as I looked at the photos when I pulled them out of the packet from the drive-thru one-hour film kiosk.

"What's this about?" Butler asked. "That murder's not mine. Never saw it before."

I had been too young and ignorant and had screwed up a simple suicide investigation that had obviously been a murder. Confirmation. Butler saw in the photos the same thing I did: Franklyn Shearer still had his shoes on and the shotgun had a thirty-six-inch barrel with a poly choke that made it that much longer. No way could he reach the trigger with his hands not and put the barrel in his mouth.

"What's this got to do with Elise Stoner?" Butler asked.

I didn't want to answer him. He'd been straight with me as far as I could tell, and I didn't want to lie to him. I handed him the next file.

He took it. "What the hell's going on?" He looked at the file and scowled. "Ugh. This is the one I thought you'd be asking about long before now. Jessica DeFrank. Damn shame."

I said, "I don't remember much about it. I was—" I couldn't finish the sentence.

"I can imagine with that shovel you took to the face it scrambled your brain. You mumbled and left out words for a couple of days after. This case is exactly the opposite of Elise Stoner. There wasn't clue one, not one iota of evidence left at the scene."

I read the report the night before. I had to force myself to read the words. I didn't want to get transported in time back to that horrific event. Being in that trench next to poor Jessica DeFrank, the dirt tossed on us, her clear-plastic-wrapped face inches from mine, her eyes pleading. The six flashes my gun made, the way it kicked in my hand. The acrid odor of gun smoke. The suspect backing up as each round struck him in the torso. Or at least it seemed they did, I was no longer sure of what was real and what wasn't.

In the short time that I was a cop, I had come to believe the adage that *cops like their whiskey from a bottle, the sun in their eyes, and blood on the ground.* Whoever said it had never been in a slit trench with the corpse of a young girl wrapped in plastic, staring at them from inches away.

As soon as I had started reading the Jessica DeFrank report the night before, it all flooded back, memories I'd worked so hard to bury and keep tamped down.

Jubal continued to talk after words fled my brain making me mute and deaf to the world.

Then he came back into focus.

"The whole station was out looking for you when you didn't answer your radio. I remember like it was yesterday. The more time ticked by, the more frantic the supervisors and officers got. We even had the sheriff's helicopter up...until you came on the radio."

Jubal's words bounced off me like little rubber balls, penetrating hardly at all.

He said, "I got there a couple of minutes after Johnny Maslow. Second unit on scene."

I snapped out of my trance the rest of the way and listened, intent now.

"He was sitting on the ground, his back to the side of the cop car, holding you in his lap, his arms wrapped around you, crying like a baby. Your face was a bloody mess. Mush. The suspect must've hit you a second time when you went down. Just to be sure. Maybe even a third time."

A lump rose in my throat. Back in the jail, I had treated Johnny poorly. I had to go back and apologize to him.

Jubal said, "If there had been any chance of tire tracks and foot impression from the killer, they were obliterated by all the cops rushing down that little dirt track along that eucalyptus hedge." He looked over at me from his wheelchair. I wiped the hot tears from my cheeks. I didn't care if Jubal saw me blubbering like a kid. I stood to leave.

"You have the report to that suicide?"

I handed it to him.

He looked at it then looked up. "You were the investigating officer?" He could've easily said something about screwing the pooch on this one, but didn't.

I nodded. He read on.

"Huh?"

"What?"

"It's real skinny, but—"

"What?"

He'd lost the slur and straightened in his chair.

"What?" I asked again.

"Didn't you say in your statement, after you took the shovel to the face, and after we found you, that two guys at the store said they saw an orange car by the hedgerow that looked suspicious and that was the reason you drove out there?"

"I don't remember. I'm sure I said it, but it's just no longer clear in my memory."

"You did. It's written in your statement."

"I know it is. I just don't have an independent recollection. So?"

He held out the suicide of Franklyn Shearer. "Right here in your report of the suicide, you say the car in Shearer's driveway was a 'burnt-orange Opel Kadett.'"

"That's a long shot to hang your hat on just a color at two different scenes."

"Kid, when you got nothing else, you play the long shots." He torqued his torso, reached behind the chair, and came back with the phone. He dialed from memory. "Yes, this is homicide detective Jubal Butler, is Sally Struthers there?" He put his hand over the phone, "Her name's Nancy, but she looks like Sally Struthers. She works for the coroner's office."

This tone and playfulness didn't match the Jubal I'd known and didn't at all suit his appearance.

He chuckled into the phone. "Yeah, Nance, I did retire. How you doin'? Good. Good. Hey, I need a favor. I have one of my old cases nagging at me and keeping me up at night. Could you work your magic on your computer and pull up the Administrative property review on a DB? Yeah, sure, it's—" He read off the case number from the Franklyn Shearer suicide. "Yeah, Nance, I'm looking for the disposition on a burnt-orange Opel that was in the decedent's driveway at the time of death."

He paused, then said, "Is that right? Can you check through the property list to see if anything else catches your eye?" He held his hand over the phone and spoke to me: "No Opel at all on the inventory, though it shows on the DMV readout that he had owned one and it was registered to him at the time. It's listed as unknown disposition. You going to tell me how all this shit is linked together?"

"That car was in the driveway when I walked up on that house." He already knew that, but it was all I had.

Jubal gave me the evil eye. "You have a staged suicide, a slam dunk homicide at a hotel, and a go-nowhere murder with a cop knocked galley-west with a shovel. Don't yank on my dick, you're onto something or you wouldn't be here. Are these three cases linked?" His eyes left mine as he again listened. Then he spoke into the phone. "Thanks, darlin'. What's that? Okay, okay, I owe you a lunch. Can I send my boy by to pick up a copy of that dispo, pretty please? Thank you, darlin'." He hung up and stared at me.

I said, "You gonna tell me what Sally just said?"

"You going to tell me what's going on?"

"I only came here to ask you about the Elise Stoner killing. I had pulled these other two just because I was there in the file room." I told him a little white lie. "Now you think they're related?"

When I'd walked into his mobile home I had thought two were related, Stoner and Shearer but not Jessica DeFrank. He'd made that leap on his own, and it was a long leap. But I saw what he meant. Two orange cars, one missing when it should've been logged in by the coroner at the time of the report, and the orange-colored car at the scene of the Jessica DeFrank killing that was also missing.

He pointed to the phone. "Shearer originally hailed from Ohio with a sister here in California. He also had a verified PI license issued by California Consumer Affairs."

"A PI?" My mind spun at the implications. Had Elise Stoner hired Shearer to look into something and that's why he was killed? That's why Elise knew his death wasn't a suicide and wanted Johnny to look into it?

"Hello?" He waved his hand trying to get my attention. "You going to tell me what's going on?"

"What?" I suddenly thought of something, grabbed the Elise Stoner report, and checked the victim's address. She was from Ohio. Coincidences had no business in homicides. Shearer used to live in Ohio before he moved to California.

Jubal leaned over as far as he could to get as close as he could before he said, "What keeps me from picking up the phone and calling West Valley homicide? Tell them about this. About you and how all this is fitting together and points right at you?"

"Points at me? What are you talking about?"

"Think about it, kid. You're the only common denominator in all three of these cases and when that happens you become suspect numero uno." He pointed, his finger more a spear.

"In what? What are you talking about?"

In all three of these murders.

The way he said it made me sound like I was the only suspect. "That doesn't make sense. Then why am I here trying to figure out what really happened?"

His expression shifted from downtrodden on his last legs to the eyes of a predator ready to leap. "Historically, cops who have killed investigate the murders they've committed in order to steer the investigation, or to at least keep track of, the progress, keep an eye on how close the cops are getting." He smiled, showing yellowed teeth.

"What about the shooting?" I asked. "I shot the suspect six times."

Unless that was something that I had imagined, which was entirely possible. A few of the words Jubal had said kept ricocheting around in my head: a face that looked like mush.

Jubal stared at me and then said, "That bothered me as well. No blood, no sign at all that the suspect had been hit. Your backup gun empty. No sign the suspect fell or flopped on the ground. No orange car left at the scene, nothing."

He too thought that I'd hallucinated the shooting due to head trauma.

He said, "Back when I worked homicides, and I couldn't get traction on the case, I went go back to the scene, sometimes sit there for hours. This one stumped me, and I went back several times."

I'd done the same thing while investigating tough homicides.

Jubal pointed. "Over there on the window ledge, the blue ashtray." I got up and went over to the ashtray. "You wanted something not in the case file, well there it is. I found those two expended rounds in the dirt on the other side of that eucalyptus hedge, thirty, forty feet from where you said you shot the suspect, the place where in your statement you saw the orange car. As you know, that whole area is used by recreational shooters and those rounds could belong to anyone."

I picked up the mushroomed rounds. They were semi-jacketed hollow points, the kind of bullets I carried in my backup .38, the one I'd fired at the guy while he threw dirt on me in the slit trench. But Jubal was right, there was no way to link them to the shooting.

I asked, "These were just in the dirt? Nothing around that they could've hit and fallen from—"

"Yep, just in the dirt all by their lonesome."

"Then why did you keep them?"

Jubal waved with his hand. "Why is the sky blue? Over there in the desk drawer, there's a magnifying glass. I never looked at them under a glass until I was already out of the job and stuck here in this damn chair, a damn reject from a circus act."

I pulled out the magnifying glass and instantly saw what he meant. A couple of minute fibers were tangled in the lead. I looked up at him.

"Clothing the suspect was wearing?"

He shook his head, shrugged, picked up the green glass bleeding with condensation, and took a slug from his greyhound.

"Do you mind if I take these?" There was so much about the case I didn't know, and I needed to play catch up. I'd waited too long to look into it. Time erodes memories and evidence like the desert sun.

"On one condition: You keep me caught up on what's going on with these cases. The hound dog in me doesn't want to roll over and play dead. Not just yet."

"You got it. Thanks, Detective."

Chapter Seventeen

I drove down the Cajon Pass headed for Sheriff's Headquarters to face the music, listen to Lieutenant Sims rant and rave and kick his desk. Put me on admin leave, the rubber gun squad. Jubal Butler's words continued to bang around the inside walls of my brain looking for a way out.

The problem I couldn't shake was that he made absolute sense. If I tried as an unbiased investigator to displace myself from the emotional and personal attachment to the three cases, I'd come up with the same conclusion. I *would be* a likely suspect.

Each time I ran the facts the world closed in; claustrophobia snatched at my breath. The thought of prison, the thought of ending up the same as Johnny behind those bars looking out—I shivered and then tried to shake it off.

I dumped the car in the Sheriff's Headquarters back lot, all the way in the southeast corner. The slots closer to the building were filled with plain-wrapped detective cars. Lazy asses, didn't anyone work anymore? The job was all about shoe leather, not desks and telephones.

I entered through the back door. On their own, and out of unison, heads popped from their cubicles. The prairie dog syndrome. How did they know I'd been the one to come in? This time no cat-calls or throwing paper balls; the silent heads came up and went right back down, a bad sign. Two groups of two detectives grabbed their war bags and headed out. The best place to weather the storm that loomed on the horizon was in the field where they couldn't get hit with the slop-over.

I didn't bother going to my desk but instead went right into Lieutenant Sims' office, closed the door, and sat down. He threw his pen and it clattered away, his face flushing red with anger. He stared.

I cringed and tried to get small. I finally said, "You better take a breath. I'm not gonna do CPR on you."

"Not funny, Beckett, not funny at all. I got a call from West Valley Homicide and they are not happy over there. Seems a sheriff's detective stuck his big fat nose right in the middle of their business."

"I figured as much."

He jumped to his feet. "You figured as much?" He put both hands flat on the desk and leaned forward. "I guess so, anyone who kicks over a hornet's nest would know it. They claim you stole a report from their homicide files and they want it back."

It was four files, but I wasn't going to correct him. I could only shrug.

"Then—" he said and took a breath. "Then, the captain over at GHRC calls and asks if I knew one of my detectives had been over there stirring up trouble interviewing a convicted murderer who is restricted from contact?"

"Yikes."

"This isn't funny, Dave. Unless you have a good explanation, I'm tempted to take your star and gun and turn this whole shit-show over to IAB.

"You going to get out the noose or are you first going to listen to what I have to say?"

He took several deep breaths and eased into his chair. "I've gone over it and gone over it. I even tried to draw a diagram connecting all these screw-ups, trying to make some sort of reasonable justification for— Never mind, start talking, and you better make it good."

The three files in my hand were damp with sweat. If I told Sims everything I'd found out, would he draw the same conclusion as Jubal Butler? That I was the common denominator, place me in cuffs, and call West Valley Homicide? Which would end up being Fletcher Fletcher—Twice. Sims would tell them to come and get me? I'd be arrested by Twice just as Johnny had been.

"Well?" Sims half-yelled.

"I'm…ah just trying to decide where to start."

"Try starting from the beginning, cowboy."

"Okay." I handed him the thinnest folder, the Franklyn Shearer file.

He opened it, looked at the photos, held them up. "This is all about a shotgun suicide?"

Sims had been promoted from sergeant, a supervisor in SWAT, to lieutenant in homicide who now managed four sergeants, his span and control. Since he managed, he didn't have to know much about homicide. It helped to have a working knowledge, but he didn't yet. He'd taken the beginning homicide course and had yet to take the advanced one. Nothing was as good as OJT, on-the-job training, seeing the dead body up close and personal. Smell the copper-penny scent of blood, see the opaque, lifeless eyes.

"Talk to me, what am I looking at?" He set the photo's down and picked up my report. "This is yours, you wrote this, what…seven years ago. While you worked for West Valley PD?"

"That's right, and I screwed up. It's a homicide that I missed."

"Show me."

"Look at the photo again. Franklyn Shearer still has his shoes on."

Anyone else would've said, "So?" Sims stared at it until he put it together. "The shotgun's too long, he couldn't have pulled the trigger with his hands."

"That's right."

"You had to be brand new when this went down; nine out of ten rookies would've missed it. If I went out there today, before you said anything, I would have missed it."

That wasn't the point. *I'd* been the one to miss it, not nine other fools.

"In the report, you'll also see that all his personal papers were laid out on his kitchen table, including his will. The call came in as a 5150, welfare check. Supposedly, the psych had called to say Shearer had missed his appointment and wanted him checked on. I haven't checked yet, but my guess is Shearer wasn't seeing a shrink."

Now Sims looked interested. "Someone went to a lot of trouble to make this look like anything but a homicide. Even so, this belongs to West Valley and has nothing to do with the Sheriff."

I handed him the Elise Stoner homicide file. He opened it and read. "I remember this one in the news, this dipshit copper gave us all a black eye. You wrote this one too." He looked up. "I'm not going to read this whole thing, not right now. Talk to me."

"I went to GHRC to talk to Johnny Maslow, he was my training officer when I just started out. He told me something that wasn't in the Elise Stoner murder book. He admitted to me that he did see Elise Stoner the night she was murdered. He said he was in love with her."

"That only strengthens the case against him."

I nodded. "But, Johnny says Elise was only using him, that she wanted Johnny to investigate a suicide."

Sims held up the photo of Franklyn Shearer, the one with his head missing, just the bottom jaw present, the rest a bloody dished-out neck.

"That's right, Elise wanted him to look into it, she insisted that it was a homicide but wouldn't tell Johnny why."

"Still, you're not giving me a reason why you've suddenly decided to stick your fat nose into a mess that doesn't remotely belong to us."

I handed him the fattest file, the Jessica DeFrank killing.

"What's this one?" he said, as he opened the file and saw my photo stapled to the inside flap and my name on the victim line. He let out a long sigh. "All of this is about your case, when you took the shovel to the face." He stared at me.

I waited.

He pointed at the thick file on the desk. "This went unsolved. I looked into it a little when I took over the division and found you on my roster. I was worried this might resurface. We can get you help. I can make you an appointment with the department shrink."

His words stunned me. I had gone over a hundred different reactions he might have as I drove down the Cajon Pass, but this wasn't one of them.

"There's nothing wrong with me."

"Hmm?" He paused, then said, "So, what you're saying is that all three of these cases are related and there is a serial killer on the loose?"

"Well, yeah." I had not thought of it that way either. I was slipping. Maybe I *was* too close to the investigation.

"Talk to me, because right now this is nothing more than a fairytale that belongs in West Valley's lap."

"Shearer was a private detective."

His mouth went to a straight line, an expression that meant I'd interested him enough that I was no longer buried as deep in the doghouse. "What else?"

"There was a burnt-orange Opel Kadet in Shearer's driveway when I was on scene. The car disappeared before the deputy coroner could disposition it."

"And?"

"Shearer had an Opel Kadet registered to him."

"And?"

This was the part that made me sound like a sketchy speed freak right off the street. "That day..." I pointed to the Jessica DeFrank file, "I was contacted in front of a store. I was getting something to drink, a coke and some peanuts, when these two guys came up and contacted me. They said there was a burnt-orange car in the vineyards. That's why I went out there to check on a suspicious vehicle. That's how I found the slit trench with Jessica DeFrank."

I waited while he digested this new information. He was going to slam me in the booby hatch over this one.

He said, "A burnt-orange car in the driveway of Shearer's house and one in the vineyard does not a homicide make."

I said nothing and waited.

He looked me in the eyes. "You are not my best investigator by any stretch, but you have the best instinct of anyone I have ever worked with. You've pulled some tough cases right out of your ass, ones I thought would never get solved, let alone get a conviction. You say this is something, I'm willing to give you a little rope. But you *will* work with West Valley on this. If, they want you. And you will keep me updated, you understand?"

"Yes, sir." Not much chance of Twice wanting me to work with him.

"I want a call every four hours while you're in the field."

"Yes, sir."

"And you will answer your pager when I page."

"I will, I promise." I got up and took a step toward the door."

"Dave?"

I turned.

"You realize you are the only common thread in all of these murders?"

He was sharper than I gave him credit for.

"Yes sir, I know. That's one of the reasons I have to find the truth."

I couldn't help it, my eyes made a quick glance over to his uniform covered in clear plastic from the dry cleaner, the one that hung on the hat rack. He caught my glance and stepped over to his uniform.

I quick-stepped from his office, trying to make it to my cubicle. I thought enough time had passed and that I could get away with it again. I had replaced his nameplate on his uniform with "Arthur Ritis."

From his office, Sims bellowed, "Son of a bitch!"

Chapter Eighteen

I sat at my desk in my cubicle, kept my head down, and filled out the pink form that requested evidence be tested, specifically for the fibers enmeshed in the lead of the expended bullets I got from Jubal Butler. I didn't have a Sheriff's case number to reference, so I used a cold-case homicide number and hoped no one would notice the huge violation of policy.

Sergeant Henry Espinoza slid into my cubicle, sat in the chair next to my desk, and stared. He had been my team sergeant before I was bounced from the teams. We got along great, but he took a torpedo right along with me over the meth lab in the desert. He was responsible for my leash and he had not yanked hard enough. He'd get over it. Hopefully.

He kept his black hair moussed and combed straight back. He believed in looking professional at all times and spent his overtime money on his suits. He looked sharp. Two years earlier he took a spill on an off-road motorcycle and cracked two vertebrae in his neck. The docs drilled holes in his head and attached a halo with a plastic and leather rig to his shoulders that kept him from moving his neck. He had to turn his shoulders from side to side like Frankenstein in order to see. After a couple of months, he came back to the job on light duty wearing his new rig working the desk. I inadvertently tagged him with a new moniker, Frankenoza. It stuck. Well, maybe not so inadvertently.

I stared back. "Can I help you with something, Sarge?"

He leaned over conspiratorially. "What did you do to the LT this time?"

I eased up and peeked over the top edge of the cubicle, then came back down.

"You can't tell a soul, you understand?"

He made a move with his fingers like he was locking his lips.

"Okay, look, I did this a while ago and it was like a silent running torpedo that chose right now to blow up. My timing hasn't been the greatest, lately."

"Come on, give me the rest of it."

"Okay, but I'm tellin' you, you have to keep it to yourself, he's hot enough over it already. If you guys start poking him about it, I'm really going to be in the grease."

"Sure, sure. You know me."

I opened my desk drawer and showed him the lieutenant's nameplate with his real name. Henry caught the meaning, threw his head back, and let out a little squeal as he tried to suppress a full belly laugh with his hand but couldn't.

"Sssh, Sssh, what's the matter with you?"

He held up his hand, his face turning red trying to hold back his laughter, which made me want to laugh right along with him.

"What name did you use?"

"Arthur Ritis."

He howled with laughter and slapped his leg.

"Come on, man," I whispered through my own laughter. "Seriously?" I stood and peeked over the top of the cubicle. The lieutenant's office door was still closed. Other prairie dog detectives popped up wanting in on the joke.

Henry stood. "One of these days, Dirty Dave, that man in there is going to cut off your nuts. I'm glad I'm not your keeper anymore." He took a pink While-you-were-out slip from his shirt pocket. "You got a bag-of-bones call, in the West End."

"Ah, man, not now. I got too much going on."

"This is per Arthur Ritis himself." He tried to keep a serious face and couldn't.

"Man, I'm begging you, don't be putting that out or he *will* cut off my nuts."

"You can trust me, bro." He walked out of my cubicle and into the row. "Hey Mikey, come here."

I grabbed my gear and fled.

The pink slip said exactly that, "Bag of Bones," with two cross streets listed that I didn't recognize. I checked the Thomas Guide and found the location at the extreme west end of San Bernardino county right on the border of Los Angeles County, at least a forty-minute drive.

I dropped off the two expended bullets at the crime lab. After working homicide for four years, I had cultivated a couple of friends over there who moved it to the front of the line. I asked if they would also classify the bullets in Drugfire, a new program that registered and documented shell casings and bullets, all of which are individual to only one weapon, the same as fingerprints are to one person.

Drug/Fire was the national database that would tell me if the bullets Jubal Butler found at the scene matched any gun or crime anywhere else in the US. There wasn't much of a chance they came from my backup weapon. The rounds I had fired thumped into the shovel-wielding suspect. With all the recreational shooting that went on along that hedgerow, the bullets had to have been fired from a different gun. In a homicide investigation, you had to check all the boxes and leave nothing to chance.

I headed west on the IS10 Freeway, got off at Mountain Avenue in Upland, and headed north. The location was almost at the top of Mountain Avenue along the only road to Mount Baldy. I wished I had my hiking boots in the trunk; this call was going to be a trek. All uphill. Note to self: get a day pack with water, snacks, camera, extra film, some rope, first aid kit, and one of those space blankets in case I get lost on one of these forced excursions.

Forty-five minutes after leaving San Bernardino I made a long sweeping turn almost to the top, just south of Mt. Baldy, and came across a fire truck, a highway patrol car, a Los Angeles County Sheriff's unit, and two San Bernardino County Sheriff patrol cars parked on the downward side of the road. *All this for a bag of bones*? Something was up.

Glen Connelly, the Chino Hills station sergeant, walked down the street toward me. He was a good guy; I'd worked with him in the high desert when we both worked patrol. He said, "Hey, it's the new Bone Dick."

"Yeah, I guess news travels fast."

His green uniform pants and beige uniform shirt were scuffed and dirty. "You bring your Swiss seat? This is a rappel job."

"Ah man, I don't get paid enough for this crap. I got real work to do."

I grabbed a Polaroid camera from the trunk, two extra film cartridges, and leather gloves. Glen stood next to me watching.

I asked, "Whatta ya got?"

"Car over the side."

I stood up from rummaging in the trunk for a bag to carry the gear. "Car over the side? That's a crash, not a bag of bones. Why doesn't CHP handle it?"

"Dispatch notified homicide and a Lieutenant Ritis said he was sending his Bone Dick. I never heard of a Lieutenant Ritis."

I slammed my trunk. "Yeah, he's my boss who apparently can't take a joke."

"Bone Dick, that's a good name for you."

We started walking to the fire truck. He said, "Car's been down there a lot of years. I took a look but didn't touch anything. It could just as easily be a homicide as a crash. It's probably right to have Homicide on board just in case."

I stopped in my tracks. No way. "What kind of car is it? Is it an Opel Kadet, burnt-orange?" That would be too much of a coincidence if it was located today, seven years after the Shearer suicide. After I'd just started investigating the murder.

"Don't know. Too much dirt covering it. I didn't look that close, didn't want to disturb the scene. There's a dead guy sitting behind the wheel though, and—"

"Who called it in? How did we get on to this?" Maybe someone was pulling the strings like he did back during the time of the suicide. When the call came in from a shrink as a welfare check on a 5150. That shrink call was something else I had to backtrack.

"You're not going to believe this," Glenn said. "It was one of those kite jumpers. You know the giant kite thing you strap into and hold onto the bar and jump off the side of a mountain? Crazy bastards. We get a couple of them killed every year up here. Anyway, this guy says he rode the thermocline up and was coming down this canyon and spotted a reflection, made a couple of turns overhead, and saw it was a car. Otherwise, that crashed car would've been down there forever and a day."

"You believe him? You were down at the car, could someone from above see it?"

"I didn't talk to him, dispatch did. The car is down in heavy brush with some tree cover. I guess he could've seen it from the air, a reflection maybe. Why?"

"You called a Bone Dick and that's a question a Bone Dick asks. Come on, I wanna go down and take a look."

Chapter Nineteen

A fireman I didn't recognize named Gus helped me into a Swiss seat, nylon webbing that went around my legs under my crotch, and around my hips. He attached a figure-eight to the D-ring, all the while explaining the rappel.

"This is a gentle slope as far as rappels go, but take it slow, it can still be treacherous with all those rocks and brush. I'll be right alongside you. If you start having trouble for any reason, don't be afraid to say something." I nodded, trying the entire time to peek over the edge, down to the car to see if it was an orange Opel. It had to be.

Gus told me how to let out rope and how to brake.

I had a nylon war bag handle around one shoulder; it was a bag, not a backpack. Our rappel ropes were tied off to a large chrome hook on the front of the fire engine. I moved to the edge and started down. I couldn't wait to see the guy behind the wheel, the guy who had killed Elise Stoner and Franklyn Shearer, the guy, who in all likelihood had also killed Jessica DeFrank and mushed my face with a shovel.

I could just imagine what had happened. After his violent crime spree, he needed to dump the car and drove up this way late at night with the streets empty, using darkness as a coconspirator. The vibration from the shovel handle still ringing in his hands and arms, a fresh memory he would relish. He must've been going too fast, missed the turn, and gone over. Poetic justice. Three murders cleared just that easy. Like Jubal had said, a simple turn on the wheel of fate.

The rope hissed through the figure eight as I descended. Gus yelled, "Hey, slow down, buddy. And keep your hand away from that figure-eight. It'll pull your hand right in, tangle, and take off a finger."

I preferred buddy over Bone Dick. I didn't slow until I hit the shrub line. Someone, probably the firemen, had hacked a path through the choke cherry, poodle dog bush, and the dense mountain whitethorn. A little farther down, the branches of several canyon live oak cast the shrubs and car in dark shadow. No way could it be seen from the road. I stopped and twisted to look behind me. I couldn't confirm the car was an Opel, not yet.

Gus caught up. "Go easy, cowboy, or you're gonna lose your footing and this will turn into a rescue."

"Got it, sorry." I started off again, same speed.

The fresh-cut greenery smelled strong and humid. The temperature cooled as I entered the dimness created by the overhanging branches. I slowed even more as I approached the car, taking it one step at a time. I didn't want to disturb anything if it did happen to be the Opel and a crime scene.

It had to be the Opel.

The side of the car had smudged handprints in the dirt, exposing the paint, handprints used for sudden support to keep the first fireman from going farther down the hill. The color didn't look orange, at least in the dimness under the trees, the shrubs, and layers of dirt. No sun rays penetrated the tree canopy. How could the hang glider spot this derelict under such cover? I got on the handheld radio and asked Connelly to have 40k, the Sheriff's helicopter, make a pass for photos before we pulled the car out. He acknowledged.

I fed out more rope to move down closer to the driver's window, leaned back, and took in the entire side of the car.

It wasn't an Opel. Damn. It was a Nissan or Toyota. This was just a bag of bones, a separate investigation from what I had going on.

Someone had opened the door, rolled the window down, and closed the door. Dirt had piled on the frame from the window going down. I pulled out the Polaroid and took a couple of snaps, putting the photos in my shirt pocket while they continued to develop.

Inside the car, the driver was leaning forward, his head resting on the steering wheel as if frustrated with a traffic jam. The front of the car's hood was crumpled and wrapped around the trunk of a thick, hundred-year-old live oak. The driver wore a ballcap, his hair desiccated and straw-like. With the windows closed and the driver's compartment uncompromised, the larger predators couldn't get to the body and left the decomposition job to small insects. He looked mummified. Had he died on impact or were his legs pinned and he died slowly, screaming for help, honking his horn no one could hear? What a way to go.

The driver wore an older-style shirt, the kind with a small animal over the left breast that declared the brand, but I couldn't see that part. Heavy dust covered his ghostly thin shoulders. He wore denim pants and had a large ring on the finger of his right hand, like a school class ring.

I reached in, my hand shaking slightly, and was glad no one stood close enough to see it. Not a great attribute for a Bone Dick, being squeamish over a bag of bones. The odor that came from the car was one of dry dust and nothing more. The interior had acted as an oven, baking everything down to a corn chip. This guy was nothing but a big bag of dust. I leaned him back in the seat. He crinkled and cracked. Brown desiccated skin stretched across his face, his eye sockets vacant holes.

Before I touched anything, I was supposed to wait for the coroner to come take control of the scene and inventory this guy's property; It was protocol, policy, the law. The coroner wouldn't rappel down; he or she would wait for a tow truck to string a cable down, hook it up, and drag it to the top, banging and jostling any evidence there might be.

My curiosity was killing me, I wanted to know this guy's name. Most guys carried their wallets in their back pockets. I stuck my arm deeper into the car.

Behind, at the back of the car, suspended from a separate rope, Gus said, "Hey, are you supposed to be doing that?"

I ignored him. Of course, I was allowed to frisk him, I was the Bone Detective. I chuckled to myself, more nerves than mirth as I began to like the new job. How many people, or cops for that matter, get to hang from a hundred-and-fifty-foot rope and frisk a guy who'd been dead for years? I laughed a little more at the ludicrous situation.

I had to pick up the guy's left arm, which hung down to his side, so I could get to his back pockets. His tissue-paper skin slipped and slid under my fingers. I laid his arm across his lap and immediately *stopped* laughing. All the air suddenly left the world. My knees wobbled.

On his wrist, he wore a macramé wristband with little white squares and black letters woven into the band.

The letters spelled *Beth.*

I forced air back into my lungs. Dizziness made the air an ebbing heatwave.

This had to be Cole Adler, my wife's long-lost fiancé. She had a similar wrist band with *his* name. I'd found it in a shoebox of high school memorabilia she kept high up in the closet.

The day turned hot and blood rushed from my head. I swooned. The rope slipped through my brake hand. I jolted.

"Hey! Hey!" Gus yelled. "What's wrong? You okay? Look at me. Look up here."

I put my hand on top of the car and took in several long breaths. I waved at him with my free hand. "I'm okay. Just a little hot out here, that's all."

"If the heat's too much, let's go back now. I don't want to have to bring down a stokes."

I ignored him, swallowed hard, and waved again.

Cole Adler, what the hell? Will there never be an end to him? I guess in a way there was now.

Then it hit me. How do I tell Beth? It had to be me to tell her. For all these years I had been the roadblock between Cole and her. The same roadblock that kept us from achieving true intimacy. It wouldn't be logical, but my wife was going to blame me for this, for Cole's reckless ride up the Baldy grade. Blame me for all those lost years. Years she fretted over with desperation, holding out a glimmer of hope that diminished a little more with each passing minute. And at the same time getting more inflamed with the sense of something lost that she never truly had.

I *had to be* the one to tell her. I couldn't let anyone else do it. My stomach knotted into a tight little ball at the prospect, at the words that would absolutely crush her. How could I do that? What would I say?

Maybe it wasn't him? What were the odds?

I shook off the bone-crushing emotions, leaned into the car's compartment, shoving the bag of bones over—Cole. He crackled and snapped. Dust puffed into the air. I felt around his back pockets and came up with his wallet. My hands shook. I opened it and found his ten-year-old driver's license with his name and address. *Cole Adler*. Opposite the driver's license, Cole kept a photo of my Beth. A younger Beth, alive with a vivaciousness I had rarely seen, something she kept hidden, afraid to show anyone but Cole. To be fair, that could've been my imagination.

Chapter Twenty

I pulled up and parked in front of the house in Redlands, the nice part south of the boulevard. The house, a two-story prewar monster, sat on the ridge overlooking the valley and the San Gabriel Mountain range to the north. Previously, I had stopped at the coroner's office and met with Jubal's friend Sally Struthers—Nancy—who gave me a copy of the Shearer decedent file. All of Shearer's personal property had been turned over to his sister, a Mrs. Ruth Brock of Redlands. I had the disposition list, the last of kin signed for but it was too nebulous. I needed a look at the item listed under *Misc. files and papers*.

I sat in the car and stared at the macramé wristband with the little white blocks, the letters in black spelling *Beth*. Tears burned my eyes. I'd cut the band from Cole's desiccated wrist and taken it from the scene of the crash without permission from a deputy coroner named Pam Sokolik. The wristband created an imaginary heat in my pocket while I stood in the road that led up to Mt. Baldy, the road above the Datsun 260Z being winched up from its final resting place. Cole Adler's makeshift tomb.

I'd asked Sokolik for a favor—to let me tell Beth before Sokolik made notification to the family. Sokolik had kind eyes and offered to give me two days. I told her I only needed 24 hours. If given the offered two days, the emotional monster would fester and I'd end up chickening out, imploding. I put the issue with Beth behind a door I kept in the far recesses of my mind, slammed it, and locked it, to be taken out later and dealt with. It wouldn't stay there long; it'd eat its way through.

Now sitting in front of the Redlands house I found it difficult to focus on the case at hand. I wiped my eyes, grabbed a notebook, and got out of the Mustang just as my pager buzzed. I checked it: Lieutenant Sims. He'd probably calmed down enough by now, and instead of cutting my head off he'd just yell and scream over the latest Arthur Ritis debacle. I'd call him later. I wasn't up for his harsh words.

The front walk up to the Redlands house had an ancient elm shading the entire yard. The sweet tang of rotting oranges wafted on the warm air. Fifty years ago, Redlands supplied a good chunk of the nation's citrus. Tracts of acre- or half-acre orange groves still existed in a patchwork all over the city, a dying era refusing to let go.

I stepped on the porch and knocked on a wide front door made of hardwood and highly polished with beveled glass insets. Inside, the old house had hardwood floors that allowed the footfalls to echo and bounce and vibrate off the windows in the quiet afternoon. The beveled glass panes at eye level in the door shadowed a second before the door opened to a well-put-together middle-aged woman in a nice dress.

"Yes, may I help you?" Her graying hair was pulled back and tied with a blue ribbon that matched her dress. The woman had not spent much time in the sun and had a light spray of freckles across her nose that she'd tried hard to mask with makeup.

I showed her the star clipped to my belt. "Detective Dave Beckett. Mrs. Ruth Brock?

"Yes, that's right, how can I help you?"

"Can I have a minute or two of your time? I'd like to ask you some questions."

"Of course." She stepped out, closing the door behind her. This odd move wasn't for security reasons. I sensed that someone of my socioeconomic class didn't rate entry, and that she would probably have preferred this conversation take place at the back door, out of view of passing neighbors who would run right to their phones to rat-a-tat-tat on the gossip drums.

I wasn't in the mood to play her games, turned my head, and pretended to sniff my underarm as if my body odor had caused her to act that way.

She scowled. "Young man, please get off my porch."

"I'd like to ask you about your brother Franklyn. Did you keep any of the property the coroner released to you?"

"I don't think that is any of your business, now please leave or I will notify the authorities."

Her expression said that Franklyn's suicide would forever remain a black mark on the family name.

She turned to go back inside.

"I work homicide. Your brother was murdered."

She froze. Her back stiffened. When she turned, she'd retaken control of her emotions. "Please, come in. Would you like some iced tea?"

"Sure, that would be great."

She led me into an expansive library filled with dark, highly polished cherrywood shelves, oriental carpets, and plush easy chairs. I wanted a minute or six hours to disappear in all the ancient, dust-free books. She guided me with an extended hand to a divan with delicately tatted antimacassars on the arms and backs. She sat across at a low coffee table on the edge of a comfortable easy chair, her back ramrod straight.

I opened my notebook on the coffee table, ready to take notes, and wondered if she'd keep her promise about the iced tea. I hadn't realized my thirst until she made the offer. As if on cue, a matronly woman in a plain blue dress with a white apron entered the library, carrying a tray filled with two glasses, a pitcher, and a china sugar bowl with a silver spoon.

"Thank you." I took the glass from the tray and drank it down. She placed the tray on the table and refilled my glass from the pitcher. The liquid cooled all the way down. The maid gave a little bow and exited.

I asked, "Is it possible for me to take a look at Franklyn's things?"

"All of that stuff went to the dump the day I took custody. Now tell me why, after all these years, this is suddenly a murder?" The word murder left her lips with an air of disgust.

I figured his things had been discarded as soon as I caught sight of the neighborhood. "It's now an ongoing investigation and at this time I really can't discuss it with you."

"What is your name, again?" she asked. "I will be calling Walter to inform him of your insolence."

Walter Goggin was the chief of police for Redlands. He carried no sway over a Sheriff's detective.

"Did Franklyn ever talk to you about cases he was working?"

"Are you going to answer my question?"

"My name is Dave Beckett, I'm with Sheriff's homicide. Did he ever mention a woman by the name of Elise Stoner?"

She stared at me and finally said, "So…so he did not shoot himself?"

I shook my head.

Her throat worked hard to swallow, and her eyes filled with tears.

"I'm sorry," I said. "I know this must be difficult."

"This Elise Stoner woman, is she the one who killed him?"

"I'm really not at liberty to—"

"Young man!"

"No, she was also killed."

Her lips mumbled the words, barely audible: "Oh, my dear Lord."

I stood to leave. "I'm sorry to have bothered you. Thank you for the tea, it really hit the spot. One more question, did Franklyn ever see a shrin—a psychiatrist?"

"No, of course not, he was the sanest man I ever knew and a great police detective."

"He was an ex-cop?"

"That's right, back in Toledo. He left the job to come out here to live closer to family. He was just getting started with his private investigator's business. And he was doing quite well, I might add."

"Thank you again, I won't be bothering you anymore."

I made it halfway to the door, my feet loud on the hardwood floor when she said, "Detective Beckett?"

I turned and followed her to a closet door under the stairs that led to the second floor. She opened the door. "Back there against the wall, behind all the coats."

I squatted and duck-walked, careful to move the coats out of the way. They puffed up a musty-mothball scent strong enough to choke a stuffed shirt. To the right, deeper into the closet, I found a standard-size file box with the words "Franklyn's papers" written in black felt tip. Bingo. Like Jubal said, sometimes investigations just fall into place.

Chapter Twenty-One

I drove to the Cool Cactus, a family restaurant that served excellent Mexican food and was extremely cop friendly. It was just down Redlands Boulevard a few miles. I carried the file box inside and set it on the table, anxious to get into it, then walked to the counter and ordered the enchilada plate and a jumbo coke at the counter.

Sue, the daughter and part-owner, smiled and looked me up and down. "Been out in the sticks, have we?"

I gave her my best Elmer Fudd. "When you're hunting wabbits, you have to go where the wabbits are."

Sue slid the coke over to me. "You better not hurt the Easter Bunny, David Beckett, or your gonna answer to me."

"Gottcha, Bugs, no Easter Bunnies."

"Take a seat, I'll bring your food out."

I offered her a well-used twenty-dollar bill, one I kept in my wallet for just such an occasion. She scowled. Most cops got HO, half-off; she wouldn't even take that from me. "Thanks, Sue." One of the few benefits to those who hunted the worst of the worst. If she found out I'd been dumped back to Bone Dick, I'd have to pay for my meals.

I hurried back to my file box, wanting to dive in. I set the hand-held radio on the seat next to me and took the lid off the box. I found a pile of papers, tossed in willy-nilly and shaken, not stirred. I sat back in the hard plastic chair as I flashed on the memory seven years ago, standing in Franklyn Shearer's kitchen seeing his death papers laid out in tightly regimented order on the kitchen table. And the moment that I realized

I'd missed something. Then I found Franklyn in the garage. I was too late—seven years too late—and at the same time, I had missed something even more important: justice for Franklyn. Something he'd expected from me, something I was paid to sniff out. I'd been derelict in my duty. I shook off the nasty nostalgia, stuck my hand in the box, and pulled out a handful. I sat in the corner, my back to the wall. I could see the counter and the doors on both sides of the restaurant.

Mrs. Ruth Bock, as it seemed, had just grabbed a bundle of papers with no other intent than to have something with her brother's name on it for memory's sake. None of the jumble would do me any good. I was an archeologist digging through the strata looking for clues to an ancient mystery with nothing there to find. The first level was bills needed to run the house: taxes, electric, water, trash, and the phone. I put the phone bill aside to look at later. At first glance, the area codes on some of the calls looked like they might be Ohio.

The next level in the jumble was a waste of space, ads for oil changes, and pizza delivery, sales on plants from the local nursery, and the like. Next, an old newspaper and *Newsweek* magazine that listed Franklyn's name and address, dated the week of his demise. Under those, I discovered the jackpot: all the contents from the top of his desk. There was one of those small frames with hanging steel balls in a row that clanged together, a yellow metal pen and pencil set, a small globe of the world, a monument that read "Franklyn Shearer, Private Investigator," and a block of clear resin with his Toledo, Ohio, police badge suspended inside. At the very bottom, a datebook from the last year of his life. I picked it up with reverence.

I put aside the datebook, the resin block, and the phone bills, and shoved the rest back in the box.

Sue brought over the tray with my enchilada plate. "Doesn't look like there are any wabbits in there?"

Whenever I took a giant step forward in a case, my heartbeat pounded at the back of my eyes and a smile wouldn't leave my face. This was one of those times. I was onto this guy, this murderer, and could almost smell him, see him off in the distant ether trying to shamble away. I said to Sue,

"These wily wabbits hide in the most peculiar places."

"You're a weird duck, Dave."

"Thank you."

I started wolfing down my hot enchilada and beans and rice, hardly tasting them as my other hand skimmed through the datebook, starting in January, resisting the urge to go right to the week before Shearer died.

"Hey, look who it is. It's our very own Bone Dick."

I looked up, startled. My good friend, Jimmy Mora from Violent Crimes.

I'd let my desire to find a clue buried in Franklyn's handwritten words jeopardize my awareness. Seven years ago, I swore that I would never let it happen again. You let your guard down for even one second and you got a face full of shovel.

"Hey, Jimmy."

"Scoot over, let me in."

I did.

"This a working lunch?" he asked.

"You act surprised. This is what Bone Dicks do."

He chuckled. "Yeah, I heard what Bone Dicks do, it's all over HQ. You're lucky your LT doesn't launch your happy ass out to Trona as the new resident deputy."

Sue came over with a plate that contained a fat burrito and set it in front of Jimmy. "Thanks, doll." She smiled and left.

I asked, "How did you get that without going to the counter and ordering?"

He shrugged, took a giant bite, and spoke around the food. "I only ever order one thing, so as soon as they see my car pull in, they start putting this baby together. Though, I gotta eat fast and get back to it. No time for talkin' smack."

"What are you working?"

He looked around and then lowered his voice. "You heard of the Oakmont Shooters?"

"Yeah, out in Texas, armed robbery spree, ambushed two cops, killed them. Armed with assault rifles, handguns."

"Yeah." He winked.

"You got a line on *them*?" A caper like that did make my archival hunt for a murderer into a cartoon from Warner Bros. A takedown of that magnitude came along once in a career.

"Yeah," he said. "You want in? This is going to be historic, buddy boy. I can get you on board if you want."

"What's the setup?"

He looked around again, leaned in. "We got word those two boys are coming into San Bernardino. It's too hot for them in Texas right now. They'll be here in the next forty-eight hours, depending on how long they take to drive out here and if they decide to make any stops to kill any more grocery store clerks or cops."

"Where?"

"You in?"

"Man, I'd love to, but I'm already on thin ice. Maybe if I get this thing cleared up by then."

"Okay, but you can't tell a soul, I mean it, this baby is code purple with gold clusters." He grabbed a paper napkin and drew a horseshoe. This is The Lucky Shamrock."

"I know the place."

"Two-story fleabag motel. We have four rooms, two on each side, upper and lower, with a van at the bottom of the horseshoe. We have a car down the block ready to roll in and block the bottom of the horseshoe, trap them."

"Jesus, that's going to be a massacre."

"We'll give them every opportunity to give up. Well, just one. We're not going to take any chances, they've already killed two cops. He chuckled. "It's going be like Butch Cassidy and the Sundance Kid. You know the scene I'm talking about? The one at the very end when Paul Newman and Robert Redford think there are only a few police left outside the cantina where they're hole up and they go running out into the guns of the entire Mexican army."

"Yeah, I know which scene you're talking about." Another one of Johnny Maslow's favorite movies that he could quote word for word. I said, "Are you going to be the fat Mexican general that yells 'Fuego!'?" The last word that echoed again and again as the movie freeze-frames Butch and Sundance running out.

I missed Johnny. I missed those days working a patrol car with him. I'd get him out of jail. I was close to getting it done. Closing in on the real killer. Then I realized I'd let my emotions enter into the equation. Johnny hadn't been ruled out. Not entirely. He could still be a murderer.

"Hey, watch it, amigo. I'm not fat," Jimmy Mora said, in reply to my comment about being a fat Mexican general.

"You're gonna be, you keep eating those kitchen sink burritos."

He had to use two hands to eat it. He let go, balanced the jumbo burrito with one hand, and picked up the badge from Toledo suspended in clear resin. He set it down and picked up the phone bill. "You're on to someone, aren't you? Crawling right up his ass. I can see it in that prepubescent face of yours."

"Yeah, I'm closing in on him and—" As I said it I turned a page and came across an entry in the datebook. "Come on, scoot out, I gotta go. I gotta go right now."

"Take it easy, *mijo*, you gotta stop and smell the roses or life's gonna zip right on past you. Sit a minute, talk with your best amigo."

"Yeah. Yeah."

"Hey," Mora said. "You want in on the Lucky Shamrock caper, page me. But don't wait too long. It's going down any time between now and Wednesday."

"Sorry, not going to happen, not this time, but keep me in mind for future gigs, okay amigo?"

He'd again just reminded me of similar words from Johnny and Jubal about taking life more seriously, not letting it slip through my fingers. After this case, I'd take some time off, slow down, find a solid hobby before I went back to work. Make Luce my hobby while she was still young.

I grabbed my stuff and headed out. I stopped at the door and yelled, "Thanks, Sue!"

She yelled over the lines of customers at the counter. "Is it going to be wabbit stew for dinner?"

"If I'm lucky."

She smiled and waved. And I was out the door.

Chapter Twenty-Two

The most logical place to make the phone calls was back at HQ, but I didn't need the heartache from the ass-chewing that I had coming. I kept a roll of quarters in the Mustang's console and had long ago scoped out the best payphones in the area where I could pull up, and without getting out of the car, dial and talk.

This method turned my car into a mobile office. The county gave everyone in the detail a department phone credit card, but it was a real pain, twelve numbers for the card, seven numbers for the access code, and then the telephone number. That's a butt load of numbers. If you have a lot of calls to make, the tip of your finger actually gets a blister from punching the little metal squares.

I parked at my regular payphone in the parking lot of the drive-thru hot dog joint, one with a red A-framed roof. This phone, a popular one for drug dealers, pimps, and hookers, would now be busy for a while. I kept my eyes on the mirrors to make sure no one walked up with a shovel. I took out my Colt .38 and stuck it under my leg for easy access.

But first I took a moment to look the gun over. I'd had it a long time and it had always provided a strange sense of comfort in a violent world. The gun had become a close friend, always there in case I needed it. Ready to speak loud and angry for me at a time when there was nobody else.

I turned the Sheriff's radio down low, used a couple of quarters, and dialed Jubal Butler's phone number. His phone buzzed and buzzed without an answer. I finally hung up, dialed the number again, let it ring twice, hung up, dialed it again let it ring once, hung up, and dialed again. We had not arranged for any kind of secret code, but the uniqueness of the pattern might spike his curiosity. Or make him mad as hell.

The phone on the other end picked up on the seventh ring. "Kid, you're worse than an itch on my long ropy hemorrhoid."

"How did you know it was me?"

"Don't be ignorant. What do you want?" His voice gravelly and slurred.

"Straight to business. All right. I tracked down a box of Shearer's personal stuff from his next of kin."

"You going to tell me or am I gonna yank this phone out of the wall and get back to some serious drinking? I have a half-gallon goal and I'm well on my way to making it happen."

I had not meant to pause, I just didn't know how to broach the question. "Shearer's datebook has an appointment listed with your name."

He said nothing.

I said, "The date of the meeting was supposed to happen two days after he was found murdered. He was killed before he met with you."

He must've put the phone closer to his mouth; a heavy rasp came over the line, his breath coming faster.

Two hookers walked by on the sidewalk trying to draw the attention of motorists on Waterman Avenue. Behind them, a homeless woman in ragged clothes ambled along without a destination, looking for something to scavenge or for something she never realized she lost: life.

"You there, Jubal?" I thumbed through the rest of the datebook. I'd bailed out of the Cool Cactus before I'd finished reading the whole thing.

Jubal asked, "his name's Shearer?"

"That's right, seven years ago, a Wednesday, 9:30 a.m., and it has the notation 'The Iron Skillet.'"

"Is there any notation why he wanted to talk with me?"

"No, just under the date and time, West Valley, Detective J. Butler."

"Sorry, kid, my mind's been submerged too long in alcohol without coming up for air. I don't remember anything about it."

"What about in *your* datebook, or your desk blotter?" I was reaching now, scared this lead would die an untimely death and take the truth with it.

I came to the last pages of Shearer's datebook while I waited for Jubal to reply, the blank pages used for notes. My heart skipped. I sucked air, took small gulps trying to catch up, unable to breathe.

Jubal started to answer my question about his datebook and blotter, but his words warbled as if he were speaking through water submerged in a far-off mirage.

I stared at the notation on the last page of Shearer's notebook, hastily written in a column instead of horizontally:

- *TB Killer*
- *Moved to West Valley from Ohio*
- *WV Cop?*
- *Joined dept. 5-7yrs ago*
- *Meet with Det. JB...Risky. No other option.*

I needed time to think. Shearer thought the killer worked at West Valley Police Department and had joined the department five to seven years ago. Which, now, really meant twelve to fourteen years ago. The way it was worded Shearer also didn't know if Jubal was the TB Killer and was taking a chance meeting with him.

"Jubal. Jubal, sorry to interrupt you, man, I have to go. Can I call you back in a few minutes?"

"Sure, what the hell, I don't have a life." He hung up.

I sat in the front seat of the Mustang, the sun beating down on the windshield, heating up the interior. Sweat rivulets ran down my forehead and into my eyes, stinging. I swiped at them as my mind ran far out ahead, jumping from point to point like crossing over rocks in a small rill.

Instinct kicked me out of the funk. An African American, dressed in pants five sizes too large and cinched up with a belt, with lots of gold hanging around his neck and a bowler hat on his head, ambled my way. He had his hand in his pants pocket. He wanted his phone back, the little corner of his world he thought he needed to control. I didn't have time to mess with him. I picked up the Colt .38 and rested the barrel on the window sill of the Mustang.

He raised his hands. "Whoa. Whoa, no problem my man, I'm movin' on." He stopped, took several backward steps, turned, and fled.

I was a visual learner and had to see the information on a broader scale in order to correlate it, especially if the information became too immense. Too mind-blowing. I took out a blank report form and turned it over. I drew squares for all three murders, Franklyn Shearer, Elise Stoner, and Jessica DeFrank. I added the dates and stopped. The note about the killer being a cop was a huge black mark against Johnny Maslow. But he came from Oklahoma, right? Wasn't that what he'd always claimed? He had the drawl to prove it. I put his name in a box and drew a line to Elise Stoner. Then I put my name in a box and drew lines to all of them.

Shit. This looked worse than I thought. *And I'd even been the first cop on scene at the Elise Stoner murder.*

My pager beeped. I checked the number. Sims. He'd added a 911 after his request to 1021, which meant to call him right away.

I reached out the window and dialed 411, information, and got the number for the Toledo Police Department. This call would take too many quarters, so I punched in the long phone credit card number, the access code, and the police department number. My arm ached from reaching out of the Mustang.

And at the same time, I realized I'd waited too long. The issue with Beth worked its way to the forefront of my brain, causing my anxiety to dominate everything else. I'd have to deal with it. Now.

A woman picked up and announced, "Toledo Police Department, how can I help you?"

I asked for homicide and was immediately transferred. Another woman picked up. I asked to speak with the lieutenant. I was again immediately transferred.

"Homicide, Lieutenant Thorpe."

I took a deep breath, identified myself, and started at the beginning, giving him deep background, talking a mile a minute without giving him a chance to interrupt, to disrupt my momentum, my need to get this over with so I could talk to Beth.

Chapter Twenty-Three

Lieutenant Thorpe finally interrupted me after I'd droned on about Johnny Maslow and Elise Stoner and that I thought a serial killer from Toledo had migrated to our area.

"Hold on there, son. I'm going to stop you right there. Where'd you say you're from? San De Angelo?"

"No, San Bernardino County Sheriff's, homicide, in Southern California."

"I don't know you from a bar of soap. I'm not going to acknowledge anything you've said or give you any sensitive information over the phone."

I was afraid he was going to say something like that. "Can you call San Bernardino County Sheriff's Department and ask for homicide? They will verify who I am and then you can call me back at this number, I'm on a payphone." I gave him the payphone number.

"I can do that, but in all your jibber-jabber I want to be crystal clear. You're saying you have a serial killer out your way and you think he came from Toledo?"

"That's right, an ex-officer from your department referred to him as the TB Killer."

On the other end, Thorp sucked in a deep breath. "Son, you stay right there by that payphone. I'll confirm your bona fides and call you right back. You hear? You stay right there."

The case was coming together. I waited five, ten, fifteen minutes. I should've been trying to fit more of the pieces together and couldn't. Beth stayed in my thoughts, the wonderful feeling of sleeping next to her the night before, the rise and fall of her chest, the warmth of her arm when I laid my hand on her bare skin, the contented peace in her lovely countenance as she slept. All of that was now at risk from that dumbass Cole Adler. My life balanced on a razor edge ready to take the big plunge over an emotional cliff and there wasn't anything I could do about it.

The payphone rang. I reached out and grabbed it up.

"You're a real asshole, you know that?"

Sims.

"Yes, sir."

"You lit a big fuse under a lieutenant in Toledo. I just got off the phone with him. He's already assigned two detectives, they're on their way to the airport as we speak. They are flying out here to talk with you. You of all people."

"What? I haven't given him any informa—"

"Apparently, you said two magic letters: TB."

"Yes, I did do that. I found it written in Shearer's datebook."

"According to this lieutenant, TB stands for the Teen Beast, a serial killer from fourteen years ago, who went dark. They have nine unsolved murders behind this guy."

"No shit."

"No shit. Get your ass in here now so we can put something together to show the captain, who is going to have to show the sheriff."

I didn't know how to answer him. Beth moved into my thoughts again. I came back to earth and heard him say, "I don't know how I'm going to explain this."

"What?"

"You're supposed to be the Bone Dick, working the desk, and under no circumstances were you to leave the station without my permission. You're on double-secret probation. The chief's going to have a piece of my ass over this."

"It's a serial killer." Sims forgot that he'd assigned me two different investigations, the leg bone, and the bag of bones. I couldn't very well handle them from my desk. He must've thought the two callouts harmless, that any three-year-old chimp could handle them without screwing up.

And he was right. I had colored outside the lines by continuing to follow up on Shearer.

"Not in our jurisdiction," he said. "It's all Ohio and West Valley PD's. Come on in, let's get this written up nice and neat. We'll put a big bow on it and hope the shit hits the wall instead of us."

"Are you pulling me from this case?"

"Hell no, this is great work, but I don't know how to give you an atta-boy for something you did while stepping on your dick."

"I have to run home for a minute."

"Are you kidding me?"

"It's personal, and I wouldn't ask if it wasn't important."

"Hurry, Beckett."

"I'll do the best I can."

"Dave?"

"I'll hurry." I put the phone on the hook, pulled back into the car, reached for the key in the ignition, and fired up. My hand was on the gearshift, ready to roll, when the payphone rang. That would be Lieutenant Thorpe in Toledo. Did I want to answer it? The phone rang again. The Mustang's engine rumbled. I needed to get the emotional gorilla off my back. I needed to talk to Beth.

I turned the car off, reached out, and picked up the phone.

"Thought you weren't going to answer."

"I almost didn't. I got a lot going on right now."

"I understand."

No, he didn't, not even close.

He waited for me to talk.

When I didn't he said, "Your lieutenant speaks very highly of you."

I thought of what Beth's eyes would do when I told her. The grief. Just the thought of hurting her that deeply was like a knife to the gut. I bent forward, my arm around my stomach. There was no way around it, I had to tell her now. Right now.

I came back to earth. Get this call over with fast and go home. Home? It hadn't been my home for the last six months. I'd only been back in for the last twenty hours. And now—

Thorpe said, "I have two detectives on their way out there with copies of all our cases, nine of them, all young girls."

I closed my eyes. "Why? Before we even talked?"

"This guy, the TB Killer, went dark fourteen years ago. It's a huge black eye for the department, not to mention the families that have had to live with not knowing—not having closure."

"Who is Franklyn Shearer?" I asked.

"He was the case agent. He worked back in the detective bureau before my time. I was a rookie on the street when he worked homicide. He was good, the best. Had the highest clearance rate. He took all his cases personally. Nine young women raped, strangled, and buried in trenches. Not solving them just about killed him. He left the job over it."

"Young girls in slit trenches?"

"That's right. Your lieutenant said you met the Teen Beast up close and personal, said that you even put a few slugs into him? Good for you, son. Damn fine work."

I picked up the Colt .38 and looked at it, the steel warm in my hand. I nodded to no one, a lump rising in my throat. I wanted to meet the Teen Beast one more time and give him six more.

Chapter Twenty-Four

I parked in front of our house in San Antonio Heights, didn't hesitate, and got out. If I sat in the car for even five seconds I wouldn't be able to work up the nerve to tell her—to emotionally demolish her.

I loved her too much to hurt her, but I had no choice. I couldn't let her find out from someone else. I left my hand-held radio in the car. She didn't need the added aggravation of the background noise—my job shoved in her face.

I raised my hand to knock at the door when it opened. Beth stood, doorknob in hand with a ravishing smile, one that cut right to my core and made me ache for her. She genuinely wanted to see me. Guys at work railed about their wives, complained about this and that, said things they would never say in front of their mates. Not me. I never got tired of looking at Beth, her beautiful eyes, her cute half-smile. I didn't understand how their relationships could be so different from mine. Those guys were really missing out.

She wore an aquamarine dress I had never seen before, one that exposed her shoulders and hugged dangerous curves that if driven too fast would throw you to the pavement. "Hey, you," she said.

I drank her in, trying hard to remember her this way. When I didn't move, she took a half-step out, went on tiptoes, and kissed me on the lips, light and moist, her eyes closed.

She came down, her head craned upward, her eyes big and dark. She put a warm hand on my arm. "Dave, what's the matter?"

I wanted to turn and run. This was the most difficult thing I had ever had to do. I took her in my arms, buried my face in her neck, and hugged her while taking in her scent: green apple shampoo with an essence of Opium perfume. Still holding her tight I whispered in her neck, "Baby, where's Luce?"

Beth squeezed me tighter. "She's at her grandmother's for the night. What's going on, Dave? You're scaring me."

I took her hand and led her deeper into the house. "Come on, let's sit down."

"Tell me. You're scaring me. Tell me now."

In the dining room, she'd set the table for two, with two tapers burning and flickering in the fading orange of dusk that sliced through the front door we'd left standing open.

The night before, she too had experienced our rekindled love and wanted it to move forward. It made my heart swell.

The house smelled of lasagna she had made from scratch, even the noodles. I couldn't remember the last time she'd cooked my favorite dish. She was trying hard to put *us* back together.

I sat on the dining room chair and eased her onto my lap. I needed her close. I had to be touching her to make her real. I tried again to bury my face in her neck, an ostrich hiding from the dangers of the big bad world. She wouldn't let me; she put her hands on my shoulders, her face inches from mine. She didn't have to ask me again, she knew I would tell her. Without taking my eyes from hers, I reached into my shirt pocket and pulled out a photo. I didn't want to show it to her. She slowly took it, her voice husky, "What's this?"

I didn't answer.

"Oh," she said, "This is a picture of me in high school. Why didn't you want to show me this? Where did you get—" She turned it over and read the back, her own cursive writing: *I'll love you forever, Babydoll.*

She stared at it, her eyes filling with tears. "Dave? Dave, where did you get this?"

My eyes burned with tears. I couldn't answer, the lump in my throat had grown too huge.

She tried to stand. I held on to her. Her chin quivered. "This...anyone could've found this and—"

I shook my head as tears wet my cheeks.

"No...don't." She put her finger up to my lips, so I wouldn't say the words.

I reached into my pants pocket. She took hold of my arm to try and keep me from bringing out anything more, instinctively knowing it would cause a pain like no other. "No. No. Don't. Dave, don't."

I held my fist out to her. I wouldn't show her unless she wanted me to. I'd gladly continue to live the charade if that's what she wanted. No way did I want to hurt her anymore. She took hold of my fist, her eyes burning into mine, my vision blurred with tears from her pain. She shook her head from side to side. She looked down at my fist and gently peeled back my fingers. She saw the macramé wristband she'd made a thousand years ago with her name in white block letters. The one she'd made for Cole.

A keening wail rose up from the bottom of her heart. Her entire body shook. I held on tight. She banged her head against my shoulder, buried her face there. I rocked her and cooed in her ear. We stayed that way a long time. Darkness crept in the open front door as if the world knew better than to shine bright.

Her body finally quit shuddering from weeping, my shirt wet with her tears. She pushed away from my chest and stood. She leaned over and kissed my forehead. I held on to her hand as she walked away, our fingertips the last contact before we parted.

"Beth?" I whispered.

She didn't turn around and continued down the dark hall to our bedroom, disappearing into the dimness. The door eased closed with a finality louder than if she'd slammed it. I realized she'd taken the wristband. She'd taken Cole with her into the bedroom.

I blew out both tapers and sat at the table in total darkness. If Cole Adler hadn't died in the car accident, I'd have hunted him down and put a bullet in him for hurting Beth like that.

Chapter Twenty-Five

I stood at our locked bedroom door, my forehead touching the wood, Beth's mewling coming from the other side. My legs shook from standing there too long. After several hours, the bedroom finally turned silent. The house creaked as the day's heat bled off and the wood settled. She'd cried herself to sleep. I ached to be with her, to cuddle up to her, stroke her hair. The bedroom lock could be picked easily with a narrow, flat-nosed screwdriver. But going in too soon was a mistake. She needed time to herself to deal with her emotions.

I couldn't stand there any longer doing nothing. In the living room the front door stood open—big mistake. Not because of any criminal element but because San Antonio Heights was still semi-rural and rattlesnakes could come in and make themselves at home. I quick-checked for unwanted visitors, then picked up the phone. I called West Valley and asked for the front desk. I got Smith's home phone number and called him. He sounded awake at ten o'clock. I told him I had to talk, that it was important. He didn't ask why. Good friends never did.

He said, "The Iron Skillet in twenty, you're buying the coffee and blueberry pie." Who liked blueberry pie? Not me.

I wrote Beth a quick note that started to turn into a tome of *Gone with the Wind* proportions. I crumpled it, started again, and signed it "Love you always." I ran out to my Mustang, started up, and headed for the meet. Without traffic and with a heavy foot, the drive took twenty minutes. I parked around back.

The Iron Skillet sat on the west side of Euclid Avenue—the main drag through West Valley—and had been a police department eatery for decades. Good service, good food, and a decent price. What more could a customer ask for? Well, HO for a start.

Inside, the tables were a checkerboard of customers eating quietly. I found Smith in a back corner booth, sipping coffee. He wore his standard replica World War II leather flying jacket, something I'd love to wear but knew I couldn't pull off.

I had developed the same survival instincts drilled into me by Smith during training. Sitting across from him with my back to the front where I couldn't see who walked in made the hair on my neck prickle, adding to my emotional jitters.

He smiled and reached across the table to shake my hand. I shook and sat down just as the server appeared and set a slice of blueberry pie à la mode in front of Smith. I ordered a patty melt, fries, and a coke. I wasn't hungry but needed to eat. Smith took a bite of pie and sipped his tan coffee. He liked it lukewarm. Ugh.

He said, "Don't see hide nor hair of you for seven odd years and now twice in one week. Should I be honored or feel used? I'm votin' for used."

I said nothing, as I mentally tried to put together the whole serial killer case, all the many pieces, the ones present and missing.

He said, "You really put me on the cross coming in like you did and using our friendship to get at our files."

"I'm sorry about that, I am. But this is really important."

"Then tell me a story."

I was already tired of telling it, so I slid the Shearer datebook across the table to him.

"What's this?" His brown hair hung across his forehead like a high school kid, only his skin looked aged from too much sun and too many cartons of unfiltered Camels.

"Look at the page I paper-clipped."

He opened to the page of the meeting scheduled with Jubal Butler.

"Okay," he said. "These initials, this is a meet right here at The Skillet with Jubal Butler? What, seven years ago?"

I nodded.

He held up the datebook, "Who's this belong to? What's this all about?"

I reached across and opened the book to the last page, to Shearer's notation:

- *TB Killer*
- *Moved to West Valley from Ohio*
- *WV Cop?*
- *Joined dept. 5-7yrs ago*
- *Meet with Det. JB...Risky. No other option.*

"What?" Smith said. "You think Jubal is this TB Killer?"

I sat back in the seat. I had thought of that, but it wasn't the first thing I went to. Not like Smith just did. What was the matter with me? I knew, though. Cole Adler was like a railroad spike pounded into the center of my brain, short-circuiting my common sense. Smith was fresh on this investigation, and smart. He went right to Jubal being the number one suspect.

From the time I was a cadet, to the time I was a patrol officer, I viewed Jubal as more a decrepit old man without the physical ability to snatch teenage girls like Jessica DeFrank off the street. "Why would you say that?"

"Well, the meet written right here is JB and Jubal's from the Midwest. I'm not sure of the state. It could very well be Ohio. I know for sure it's the rustbelt, though. You didn't answer me, who's this book belong to?"

"Jubal, he's from the Midwest? Are you sure?"

All business, Smith held up the datebook and waited for an answer.

"The book belonged to a guy named Shearer. It was my first suicide investigation back seven years ago, right out of your training car. Shotgun to the head. Real ugly."

Smith sat back, his smile gone. "This is about a suicide seven years ago? Is that why you came in and grabbed the Elise Stoner case file? Is this Shearer suicide somehow related to Stoner? That one's closed, my friend. You know that. Is this about you trying to get Maslow off the hook on a wing and prayer by trying to tie it to Shearer?"

I stared at him. How could Smith believe Johnny could do something like murdering a woman in a hotel room? I guess for the last seven years, I too had believed it. But after talking to him at GHRC, and without any factual basis, the scales of justice tipped a little more toward innocent. I couldn't displace myself emotionally from my friendship with Johnny and at the same time draw logical conclusions. Apparently, Smith could.

"He's your friend," I said.

Smith shrugged. "So's a Rottweiler, until he bites your hand." He pushed away his plate of half-eaten blueberry pie and melting vanilla ice cream. The server dropped off my meal. The greasy reek disgusted me. I couldn't eat and pushed it away.

Smith sat back, bumped out a Camel, and lit it. He stared at me, his eyes squinting from the smoke. He pointed at me with the cigarette between two fingers. "I always thought Johnny might've also done in Jessica DeFrank."

"What? You're kidding, right?" The dim jail image bubbled up, Johnny behind the bars as he lifted his shirt for me to see his abdomen and chest. No bullet scars from my .38 Colt. But there might not have been if he'd worn body armor. If he'd gotten really lucky.

Smith shrugged. "The killer hasn't hit again, not since Johnny's been locked up. Coincidence?" He shrugged again.

"No. That's crazy talk. You think he was the one who hit me with that shovel and tried to bury me? We were friends. How could he…no. No way."

He shrugged again and tapped ash into the ashtray. I glared at him. In that moment I'd lost a little respect for Smith. I was wrong; Smith's die-hard competitiveness wouldn't let him view the big picture without bias.

"Come on," I said. "Who else could it be? There's ninety-seven other cops who work at West Valley."

Smith's brown eyes drilled into me. He let a little smile creep out.

"What?" I asked.

"Fletcher's from Bowling Green. Not Toledo, but close enough. Sedge is from Ohio, don't know which jerkwater burg."

The way he said it sent a chill up my back, the way he could, without hesitation, toss Twice and Sedge under the bus.

My pager went off. Lieutenant Sims asking me to come to headquarters. He'd added in three 911s at the end. He meant business. I had a feeling I was going to catch a midnight transfer to MCJ, Men's Central Jail, turning keys, smelling ass, and eating stale cheese sandwiches.

Smith said, "You know the turnover at West Valley PD. The pay's crap. Guys come in, get a little experience, and move on where they can make some real money. You did it. You went to the Sheriffs. If…and this is a big 'if,' if your killer had worked at the PD, he's probably moved on by now. That's a lot of years you're talking about. Doesn't seem like it, but it is."

I didn't leave because of the money. I was running away from a shovel to the face. In my dreams, I still heard the twang of metal off skull bone, smelled the warm iron scent of my own blood, saw bright lights swimming in my vision, choked on the dirt in my mouth.

I said, "Twice is an asshole, everyone knows that, but being an asshole doesn't make him a serial killer."

"Wasn't Twice a cadet who handled the fingerprinting for the department? That could be how he snuck in under the radar and got the cop job."

"I was a cadet too." I'd said it before thinking. Another link that tied me to the killings. But I'd never been to Ohio. The cadets fingerprinted all new hires. When Twice was promoted to patrol officer from cadet, it would've been simple for him to send in—as his own—someone else's ten-print cards.

Smith smiled. "Yes, you were a cadet, a damn good one. But look at his name, Fletcher Fletcher. Who named a kid that? Fletcher Fletcher has to be made up." Smith was talking himself into it.

"Before we do anything else," I said, "I want to look at the personnel files, see how many officers or detectives have roots in Ohio. See if their backgrounds have any holes in them."

"I don't think so, this isn't your case. It's West Valley's. I'll take all your notes, this is my investigation now."

"Come on, you're not going to squeeze me out. I brought this to you."

"No, you didn't, kid."

He was right. I'd come in, conned him, walked away with the case files and he'd figured out what'd I done and why.

"Twice is *your* homicide dick, how are you going to give this to him to investigate?"

"I'll vet him first, then he and I will take it from there."

"How are you going to vet him? It'll be a huge conflict for you to interview him. I'm from a different agency. It makes sense to let me in."

"I'll do a deep background before interrogation, see if the dates match with any of his shifts."

"He'll tumble to you doing the background. He's not a fool. Especially if he *is* the one. He's been smart enough to get away with it until now. Let me in on the interview."

Smith slid from the booth, took out a ten, and dropped it on the table. "No chance, kid." He walked to the payphone on the hallway wall and dialed. I stared at him. He looked back while he spoke, his words too muffled to hear. He hung up. He stopped at the table. "Thanks, kid, I'll take it from here. I want those case files back by eight tomorrow morning, *with* all your notes."

"Wait. Fletcher could be a homicide suspect, a serial killer. You want to interview him by yourself?"

He opened his leather bomber jacket and showed me his long shoulder holster with his model 19 Smith and Wesson .357, the one he'd always carried. "I won't be alone. I got my friend to back me up."

I stared at him, willing him to let me back into my own case.

Finally, he asked, "How would you interview Fletcher?"

He's a cop, he's had homicide training, that means he knows all the interrogation tricks. He's going to be tough to crack. I'd put him off his game."

"How?"

"I'd...I'd interview him in the vineyard alongside that eucalyptus hedgerow, right there where Jessica DeFrank was thrown in the ditch. If it's him, it'll shake him, make him think we know something."

Smith rubbed his chin and nodded. "That's good. I like it. Okay, you just earned yourself a ticket to the interview." He turned and walked quickly to the payphone. He dialed again, spoke in low tones like before, updating Twice on where to meet instead of the interview room at West Valley. I slid out of the booth, dropped a ten on the table, and grabbed half the patty melt. I was suddenly hungry.

Chapter Twenty-Six

I stuck the remaining half of the patty melt between my teeth while I unlocked my trunk. Smith stuck his nose in to see what I had stored in the dark recesses. "What are you doing?" he asked.

I took the sandwich from my mouth. "I'm putting on body armor." I stopped short of saying he should do the same. This was Smith, my mentor. Who was I to tell him what was best?

He said, "Twice is one of us. He'd never throw down on me."

I stared at him as if not understanding his words. I nodded, put the sandwich back in my mouth, and donned my threat level three Second Chance vest. I took out a dark long-sleeve shirt and put it on to cover it. I didn't want Twice to have a tactical edge seeing the vest. I took the Colt .38 from my back pocket and stuck it in my waistband. I had my 4-inch .357 on my hip in a pancake holster loaded with magnum rounds.

We got in the Mustang. I fired it up and pulled onto Euclid. It was nice having Smith in the car again. The same feeling returned from seven years ago, the one I had while on training. With the two of us, we could take on all comers. A foolish, youthful sentiment that had ended abruptly one night with a shovel to the face in a dark vacant field.

I made a left turn onto G Street east. Smith rolled down his window and lit up a Camel. Back when I was with Smith I was tempted to start smoking but realized the urge came from peer pressure and the overwhelming desire to fit in—to be accepted in the new world I'd chosen as a career.

We rode in silence. The excitement grew with each passing mile.

Smith finally spoke; the cigarette still in his mouth wagged up and down with each word. "This is some good work, the way you put this whole thing together. Why don't you come back to West Valley? I'll have you working for me in the bureau in no time at all."

I didn't answer. My nerves suddenly rose up to block out the excitement. I should've taken the freeway; it would've been faster. We'd just passed the Holiday Inn where Elise Stoner met her demise in a most violent manner and realized I was headed back to the hedgerow, a place I'd not been to in seven years, a place that was the source of too many nightmares. My hands turned sweaty on the steering wheel.

The passing streetlights lit up the Mustang's interior in flashing nickelodeon style. Smith stared at me. "You okay, kid? You look like you're about to drive us off a cliff."

"I'm fine. I just don't want it to be Twice. I never got along with him but—"

"I learned a long time ago, you play it by the facts. You leave out all that romantic emotional bullshit that can get you killed and play it strictly by the facts. You can't go wrong if you do."

I nodded and then chuckled at the flash of memory, the perfect example of emotional bullshit—Johnny sitting in my living room drinking Miller High Life, the champagne of bottled beer, as we watched *Tell Them Valdez Is Coming*. What he'd said later after the shooting on Rosewood: "More like a thousand."

"What's funny?" Smith asked.

"You ever watch *Tell Them Valdez Is Coming*? It's with Burt Lancaster."

"No. And that's exactly what I'm talking about. That's the romantic bullshit that'll get you killed. Life doesn't work anything like the movies. This is real-world shit we're talking about here. I thought better of you, kid. Keep your head in the game tonight or you'll get us both killed." His expression turned morose. He flicked his lit cigarette butt out the window and lit another one. He said, "If nothing else, you gotta keep your perspective. In the big scheme of things, in this infinite universe of ours, we amount to nothing more than a popcorn fart. Don't ever forget that."

He had a unique perspective in a place I wasn't so sure I wanted to own stock.

Ten minutes later I slowed almost to a stop to make the turn into the rutted road. The hedgerow was off to the right, dark and ominous. The headlights lit up the debris in the vacant field to the left: a couch, the shot-up refrigerator, and the holey fifty-five-gallon drums. Nothing much had changed.

The span of the headlights caught the reflection of a car on the other side of the eucalyptus hedge, the dark image of a sleek black El Camino parked right about where the slit trench had been seven years ago. Had Twice parked there on purpose? Was he playing mind games?

The darkness, the hedgerow, just being back in the area made it difficult to breathe. I thought I'd be able to handle it and wasn't doing a good job controlling my emotions.

Smith said, "Let's take this slow, let me lead the interrogation. When I look at you, that's when you toss in a fact concerning the case, just one at a time, though. Whatever you do, no matter what he says, don't fly off the handle. Be professional."

"Yes, sir." I'd reverted back to training, my mind running a hundred miles an hour.

We got out and stood by the closed car doors, waiting for our eyes to adjust to the ambient light cast by the stars and the glow of the city to the west. I reached back in and pulled the hand-held radio. I carried it in my left hand to keep my gun hand clear. I switched the secondary channel to Talk-Around, so the busy dispatcher noise didn't disrupt our interview.

We picked our way between the hedgerow to the other side. A shadow stood by the driver's door of the El Camino. The shadow reached inside the car. The headlights came on and blinded us.

"Fletcher," Smith said. "What the hell?" We both had our arms up blocking out the light.

Fletcher reached back in and shut the lights off. Except for the running lights. The amber glow made us all shadows and ghosts that danced in our vision.

Twice said to Smith, "What the hell is he doing here?"

At the same time, the radio in my hand burped. "Dave, you there? Answer up, buddy." Jimmy Mora on the Talk-Around channel, he knew that's where to check for me if I didn't answer on the primary channel.

Smith heard it too. "Not now. Turn that damn thing off."

"Dave, you there, go ten-thirty-five." The code for confidential information. I keyed the mic. "Jimmy, I'm busy, let me get back to you."

"No, listen. I just got paged and called in. They want to pull me from this gig to go looking for you."

"What?" That didn't make sense, not with something as important as what Jimmy had going on. This time, talking a little lower, I said, "Why? What's going on?" But I knew: I didn't come right in when Sims wanted me to. I didn't answer his pages, so now he wanted to sic the hounds on me. Before he could answer, I said, "Give me an hour, I'll be in."

"No, *mijo.* Listen. There's a warrant out for your arrest."

Smith had been looking at Twice. His head whipped around. He'd heard it too.

I stepped further away, put my hand over the radio, and spoke low. "What? Are you crazy?"

"It's something about two bullets you put into Drug/Fire to be analyzed. Those bullets come back to a murder. To a Stoner, an Elise Stoner."

In my stunned shock, Smith was able to do it again. He sneaked up on me. But not with a shovel; instead he used his .357. He put the gun right to my shoulder above the body armor and pulled the trigger. The loud bang deafened my left ear. Made it ring. The world froze in time, stopped its rotation. I'd become nothing more than a popcorn fart.

Chapter Twenty-Seven

I crumpled to my knees and fell forward into the dirt.

Smith put his knee in my back, pulled my hands behind me, and cuffed them. He yanked my duty weapon from the pancake holster. Under the body armor, warm blood on my skin ran down my chest to my pants. I gulped for air. How had this happened? Why had Smith shot me? What was Jimmy talking about? My mind kicked back into gear everything fitting into place all at once.

Smith had killed Elise Stoner with the .38 Detective Special, then that same night or soon after, came over to my apartment and gave me the gun as a gift, knowing I'd have to shoot it at the range, have the bullets logged. He'd set me up seven years ago for the Elise Stoner killing. But then Jubal Butler must've found the information about Johnny Maslow having a prior relationship with Elise, and Smith found Johnny to be a better patsy. Why not have two patsies?

"What the hell, boss?" Twice yelled, as he drew his gun and covered me on the ground. The gunshot still echoed in my good ear, the gunshot that came like a painless sledgehammer blow, knocking me flat on the ground. Dirt in my mouth. The numbness wore off. The pain all but blinded me.

"He's a serial killer," Smith said. "He brought us out here to kill us both."

Fletcher stood up straighter, stunned. "No, shit. And you figured him out. That's beeeauutiful." He giggled like a little kid.

I breathed in dirt and coughed. The words came out garbled. "Shoot him, Fletcher! Shoot him!"

Fletcher chuckled, but not as confident. "Right, like I'm going to—"

Smith shot Fletcher in the head with my duty weapon.

Fletcher crumpled where he stood and landed next to me, his eyes open and without emotion. He stared at me with the new third eye in his forehead.

Smith grabbed the back of my collar and dragged me to the El Camino's amber running lights. I dug my heels in and kicked but it didn't matter. He propped me against the grill, the shoulder pain excruciating, my left arm useless. With my right, I reached across my body and took hold of his retreating hand. "Why?"

He shook loose from my grasp, backed up a couple of steps, and squatted on his heels, the .357 resting in his lap as he casually lit another Camel. He took a long drag off the cigarette. The cherry glow gave his tan face shadows with sinister intent.

I tried to struggle higher in my sitting position and said, "I shot you seven years ago."

He cocked his head to the side and smiled. He put the cigarette in his mouth, squinted from the smoke, and pulled up his shirt to expose a puckered scar on his right shoulder. "You hit me three times. Damn good shooting, considering. Two hit the vest. I thought tonight I'd return the favor. You get one more question, then you're going to answer some of mine. Make it a good one, kid."

"You killed Elise Stoner because she'd hired Franklyn Shearer to ferret you out. And then you framed Johnny Maslow for Stoner."

He shrugged and smiled. "Is that your question?"

I still had the Colt .38 in my waistband and inched my right cuffed hand toward it with both hands still cuffed behind my back. "Did you kill all those girls in Ohio?"

In the squat, he pointed his cigarette at me, his other hand on the stock of his gun. "Don't do it, Dave. We're not done talking yet. And I'm sorry, but I have to take the fifth on that question. Besides, that's ancient history. I thought you might want to know how I created this new life without anyone figuring it out."

I nodded toward Fletcher. "You charmed him when he took your fingerprints. He must've been a cadet when you applied for a job at West

Valley. You owed him, that's how he made detective in homicide."

Smith set his gun in his lap, put the cigarette between his lips, and clapped. "Very good, Dave." He got up and walked over to me. "Now it's my turn to ask the questions. What do you know for sure, kid? Tell me and make it easy on yourself." He stepped on my right hand I used for balance and ground it into the dirt.

I grunted around the pain to get the words out. "I know one thing for sure, you're going to burn."

"Why's that? Tell me." He stuck the gun barrel in my shoulder wound and pushed down. Bright red, blue, and white lights exploded in my vision. I tried not to give him the satisfaction, but a pathetic yelp escaped my lips.

He eased off. The world came back into focus. My chest pumped hard for air, my face wet with tears of pain.

"We can do this all night, kid. Tell me why you think I'm going to burn? What do you know?"

"Screw you."

He stuck the barrel against the gunshot wound and pressed down, leaning into it this time, gritting his teeth, his eyes alive with an anger I'd never seen. I passed out.

I woke to the same nightmare. Smith crouched in front of me with the ratchet end of Twice's handcuffs open as he heated the tip with his Zippo lighter. He'd been working on it for a while; the tip glowed red.

"I really don't want to do this, Dave. Us being friends and all."

"You're a sociopath and aren't capable of having friends. Or emotions for that matter."

He smiled. "Okay, you got me there. But here's the deal. You don't need your eyes to talk, so those two are going to go first. They'll sizzle and pop when I stick them with this. And pain…there will be pain like you've never experienced."

"What do you want?"

"You know what I want."

"Two detectives from Ohio are on their way here. They've probably already landed."

"That's a start. Why are they here? You better hurry and tell me, you're losing a lot of blood." He continued to hold the flame under the ratchet tip.

"To...to debrief a witness."

He stopped and looked at me. "What witness, Dave?" I was the witness, but I couldn't tell him that.

"You'll never get to her in time, not now. She can place you at the kidnapping of Jessica DeFrank. From there it's an easy stepping stone to all the rest." I was lying. That was all I had left to stay alive, a thin, feeble lie.

"Where is she?"

"A safe house."

"Where?" His hand with the glowing red ratchet moved toward my shoulder.

"No, don't. Wait. Okay. San Bernardino. She's in a house in San Bernardino."

"That's good, kid. You did good." He put the red-hot metal to the wound in my shoulder. Sizzle. Severe pain came hand in hand with oblivion.

Chapter Twenty-Eight

I woke sitting in the passenger seat of my own Mustang. Smith sat in the driver's seat. He reached across and pulled the seatbelt, buckling me in. "Wouldn't want you to get hurt." He winked, his humid breath thick with the reek of burnt Camels and, oddly, the essence of blueberries. He started up and backed the Mustang down the dirt path along the west side of the hedgerow to the asphalt street. Nobody ventured out this far east except for the occasional illegal shooter. Twice wouldn't be found for days. Smith intended to take out the make-believe witness I'd offered up and then bring me back, dump me dead alongside Twice. Since Smith headed the detective bureau, he'd be the one supervising the investigation: a murder-suicide. Perfect. If any flaws in his plan were discovered after the fact, he could fix them on the fly.

All I had left was the lie, and that wouldn't last long. Smith's cunning had kept him alive too long.

Smith had left the Colt .38 in my waistband, but with my hands cuffed behind my back and seat-belted in, I didn't have a chance to bring it into action. He'd leave it there; the gun proved me the killer of Elise Stoner. Maybe they would let Johnny Maslow out and he'd take a run at Smith. Somebody had to bring him down.

Smith smoked and drove. "Don't know how I missed that datebook of Shearer's. Where'd you find it?"

I watched the passing streetlights as we headed west and didn't answer him.

"Which way?" he asked. "And you better not be yanking my dick here, kid. It'll only make it worse for you."

"You're just going to kill her."

This time he didn't answer. I needed time to think, my mind foggy with shock or blood loss.

"Which way, I'm not going to ask again."

My only chance was to get him pulled over. Get him on the freeway and hope to see a cop, a California Highway Patrol car. Kick the steering wheel, reach over with my foot and slam on the brake. What were those odds? And what if the cop did pull us over? Smith would only tell him he was transporting a wounded prisoner to the hospital, he'd show the cop his lieutenant's badge. If the cop got nosey, Smith would just shoot him.

"Take the freeway east, get off…get off at…" Suddenly I had a plan. "Get off at Alabama, go north to Lugonia, and turn left."

"Good, now you're thinking straight. What's this girl's name?"

Details tripped up the liar every time. I couldn't afford to tell him too many details.

"Emily."

"Her last name?"

I didn't answer.

"How old?" This time when I didn't answer he shoved me.

"Eighteen. She's eighteen now."

"Hmm."

He got off at Alabama and turned north. "How far before we reach Lugonia?"

"Not far, just two or three long blocks."

He made the turn on Lugonia. "This is a commercial area, not residential."

"There, on the right, the motel. I got her stashed in that motel."

"In a fleabag like this?" He chuckled. "You coulda done better, kid, much better." He pulled into the Lucky Shamrock's parking lot. Most of the lights had burnt out or had been broken out by those who didn't want to be seen. The low-level light left the place in spotty shadows.

"But you're right," he said, "this is perfect. There's hardly anyone here. Which room?" His pupils had dilated, absorbing the brown irises, making them pure obsidian, made them not of this world. All he lacked was a lizard's tongue.

"Let me out. It'll be better if I get her to open the door. You don't want to kick it in."

"Which room?"

"Seven. Lucky number seven."

He came around to my car door, grabbed me by the shoulder strap of the body armor, and dragged me out. I gritted my teeth to eat the pain. He had me by the elbow and we headed toward room number seven. We only took two steps before I eased down to my knees.

Smith leaned over and in a harsh whisper. "If this is your chickenshit plan to get away, it won't work."

I eased forward to prone on my belly, then rolled over on my back so I could see his face. I said, "If chickenshit is all you got, you go with it."

He pulled his .357.

I said, "Thank you for doing that."

"Doing what? Get your ass up, now!"

I yelled, "Jimmy! Fuego! Fuego!"

Upstairs, Jimmy Mora stepped out of the motel room, his gun at the ready, and fired at the man holding a gun on his good friend.

All the other Violent Crime cops on his team, in the upstairs and downstairs motel rooms and the two in the van at the U in the horseshoe, had their fingers on their triggers taking up the slack, not knowing what was happening. When Jimmy fired they did too. Shooting Contagious.

I stared up at Smith. Bits and chunks separated from his body, flung far in a mist of moonlight black, the hot steel and lead doing the job. The first bang of Jimmy's shot was immediately drowned out by the fusillade that followed.

Smith thumped to the asphalt and, as Johnny would say, DRT. Dead right there.

Lights came on. The hunters of man ventured from the rooms and the van, guns in hand ready to kill the beast a second time if he raised his head. The billowed smoke smoothed into a continuous bank. Gunshots echoed in my brain.

Jimmy came over and helped me to my feet. *"Mijo,* who did I just kill?"

"He's a lieutenant from West Valley Police Department."

"Aye Dios Mio."

The look on his face was priceless. I wanted to do what Johnny had done for me, get down on one knee and say to Smith, "Goodbye, asshole." Instead, with the relief of having it over, and a dangerous monster taken off the street, my sick sense of humor returned. I said to Jimmy, "Man, I was just kidding when I yelled fuego. Why'd you shoot him?"

Jimmy Mora's mouth sagged open, his eyes going wide.

I patted him on the shoulder, I was going to owe him for a very long time.

Author's Note

I have tried to write a memoir four times and couldn't find the glue that held all the stories/true incidents together. The fifth try I added a couple of fictitious plotlines: the love for Beth and the killing of Jessica DeFrank, along with a theme that was all too real. In all of my novels, I try to give the reader a glimpse of what it was like to work the streets.

In *A Fearsome Moonlight Black,* I did my best to depict what it was like being a young kid who'd been given a badge, a gun, and a fast car, and let loose on the street. Not so much what happened on the street but more what the street did to the kid. Many events in this novel happened more or less just as I wrote them—how I remembered them. I did compress time for dramatic effect. The incidents that really occurred are everything in the first half up to chapter Twenty-Nine. The murder of Jessica DeFrank did not happen.

To this day I wonder if I erred while investigating the Franklyn Shearer suicide. The car crash happened at Sixth street instead of Fourth and my mother was run off the road. The driver got away with manslaughter. My first murder investigation was at the Holiday Inn with Elise Stoner, a shock to my world, to my way of thinking, to see a woman naked, hog-tied, and shot in the head. This murder was committed by a transient truck driver who was captured the next day at the 76 Truck Stop. By Homicide detectives, not me.

The robbery of the Market Basket where I experienced my first officer-involved shooting happened just the way I wrote it, even with the comment from the movie Tell Them Valdez Is Coming made by a good friend and training officer. The Market Basket was the store I grew up shopping in with my mother. The clerk was pistol-whipped.

The shooting on Budd Street had one of the biggest impacts on my life, standing next to a father with his boy in his arms dying and there was nothing I could do. The native, volcano barbeque, and tikis were real and did cause car accidents. The city made my mom take it all down.

The storyline with Cole having gone missing was another event that stunned me. I did know him in high school and I did have a crush on his girlfriend, Beth. Eight or ten years after high school and when I was working violent crimes manhunting murderers, I stopped at a small market in the Fontana/Bloomington area for a coke and a bag of peanuts. I was wearing my usual garb, the khaki work shirt with a patch over the left breast that said Grace Trucking and a name patch, "Karl," over the right breast. I had on denim pants, a hat, and sunglasses.

When I came out of the store a girl said, "Hi, Dave." I looked at her, didn't recognize her, took my sunglasses off, and still didn't know her. She said, "They found Cole." I had not known he'd gone missing. As she continued to talk I realized that this was Beth and Cole was the guy I knew as her boyfriend in high school. Time had not been kind to her. She told the story first thing, meaning it still played a major part in her life. I was shocked when she said Cole had been found ten years later, his mummified corpse sitting in his wrecked car at the bottom of a ravine.

Everything in Part One of the book is true with the exception of the romance with Beth and the slit trench murder with Jessica DeFrank. Part Two of the book is fictitious. I also changed all the names.

About the Author

During his career in law enforcement, best-selling author David Putnam has done it all: worked in narcotics, violent crimes, criminal intelligence, hostage rescue, SWAT, and internal affairs, to name just a few. He is the recipient of many awards and commendations for heroism. *A Fearsome Moonlight Black* is the first book in a trilogy. Look for the second book, *A Lonesome Blood-Red Sun* coming out in 2023. Putnam lives in the Los Angeles area with his wife, Mary.

SOCIAL MEDIA LINKS:

https://twitter.com/daveputnam
https://www.facebook.com/davidputnambooks
http://davidputnambooks.com
David@davidputnambooks.com

AUTHOR WEBSITE:

http://davidputnambooks.com

Also by David Putnam

The Disposables

The Replacements

The Squandered

The Vanquished

The Innocents

The Reckless

The Heartless

The Ruthless

The Sinister

CPSIA information can be obtained
at www.ICGtesting.com
Printed in the USA
LVHW032301101022
730380LV00003B/157